La Dolce Vita

AN ANTHOLOGY OF CONTEMPORARY ITALIAN EROTICA BY WOMEN

EDITED BY
MAXIM JAKUBOWSKI

TRANSLATIONS BY
JUDITH FORSHAW

RUNNING PRESS
PHILADELPHIA · LONDON

Selection & Introduction © 2013 by Maxim Jakubowski ; © 2013 individual authors with the exception of story by Valeria Parrella © 2011 Valeria Parrella/Agenzia Santachiara

Cover Photo: ©iStock/PhotoGraphyKM

Published by Running Press,
a Member of the Perseus Books Group

All rights reserved under the Pan-American and International Copyright Conventions
Printed in the United States

This book may not be reproduced in whole or in part, in any form or by any means, electronic or mechanical, including photocopying, recording, or by any information storage and retrieval system now known or hereafter invented, without written permission from the publisher.

Books published by Running Press are available at special discounts for bulk purchases in the United States by corporations, institutions, and other organizations. For more information, please contact the Special Markets Department at the Perseus Books Group, 2300 Chestnut Street, Suite 200, Philadelphia, PA 19103, or call (800) 810-4145, ext. 5000, or e-mail special.markets@perseusbooks.com.

ISBN 978-0-7624-4848-7
Library of Congress Control Number: 2013931280

E-book ISBN 978-0-7624-4849-4

9 8 7 6 5 4 3 2 1
Digit on the right indicates the number of this printing

Design by Joshua McDonnell
Edited by Jennifer Kasius
Typography: Adine Kirnberg, and Bembo

Running Press Book Publishers
2300 Chestnut Street
Philadelphia, PA 19103-4371

Visit us on the web!
www.runningpress.com

5	INTRODUCTION	MAXIM JAKUBOWSKI
8	THE LOVER	BARBARA BARALDI
28	CHANCES	LIVIANA ROSE
42	A DANGEROUS GAME	ANNA BULGARIS
62	A SERIOUS STORY	VALERIA PARRELLA
67	THE BIRD OF PARADISE	CLAUDIA SALVATORI
86	JUNE 1978	KATIA CECCARELLI
96	INSIDE THE BODY OF ROMA	SOFIA NATELLA
120	MR. BABY GIGOLO	MARIROSA BARBIERI
132	THE STEEL-SCALED MERMAID	MARIA TRONCA

143	HAVE YOU COME YET?
	FRANCESCA CANI

162	THE GALLANT ADVENTURES OF COLETTE AND RENATE
	MAYA DESNUDA

176	THE NIGHT I WENT AWAY
	CRISTIANA DANILA FORMETTA

194	DOROTHY IS GOING HOME
	ELISELLE

209	RANDOM CONSTRUCTIONS
	ALINA RIZZI

226	THE FEELINGS DON'T COME BACK
	GRAZIA SCANAVINI

243	THE SPA
	HEATHCLIFF

256	THE HILL OF THE GOATS
	GIORGIA REBECCA GIRONI

277	A DYPTICH: ABSINTHE & PIERCING
	FRANCESCA MAZZUCATO

Introduction

As much as any of us is fascinated by the imagined private lives of others, we are similarly intrigued by the veil of discretion often drawn across the sexuality of strangers, and even more so when it comes to the world of desire beyond our knowledge and understanding.

Until recently, this was a curiosity we kept concealed for fear of attracting disapproval, but since the success of the *Fifty Shades of Grey* erotic book series, the secret is now out in the open and it has become almost acceptable to admit to an attraction to matters sexual on the page, if one considers the millions of readers all over the world who lapped up the romantic, if steamy saga.

This is of course nothing new for me, since I have been both writing and editing erotica for a couple of decades and am highly aware of the underground current of interest in the subject. But until now it was a guilty pleasure, which I had to share with a minority. So a great vote of thanks to E. L. James for, despite her clunky style and cumbersome clichés, making erotic writing acceptable again.

In many foreign countries though, the acceptance of literary erotica has never been in doubt, and it has represented a strong intellectual tradition for a long time. Some twelve years ago I assembled the *Mammoth Book of International Erotica* in which I offered examples of outstanding erotica translated from more than fifteen languages, and the volume has gone through numerous printings, a couple of editions, and is still in print and selling steadily still.

In Europe they have a different and healthier attitude toward writing about sex, and in *Ooh La La!*, which I edited with French editor Franck

Spengler over five years ago, I presented a compendium of modern French erotica by women writers, which proved provocative, eye-opening, and compelling. These were the granddaughters of the Marquis de Sade, the successors to a healthy strand of libertine and surrealist writers of the French past, and a collection of authors who felt no shame writing explicitly to arouse and entertain. But then you would have expected no less from France!

But writing erotica is not just a French tradition, as the present volume I think ably demonstrates. I have been fortunate to live for several years in Italy and return there frequently, and as a result I have learned the language, which has given me the opportunity to discover much of Italian literature that is still unknown to the exclusively English-reading public. And yet again, we find there is a fine heritage of erotica: Ovid, Boccacio, the Decameron, Casanova, and so much more . . . so is it any wonder that, to this day, the art and practice of literary erotica is particularly strong in Italy? And that many of its finest practitioners also happen to be women.

Many of the contributors to this anthology are celebrated in Italy and, in addition to their short stories, have countless novels to their credit. Indeed, I was sadly unable to include authors like Isabella Santacroce, Melissa P., Simona Vinci, and Tenera Valse, because they seldom write at shorter length in the erotic genre, but I urge you to investigate them at the first possible opportunity.

Some are also active in other genres: Barbara Baraldi, Claudia Salvatori, and Maria Tronca are well known for their crime thrillers and even horror; Georgia Gironi is known for her science fiction; Sofia Natella and Cristiana Formetta are leading bloggers and journalists; Francesca Mazzucato and Valeria Parrella are recognized as some of Italy's most challenging literary authors, and some even write for young adults, erotica being just one of their many talents.

To contradict our title, not all the stories are even sweet or upbeat, but how could we not tip our hat to Fellini and the Italian cinema, which has also been a fertile field for the unique accents of Italian-style erotica over the decades: Pasolini, Tinto Brass, early Dario Argento are all echoed here in subtle ways.

We of course already knew how beautiful many Italian women were: from Sophia Loren, Gina Lollobrigida, and Claudia Cardinale onward, Italian actresses have illuminated the silver screen with their sensuality and effervescence. But now is the time to recognize that when it comes to celebrating the giddy whirlpools of sex and sensations, Italian female erotica writers are in world of their own.

To which you have a passport in the pages of this book.

—Maxim Jakubowski

The Lover

BARBARA BARALDI

A Shell

I am in the dark in the car park behind the supermarket. I am waiting for him. I'm wearing a black silk slip dress, as light as the merest hint of a caress. I'm shut inside. My car is a shell and I'm a pearl with opalescent skin. I look around nervously.

The sense of fear is mild but it gets stronger with every minute that passes. The feeling will fade as soon as I see the headlights of his car cutting through the darkness and lighting up the inside of mine with two quick bursts on full beam, the signal we agreed. Then my nervousness will dissolve in a rush of desire. Not now. Not yet. My body is rigid, my muscles tense from waiting. My hands are manicured, the nails varnished—rouge noir—the color Fernando likes best. I use the same color on my full lips. I have light-colored eyes, sparkling and full of promise. Because of this, I have never believed that they are the mirror of the soul. So clear, as bright as splinters from a diamond, they definitely don't resemble the clouded well that is my soul. All seven deadly sins are there, one on top of another, one fighting against the other to gain supremacy in an oasis of suppressed virtue. There's Lust, undisputed mistress in the Garden of Eden of my vice. I have called it Love to disguise it and keep at bay any sense of guilt. And then there's Pride, which makes me believe that I deserve all the pleasure I can get, even if to get it I have to trample on the feelings of other people. And finally there's Wrath, domineering and dazzling, which flares up every time I think about the woman who holds the official position by Fernando's side. She occupies his bed while I get toilets in public places, the backseat or the hood of the car, the desk in his office—but only occasionally, otherwise his secretaries might become suspicious. And more: hotel rooms rented by the hour, and once a park bench. And how could I forget New Year's Eve: our first time, biting cold, he and I on the terrace, him on top of me, inside me.

I remember the lavish apartment, crowded with people I didn't know. Friends of Simona, the girl I used to go around with at the time. That night Fernando and I noticed each other. A first lingering gaze, the sort of gaze you could lose yourself in, then quicker looks to find each other again, to follow each other. I danced in front of him in the living room. I heated up the atmosphere by rubbing up against Simona: blonde, boob job, and perfect body. Me: brunette, naturally seductive, wearing a red dress, slit up to here at the side, and silver sandals with vertiginous heels.

I did nothing more than follow the rhythm, careful not to lose contact with the grey eyes of the stranger with the salt-and-pepper hair, so elegant and apparently full of confidence. And he was always there, every time I looked up.

"It's just like you," he said shortly afterward, finally speaking to me. "Your hair, I mean. Every sinuous twist of your curls is an invitation." I smiled, kissed a lock of my hair, and held it up to his lips. He took me by the arm in the midst of the chaos, a grasp that was firm but gentle at the same time. A few minutes before the countdown to the new year, we reached the bedroom at the end of the corridor through the steady stream of people trying to get to the living room or the kitchen for the midnight toast.

I let him do it. I was a bit tipsy, incapable of putting up any resistance to his will, which crushed any moral resolve I might have had. His taste was unusual, slightly spicy. The strong aftertaste was because of the cigars he smoked, as I found out later. His hand travelled over the curves of my body, more and more persistent. It slipped through the slit in my dress and up to my pleasure point. When my knees gave way, I had to lean heavily against the railing. He whirled me around and took possession of me.

The headlights cut through the darkness, two quick bursts on full beam. I am in the supermarket parking lot. And he, at last, has arrived. I grip my thighs and try to control my excitement.

The Doll

Excuses. Excuses yet again. He can't leave her, it's a bad time. I have to understand, put myself in his shoes. But he doesn't even think about trying mine: too uncomfortable. A wardrobe of figure-hugging dresses, low-cut tops, short skirts, sky-high slits and stiletto heels; just as Fernando likes me. That's how he cheers himself up. It's the norm for me to always be perfect and smiling and flawless. A sexy Lolita, Venus made flesh, the woman of your dreams, but also understanding and rational when needed.

Lovers have to be perfect. Men already have imperfect wives.

"I can't now, sweetie. You know it's a crucial time at work. I can't possibly cope with a divorce and all the stress it would cause." As I think over what he said I increase the speed on the display of the treadmill. I run, fists clenched, the sweat runs down and washes away with it all the tears I don't want to cry.

I knew what I was letting myself in for, going out with a married man. I knew I would always come second, that I would spend the holidays alone and that I would have to smile at his tomorrows. Tomorrow is another day, I repeat to myself. Another day.

I am the lover, she is the wife. Sara: I hate her without even knowing her.

When I try to picture her I give her the worst faults of the entire female gender. Is it possible that she hasn't noticed anything in all this time? I would realize if my man were screwing another woman. But Sara is the fragile woman; Sara who is devoted to her family; Sara who needs him; Sara who lost a son two years ago; Sara who has suffered so much and hasn't yet gotten over it.

"Don't worry, sweetie, she and I haven't touched each other for ages now. We're like brother and sister. I have to stay with her for now, but as soon as she's back to normal I'll talk to her and then it'll be just you and me." Promises. I'm tired of promises and I increase the speed another level. Now we'll do things my way. I smile, determined.

A Crazy Idea

It was exciting asking for the morning off and lying in wait in front of the house where my man lives. I waited; I saw him leave the house in a hurry, handsome and sure of himself, as always.

I'm waiting for Sara, his wife. Today I'll put a face to the name. I'll follow her and then we'll see what happens. Perhaps it will be enough for me just to see her, homely and pale, to stop myself worrying. Or perhaps I'll speak to her to hear what her voice sounds like; I'll smell her skin as I pass close by her like the subtle touch of the autumn wind. I want to know. I have to know.

There she is, her movements as light as a butterfly. She glides from one aisle to the next in the supermarket, leaning against the shopping cart. She buys ten items at the most. I follow her for three days; she thrives on routine.

Sara is blonde. Her ash blonde hair tamed by a ponytail. She is tall and slim. She has small blue eyes that swim in a perfectly oval, pale face. Sara dresses simply. She isn't flashy; she looks like she doesn't need to be. She seems to glide through the air as she walks along and she doesn't make a noise.

Sara has small breasts; she doesn't confine them in a bra. So, in the refrigerated aisle her nipples get hard and lift the cotton jersey of her T-shirt, a touch of femininity that annoyed me. To start with I found her insignificant, then nice.

Today Sara is beautiful, beautiful enough to give me a twinge of pain in the pit of my stomach.

I have lost sight of her. Where can she have gone? I'm tired, and I realize that only now, lost in this labyrinth of canned food and promises printed on colored cartons.

I've been off work for days; not a problem, there's not much to do and I can take my time off when I want. Anyway, a holiday with Fernando is something I can only dream about. Holidays are for wives.

My body feels warm, a sign that I'm ill.

I swing around a corner to get to another aisle. Frozen food. The collision is inevitable and violent. The shopping basket falls from my hands; two apples in a bag, a small tin of peas, and tuna chunks in brine scatter across the polished floor.

"Excuse me, I'm very sorry," a soft, caressing voice.

"Don't worry. I was miles away. I'm the one who ought to apologize. Did I hurt you?" I say and look up. I recognize her nipples outlined by the light cotton of a white T-shirt. I melt like snow in the sunshine, my knees give way, and so I bend down to pick up my shopping.

"Leave it. I'll help," she smiles, and her eyes light up for a moment.

"No, please don't bother," I say firmly.

"It's no bother." She is polite but clear about what she means to do.

Her hands around the apples. Eve versus Eve in the supermarket. My shopping is returned to its basket, and she gets up and holds out her hand to help me stand. My legs feel heavy. I accept her help even though the voice in my head is whispering that I shouldn't touch her.

A warm hand, a reassuring touch, not a trace of sweat. Mine, on the other hand, is clammy with embarrassment. I snatch it back and wipe my palm on my denim miniskirt that shows off my slim thighs, elongated by the four-inch heels of my silver-colored sandals that accompany me during these days spent tailing her.

"Let's not be formal. I'm Sara," she says.

"Mimma. Pleased to meet you."

It's strange. Now I don't know exactly what I feel any more. Confusion perhaps; that's all that's left. Everything happened so quickly. Sara is no longer the personification of my fears. Sara has a face, and together with the face I have caught her very essence, the color of her hair, of her eyes and of her skin, and now I can add the tone of her voice, the softness of her hands. I am intrigued by Sara. Sara the wife, Sara the saint sent by heaven,

Sara the fragile woman, Sara devoted to her family, Sara who needs him because she lost a son two years ago, the woman who has suffered so much and hasn't yet got over it.

"I've finished my shopping. If you like, could we get a coffee together?" I ask without being conscious of doing so.

"Of course," and she smiles. Now I've done it, I think to myself. I can't turn back now, the cogs have started to turn, the gears are screeching. I try to convince myself that there's no harm in it. Fernando will never know, and anyway I have the advantage. I know things that she doesn't. Better to know one's enemy, it makes you stronger. I am the perfect lover, and I am weaving my web.

Your Voice

We sit opposite each other at a table outside the bar next to the supermarket. The stillness of her features is a calm pool matched by the low, even tone of her voice. She is the opposite of me, everything that I am not and could never be. I am fire, impulsive, and sensual. I am earth, skin that tans easily and is hot like the summer air at noon. She is air and water, cold hands, proud and with a look of detachment. But fragile at the same time; a delicate and regal swan on that pool of stillness that rules her face.

We chat for an hour or so. At the start, to break the tension, I bombarded her with a mass of information, true and false, all mixed together: I go to the gym four times a week, I don't use sunbeds because they give you wrinkles, I'm lazy and prefer to lie in the sun like a lizard. It's true: it's contradictory to be lazy and to go to the gym so often. I like to please myself and, why not, also to give pleasure. I work part time as a receptionist in an office on Via Amendola. I'm originally from Puglia. No, I don't believe that everyone from Puglia has dark hair and eyes as blue as the sea. I even ended up talking about my mother, too much like me for us to get on. She listened to me attentively, her small, light-colored eyes always on mine. I look down at my hands, and I'm amazed how natural it is to be here, together. For now, there's no sense of guilt, nor of hate or jealousy, just curiosity and an intense desire to know more about her. I realize that I have hardly let her say a word and now she is looking at her watch. Damn!

"It's getting late, I have to go. I'm meeting someone for lunch," she says with an apologetic look.

I can't miss the chance to see her again. I have to know what sort of a relationship she has with my man, if it's true they haven't touched each other for ages, or if she really loves him. Or perhaps there's more. Morbid curiosity, I tell myself, and I grab my chance: "Why don't we have lunch together one of these days? I'd like that. And anyway, I did all the talking today, I feel terribly guilty," I splutter, biting my lip. I always do that when I'm embarrassed.

"I'd love to. Is tomorrow okay for you?"

"Perfect."

We swap mobile numbers and as I'm saying good-bye my cell phone vibrates. It's a message from Fernando: see you this evening at the usual place.

A Walk

I'm wearing a pair of wide-legged white trousers and a matching blouse with the last three buttons strategically undone. I wanted to arrange the meeting with him in a village on the Via Aemilia, not far from Bologna but far enough to avoid meeting anyone we know. We are strolling along a tree-lined avenue, he has his arm around my shoulder and seems, for the first time since we met, surprised. I haven't behaved how he would have expected me to.

"I want to go for a walk," I told him. I got the urge to have an ice cream and then walk some more. I didn't wait for him to suggest something; I didn't passively go along with what he wanted. For once the perfect lover, always ready to welcome him with her red-hot body and her fixed smile, has chosen instead of letting someone choose for her.

He stops and pulls me closer. He embraces me under the leaves of the trees that hide the face of the moon. I lose myself in his smell and I feel his desire growing. Our tongues intertwine; they speak the language of seduction and prepare our bodies for the battle of love. He rests his hands on my buttocks and then moves them up my body to the breasts that are bursting from my tight-fitting blouse. He can't resist the lure of my body, he shudders and I feel powerful as never before.

I want to make him desire me for a while longer, so I move out of his grasp.

"It's hot, isn't it?" I say with a mischievous smile.

We walk in silence to the car. I sway my hips, breathing deeply the flower-scented air of midsummer. He opens the car with the remote but I still want to take a bit more advantage from the situation.

"Will you buy me a coffee?" I ask in a deliberately indifferent tone of voice. There is a bar right in front of the parking space.

He waits, uncomplaining, as my lips settle on the small cup. I drink slowly, keeping my eyes fastened on his. The first sip of scalding coffee makes me jump. I put the cup down and run my finger over the lipstick-stained rim.

"Are we going?" he asks with a grimace. He never asks—I have to deduce, but not today.

I drink the last mouthful of coffee and I head for the car, following a step behind him.

I don't have time to sit down before he locks the car doors, looks around feverishly—it's eleven o'clock on Thursday, and there's no one around. He practically jumps on me; our breath is a heavy blanket that envelops us and muffles the sound of the bells ringing in the distance, of the occasional car speeding past on the nearby road. He bites my lip, he licks me and seeks out my flesh under my clothes. In an instant I find myself with my trousers and panties pulled down; there's no room for foreplay. He enters me as if he wants to punish me, without realizing that he's actually giving me power. He hammers down on me to destroy my arrogant femininity; he drives forward with regular thrusts and groans more than usual. My cries merge with his. I feel an earthy pleasure. After a few seconds he's out. He withdraws just in time, staining my blouse with a spurt. I smile.

Hidden Persuasions

I have dressed with care: I see myself as being different. The old clothes don't go well with the new woman who has risen from the ashes of my old instincts. The vain phoenix looks at herself in the mirror and asks: "Was it meeting Sara that has changed you so thoroughly?"

The reflected image is motionless and observes the black satin pencil skirt, the voile blouse and the black leather court shoes with high heels. Elegance and femininity. Minimal make-up, a bit of mascara and a touch of lip gloss. Natural-looking hair, a mass of dark curls that fall onto my shoulders: a total weapon of seduction.

"I don't think Sara has anything to do with it. She's just a drop in this ocean of ambition. The change germinated inside me and came out all at once," the reflected image finally replies.

It always happens all at once. The meeting with Fernando knocked the old equilibrium off balance. In an instant I became the lover. The one who says yes.

What sort of a wife could Sara be? Today I'll find out.

I drive, lost in thought, and find myself in front of the salmon-colored house that looks out onto a well-kept garden. Today I will immerse myself in their world. I sense a new awareness inside me; I don't know where this game will lead us, but I'm the one directing it.

I ring the bell. Sara looks out of the window and then materializes in front of the door. She is wearing a simple yellow cotton dress and a pair of matching ballet flats. They say that blondes don't look good in sunshine yellow, but she is the exception. Her hair is tied back, as always, in a ponytail that leaves her aristocratic face bare. She seems happy to see me, perhaps she doesn't have many friends. I was surprised that she invited me to her house rather than to a bar for a quick snack. She said we would be more relaxed this way. "And anyway, it's no bother," she let me know. "I'll do a rice salad."

She shows me into a room and says: "Make yourself comfortable. We'll sit in the living room. I've made a fruit cocktail." The voice has that soft, low tone that sets her apart.

"Thanks," I smile and look around.

The living room is decorated tastefully, with lots of light. It looks as if it has come straight off the cover of one of those magazines that show the most stylish houses. Nothing has been left to chance.

"What a lovely room. Did you decorate it?" I ask.

"No, we left it all to an architect from Milan. A friend of Fernando, my husband."

Fernando controls things and loves to be in charge at home, too, it would seem. The sudden thought of him makes me wince. My body still bears the traces of his anger, bruises and the odd scratch.

"Cheers!" says Sara and raises her crystal glass.

"To our meeting and to a new friendship," I reply and drink it all in one go.

We eat in the kitchen with plastic plates and cutlery. "For me, this is an act of total anarchy, and you're my accomplice," she says, trying to catch my eye.

"What do you mean?"

"My husband would never let us eat like this. Disposable plates, a single quick course. He says mealtimes are sacred. He insists on me laying the big table in the dining room and that everything's perfect, even when we're alone. Just imagine if he knew I'd entertained a guest like this."

I don't find it hard to believe, but to get her to talk I prompt her with a "Really?"

She smiles and her whole being lights up. Today Sara is incredibly beautiful. Her beauty isn't a showy beauty; you wouldn't notice it unless you stopped to look at her. I continue pouring red wine into our glasses and I intoxicate her with chatter. I talk about the man I've been seeing for more than a year. I feel the need to broach the subject even if it's in an indirect way. I mention the fact that we never have much time to see each other and that he loves to be in charge and keep everything under control. I confide in her that I've always liked this. I used to find it reassuring, perhaps because, in contrast, I grew up with an absent father.

"I feel I've changed lately and as a result the relationship is evolving. Even if I don't know yet if it's moving in the right direction," I add.

"To changes!" she says and lifts her glass with a strange light in her eyes. "To changes!"

Paradise

Sara takes off her shoes and makes coffee. As light as a butterfly, she moves silently. When she puts down the steaming cup in front of me I find myself saying: "You're very beautiful, Sara."

"Thank you. You're stunning. I'm largely insignificant, just pretty. My husband is a handsome man, you should see him. If you see us as a couple, he's the one who stands out."

I fight off a rush of annoyance. It isn't because Sara has talked about them as a couple; I feel a strange, insane desire to reassure her, to make her realize that the husband she admires so much is after all just a . . .

A what? A man who made me completely lose my head and who took me to bed. In fact, someone who fucked me against a railing, the first time we met. Should I tell her that? And perhaps I should add that our relationship is based on a multitude of uncomfortable and decidedly unusual places where he has taken me, anytime and anywhere. I've only ever needed to have him, to smell and taste his odor of tobacco and aftershave on my skin and in my mouth and to let myself be taken in by his promises.

"You're an extremely beautiful woman, Sara. The incredible thing is that you're gorgeous without make-up, without flashy clothes," I say, pushing behind her ear a lock of blonde hair that has escaped from her ponytail. My grandmother used to do it when I was a child, after I'd tried to tame my hair by plaiting it or putting it in pigtails, but the mass of curls would rebel and try to escape.

She holds onto the cup, slightly embarrassed. She takes a quick mouthful and then says: "Fernando doesn't like me dressing flashy. Sometimes I'd like to look different, perhaps more sensual, a bit like you. He doesn't agree. Once I wore what I wanted and he made a scene," she admits, lowering her voice.

"What?" I can't believe my ears. He criticizes his wife's femininity and then plays the part of an aggressive lover. I'll punish him properly when we next meet, I think to myself.

"Don't get me wrong, he doesn't let me want for anything. It's just that sometimes . . . ," she leaves the sentence incomplete and I have an absurd desire to hug her and tell her everything will be alright.

She gets up and starts to clear the table. We throw the plastic plates, cutlery, and glasses into the bin. So much for Fernando, I think. We joke around a bit; she's cheerful again, her bare feet dart across the floor.

"Try my shoes on," I suggest, enjoying myself. I take them off, revealing my tanned feet with purple toenails. She puts them on and they fit like a glove.

"Definitely sensual," I say, admiring her legs, the muscles taut because of the heels.

The effect of the wine is wearing off and so I suggest a toast to high-heeled shoes. She takes from the cupboard a bottle of Montenegro liqueur and two small glasses, but I forestall her.

"Wasn't it a day for anarchy? No glasses," I challenge her.

"Okay."

She takes a mouthful of amber liquid straight from the bottle and I do the same, one foot on the other on the cold floor. We take turns with the bottle like two teenagers pretending to be grown-ups. The whole situation is very weird.

My head is spinning slightly. She is so defenseless, beautiful, dominated by a man who I wanted to please until yesterday, but today I want to punish.

"Try to see yourself as totally different. It's a game I used to play with my senior-year school friends. We used to pretend to be each other. I'll be Sara and you can be Mimma," I suggest.

Without saying a word she has another mouthful of liqueur and slips off her yellow dress. Straight away she feels a wave of embarrassment and holds the dress in front of her body to cover her breasts while I begin to calmly unbutton my blouse.

"Be quick or I'll change my mind," she begs me. She smiles that smile again.

"Help me. Maybe I've had a bit too much to drink, and with all these buttons I can't see straight."

She extends her arms and focuses on the last, tiny, mother-of-pearl button that she holds in her fingers. The yellow dress falls onto the floor. She doesn't seem to notice straight away, her attention caught by the round, glittering buttons.

I look at her small, perfect breasts that point upward, the swollen nipples, her flat stomach. Her unblemished skin contrasting with her black pants, her feet bent into my shoes.

My mind is a sheet of white paper where I want to write the words to describe those girlish breasts, those bright eyes, those tender lips. I find myself thinking that he doesn't make her smile the way I have done. I find myself wanting her. My blouse falls to the floor; I unfasten my bra. She leans against the stove and doesn't move. The zip hisses like the tempting serpent suggesting the next move. Eve versus Eve again, or perhaps she's the apple. And all I want to do is pluck her from the tree.

A Pleasant Madness

I reach out my hand and untie her hair, which falls like threads of silk onto her slender shoulders. I notice that she's trembling. I move closer to her and stroke her gently. First her hair, then her face, her neck.

I can feel that I'm wet down there. She is a frightened deer and I'm the hunter; I have set my trap. I have done it to punish her or perhaps to puncture her pride. But now that I've caught her I realise that all I want to do is lose myself against her pale skin, make her cry out, give her pleasure.

I'm scared that she will push me away; if she does that I will die. I have to know, my desire is too strong. I'm a breath away from her lips. A whispered kiss. I move away and look at her.

"I'm afraid," she says quietly.

I give her a kiss that forces open the slight resistance of her lips. I find her soft, yielding tongue. I rest my hips against hers, my hands on her breasts. It's not like it was with Chiara when we were girls; then it was just a game played by curious teenagers. Now it's different. Now I'm controlled by a feeling I've never felt before. I'm like a man standing in front of a frightened virgin. I want to take her virtue, fill her with the blinding heat of my vice.

"I can't," she murmurs.

This excites me even more. I bite her lower lip and slide my hand between her legs. I pull aside her panties; she too is dripping wet. My blue eyes sparkle in the sea of hers. I draw a first moan of pleasure from her and then I kneel down, a sinner with bare feet. I sink my tongue into a paradise of the senses.

Subdued Seducers

I met him one more time. The last.

For a while I enjoyed pushing him to the limit, but then Fernando overstepped that limit.

For a while I delighted in seeing him at the mercy of his emotions. He, who used to be so respectable, blinded by desire, his features transformed and his whole body quivering. At dinner I would eat slowly, then pretend I had a sudden headache and leave him in the grip of the hormonal storm stirred up by my body. I loved that unexpected reversal of our roles.

I have changed my clothes; now I dress like a beautiful and unattainable business woman, professional and detached, but with details that suggest that I know how to be sensual when I want to be. I'm always the one who decides how and when.

Fernando started to annoy me mercilessly. I gave in to him just a couple of times, perhaps to test whether I really didn't feel anything for him anymore, or perhaps, even worse, out of pity. While he was screwing me I could see Sara's face, her hair dishevelled from our amorous struggles, compliant and tremulous. I take her every afternoon, on the sofa, in the bed where she sleeps with Fernando. I leave the trace of my perfume in every corner of their salmon-colored house. I consecrate every chair with the sweet fluids of her pussy. My desire for her is insatiable.

That evening I left Fernando, two cruel and irreversible words escaped my lips: never again.

He hit rock bottom, he yelled, he cried in front of me; me, who used to love his self-control, his strength of mind, and his inner confidence. He never used to need to ask, all it took was a glance. Today he begged me. I laughed in his face.

"You've become pathetic," I told him.

The change is complete. I am the phoenix with the feral beauty that has ripped out the predator to become a wild animal.

Sara. What part has Sara played in all this?

None, I like to believe. The change had already been triggered in me some time ago, I'm sure of that.

And yet, if I think about the possibility of losing her now . . .

But this is a pointless and negative thought. Sara is mine, her body belongs to me, and only I know how to play on her pleasure. Only I have the key to the door that leads to her vice.

I am in bed and I'm thinking about her, giving myself moments of solitary pleasure.

Women of Shadow, Men of Fog

Sara has told me that Fernando will be away all weekend at a conference. I can sleep with her in their bed. I have asked her not to change the sheets. I want to cancel out his odor with the smell of our sweat and our tears of joy. I hate to admit it, but every time I get ready to say good-bye to her I can hardly breathe. I can't think about leaving her in his power until the following day. She is mine, I know that, and yet sometimes I miss her so much that . . . all I would like is to not suffer the excruciating pain of separation. She has said she has a surprise for me. She told me this with that strange light that every now and then ignites in her small pale eyes. She kissed me and whispered: "You'll be lost for words."

"I adore surprises," I replied.

"This will definitely be a surprise," she said with a kiss. Her voice is like amniotic fluid in which my whole being wants to float. She has conquered me with her fragility. I have always been competitive with other women, but not with her. I'm the one who calls the shots; she is my swan, my doe, eager for my caresses, a silent butterfly.

I have a surprise for her too. I have bought handcuffs, a pale pink-colored vibrator. I will drive her mad with pleasure, and perhaps after this weekend she will decide to leave Fernando. She could easily come and live with me. I'll be the one to take care of her; I won't let her lack for anything. I feel a rush of anger. What am I saying? Has she affected me so much that I've taken leave of my senses?

Dying Among the Violets

The bed is covered by a black sheet scattered with violets. The color of dreams, or at least that's how I imagine them. A mass of candlelight dances around us, framing the bed with a warm and caressing glow. The background music is a mellow tune; a musky fragrance hovers in the air.

I have tied her wrists to the head of the bed and have made her come until she is exhausted. I wanted her to never forget our first weekend of love.

When I thought she was tired I freed her from my bondage. I lose myself in her eyes. I kiss her gently and stroke her hair.

"You're so beautiful," I murmur.

"You are. At best I'm pretty," she replies in that low, soft tone she has that immediately provokes a pleasurable stab deep in my stomach.

"I'd like you to come and live with me," I say. The words escape like all the other times when something is bigger than me and just slips out. Almost as if my soul isn't able to hold it in.

"Can you say that again?"

"I want you to come and live with me," I repeat, saying the words clearly.

"Do you really want that?" she asks.

She looks like a goddess: her blonde hair kissed by the golden light of the candles, the body of a child woman beaded with tiny drops of sweat.

"I want it with all my being," I reply.

"Can I ask you something?"

"Of course."

"I'd like to tie you up. It's that . . . you make me enjoy it so much. For once I'd like to be able to give you the same pleasure." Sara takes me aback. I wasn't expecting a request like that after my proposition, and usually she is so shy and submissive.

"It would be a way to show me that you trust me," she adds.

"Of course I trust you," I reply. After all, there's no harm in it, I try to convince myself. Perhaps Sara wants to experiment.

I am wearing a black satin, boned corset. It encircles me like a vice; I look like a lady from the olden days in a naughty pose, my full breasts bursting from my bra. My partial nudity is emphasized by silk stockings held up by lace suspenders.

The graceful butterfly fastens both my wrists to the headboard, making use of the handcuffs. My heart begins to pound, partly because I've never found myself in this sort of situation before, partly because of the feral light shining in her eyes in that instant.

"Just a minute. I have to get the first part of the surprise," she says.

I try to relax but it isn't easy. A few moments later she reappears wearing a latex outfit: shiny boots up to mid-thigh, panties, and a lace-up bustier. In her hand she is holding a short whip made of strips of leather.

I gulp noisily. "And what do you mean to do with that whip?"

"It's my cat-o'-nine-tails. The only pet I could buy without my husband noticing," she responds with a strange smile.

Before joining me she turns up the volume of the radio, and then opens the wardrobe door. My mouth falls open in an expression that is more astonished than I'd like it to be; I can't believe my eyes.

The Thinking Butterfly

The bed is covered by a black sheet scattered with crumpled violets. The color of nightmares, or at least that's how I imagine them. For about an hour I have been falling into a dark well. I keep on falling without stopping. Perhaps because what Sara has made me experience is the ecstasy of a pleasure so unbearable that it becomes painful. She has been able to transform every one of my orgasms into a wound and she has soothed every crack of the whip on my body with the medicine of her tender tongue and her skillful fingers.

She has learned and refined the art of giving pleasure. She has blended all my tricks with those that Fernando used to use to make me moan to the point of exhaustion. Sara has made our techniques hers and has combined them with her own individual skill. A subtle skill, as sweet as venom.

My body is covered with purple-colored streaks. My clitoris is throbbing; I could die for another orgasm. And every time I came I couldn't help but look beyond the golden circle of the candles burning around us to see the pale and devastated face of a man, naked, tied to a chair, gagged. A man I hardly recognize, drained, his eyes red. A man who has observed every one of our caresses, right from the start, through the cracks in the door, unable to escape from the most agonizing and thrilling sight he could imagine. The staging of a double betrayal. His wife and his lover locked in the ecstasy of pleasure.

"Let's begin, sweetie," Sara said before starting to play with my pussy.

Sweetie: the pet name that Fernando used to call me when we made love. Then I understood that I wasn't imprisoned in a nightmare. The cruel, striking reality was standing before me.

Sara, the graceful butterfly, or perhaps the patient spider who had woven the web of her revenge. While she was arousing me with the silicon vibrator she told her story in a musical voice. That afternoon she sedated Fernando by slipping a massive amount of benzodiazepine into his glass. Then she arranged everything so that he couldn't miss even a second of the show staged for him. And for me.

Me, who thought that I was directing the game; me, a stupid woman ruled by my ego and the seven deadly sins in never-ending conflict. I changed from victim to tormentor of my man, only to discover that the one real victim in this whole affair was also the real tormentor. Sara. Who knows for how long Sara had been following us. Who knows for how long she knew everything . . .

You seem satisfied now. You stand up, you move away from my body and for me it is an excruciating stab of pain, worse than that caused by your whip. You put on a pair of jeans and a white T-shirt, like the first time I met you. You pack a suitcase.

"Untie me right now!" I shout.

You don't seem to be paying any attention to me. Fernando stirs and groans from his vantage point, the front row at the great spectacle of his downfall.

You switch on the light; extinguish the candles with a gentle blow. Me, make-up smudged, humiliated in both body and spirit. Fernando a disjointed puppet, groaning grotesquely.

I close my eyes, I am worn out.

Shoot Me in My Heart

I open my eyes to find myself aching in an unmade bed. I am free, my wrists are burning, the wounds on my body cry out. Fernando is opposite me, tied to the chair in the same position as last night, his head hanging to one side. He must have fainted or perhaps he fell asleep, just like me. On his legs he has the same red streaks that decorate my skin. Dried tears on his face, dried sperm on his stomach. Seeing us together must have hurt him and at the same time aroused him.

"Pain and pleasure, Sara's punishment. A letter on the pillow."

"Good-bye Mimma. I told you I would give you a surprise that you would never forget. I leave you with a kiss and a tear for what will never be again. I forgive you.

"Now I am free and I will make sure my life from now on is a happy one.

"Sara

"P.S.: I'm pregnant."

And so Fernando always continued making love to her, even when he was promising that he didn't touch her anymore. Or perhaps after the red-hot afternoons in the company of her lover, Sara also gave herself to her husband, preparing her revenge. The tears stream down my face, salty; they burn more than all my wounds. I can't lose her. Sara is inside my flesh now, she flows through my veins, she has entered me silently like an illness infecting my senses.

"No!" I scream. "I can't lose you!"

I cry, unable to move. My skin is cold as never before, the pain of separation is like a dagger.

Fernando moves suddenly in his sleep but doesn't wake up. There is a note for him too.

The signed papers for the divorce are on the kitchen table.

"It's not worth you making trouble, I have proof of your adultery—photographs and videos. I could take you to the cleaners. Don't ever try to find me. My lawyer will contact you.

"Sara"

Sara's perfume fills the air. Obsession. My hand moves all by itself and I don't even realize that I have started to caress myself again.

Chances

LIVIANA ROSE

I stop at a traffic light, one of many red lights, on a shitty day that shows no sign of ending. Even in my head, I put a "fuck" or a "shit" after every word I think.

Why must I live in one of the most congested cities in Italy?

Because it's fashionable.
Because there are so many opportunities for the child.
Because you have better opportunities for work.
Because all our friends live here.

Because you can pay a king's ransom in order to breathe the black air that will give your lungs a lovely cancer.
Because it's really cool to pay the equivalent of a normal person's salary to insure the high-performance car that someone will definitely try to steal.
Because you're a poor nerd.

And, fuck, it never turns green.
I'm never the first in line so I can't even try to challenge the cars that are next to me over who manages to set off first.
I was forgetting: I couldn't win anyway—today I've got my wife's Jeep.

The only good thing about it is that I can look down on the tie-wearing pretty boys on their scooters and the posh young ladies in smart cars.

Like this one to my left. Look at those thighs. She's wearing a miniskirt that would make you wolf whistle in the street seeing it wrapped round that arse, in her car I'd say it looks more like a belt. Leather. Black. Into S&M, that young lady. Young, so to speak. Judging by her hands and the jewelry she's wearing on her fingers and wrist, I'd say she's at least forty. A pity I can't see her face. She's sitting with her thighs slightly apart—who knows how hot it is down there. Look, look at what magazine the honey's flicking through. It's only the catalogue of the best known sex shop in the city: I recognize it from the logo.

The light turns green, but at the next traffic light I arrange it so I'm next to her again. I don't know whether she's noticed my interest or not and whether she's doing it on purpose but she carries on thumbing through the magazine. There are unequivocally pornographic photos: sex scenes to advertise this or that product for forbidden games. I'm a bit further away than before—this time I manage to see her face. She is a really beautiful woman, one of those women who gives you a hard-on with a single glance. Despite the leather skirt, her hair and makeup are very sophisticated: the overall effect creates a truly intriguing contrast. For just a second our eyes meet: now she knows perfectly well that I'm watching her.

Green again, and again I follow the mysterious woman.

At the next traffic light I manage to be near her again. Distractedly, she flicks through the newspaper lying on the passenger seat, then moves her hips a bit further forward on the seat, opens the glove compartment, and, fully aware of my gaze following her hands, takes out a fairly large vibrator, wets it with a bit of saliva, opens her thighs and slides it right inside. She looks at me, smiling, perhaps teasing me, seeing my staring eyes and my slightly open mouth, and starts to move the fake penis backward and forward. Every time she takes it out I see the reflections of the sun making it shine: it must be very wet and hot . . . I'm exploding inside my trousers.

I would like to get out of the car and fuck her. Perhaps I could follow her home and ask her to let me in, or . . . A blast from a horn wakes me from my daydream. It's green and I'm holding up the traffic. The woman next to me, however, has already gone and there's no trace of her.

※

In order to be able to move into the new house, we had to wait for about a year and a half beyond the due date. An immeasurable pain in the ass. Also because the builder did some truly crappy work. For example, the slope of the terrace floor was wrong, and when it rains I appear to have a swimming pool right outside my bedroom.

Also, the tiles have big black marks that can't be cleaned off. I called the company that supplied them several times until I finally spoke directly to the owner. The lady assured me that she would come in person to rectify the problem.

Here she is: a woman of about fifty who smiles at me and shakes my hand. She has a very pleasant jovial smile and a spark of vitality. She is still a good-looking woman, thin but with quite an ample bosom on display—anyone who cares to look can check it out thanks to her low-cut blouse. She carries her years with confidence, and this makes her even more attractive. I show her the problem with the tiles on the floor. She examines them for a moment, ferrets about in her case and takes out a product she tells me is miraculous for these sorts of black marks.

"You just have to wipe it on with a sponge and then rinse with a bit of water and vinegar," she says.

And, elegantly dressed in a designer suit, she gets down on her hands and knees on the floor and starts scrubbing energetically.

I am amazed: not so much by what she's doing but by the stupendous view she's providing me with. Right before my eyes there's her lovely arse moving backward and forward, hugged and emphasized by her pencil skirt. There's no visible sign of underwear but above the waistband of her skirt peeks out a border of black lace, so she must be wearing a thong. I'm delighted, and I don't listen to the part of my brain that keeps telling me to look somewhere else or at least to move away from the fantastic sight.

I'm wearing a pair of lightweight tracksuit trousers and I think my arousal is starting to become rather too obvious. Just at that moment the woman stands up, her gaze lingers for a moment on my erection, and she says to me:

"The stains have gone now, but if they should recur don't hesitate to call me."

She smiles wickedly and, as she leaves, she puts in my hand a business card with her private number.

Every now and then I too have moments of respite. For example, when I meet up with my young lover in some shopping center or other to eat ice cream.

She always has a cone with cream and strawberry flavors; I have a cup with hazelnut and chocolate mousse. If I haven't seen her for a while I get them to add a bit of whipped cream as well and I offer her a taste.

I like watching her as she moves her little tongue up and down the cone and how she relishes it.

I still haven't worked out if it's just lust for ice cream on her part or if it's a premeditated sexual ploy, although I'd plump for the second hypothesis.

However, there's no need for her to act like this because all I have to do is think about her when she's in the car with me to get aroused. She has a sort of habit that is truly delicious. Every time we stop at a traffic light she says "It's red," she turns toward me, sticks her tongue out slightly between her lips, puts a hand on my thigh, strokes the fly of my trousers with her fingers, and invites me to kiss her with an extremely cute look, a mix of femme fatale and seasoned porn star. I smile at this behavior, so out of place in this sweet young woman, I return her kiss and then I look around.

Usually I realize, only after the kiss, however, that the car next to mine belongs to a colleague of my wife, or my bank manager, or the family greengrocer.

I retreat gracefully, hoping that no one has seen me, and I think about something genuinely tragic, like my secretary's cellulite or my neighbor's snoring, to try to make my dick deflate, which, from the constraints of my trousers, is begging me to stop in the first blind alley and fuck the tasty little morsel sitting next to me.

I double-park in front of the shop in the city center to wait for my wife who has to buy something or other. Evidently they must still produce the something or other because I have to wait for quarter of an hour. I watch people passing by and I notice how everyone's in a hurry. Always in a rush, always out of breath, cell phone in one hand and umbrella in the other. It's just stopping raining after a heavy downpour.

And then a flash: a woman wrapped in a black coat, hair tied back, dark sunglasses, black shoes with towering silver stiletto heels, a measured and very sensual way of walking.

I feel turmoil in my stomach, and I watch her cross the road in front of me with the intriguing sensation that under her raincoat the woman is completely naked.

The thing I hate most, among all the things I hate most, is having to take out the rubbish in the evening, straight after having finished supper. I would like to stay on the sofa enjoying a film, channel surf for a bit . . . I would even watch a game of soccer rather than take the garbage out. Can't one do it in the morning before going to work? No, in the evening, otherwise it smells. I could buy some scent . . .

The fact is that almost every evening I go out on foot, if the weather allows it; if not, I get no further than the parking space for the car. I do a route that covers almost the entire neighborhood, because, where I live, the rubbish collection is separated, to be environmentally friendly. And the bins are further away.

On the way there I walk by the houses, from which emanates an amazing variety of noises; on the way back I like to cross over to the cool of the bay hedge that surrounds the public swimming pool. It's a stupid idea, but I feel that the greenery helps me breathe better. Every now and then in summer I hear voices coming from inside. I don't know why, but I decide to take a peek through the thick growth of leaves. It seems strange to me that there are still people there at ten o'clock. I search for a spot where the vegetation is a bit thinner and I look through. In the water there are two very distinct figures: a man and a woman. I immediately recognize the girl—I could hardly do otherwise given her bulk—it's the caretaker at my son's nursery. She has two shoulders as wide as a four-door wardrobe and her walk resembles very closely that of a hippopotamus. She has, I have to admit, an exquisite complexion, fresh and smooth skin, and her face is lovely, like with most fat women. I don't know the small man who's splashing her. But he is thin and short, and his coloring, as far as one can gather in the dim light, is rather dark. He must be from North Africa, or possibly Turkey. They are playing in the water: they chase each other, they push each other under, and they compete to see who gets to the side first. I smile, pleased and accommodating: I'm happy that they're enjoying themselves and cooling off. I too would gladly have a swim, what with this mugginess. I've no idea how the caretaker manages to be there after closing time. I am about to go when I see her coming out of the water completely naked, her rolls of fat clearly on display: she has such enormous tits they could do with a sign saying OVERSIZED LOAD. And between her thighs sprouts a thick clump of coal-black down that contrasts with her very pale skin. The Moroccan gets out of the water—he's naked too—and strokes her cheek. She then grabs him by the wrist and pulls him toward her, starting to kiss him and to play with his dick. When its hardness is to her liking—and I have to say that the man is tiny but his equipment is rather well developed—the caretaker opens her legs and slides it into that . . . that . . . technically I'd call it her pussy, but my brain keeps using the term "chasm."

All the poor man can do is pump away in the hope of coming, or making her come, as soon as possible.

It would be better for me to go. I put back the branches that I moved and go home.

An overwhelming desire to have sex has come over me.

When I get home I can hear that my wife is in the shower. I join her, and maybe I'll get a nice blow job.

I don't know why but I decided to take my lover, Juno, as I call her—though only to myself—for a turn around a book fair. In general, lovers are for hotels or pieds-à-terre. Perhaps I like to play and to feel that I'm desired the way she makes me feel. And I want the whole world to see that: there's nowhere better than a nice, crowded fair.

The girl flaunts herself, she dances around me, every so often she kisses me, bites my ear without restraint, teases me, whispers strange, exciting things to me. It's an enjoyable game, watching her, so exuberant and passionate.

It relaxes me to drive her mad. And she, to get her own back, puts a hand on my dick and makes an irresistible desire to fuck her grow inside me.

She finds any excuse to punish me like that: she stands next to me, and when I least expect it she gracefully extends her hand and squeezes. We are walking past a stand displaying Catholic publications and a member of the staff in a prim, masculine suit is showing a book to a potential client. Her glance wanders over to me for a fraction of a second: perhaps I interest her, perhaps I've made an impression on her. The grey-haired woman is aware of me. She stares.

Juno is reaching out with her hand to my dick and the woman suddenly widens her eyes: scandalized or interested, I don't know.

I stop the girl's hand and whisper in her ear that people are looking at us.

She smiles at me, pulls me by the hand toward another stand, and the joke is forgotten. I turn toward the woman with purple cheeks and her blatantly voyeuristic stare still directed at us.

I stop Juno, hug her and kiss her, while with one hand I give her bottom a good squeeze as if I'm about to slip a finger into her petite arse. I kiss my young lover and look the woman straight in the eye; she isn't able to divert her attention.

After a good two minutes we draw apart, turn the corner, and bid goodbye to the Catholic publications.

One of my clients has arranged to meet me in the square by a gas station on the highway. I get there a good hour and a half early but wouldn't know how to pass the time in any other way. It is truly scorching hot. And in the gas station, there's no shade at all, not for love nor money. However, there's a small bar, a fairly dilapidated hovel. With every step I take toward it, my stomach rebels at the thought of ordering anything because, from its appearance, the place gives me the impression of being filthy. In front of the door there's a huddle of truck drivers downing cans of beer. If I did that I'd be fucked for the rest of the day—I wouldn't stop sweating for a second. I go into the cramped bar, and there's no one behind the counter. On my left is a cabinet full of prepackaged ice cream, the only thing my brain will let me risk buying. Leaning against the fridge there's a young woman—typically Mediterranean amber-colored skin, quite a cold type—who's reading the paper. She is, undoubtedly, the girl who works there. I can tell from the slightly annoyed manner with which she's looking at me. She's used to seeing strangers, but she's miffed about having to move. I ask her for an ice cream and she gives it to me without saying a word. While she leans on the cabinet, she kindly shows me her behind: she's wearing a very short miniskirt and an abbreviated vest, on her feet a pair of slippers that leave her feet, beautiful feet, practically naked.

She's an attractive girl and she knows it, just as she knows perfectly well that those truck drivers outside are there just for her tits and arse.

I sit down at one of the two tables inside the bar and, trying to ignore the dirt as much as I can, I start to eat my ice cream and to watch the comings and goings.

Regular customers. They say hello to her, they know her, some try to make themselves look good in front of her, others ask her how things are going and if she's well and pay her compliments about how pretty she is: all with the sole aim of trying to get her into bed. Behind the counter she is leaning with her elbows on the rack of dirty glasses and generously thrusts her breasts forward. It's clear that her stance is deliberate, slightly false—it's the price she has to pay to have a full till at the end of the day.

I feel sorry for those poor regulars who go to all that trouble needlessly: it's not as if she'll ever give herself to them.

My client has arrived. I get up from the table, greet him with a nod of the head, and I realize I've got an erection. Luckily I've got my rucksack to cover it.

Another thing I hate is doing the shopping at the supermarket. Outside it's boiling hot and inside you almost freeze.

Then I happen to run into the caretaker who invites me to go, with her, to the swimming pool after closing time.

You go through a side entrance that they never close—she tells me—and then the water is cool, inviting . . . I knew what she wanted to invite me for . . . Just the thought of being confined between those rolls of lard brings on an attack of claustrophobia.

I say good-bye, thanking her, and I go to the fruit and vegetable section. I take a bag and put a few lemons in it. I look at one and think about the poor man I saw with her in the pool: she must have really squeezed the juice out of him.

Sunday afternoon I go to the bar under the arches to have a coffee. I always go to the same place because the coffee is good there. Before finding and trying this blend I used to drink my coffee with no sugar, but now I always put a packet in just for the fun of seeing how the little heap of sugar floats on the thick and glossy froth and then gradually sinks sweetly.

The television is switched on, with pictures but no sound, and the radio squawks out a commentary on the soccer matches.

The girl behind the bar doesn't even ask what I want anymore and just gives me a hint of a perfunctory smile. I drink only one cup of coffee: I'm not a good customer.

I never talk to anyone. I listen while the others talk.

I pour in the packet of sugar, stir carefully, drink my coffee, and stand for ten minutes at a table where they're playing a card game.

A group of women who for twenty years, on every Sunday and every bank holiday, can be found here from two in the afternoon until seven in the evening playing cards: there have been wars, the country has gone through economic crises, there have been three floods and a tornado, Italy has won the World Cup, lots of extraordinary crimes have upset public opinion. They have always been there.

Everyone is ready to discuss this or that in the bar. It seems like an agnostic confessional. Then you ask questions. Then you develop an interest in their lives and the adventures you imagine they have, following the series of glances that intersect.

You listen to what they say and what they tell you and you draw your own conclusions. Then there are things that you wouldn't want to hear, but that force their way into your ears and are like a worm in your brain. And your assessment of the person goes up and down like a haywire elevator. Like that time when a couple had sex in the bathroom of the bar and I'm sure I was the only person who noticed.

Once they asked me if I wanted to join in the card game with them. I declined their invitation politely.

In the little group of spectators I saw envy and displeasure, because even the lives of those who stand around the table intertwine with those of the players. Everyone would like to be the dummy who finds a place at the table every now and then.

They smoke, they cheer at touchdowns, they drink, they nibble at bar snacks, they get annoyed about a trump card not played, they talk, they gossip, they look to make sure that the others are looking at them, they answer their cell phones quietly to make the others think that the call is spicy and private, they hope that seven o'clock will come around as late as possible, they live.

Sometimes I would like to know whether they talk about me as well.

But I never talk about my wife, I don't have a tumor, I don't have dogs, I'm not well endowed, I'm not handsome, I'm not nice, I don't have a cool motorcycle or car, I don't follow a soccer team.

They'll only be able to say bad things about me because I'm a boring man who has a coffee with a packet of sugar every Sunday, watches ten minutes of the card game, and then leaves, barely saying good-bye, perhaps thinking that his life is much better than theirs, as for twenty years they've always sat at the same table in the bar under the arches.

———

I need a shower.
    After this shitty day I can't think of a better way to switch off.
    Arguments, silences, anger, they all seemed determined to pile up today.

I touched bottom at lunchtime, in the canteen, at my usual table in the corner, while I was picking at a plastic salad and writing down ideas on a wretched notepad with the unmistakeable logo of the company I work for.
    I was writing and my colleagues repeatedly came up to me, not looking me in the eye but trying to peek at the inky words.
    But you should be ashamed of yourselves. Go away!
    A dull fit of rage rose from my stomach but I couldn't scream. That suffocated scream is still stuck in my throat and it won't go either up or down.
    Shower, shower, shower.
    I turn the tap to blue and wait for the cold water to start flowing and wake up my body.
    I close my eyes and bend my head under the icy jet, letting my thoughts run through my mind and glide away like the water flowing over my body.
    I haven't eaten this evening.
    My wife is at our house by the sea with my sister-in-law.
    I hope my brother, who's staying with me at the moment, has done the shopping.
    I need to pick up my trousers from the dry cleaners.
    There's a phone bill that needs paying.

I've still got two weeks to service the car.
That shit of a neighbor has parked his car in front of our gate again.
Juno hasn't called.
Those idiots I work with keep on harassing me with their forced smiles and those fake indulgent winks and as soon as you turn your back on them they backstab you.
I finished work at ten.
Fifty, fifty-five minutes of traffic to get home.
What a fucking awful life.
The house is silent except for the noise of the water gushing from the shower.
My brother is sleeping in the living room.
It's after midnight.
I'm hungry, I'm tired, I'm restless.
I turn off the tap and get out of the shower.
I'm so cold my teeth are chattering.
I put on my robe, which gives me a warm hug.
The annoyed thoughts and the lump in my throat are still there, more unsettling than before.
With my robe open, not caring whether I might bump into anyone, I leave the bathroom and go into the kitchen.
In the dark.
I pick up the remote control from the breakfast table and switch on the TV to a random channel.
Crap, crap, crap, unadulterated crap.
I switch it off and am in the dark again.
I blindly feel for a piece of fruit in the center of the table.
I sniff it. It's an apple.
I don't know why, but before I take a bite I wait for a few seconds.
With my free hand I punch the wall.
It hurt. Fuck.
But I definitely feel better.
I am standing with an apple in my right hand, my robe undone, and a

gentle breeze that's coming through the slightly open window that tickles my pubic hair.

With my left hand I'm about to pull my robe closed then I have second thoughts and I begin to touch myself . . .

I feel the tension gradually relaxing.

I slide my hand up and down slowly.

In an instant my dick is hard and ready to come.

My mind is completely and finally empty.

Anyone could come in the kitchen and find me like this.

I don't give a damn.

It's the right thing to do in this moment.

I throw my head back and feel my breathing getting heavier.

I bite into the apple and find it sweet and juicy. Crunchy.

I come between my still cold fingers.

And the world can go fuck itself.

A Dangerous Game

ANNA BULGARIS

It's now two weeks since he left.

I don't like being on my own; I miss him more and more—sometimes it's unbearable. I miss his smile, the exotic sound of his voice, the way he pronounces his words. And then there's that need, the continual throbbing between my legs, the dull desire to feel him inside me.

I could take the edge off the feeling but I won't, because when he calls me he'll hear how much I want him.

He's what I want, not some fleeting pleasure, nor another man, someone I could seduce without even having to put too much effort into it.

I get out of bed, and after having a shower I get myself ready for a tedious and meaningless day at work, a day like all the others.

I don't like my job. We have talked about it and he asked me, after having looked at me intensely, why I don't change things. For him life is simple, and I'm starting to believe that he's right after all.

Before him there were commitments, duty, set patterns to follow, and unhappiness; nothing tragic or profound, just a faint melancholy, a continual feeling of sadness.

If I had to describe my old life with a color, I would choose grey. Not a pearly grey or the rich grey of a dark sea.

No.

That sea grey, under the swirl of the eddying waters, becomes pure energy, powerful, terrible, but magnificent.

The grey that I'm talking about, on the other hand, is the monotonous and unchanging color of asphalt scorched by the sun.

Before I knew him there was nothing beneath the paper-thin surface of my life of pretense and lies.

Now I'm beginning to know myself, to understand myself.

I sigh and put on the pink dress with sky-blue flowers, the one that has a short slit at the back. I don't put on any underwear. I want to feel free, I want to think about him, about the man I know nothing about, and who paradoxically has made my life different, intense, and amazing.

As I walk my legs rub against each other, creating a delicious current that runs through me. I feel the muscles in my vagina tighten and quiver with longing. I breathe in and then out again; I have to calm down or I won't be able to get through to the end of the day.

I pin up my hair, I put on a bit of makeup, I even try to sing something, but that dull throbbing, the pulsing between my legs, doesn't go away. I look around to check that everything is neat and tidy.

I have just picked up the car keys when my cell phone rings. I look at the display and recognize his number. My heart feels like it's about to burst with happiness and I grin idiotically.

"Yes," I answer quietly.

"I like your voice, and the way you say 'yes' to me." A shiver runs through me from my head to my toes. I sit down. I sense that I will have to soon anyway. "Did you sleep well?" His question is polite, his voice melodious, but what's going through his mind is quite a different matter. I know; I'm as sure of it as I am that day follows night.

I nod, but then I realize he can't see me and so I clear my throat.

"You know I don't sleep well when you're not here."

He doesn't reply, the silence that follows is charged with meaning.

"Did you touch yourself?" His question ties my stomach into knots. "No. But I would have liked to." I can hear his breathing, which hardly quickens. "Remember that you're mine. And you don't do anything until I grant you permission."

I don't respond. I raise my head and open my mouth. I need air. The hall mirror reflects my image back at me. Only now do I notice that my hands are shaking.

"Are you about to go to work?" he asks me calmly. "Yes. I was just leaving." He sighs. "You're not late. There's time." It isn't a question. I moisten my dry lips, I close my eyes a little, and I wait.

"What are you wearing?" I'm ready for his question. "The dress with flowers. Nothing else."

I can hear him as he holds his breath and then breathes out, slowly.

He likes this dress. It is loose and light. It glides over the skin like a caress when he lifts it up, a moment before he sinks into me.

"Lift it up."

I do, and I keep watching myself in the mirror as, an inch at a time, my pale skin appears in front of me. I continue raising it higher, until I can see the mound of Venus, no hair. That's how he likes it.

When he licks me, he wants to feel my smooth skin under his tongue. He explained this to me explicitly, and I keep him happy.

"Open your legs."

My breathing quickens, as does his. "Are you wet enough?" His question is precise. He doesn't want to make conversation. I inhale; suddenly the air seems to have become heavy. "Yes," I reply. "Good. You know what to do."

I frown, and for a second I think about making an excuse.

But his voice is like steel.

I shudder as I make my way to the bathroom. I take the vibrator from its velvet case and I get it ready. Then I go back to where he is waiting on the phone. I sit down in front of the mirror, spread my legs and then switch on the speakerphone. He wants to listen to me while I'm doing it. "Put it in now." His voice has lost any trace of gentleness.

Total control.

I tremble with desire. I arch my back and lift up my heels, placing them on the arms of the chair. By now I'm wide open. I use my fingers to help push in the bulky vibrator, parting my flesh. I tremble as I feel myself dilating around it. It's large, and long.

Not like him, but close enough.

"Move it now. Imagine that it's me fucking you."

And I do. I push it deep inside, and then I slide it out. My breathing becomes heavy, the desire grows and centers in my vagina. "Turn it on." I swallow and then push down on the little button.

The slow movement of the vibrator is torture. I bite my lip and keep moving it back and forth. "Speed it up, and then wait till I tell you."

I bite down on my arm as the arousal becomes uncontrollable. But all I can do is obey him, while a film of sweat forms on my body.

How can I resist?

"Good girl."

That self-satisfied tone of his cajoles me and turns me on.

His pleasure is my pleasure. I start to writhe as I feel the orgasm getting closer. I close my eyes and let myself be carried along by the undiluted desire of his voice. With each breath I feel the tension mounting, my nipples are getting swollen, yearning for his touch.

"Not yet." His command is peremptory. For an instant I am tempted to tell him to go to hell and to come when I want, and I'm about to do so when he groans, and then I open my eyes wide.

He's touching himself; I can hear it. His breathing becomes quicker, the faint noise more frequent. I know that he wants to hear me come as he does, together. Me and him.

And so I wait and I imagine that it is my man pressing inside me, thrusting and filling every inch of my vagina.

"Now, now. Come for me!" Power and a plea combined.

And I do, while I lose myself in the stifled cry that rises from his throat.

We remain in silence for a moment, while our breathing merges with faint gasps, still caught up in the web of passion.

It was nice, but that knot I have inside me will only unravel when he possesses me.

I know that absolutely.

"I'll be back soon. And I'll bring you a present."

A moment later he hangs up.

I need another minute to recover. I stay there, breathless, legs stretched apart, while the final spasms are still running through me. Then I go back into the bathroom, clean myself, and go to work.

Another long day that seems to never end, without him.

And that constant fear won't leave me: the thought that he might decide not to come back to me.

When did I start to love him? I don't know. But I honestly don't even know if the feeling that burns inside me is love or obsession. I only know that my days have meaning when he is with me, that I breathe, dream, live for him.

And this is my greatest weakness.

I have decided to eat in a small trattoria; I don't feel like cooking. I feel sad. He hasn't called me, and this means that he hasn't been able to conclude his business affairs.

I climb the stairs and enter the apartment. A shower and then bed.

As I let myself drift off, my last coherent thought is of him.

We are such stuff as dreams are made on.

I've often thought about this phrase, and now I fully understand its meaning. At least, at this moment I think I do, when his warm skin slides over me and I wonder whether I'm really awake.

His breath is soft, it tickles my neck, it makes me think of a large, contented cat. When he gently bites me, leaving a moist trail, shivers of pleasure run through me, like rays flowing through me, until they reach my vagina.

I snap open my eyes. Around me there is silence and darkness.

The feeling of loneliness that floods over me when I realize I am awake is overwhelming. I kick off the sheets and I feel a lump in my throat.

He hasn't come back. The disappointment is unbearable.

Another long day in the office. A night, and then another day. Hours marked by need, fear, and anger. Like magma bubbling under the skin and increasing in volume.

Yesterday he called me, after five long days of silence.

I didn't let him speak or explain. I am well beyond being angry.

"You're not what I want! Forget about me, forget about what there was between us. I don't want to see you ever again," I said to him before hanging up.

He didn't reply, he just laughed, a slow, deep, heavy laugh, almost threatening, which made me shudder. That grating sound echoes through my mind, and the implicit threat makes me stay on the alert, wondering what he will be capable of doing now that I have defied him.

And I also wonder what I'm capable of, when, at night, I hug his pillow and breathe in his smell, and then I curse him because I miss him, and nothing can lessen that craving I have for him that makes me contorted with need and desire.

He hasn't called again. And sadness envelops me like a heavy cloak.

Who am I? What am I? Is it possible that I have become the person who completes him? What do I really want from this relationship?

All I do is wonder. The questions torment me, confuse me, and the need to feel loved, the need for the warmth of his arms, for the talks we had at dawn after having spent the night seeking and finding each other in ever new ways, becomes pure agony.

More lonely mornings, monotonous days, questions that aren't answered, and an ice-cold solitude that slowly devours me. I want to call him, to ask him to come back to me. I want to tell him that I will do anything. But I know that I couldn't bear his long silences again, his business trips, the thought that he might have another woman, a family.

And that all I am is sex—passionate, wet, incredible, but nothing more than that.

This, at least, I know I don't want, and I know I couldn't stand it anymore.

And so I let the time glide slowly past me.

I have lost count of the days now.

The only thing I manage to do is work.

In silence, shut inside my own little world.

The grey that surrounds me again, like the clothes I wear.

He hasn't been back in touch, and I have managed to summon up enough self-respect not to call him.

Now all I have left is a job I hate. Piles of paperwork. In the office life continues as before, marked by the usual pitying glances of my colleagues.

A DANGEROUS GAME

I can't bear them, but I can't make up my mind to leave once and for all the place that represents the single fixed thing in my entire existence. So I force myself to shrug my shoulders and carry on working.

"Lara, there's a parcel for you." I jerk up my head and, when I see it on the reception desk, my heart starts beating faster.

It's large, anonymous, heavy.

I know that he has sent it; I'm totally certain.

I don't want to open it in front of my colleagues.

"I'm going early; will you cover for me?" I mutter without turning to anyone in particular. My voice is trembling but I manage to keep my emotions under control. One of my colleagues nods absentmindedly.

"Okay, I'll cover."

After a few minutes I find myself in the car with the parcel held tight, my breath burning in my throat.

But I don't open it, not yet.

I continue caressing it as the tears press against my eyelashes and tighten my chest.

Is it really so easy to forget about what he did to me? But what sort of life have I had since he went away?

I put the parcel on the seat, put the car in gear and drive off with a squeal of the tires.

I enjoy driving, and I go fast. I've always wanted one of those red convertibles that rich people buy. I can imagine the fresh air brushing against my skin, the hot sun, the damp night air.

And then him. Always him.

His tender mouth, his gaze, the control he exerts over me.

I broke the agreement. I resisted him, I stopped trusting him and I ended our relationship.

So why has he sent me a present?

Suddenly I slow down and pull over by the side of the road, ignoring the horns and curses of the other drivers. I grab the box and, using my teeth and nails, I tear the tape, opening it eventually.

Nothing is as important as knowing.

A moment later and I'm breathless. I don't know what to say or what to think. My eyes widen at the dress of black silk chiffon and silver thread, as ethereal as a cloud.

"Black is your color, my love. Your hair looks like gold against it," he said to me once.

My heart beats faster as the memory becomes more and more vivid, and for an instant I think that it might explode in my chest.

With shaking hands I pick up an envelope. It is thick and heavy. I open it and inside there is a plane ticket and a hotel reservation.

Lisbon, one way. Instinctively I look at my watch. The flight is in less than half an hour; I don't even have time to go and get changed.

Why on earth am I going to Lisbon?

A flash of indecision makes me doubt myself. I plunge my fingers into the box and find a velvet bag. I open it and a long gold chain with the two ends covered in diamonds falls into my palm.

I struggle to breathe, and my heart becomes a hammer beating in my throat.

But it is the throbbing between my legs that makes me close my eyes, while images appear in my mind that soon transform into a single dull desire. His hands on my breasts, the fingers circling my nipples, arousing them until they harden, and the gold fastening on the swollen tips.

Pain, pleasure.

A hoarse moan escapes from my throat.

I sit up straight, open my eyes, and pick up the chain. It is heavy, valuable, but that isn't what unsettles me. It's what he wants to do with it. It's the desire that throbs in my vagina.

It's knowing exactly what he is asking me.

Do I really want this?

A sob rips through my throat.

A wave of embarrassment overwhelms me but lasts for only the blink of an eye. The past comes back to me, implacable, to remind me what I ought to do, the clear boundary between what is permitted and what isn't.

Then a soft, seductive whisper emerges from that same past and eases my pain, driving away any doubts.

"My love, be yourself."

He has always encouraged me to discover what I like, without moralizing or insincerity.

The decision is mine, even now. That's what the jewelry seems to be saying.

If I go to him, it will mean accepting his conditions.

I know what he will do to me.

Will I have the courage to confront my needs, my weaknesses, to accept what I am?

I swallow and close my eyes. The pain of surrender again.

Anger comes to the surface and burns me.

I'll go, but not under his conditions.

Now I understand. I'm not his toy; I'm not his. And yet, as I put the car into reverse and then take the road toward the airport, I feel as if a weight is lifting from my chest, and then an almost uncontrollable joy at the idea that I'll soon see him again. Because, however much I try to convince myself of the opposite, without him I feel like I'm dying, and even the simplest things, like breathing, eating, and sleeping, become impossible.

From the moment I leave the plane, I seem to enter a sort of dream.

Two men are waiting for me and come toward me as if they know me. I think I'm the only woman in the entire terminal wrapped in a cloud of black silk and silver. Perhaps I shouldn't have accepted his gift, the dress and the jewelry, but I didn't know how to resist. It's as if he knew that the delicate fabric, brushing against my body, would only inflame my desire for him.

So, despite a hint of fear, I want to know where this adventure will lead me, and I agree to follow them.

They are tall, dark, and menacing. They look around with their black, stone-cold eyes that remind me of his eyes.

The dark, full lips are the same as well, and in their hard, chiselled faces there is a streak of cruelty that makes them look like brothers.

There is a long, black car waiting for us. It has blacked-out windows; it is glossy and gorgeous. The way dangerous things often look.

And, like all dangerous things, it mesmerizes me.

I close my eyes as I sink into the leather seats and I breathe in their scent.

I feel as if I am being enclosed in a warm embrace. I snap open my eyes, but there's no one next to me, just my imagination playing tricks on me.

I am surrounded by luxury. I have seen fabulous hotels before, but nothing to compare with what is in front of me as I take the hand that one of the men offers me and I get out of the car.

I have never seen so much beauty. It is as if every sense is stimulated, an endless seduction. High ceilings, crystal chandeliers that drip with thousands of iridescent droplets, the lights are brilliant white and then softer, caressing. The music slow and sensuous.

I stop in the center of the vast atrium. The marble floor seems to glisten with its own light, a mirror that reflects everything, almost a kaleidoscope of colors. The skirt of my dress flutters, disturbed by a sudden breeze that reaches me from the terrace. And then, as the night progresses, the tension that has accompanied me throughout the journey also seems to move to another level. But it isn't an unpleasant sensation, it's just different. A moment later I feel like I'm being plunged into a world of sensuality, where the only thing that really matters is my burning desire, the need to see him and to know.

The atmosphere in the hotel is a whirl of conflicting emotions: the murmur coming from the fountains, the music, the lights, the pervasive scent of the flowers, the mystery.

My head is spinning. I need him; I feel lost. So I look for him in the crowd of guests in evening dress, covered in jewelry, but although I wander back and forth, although I look everywhere, my heart pounding, I can't see him.

I am afraid. The taste of fear is bitter on my tongue; it tastes of despair and loneliness.

The thought of how stupid I've been by trusting him again makes me want to turn back.

At that very moment I realize that I don't have my bag.

I feel a stab of panic in my stomach. My eyes dart around the room, looking for a way out, but there's nothing I can do without asking for help.

"I've lost my papers. Has anyone handed in my things?" I ask, barely audibly, at the reception desk. I realize that they won't be able to help me if I don't tell them who I am, and I'm about to do so when the receptionist turns toward me.

I hate the fact that I'm mumbling, and I hate the fear dripping from my words. The man at the desk, observing me, seems used to strange behavior of every kind. He holds out a hand and gives me a key.

"You're expected upstairs."

I don't know who he has confused me with, and I'm on the point of telling him that he has definitely got the wrong person. I just want my bag, and I want to leave. My adventurous streak has been shattered by the realization that I've done an immensely reckless thing.

"You're mistaken. No one's expecting me."

I'm tired, and my sense of fear has become a living thing, squirming under my skin and clawing at me.

I have almost reached the large sliding doors when someone takes hold of my arm, and, without using any force, leads me to the elevator. I just have time to raise my head to protest, but then the doors open wide and one of the men who met me at the airport gently pushes me in.

"This way, miss."

His companion is there too. I move away from them as they lean against the elevator wall. I turn around and focus on some vague point in front of me. I can hear their breathing behind me. The heat radiating from their bodies disorientates me. I grit my teeth and I try to think of a way to escape from the two of them, from their unsettling presence.

My heart is bursting in my chest. All of a sudden I feel paralyzed with dread.

"Please, please." The only thing I can do is beg.

The rest of my words are lost in the trembling of my lips, in the feeling of panic engulfing me.

I close my eyes and breathe deeply, trying to calm down.

He has organized everything. He won't hurt me. I can handle the situation. He won't hurt me, I keep repeating to myself.

By the time the elevator stops, I have decided. I know what I have to do. I'll run away and then I'll find the embassy. I'll get my office to send me some money. I'm a grown woman, capable . . . I just need time.

The doors open and I rush out, hoping to escape from my two guardians. But there isn't a corridor on the other side of the doors, just an enormous hall. The elevator has opened onto a spectacular suite, and he is in the middle of the room.

Our eyes meet, and for an instant the world disappears.

There is nothing but him, and that stare that runs over me like a caress.

Suddenly I feel unable to do anything, not even something as simple as breathing. My heart beating in my throat is the only thing that marks the passing of time.

He takes a step forward, and I step back.

But is the feeling knotting my stomach really fear?

This is him, my love, the man who knows all my secrets, every unspoken need.

I know every inch of his body, intimately, and yet suddenly it's as if I am seeing him for the first time.

He is large, his shoulders broad, his stare arrogant. His hair is tied back in a ponytail that leaves his face uncovered. He is confident, aware of his strength and of the power that swirls around him like an aura.

His eyelids are lowered, as if he were carefully assessing me. Even from here I can see his large eyes, the proud expression behind the thick lashes, the fire that burns inside him.

My heart is pounding hard against my chest, and with every step he takes toward me I seem to become weaker.

But I want to stand up to him.

Desire builds up deep inside me and starts to throb. He stretches out his hand and brushes my face with his knuckles. I close my eyes and inhale slowly.

"You've saved me an inconvenient trip. Coming to get you is something that I would have found very annoying at the moment. This is a good thing. But these two men in the room are here for a specific reason. You tried to escape me again. You know you'll be punished for what you did, don't you, my love?"

The possessive tone of his voice makes me tremble with pleasure, a shiver twists my stomach as my legs weaken. His eyes are black, hard, and burning with passion. I know that look.

"You were the one who left me . . . " I murmur. But my voice is as insubstantial as a beam of light.

"Wrong answer, my little one. You agreed to join me, and then you aren't brave enough to follow it through to the end. Or perhaps you're looking for something else, my love? Something more daring, darker even? Sooner or later I would have suggested it: there are no limits between us. But I thought it was still too soon, that you needed more time."

I don't know what he's talking about. I can't follow his thought processes. He seems to understand my confusion, and so he smiles.

"You shouldn't have broken our agreement. Now we'll start afresh, Lara. But I could add something new . . . "

"No, I . . . we have to talk."

My response makes him smile again. His teeth flash in the glow of the candles that light up the room.

"You've already forgotten the first lesson. I know what you need, words are no good. I'm in control. And I haven't given you permission to talk."

His whisper spreads out into the silence of the room. Words of protest rise to my lips, but he puts a finger against my mouth.

He spins me around, holding me prisoner in his arms.

"Take a good look at them," he whispers, indicating his men. "I can ask both of them to stay while I give you your first lesson. What do you think? The choice is yours, as always."

What does he mean? What does it mean, that they'll stay here with us?

The thought paralyzes me, breathing becomes almost impossible, suddenly the throbbing between my legs is pure agony.

A blow strikes me from behind. My eyes open wide as the realization of what he has just done fills me with dismay. The humiliation brings tears to my eyes. I can't understand.

But it isn't the pain that upsets me as much as the surprise.

Another sharp slap echoes in the silence of the room, which is charged with tension and rapid, excited breathing.

I ought to be indignant, furious, but instead I feel an overwhelming desire, a lust so intense that I drop to my knees.

Something dark and uncontrollable forces me to turn toward him, to tell him not to stop.

It was never like this between us before. I don't know what has happened, every logical thought has disappeared, there's just pleasure, desire, and emptiness inside me.

The palm of his hand lands again on the taut skin of my buttocks. The burning feeling through the silk of my dress makes me moan. His fingers caress me slowly, gently over the mild stinging. And I have to grit my teeth in the face of this intense and unfamiliar pleasure.

He keeps on striking me, and then caressing me.

My breathing is just a gasp; I suck in air through my teeth because I have to, but nothing more. Every slap brings me closer to the edge of orgasm. I feel it's so close that I have to bite my lip to stop myself crying out.

The two men still stand motionless in front of me. I can't stop myself from looking at their black, cold eyes, full of lust, devouring me.

All of a sudden he pulls up my dress, exposing me completely to the two strange men.

I ought to scream, I ought to feel wretched, but I can't take my eyes off them, aware of their desire, of their stares following the movement of his fingers between my legs.

He has started to move, sliding back and forth in the heat that burns inside me, the heat into which he has slipped a finger, moving it slowly, drawing a desperate whimper from me.

"So? Do you want them to watch, my love? Do you like the idea of someone watching while you pleasure yourself?" he whispers directly into my ear, at the same time tightening his fingers on my clitoris.

The two men follow his every move, hypnotized. One licks his lips, the other takes a step forward.

What's wrong with me? I ought to be outraged and angry in response to the words that merge with his hot breath. I ought to kick him, tell him to go to hell, but I am paralyzed by the tension, by the perversion of his actions, and by the pleasure that is increasing in me with every movement he makes.

My breathing starts to become deeper, and he slows down. He lifts the material of the dress again, showing what he is doing to the men. The throaty grunt from one of them is so ominous and lustful that it terrifies me.

"Send them away."

He laughs and sinks another finger into me, filling me and opening me up. The material falls back into place, and he gives a sharp command that makes the two men disappear behind the elevator doors that close in front of their livid faces.

"For now, my love." He doesn't say anything more, but he starts to push harder, to move his fingers backward and forward inside me.

"You are so tight, so wet. And you're beautiful."

I know I'm not beautiful, but his voice is so firm that I believe him, and so I truly become beautiful, more than beautiful. Because he makes me feel that I am. The center of everything, important, unique, vital.

I close my eyes and let myself sink back against his chest.

My world begins and ends with his deft fingers, which are making me moan with pleasure. By now my skin has become so sensitive that even the breeze drifting in from the windows seems to trace red-hot trails over my body. When his fingers close over my breast and squeeze, I want to scream.

"Don't move, don't turn around, don't do anything until I tell you to."

The erection pressing behind me gives me the exact measure of his desire. Suddenly it all seems unbearable. I sway, and a second later I find myself in his arms.

His lips are cool on my eyes and on my forehead, but when they reach my mouth they become liquid fire.

"It will pass soon, my love," and his voice is so kind and gentle that I feel like crying. But then that hard, demanding expression again.

I'm aware of him walking, he pushes a door, and suddenly he drops me onto a bed.

"Now you will know."

I have no idea what he means. I just try to stay afloat in the whirlpool of emotion that is sweeping me away, in that razor-sharp desire that is everything that I really care about.

I watch him as he slips his fingers under the neckline of my dress, ripping the material with a snap of his hands. I don't even have time to protest. He frees himself from the silk and pushes me onto the snow-white sheets.

I am naked, completely exposed.

There is something deeply erotic about a fully dressed man touching you. Now he is towering over me, the fabric of his suit brushing my skin.

"Did you really think you could be free of me?" His voice is pure steel.

He holds my legs open wide, his fingers press into my skin, and I watch him as he moves lower and lower. I arch my head back and wait.

When he starts to use his mouth on me, I cry out. His tongue encircles my clitoris, it presses down then relaxes. And the rhythm drives me mad.

"Now let's get something clear." There is complete control in his voice. I gasp for air under his touch, tears flow, and the thrill tightens my throat.

"You will not leave me; you'll never do it again. You belong to me."

I can't reply; I don't have the strength to. If I could, I would tell him he is everything to me, the air I breathe, the sky and the stars, the world. That living without him has been hell. Instead, I open wider, giving him more space, while he keeps on moving and pressing down into my flesh, burning with desire and with need.

"Please, please."

And then I hear a zipper being lowered. His hard flesh stabs at the moist folds of my body. I arch my head back as I wait for the thrust that I yearn for.

"Answer me."

"Yes, yes. I'm yours."

For a second he stops and looks at me intensely. I find what I've always searched for in those eyes, in the loneliness that his gaze betrays, in his pride of needing without knowing how to ask.

Now I understand what connects us.

The control that he has to feel able to exert; the need I have to please him.

We are made for each other. From the very first time he possessed me, making me what I am.

He raises his head, he stretches out on top of me, and he grasps my wrists, imprisoning them.

"Stay still."

But despite his command, I can't obey. I lift myself up and close my lips on his skin, biting him gently. The moan of pleasure that escapes from his throat fills me with a feeling of contentment.

He grunts. I have just done exactly what he wanted.

"Let's see if this will make you be good."

I don't even know how he did it, but suddenly my arms and legs are spread wide. He is on top of me, and looks at me with his hot black eyes like coals. He is smiling; in the dim light of the room his teeth gleam like those of a predator.

Then he finds me, ready and wet.

His lips are soft against mine, his tongue gentle, as are his caresses. He doesn't seem to want to stop as he devours me. He slides down further, between my legs.

His breath is burning hot on my naked flesh. The first touch that caresses my clitoris is as light as air, as sweet as the torment mounting inside me. He keeps on licking, tracing moist trails, until he draws closer to the throbbing that now is pain, need.

"Please, please."

And then he slides his tongue inside me. Stroking me once, and then again. His mouth closes and he starts to suck at my flesh. I arch my back, in the grip of a feeling of bliss that is unbearable, while he keeps on licking inside my vagina. But it isn't enough to bring me relief. It is torment, pain.

I want it to go deeper. I want it to fill every cell of my body. The sensation is so intense, so intimate, that for an instant I ask myself, dazed by these feelings, if one can die of pleasure.

But before I can find that relief, he gets off me and moves away.

He stands up, turns toward me, and gets undressed quickly.

I am tempted to call him back, but I know I shouldn't.

Trust is what he demands of me, so I wait even though I feel as if I'm being consumed by a fire that knows no end.

I follow the movement of his buttocks as he walks away from the bed. There is something on the table. He is looking inside a box. I can't see, but I hear him laugh. I bite down hard on my lip, while with my legs spread and my heart feeling as if it's about to burst in my chest. I wait for him to come back to me.

He won't hurt me, he won't. But knowing that he could leaves me breathless, makes me struggle against the straps holding me prisoner.

I can't take my eyes off him; he has now turned and is watching me pensively. When he comes closer I can see that he is holding the gold chain taut between his fingers, and I hold back a gasp.

"Relax." His voice now sounds razor-sharp. I hear him breathe in deeply as he puts himself between my legs. His teeth shine in the soft candlelight.

His gaze is unsmiling, penetrating. He leans over me and looks at me intensely, showing me the necklace, the one I thought I had lost.

"Do you accept my present?" There is almost a hint of doubt in his question. Suddenly I am aware of the importance of my role in this strange relationship we have.

"Yes, I want it."

I writhe under fingers that brush against my breast. The metal is cold on my hot skin.

When the clasp closes on my nipple, I feel an almost unbearable grip. A fire explodes in my head. It isn't just pain, it's something deeper, it's a raw pleasure that makes me cry out. For a moment I think I am on the edge. But I can't reach orgasm yet. He hasn't given me permission to come. I bite my lip hard, but he notices.

"I've nearly finished."

It isn't true, and I know it isn't. He has just started. He closes the second clasp on the other nipple, and then pulls tight the chain that links the two ends of the piece of jewelry.

Pain, and a pleasure that cuts short my breathing. It is just for a second, but it's enough to make me tremble, to draw a moan of ecstasy from me.

"Do you like it?"

"Yes, yes." I want to say more, that I'm ready, that I want him. I want him to fuck me until I can't move from this bed ever again. He slides two fingers inside me, opening me up. "You're so wet."

With a jerk, he raises my pelvis.

"Look at me. I want you to look at me as I take you."

His voice is hoarse, thick. I can't look away from the large, glossy penis, scored by dark veins, that presses down on me. I feel him pushing into the folds of my flesh, parting them. A blaze of heat sweeps over me. My blood roars in my veins, and everything else disappears.

His thrusts are hard, violent, then smooth, long, and gentle.

Lust, hunger, desire. There isn't room for anything else.

Forward, until every cell of my body is filled, and then back, sliding against my skin, arousing, tormenting.

Slow waves of pleasure, strong and hot. A tide that could drown me, that could dissolve reality. And then he opens his eyes, his pupils dilate. And he sinks down onto my lips, parting them as he pushes his tongue into my mouth, as if seeking refuge and comfort.

Too sudden, too strong. There are no boundaries now, just a single entity. As the orgasm overwhelms me, erupting in a savage joy, a light disintegrates the very substance of my body. All I'm able to do is cry out to him.

I have no strength, I have no breath, there's nothing left in me, everything is his.

But when I'm still in the final throes of pleasure, he clasps my face and fixes his eyes on mine. And then I see that same emotion in his velvet gaze, and I fill with a wild joy that knows no reason, no beginning, no end.

Another powerful thrust, and a cry of ecstasy resonates in his chest.

I feel him stiffen as he fills me and empties himself deep inside me, another muffled groan and then he relaxes on top of me.

His arms hold me, wrapping around my body. He lifts me up and rolls over on the bed to lie next to me.

His fingers tremble in my hair, and his heart beats fiercely, as does mine.

"My love, there are so many things you don't know about me." His voice is a gentle whisper that I could listen to for hours.

"Why don't you tell me who you really are?"

I shouldn't have asked him that question, I realize as he tenses up by my side. But despite everything that has just happened between us, I know I can't carry on living with the uncertainty, in this dreamlike world where he is the only thing that matters.

Perhaps what has just happened has marked a threshold. And I realize I need something more permanent, a real relationship, a commitment on his part.

"You know who I am, Lara. Your lover, and the man who will be your husband."

The surprise runs through me like a flash of lightning. Then his lips close on mine again.

I can't respond, and perhaps I don't want to.

Our hearts beat together, united, just as our breathing merges and our fingers entwine.

Together.

A Serious Story

VALERIA PARRELLA

"N'en frais pas. J'en duit"
"Fai le. Manjue, ne sez que est.
Pernum ço bien que nus est prest!"
"Est il tant bon?"
"Tu le saveras. Nel poez saver sin gusteras."

—Thomas Mann, *The Holy Sinner*

She lowered the magazine and the sun hurt her eyes. So she closed them, and said to herself: "No, that's wrong: with sex you have to be serious." She lifted up the magazine again, quickly flicked through the pages, and thought that it hadn't relaxed her at all. She had taken it from the reception desk of the resort, hoping to waste some time without thinking about anything, but it hadn't worked. That endless varnishing of extramarital affairs and phony weddings, or girls who brightened up two-hundred-foot yachts, editorials by television presenters and priests, stolen or permitted photographs, pixelated masks over the eyes of the children, the lavish use of words like "partner" to refer to people who not even ten days before had been flirting with someone else: this had depressed her, annoyed her. And then there was the interview with the sexologist. She read for a last time the magic ingredients; the self-styled doctor proffered them like cards from a pack: *Cunning, Guile, Complicity, Play.*

"Bullshit. Sex is something meaningful."

So she fished out of her bag the book she had finished too early in the week and searched through the pages by eye: the way you hunt for that phrase you want to find again, that you remember was on the right or the left, or more or less in the center or at the bottom of a page, and after that thing that happened, yes, but definitely before that other thing. She finally found it. Their first night of incestuous sex: Wiligis, who had had an enormous penis since he was a boy, so much so that his nannies who bathed him could spell out his future in it, and Sibylla, who didn't know that by sleeping with one's own brother one could become a wife and mother. All around, loud crows rose up cawing, and the dog let out a deep howl.

She reread it until she felt sufficiently intoxicated, excited by the joy of the evocation, of the imagination, and then she went back to her room. She scratched at the door instead of knocking—it had been their signal for twenty years—and he came to open it for her.

"You didn't last long."

"The beach was crowded."

"I was about to come and rescue you. Aperitif?"

"Not yet. What's in the paper?"

"There's a good article on absenteeism in the senate."

Rossana threw herself onto the bed, face down.

"Oh, come on! Not in your swimming costume."

"Take if off me."

"Do you want me to?"

"I want to tell you about an enormous penis."

"Mmm. For an enormous penis, give me a bit more time."

"No. But there's pussy too. There's everything. Come here."

Rossana took his cock in her mouth, touched his balls, squeezed them where, how, and as hard as she knew her husband liked, and then she told him about the night of incest, of how all of a sudden Sibylla tasted Wiligis's shoulder on her mouth, and it was the very night when the corpse of their father was lying in his coffin, in the same castle: the night when the Chosen One was conceived.

Then he started to make love to Rossana as if she were a very young woman, like the initiation of that Sibylla, still a virgin.

Then Rossana threw her head back, right over the edge of the bed and, through the opening of the window, she could see the sharp slash of the horizon that supported above it all the water of the sea, pushing the sky down below it. She lost herself.

Twenty years before, at the beginning of their relationship, the same evening that they met and got to know each other, he was coming from a dinner party during which he had been courted persistently and mischievously by a very young girl. At the end of the evening he had said good-bye to her forever, with a little kiss, just a brush of the lips, and he had encouraged her to look elsewhere. Then, five hundred paces later, under the arches of the wide central street, he had seen Rossana. Since then they had never parted, not since that evening, which ended with a glass of wine on her sofa, just chatting, confidences, telephone numbers exchanged. And he had told her about his recent little adventure of the kiss, to give himself a bit of credibility in her eyes, the way men sometimes do when they are courting.

In the last few years she had reclaimed that image, which by now was a memory that was just hers, and it had changed shape a thousand times. While she was making love, at a certain moment, when she felt passion being replaced by the constant rhythm that anticipates an orgasm, she, like a puppeteer, pulled it out of the box in her head, full of lost and found objects. She prepared her imaginary backcloth: her imagination substituted faces—like masks—for that girl, leaving him intact. He was standing, with muscles that trembled slightly under his summer shirt, his powerful smile that had never lost its honest and gentle look that made him handsome. He was pinning her against the wall, she had a very short skirt, like Nabokov's Lolita, or an unusually healthy bosom like Kubrick's Lolita, and she was offering him her mouth and all her love. Sometimes he was standing there watching her, feeling she was his: she was still, immovable in her request, while his cock was growing in his trousers. Sometimes he was asking her to pull open her blouse and show her breasts in exchange for the anticipated kiss. Yet another time he was lifting her skirt and behind them there was a shop window that reflected all the possible images in Rossana's eyes in her mind. The girl, with her swollen lips and her silky hair like only young girls have, her blouse open, the miracle of a nipple. Behind, her raised skirt, her lowered knickers, her hands with phosphorescent polish that were spreading her buttocks at his request. He was putting a finger in her mouth, letting her choose which she preferred, and then, along with the granted kiss, he would slip that finger into her behind; by now his cock was rock hard in his trousers, it was just waiting to be taken in her hand or her mouth, or in that same hole. But Rossana never got to this point, because what made her come, finally, together with her husband's finger that entered inside her, all over, in her brain, was the image of his pleasure increasing, obvious and strong, between his thighs. Then she would come, and the image broke off there, like a film burning, when films were made of celluloid and silver nitrate.

She opened her eyes.

She smiled, lay on her side in silence, enjoying the warm peace that was flowing over her. She felt free of all the demands of the world.

Her husband loved to see her like this, but he was also a bit jealous of that moment that was all her own and he would annoy her, kissing her, or else he would ask her, as he asked her then:

"What are you thinking about?"

"Nothing."

"What?"

"That when I come I would like to have a printer linked to my brain."

"What?"

"Marvelous images come to me and phrases full of meaning, but they vanish in the shower."

"You could write them down before your shower."

"Would you be annoyed if we fucked with a tape recorder on?"

"Idiot!"

Finally he braced himself against the arms of the chair and was about to sit down, but Rossana guessed what he meant to do and ran ahead to the bathroom door, making a Saint Andrew's cross with her body. She said:

"Come on! Me first for the shower. I've been in the sea."

"You're a bully, and I'm a poor paraplegic."

"But a male and gentlemanly paraplegic to the last spoke of your wheels."

Half an hour later they left the hotel room behind and went toward the elevator, looking at themselves in the mirrors because they were very good-looking and happy, and an aperitif was awaiting them, and the orange sun that heralds evening.

He pushed the button to call the elevator and felt under his fingertip the floor number written in Braille on the metal. He said:

"These blind people, eh?"

"Mmm, it's a good idea," she said, pushing him into the elevator.

"What is?"

"I have to retrieve a page of *Perfume* by Süskind."

"When we're back in town . . . "

Then the doors closed.

The Bird of Paradise

CLAUDIA SALVATORI

I remember only a few details about my mother, who died when I was too young: her tapering fingers and a ring with a black stone, her fast but rather stiff way of walking, and the short, satin pink dress that rippled as she walked away from me.

My father has been dead for a little over seven months. He was a private investigator: he used to investigate unfaithful husbands, runaway wives, disappeared children, stolen cars and other things that had changed hands.

In the evening, however, until late, he used to study and dream of great unsolved criminal cases, sinister stories that sprang from the dark and mysterious blood of murderers.

If things had been different, he would say, he would have been a master detective, he would have investigated those cases, and he would have been able to solve them.

But he didn't know why things hadn't been different.

He left me the detective agency and this house between the hills and the city, near a huge rubbish dump, in which a killer scattered the remains of murdered young women over a period of seven months.

At one time my father used to breed Japanese nightingales. He had a dozen, and one whole room in the house was reserved for them.

My mother, I think, like every woman, was suspicious of these male obsessions and was opposed to the nightingales; but he would shut himself up with his birds whenever he could, and when he came out his face was that of a stranger.

I don't know how and when the nightingales disappeared. It seems that, after the death of my mother, the reason for keeping them faded too. The empty cages were left there, as if waiting for their return.

In the room, I feel I can still recognize their smell: a mixture of disturbed air and droppings. On the ground, on the perches and on the shelves there are still fine and soft feathers.

On the blue ceiling are painted five stars linked by a yellow-orange trail; the shape of the design vaguely resembles a resting bird with a long and luxuriant feathered tail. With the same paint the word *Apus* has been written.

It is the name of a constellation close to the South Pole, which is also known as the Bird of Paradise. I think my father painted the ceiling for his nightingales, so that they could feel they were under a friendly sky that belonged just to them.

I love cinemas because they let me sink into a dark place, one that shuts out reality thanks to a velvet curtain that smells of mustiness, mildew and smoke, and one that projects me into another reality. The images, the sounds, the colors, the music get to the innermost part of me with the force of an immense, terrible impact, which has at its core a melting sweetness. It is like a painful and terrifically sensuous assault that you submit to, from the bottom of your heart.

One evening, in the film library, I hear the sound of people fleeing, thuds and crashes. It's coming from behind me.

I turn and see what looks like an avalanche of fire pouring into the theatre, making it explode with redness and heat.

I throw open a small door to the right of the screen. It is the video library where the manager files and preserves the films kept on VHS. At the back, the fire exit. On the workbench there is a cassette.

I don't know why, but, coughing because of the smoke that is choking me and burning my lungs, almost blinded by my tears, I grab that single videocassette, and I save it from the blaze.

Outside, while the firemen try to bring the flames under control, I approach the manager of the film library and hand him the cassette.

In his eyes there is a flash of recognition, and bitter amusement: in the middle of the disaster, the only thing that has been rescued is the thing that is worth the least.

"It's an amateur video I filmed a long time ago. I had meant to throw it away. You can keep it, if you want."

Later, at home, I put the cassette in the VCR. A succession of people pass in unfocused disorder in front of the lens.

There are children in a park who are playing a strange game made up of pushes and running and brief contests, as if each child were seeking their own position, their own role, with regard to themselves and the others: of assertion, submission, support or escape.

Under a junction of major roads, tangled like snakes, in the roar of the cars that speed by incessantly, day and night, there is a bar.

That's where I meet him.

"I know you," he says. Something in his hushed and suggestive tone makes me suspect that he really knows me.

"They told me you're a detective," he continues.

I observe him. His face is delicate and white, as if it were made of fog. He has pale hands that he moves like a conjurer. He says he has been away a long time, and now he has returned. He has ways of doing things that aren't like other people. Not exactly like a foreigner, but like someone who doesn't really belong anywhere. He must be about my age. He looks like me.

The day after, in my father's office, I finally remember who he looks like, other than me.

Robin.

A boy who was raped, tortured and killed.

Robin vanished about ten years ago from the park right by his house on a sunny, cruel spring day. Inexplicably and despite, or perhaps because of, the exceptional clarity of the light, they found him at night, in a ditch, in the darkness, shrouded by layers of mist, half-naked and disfigured. Forced to submit to oral and anal intercourse and bitten all over his body.

Here he is now, Robin, appearing from yellowed press cuttings, from the computer monitor and the television.

He is blond, like all martyred heroes, and smiling like someone who hasn't yet been overtaken by the future.

He reveals his smile like all children do, tilting his head back and looking upward, in a surge of both confidence and defiance.

The boy in the bar could be Robin after ten years, without the smile, raised by someone of another nationality, and as if he found it difficult to understand our language. It can't be him; and yet he has the lightness, the freedom of a dead person.

I find him near me more and more often: he anticipates my movements. I don't know where he lives, but he doesn't seem to need to own a house. He is like an image projected on a screen.

He looks at my features and my confused expression, like when I catch a glimpse of myself by surprise in shop windows. I touched him and I felt his solidity, but he seems to be made of a material that's different from flesh.

His fine and golden hair dances, moved by a gentle breeze.

He hasn't yet told me his name.

"Robin," I say quietly.

He turns, he looks at me, he smiles. It is an enigmatic smile, and it leaves me unsure about whether he has responded to his name, or if he is wondering why I'm calling him by someone else's name.

Sometimes I imagine being Robin and his killers, the tormentor and the victim together.

I am in that park in the suburbs, on an April day pulsing with renewed life. A slight uneasiness floods through me, as irritating as the truth.

I don't see the faces of the two or three men who attract me, just a charming smile, the certainty that I would like to possess, the elegance of a suit worn with confidence, a clear, measured gesture of graceful authority. I don't know how they manage to take me away, and it isn't important. They have the radiance of fictional characters, and taking their hand is like entering a film. Every child would acquiesce to such a seduction.

So, following them, I leave time, my life, myself, forever, and *maybe this is why I follow them*. Between the dread of growing up and the wish to be grown up, there's a third choice.

I then picture a sensuous darkness of fear, pain, violent hands that separate me from my innocence. But have I ever had an innocence? The mystery of sex runs through me with the sudden flash of a sacred revelation.

As they ensnare me with saliva and sperm, as my blood flows and they bite my arms and sides, I shout and cry for help, but in the depths of a remote and secret part of myself I still acquiesce.

I kill and I die in an ecstasy of obscene delight. We fall together into a single throbbing jumble of horror and languor, which has the light of the hereafter.

Robin wants me to investigate a series of murders of girls.

The monster kidnaps them and tortures them while they are still alive. He rips off their scalp, he pulls out their teeth, their eyelashes and eyebrows; he scars them with hideous burns and wounds; he leaves them to bleed to death, with their vocal chords cut.

"In your opinion, why does he cut their vocal chords?" Robin asks me.

"To reduce them to silence."

"They are singers," says Robin. "He meets them in the shopping arcade, on Saturdays."

Every Saturday, in the Paradise shopping arcade, there's karaoke. The mutilation the killer inflicts on his victims must be connected to their singing.

"The girls are all pretty, and they can all sing. How does he choose them?"

"They're talented. Maybe they have a kind of charisma onstage. They have something that excites him, and that prompts in him the desire to destroy them. Something envious, that he loves."

A bizarre, terrifying insight crosses my mind.
"They're nightingales."
"You have to catch the monster," says Robin. "I'll help you."

Saturday afternoon, in the Paradise shopping arcade. The huge sign, as insubstantial as a hologram, cuts through the clouds. It depicts a female figure with her limbs together, soaring in flight, chaste and unapproachable. Her wings intermittently appear and disappear.

Around us, behind and in front of us, gangs of nervous and jostling adolescent boys and groups of girls, all atremble, mill about. They push and pull us. There are hundreds of people under the transparent dome, around the stage. Shaved heads, semi-naked backs, fake hair, tattooed flesh, metal, a reek of cosmetics and sweat.

On the stage the DJ starts the interactive part of the show. He introduces it with long bursts of blunt, contemptuous words. He will be the one who chooses.

When he calls a girl, he holds out his hand to her, and she clings to it like a castaway hauled up onto a raft, screaming with pleasure. An interview follows, which turns into a single question: *Who are you?* Then a comment from the DJ, almost always humiliating for the girl. Thirty seconds for her performance, not a second more.

I watch lots of them pass across the stage, one after another, until a hard lump of disgust eats into my stomach, and I would like to lie down and sleep.

But there *she* is.

Tall, lithe, though slightly self-conscious. She has very pale skin, like a marble statue. Her height and her proportions are a bit larger than the norm. She is wearing a pink satin dress that reveals her long legs. Her hair is pink. Her awkwardness is because she both likes and fears being looked at; modesty fights against her delight at presenting herself to the gaze of the public.

"And you are?" asks the DJ.

I don't catch her name.

"Regina" sarcastically splutters the voice of the DJ. "We've got a queen today, guys. A real queen. I don't doubt it! Come along, darling, let's hear how you sing like a queen."

Later on, I won't remember what Regina sang; I'll recall the melody, supple and wistful, and a dark yet crystalline voice of great purity.
She will be the next victim, definitely. Regina is like the others in every way, and yet she's different, but I wouldn't be able to define what it is that sets her apart.
Her thirty seconds are over and Regina is returned to the place she came from. She goes across the stage laughing, with a little sprint like a woodland animal. Arms and hands strain to grab her, to suck her below.
She disappears into the crowd.
I shove and push; I scrape against someone's metal studs; the loudspeakers shatter my brain.
I think I see Regina's pink hair near the exit. I sense that, in some concrete point not far from me, the killer is present too.
I rush to the automatic doors; they are closing and I have to wait for them to pause, resume their rhythm and open again to go out.
There she is in the grey square. Her pose is that of a star: one foot in front of the other and turned out, like the fifth position in ballet.
I catch hold of her wrist. She isn't just wearing a pink satin dress like my mother's, but on her hand, as soft as a lily, she has a ring with a black stone.
"Hi," I say.
She looks at me. In her eyes there is a strange expression. It isn't surprise, nor curiosity or excitement, nor is it revulsion or disgust. A sort of open indifference to whatever might happen.
"Hi," she replies.
"I heard you sing. I liked it very much."
She nods, still with the same fatalism and, it seems to me, indulgence and irony.
"I'd like to get to know you better."
Yes again, with a barely perceptible nod of the head.
"Can I offer you something to drink . . . at my house?"
Yes, yes, twice.

At home, with Regina sitting opposite me, I can't help imagining.

I am the killer and I do everything to her that makes a killer out of me. I tear off her dress and her shiny silk stockings, and then her underwear, which I would like to be white and lacy. Just the act of ripping the precious materials, reddening and exposing the beautiful body they hide, is so exquisitely erotic that it almost makes me lose my mind.

Then the sequence of tortures and mutilations starts. Regina must be tied and conscious, and I have to feed on her pleas, her cries, her groans, her writhing and the fainting that sometimes comes over her. I imagine starting with scalpels, knives and welding torches. Then it's the turn of her marvelous face, her teeth, her eyelashes and her eyebrows. I carve the skin on her forehead and her temples and I bare her scalp, which I leave bald and bleeding. Her screams were a song of horror until I open her throat and snuff out her voice.

Now, only now, there is the greatest pleasure. It is found in the destruction of her beauty, which makes her resemble every other beautiful, destroyed thing, a bird, a flower. It is in the agonizing pain that she can't survive, and I can't survive either, the death that seizes us both in a sigh, peaceful at last.

I imagine all this as I look at her, and as I see myself in her as in a mirror. I am a raped child, eaten alive by monsters, who becomes a monster to devour Regina; I am Regina, raped and enjoyed by a monster child, and together we float off to some point in this universal hell.

Regina gets up and moves over to me. She kneels down slowly. Her face shines from inside, like that of an actress in a film. She smiles.

"What do you want?"

What do you want, she asks me. Not what is my name, who am I, why have I invited her to my home. What do I want, only what do I want. In this moment, when we are alone and beyond reach, she is willing to want what I want, to grant my wishes. It is the gift that she gives me today, with indifference, and she will withhold it from me tomorrow with the same indifference.

With her fingers, as if for fun, she touches my knee, her wrist laid on my thigh. My sex rises. The contact is almost immaterial; I can barely feel the tips of her fingers. I close my eyes and go toward her. The contact becomes urgent, demanding. Regina takes me, holds me, squeezes me with the palm of her open hand. I am a wave that breaks over her only to surge back and become vast in my desire.

I caress her face, her neck, her shoulders, her hips, her legs. Her pink satin dress comes undone, slips off. Her pink hair is *real*. She has small, high breasts, which I press tight, making her utter little cries, like the squawks of a bird. Her skin is as smooth as a petal. She falls backward onto the carpet, and I run my face over her sunken abdomen.

On a level with my mouth, her male sex appears, as large as mine, but I don't stop. The dizziness that grips me isn't a repudiation, nor is it surprise: after all, I have always known that Regina has something of me, something of Robin, and something of my father and mother. It is the moment of hesitation before inventing a new way of making love.

Regina invents it for me, and I don't have to do anything except copy what she does. I stroke her hard and silky sex, while with my other hand I plunge into her, and she does to me what I am doing to her. Her fingers reach a point inside me that I didn't know, a shameful place where an unnameable pleasure was nestled like a monster, waiting to be unleashed. With my fingers I touch her as she touches me.

I am above her, and together we share a wave-like and rotating movement, slow at first, to let me understand what is happening to me, to experience it, to feel it completely, until I go mad with it.

All I am is a mound of lost and throbbing flesh, and the languor that takes hold of me is like the anguish before a longed-for death.

Then we let ourselves be swept away, and we go harder, always harder, inflaming each other in this perfectly equal act, as equals. From outside in, from inside out, until we can't recognize the boundaries of our bodies.

As I am about to be completely destroyed in her, I still hold onto what I believe myself to be, and I guard my solitude.

I wake up alone, lying on the dirty floor. My sperm and my saliva have dried on the carpet.

But Regina has gone, she has left me. In some moment between pleasure and sleep she slipped away from me.

When I meet Robin again he seems to be able to tell what has happened and he criticizes me.

"You should have kept her. She goes with everyone, but only once. Now it won't be easy to get her back again. You had the chance to save her, and you lost it."

I bend my head, full of shame.

"Now we have to find the killer," Robin continues. "She'll be with him."

Robin takes me to the dump, an abyss of rubbish beaten by the rain and the wind, burned by the sun and the frost. A molten slurry of metal, plastic, bone, organic sludge, petrol, paints, rotting carcasses, corrosive solvents, rags, tar and mechanical parts of disemboweled contraptions.

We begin to descend, careful not to hurt ourselves on the sharp rusty edges, kicking the odd broken toy, a doll with its head already smashed.

We go down toward the lowest point of that overturned cone of rubbish. Robin calls me, invites me to join him.

"Look."

Mixed up with the litter, with the decaying colors of the dump, I hadn't seen it, because I wouldn't have thought it possible.

A flower.

A thriving plant, well nourished, so florid that it looks like it's made of human flesh. It has elongated oval leaves and a straight stalk. The petals, as sharp as blades, are bordered with red and have a color that fades from blue-violet to yellow-orange.

It almost as tall as us.

Robin takes photographs of the plant from various angles.

"It's a clue. It can tell us lots of things."

"What things? It's a seed carried by the wind. The wind doesn't know where it sows."

"It's a rare plant—you don't find it around here. The killer must have brought the seed with him."

"In the areas around the victims' bodies they haven't found anything that could shed light on the identity of the killer."

"They haven't looked properly, or they didn't know what to look for."

The plant is splendid, magnificent, elegant. In order to grow, it should need a damp clay enriched with sand, or else a mixture of peat and clay. Instead, it has fed on the remains of rotting food, on lead and other polluting metals, on toxic substances, on blood maybe, the blood of the victims soaked into that foul mud.

At my house, after having scanned a photo of the flower, we look on the internet until we find something similar, with the same shape petals and pistils.

"Just as I thought," Robin says, "we're talking about a rare and valuable plant, and no one would throw away its seeds. Only someone who had slipped into the dump to get rid of human remains could have lost them. Its scientific name is *Strelitzia reginae*, after a queen, Charlotte von Mecklenburg-Strelitz, the wife of the king of England, George III. It originally comes from southern Africa. It needs full sun and it has to be protected from the wind, so the bottom of the dump was the perfect environment for it. Do you know the name it's commonly known by?"

"No, what?"

"The bird of paradise."

We are in the room with the cages.

"Leave me alone, Robin, please. I don't want to have anything to do with this case anymore. I don't want to see you anymore."

"You don't understand. You *absolutely* have to solve the case. If you don't, you'll lose your life."

"Go away."

All of a sudden I feel an overpowering, unstoppable hatred toward him. I attack him with my fists, with kicks, with all of myself.

THE BIRD OF PARADISE

Then it is as if a black curtain falls, and I hit him, hit him, hit him, but I don't see him and I don't hear him cry out, and my blows have no effect, as if I were fighting wrapped in a shroud.

I end up, panting, sitting on the floor of the room. I have cut my hand, I don't know how, and the vivid blood drips onto the dried bird droppings. Between my feet there is a feather, a long and strange exotic feather that definitely didn't belong to the nightingales.

I pick it up. It is extremely long, like a peacock feather, curved and of a color that changes depending on the light, between blue, violet and yellow.

I seem to remember a conversation between my father and my mother. He was telling her about a friend who, knowing of his passion for birds, had brought him that feather from New Guinea.

Searching on the Internet I find the bird to which that feather might have belonged: *Cinnurus magnificus*, native to the southern hemisphere. A creature with a long blue, violet and yellow tail, the same colors as the flower.

A bird of paradise.

I look for Regina. I imagine her being with a lover, and then another, and another, male or female doesn't matter, endlessly. A single time with each of them, and never twice with any of them.

In my sweat-drenched bed, between sleeping and waking, between hell and heaven, I imagine being Regina, seducing her lovers, and her lovers seduced by her.

I am a man and I am a woman, I am many men and many women. I experience the dizziness of an endless orgy. I become intoxicated with my smells, with the smells of all mankind. While I kiss and bite my hands, all the parts of me that I can reach with my mouth, while I turn over and moan and writhe on the sheets, while I thrust into the body of a woman and I become that woman, who opens herself to let herself be entered, I am the world that blindly, relentlessly, joins with itself.

Regina is a chain that reaches me after passing through all beings, and can be broken only by an extreme criminal act.

There is only one house in the city with an extensive garden planted with birds of paradise, the stalks of the plants six feet tall, in full bloom.

The house is large, stately, enchanted. Peaceful, in its green oasis that the evening makes even darker.

Robin is still next to me.

"I told you I didn't want to see you anymore."

"You need me."

In the monster's house there is a light on, and we go toward it, disquiet clawing at my heart.

"It looks like your house," says Robin.

In fact, the monster's house is strangely like mine, in its fabric, shape, and colors. It is just larger, more magnificent. It resembles what we become, what we make things become, in our fantasies.

We find ourselves in front of a wall and an unkempt hedge. We get in through a gap. An intense and heady perfume permeates the air, but it doesn't come from the flowers; rather, it seems to emanate from the black mystery of that house.

Regina's voice.

We look through a window. A gigantic shadow towers over Regina. She moves her arms like wings, but we can't work out whether it's because she's trying to escape or she's going towards the other person present in the room.

I pull out my father's gun and we cautiously move nearer to the entrance.

The door is half-open.

We enter a large room lit by countless candles.

Chained to a very high perch is a *Cinnurus magnificus*, a live bird of paradise, the incarnation of the bird whose feather I own. It has bleary eyes and dull plumage. I think the bird is the god of this sacred place—but an ill and tired god, a prisoner.

Under its wonderful tail of yellow and violet feathers stand Regina and a man. She has her hands on him, she is touching his chest, his arms, his sex.

He doesn't avoid the contact but he shakes with fear and anger. He is a tall man, large, old but strong.

A hunting knife appears in his hand.

"Stop!" I shout.

I keep him within range of my gun.

The man turns, slowly.

There is no expression in his eyes, or perhaps he has the same eyes as the bird, steady, full of unease, of bewilderment at being bound in a place that doesn't belong to him.

He resembles my father to a startling extent.

The monster aims the knife at Regina's throat. Robin is a step behind me.

"Let her go!" I shout.

The monster doesn't seem to be afraid of my gun, nor of me, nor of Robin. He talks as if he were alone, or as if he were talking to an invisible deity.

"Only the male sings," he says. "Only the male is colorful."

So, this is what offends him. The beauty of a woman, her singing, the practice of her art, the assumption of an alluring plumage that in nature is reserved for the male bird, in order to win over the grey and silent females. This is what he feels he has to punish, destroying her weapons of seduction and the organs that modulate her voice. But, if it's the singing of the female that provokes his hatred and resentment, his strength and control, then he's been taken in by Regina.

"Let her go," I repeat. "She isn't . . ."

Regina starts to untie pink ribbons. She stares at the monster with defiance and, it seems to me, with contempt.

Shaking her shoulders with a proud, beautiful movement, Regina frees herself from the dress. The light and silky fabric falls in a heap at her feet. She is naked underneath.

"Someone who is male and female in the same body and in the same soul doesn't need to sing," Robin says, in a whisper.

The monster stares at Regina's male sex for a moment, astonished. Then his face contorts.

Letting out a hoarse cry he severs Regina's carotid artery.

"No!" I shout, and I start to shoot.

The bird of paradise, struck by a bullet, sends out a high-pitched death cry. The killer comes toward me, but I empty the entire magazine into his chest.

He collapses at my feet.

Regina, drawing her last breath, emits a sound that resembles singing. The bird of paradise falls onto her, covering her with its feathers.

"It's over," I say.

"No" says Robin.

"The killer is dead."

"No."

He points me in the direction of the back of the room, where a stone staircase opens up.

I grab him, push him against the wall, hold my face a hair's breadth away from his.

"But who are you? Why are you helping me?"

"You'll find the answers to all your questions down there."

Followed by Robin, I rush down the stairs. The room in which I find myself resembles a crypt, as well as my father's room of cages. Numerous cages are hanging from the walls and ceiling, enormous cages capable of holding birds as large as human beings.

And, in the light of the candles, I see that the cages contain human bodies. Some are already completely reduced to skeletons, others are in various stages of decomposition. Yet more are transfixed by the bars as if they had tried to escape, like crazed birds. Others are sunk down on the bottom of the cages, dejected and resigned, waiting for death.

Looking at those bodies where traces of wounds and mutilations are still visible, I realize that they are those of women, and that all these women must have been victims of the monster.

I fall to my knees on the coagulated blood that rained down from the cages.

On the stairs, a woman dressed in pink satin has appeared, wearing a ring with a black stone. She looks like the old photographs of my mother.

She holds in her hands an object that resembles a kite, or else a stuffed hunting trophy.

It's a bird. A bird as big as a stork, with no legs, covered in feathers all the colors of the rainbow, with a long, curving tail like a lyre.

A bird that doesn't exist.

"Do you know what the bird of paradise is?" asks the woman, in an ancient and husky voice. "Do you know what the bird of paradise *really* is? It's not a plant, it's not a real bird."

She reveals the trophy, with a sort of wretched and forlorn pride.

"It's a fantastic bird and a fable. They say it reached Europe on the only ship of Magellan's fleet that returned home. The natives used to practice exquisite handiwork using certain birds: after having removed their legs, bones, and insides, they left the bird's skin to dry, which, treated this way, stayed in one piece, although it was empty. Then they would insert lots of multicolored, exotic feathers. We Westerners, seeing this, didn't realize that we were looking at a work of art and we thought these trophies were the remains of a strange, legless bird. And this gave rise to the myth that birds of paradise never rested on the ground, eternally flying and floating, feeding on dew and nectar. They reproduced by eggs being laid on the back of the male, which had a special hollow to hold them. Later on, in the southern hemisphere, people discovered the species of bird that we now call the bird of paradise, but until the eighteenth century *this* was the only authentic bird of paradise."

"It was for this that all these women died? For the bird of paradise?"

"Only the male sings. Only the male is colorful. The male hatches its eggs itself. It's the only one in the world."

"But why kill? Why?"

"Punishment. Those women wanted to take the place of the only one in the world, singing and wearing colorful clothes."

"It's madness."

"Madness? You still don't understand. We were defending a faraway world, where legends and heroes were possible, kings and queens, gods and myths. The bird of paradise isn't just an invention: there was a time when it was both an invention and a reality. The time of poetry."

So the monster wasn't a single being but rather was made up of two entities. Like Regina. He had been killing forever. Deep down, I should have known that forever.

"At the end, my husband was insane. He started to act alone, wandering around the suburbs and the woods, and instead of keeping the bodies hidden he left them around. He was always careless."

As she was talking, the woman has come down the stairs until she has reached us, holding in front of her the bird of paradise like a shield.

When she lowers her trophy, I see that she has her husband's bloody hunting knife in her hand.

Screaming, the woman leaps toward me.

I pull the trigger of my gun, but I've fired all the shots. I am seized by a kind of death wish. I don't move; I smile. It is a moment of stark serenity that answers the smile of the gods.

Robin puts himself between my body and the killer, taking the knife blow that was meant for me. He falls with a gentle sigh, which seems a sigh of joy, or of release.

Now the woman is disarmed and sinks her claw-like hands in my throat. I feel her scorching breath, as if the decay she caused were rising from inside her. Together we fall to the ground.

We roll around, fighting on the viscous mixture of liquids that have seeped from the cages.

I see Robin through the dazzling haze that descends over my eyes, kneeling, grasping the hunting knife and using it to cut a rope.

A creak like a long groan, then a crash of metal.

A cage is plummeting down on me.

I gather my strength to escape the grip of the monster's female side. I struggle; I kick.

The cage strikes the woman, crushes her, pins her to the floor. One of the bars snaps her neck.

THE BIRD OF PARADISE

The skeleton that occupied the cage remains seated on her chest, like in depictions of nightmarish demons that ravage the slumbers of human beings.

Crawling and crying, I reach Robin. I take him in my arms. In the flickering light of the candles I see shadows passing over his face.

"Who are you?" I ask him. "Why did you sacrifice yourself for me? You've been dead for a long time, haven't you? Are you Robin?"

"Yes, I'm Robin, if you want to call me that still. Do you remember the fire in the film library? I'm on the video cassette that you rescued from the flames. My whole life is there. My image, what is left of me. I still live, breathe, move and exist on that tape. By saving the video, you saved my life, *the only one I have*. I was in your debt, and I wanted to repay you. I wanted to superimpose the imaginary on the real, the film on reality, the criminal act on innocence, the victim on the killer. To die in place of you, to save you. I have made you an artist, I have given you an investigation."

"You're lying," I say, between my sobs. "You're not a ghost. You're not an image on that video. I'm mad, and you're the imaginary friend I talk to."

"It doesn't matter . . ." Robin says, his voice getting weaker and weaker.

"You don't exist."

"It doesn't matter . . . "

Robin's final words fly away like doves taking off. He passes away imperceptibly, without the difference between life and death being visible, and making everything around me vanish.

I remember then having walked for a long time, carrying with me the bird of paradise, the fantastic bird, the fable. I remember having staggered like a drunkard under the traffic of the road, with my poetry in my arms.

Finally, I remember having returned home, or rather having woken up.

With invisible wires I hung the bird of paradise from the walls and the ceiling of the room with the cages. With no legs to walk or rest on the ground, dressed in the feathers of all the winged creatures, always in the sky, it flutters lightly in the wind that stirs it, a simulacrum of life.

I wait, puzzled.

I know that sooner or later I will have to call someone, ask someone what really happened.

Maybe they will say that I discovered the cruel pair of killers who for seven months terrorized the city. That I discovered the remains of their victims, that I didn't succeed in saving Regina but I killed the two monsters.

Or else they will say that the monster's house is my house, and I am the cruel killer. In my delirium I projected the killer outside myself, giving it the face of my dead parents.

They will say that I am Robin; that I survived but was driven mad by the kidnapping, the rape and the torture I suffered as a child. Not being able to love a woman, I hate all women and I kill them, obsessed by a world of male purity that I symbolized with the bird of paradise: I worship the fetish, I cultivate the plant and I follow the constellation.

They will say what they want, but will it be more correct, more *true*, than what I have gone through?

It doesn't matter.

Whether I'm a detective or a criminal, a man or a woman, a child or an adult, my father, my mother or Robin, it doesn't matter.

On the video that I saved from the fire there's a child that could be me.

In the park, in the middle of all the others who are seeking out their role in reality, in the future, he and he alone seems not to believe in the future nor in reality. He stands by himself, as if his companions, made of flesh and blood, vigor and health, were evanescent ghosts.

His small hand is caught in the grating, like the leg of a bird that can't fly.

June 1978

KATIA CECCARELLI

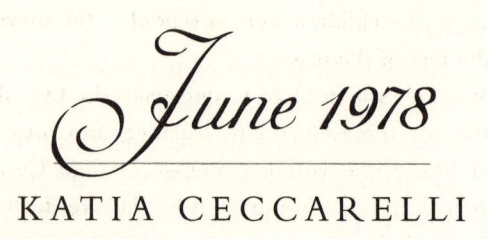

In summer everything was much easier; it was hot, the windows were left open, and everyone spent their days outside, in the courtyard, in the streets.

In June they'd buy you a colorful exercise book with holiday homework, full of little stories and comic strips—not as good as the real ones, but good enough to make the quiz at the end bearable. Luckily, there wasn't much in the way of math—less than you got during term time.

You'd start enthusiastically and then leave everything to be picked up again after the summer holiday, after the outings and the excursions out of town or to the baths at Tivoli that stank of rotten eggs but that were really good for the skin, or so they said.

The summer of '78 was bound to be special: there was the World Cup, and soccer, of course, was always an excuse for a party, to get together in the bar to watch the games, or perhaps at home with the windows open.

The Morettis could consider themselves a large family: father, mother, two daughters, two sons, and a disabled and dependent grandfather. The husband and wife slept in one room, the daughters Livia and Carolina—known as Lina—in another, the boys in the living room on the sofa and the chair-bed respectively, which had to be folded up by half past seven in the morning without fail, and the grandfather in the box room that also housed Mrs. Moretti's treadle sewing machine.

In order to avoid overcrowding, life mainly took place outside the four walls of the home; Mr. Moretti, who worked for the post office, filled up his afternoon off with a part-time job doing the accounts in a grocery store, his wife was a hospital porter and supplemented this by giving people injections at home. The children were at school in the morning and out on the street for the rest of the day.

Because it was the fashion to go to university, the two oldest—Livia and Mauro—had thrown themselves into learning and into young people's committees, while the two younger ones—Lina and Cesaretto—had the boundary of their field of action marked by the tire dealer opposite their building and the bar/tobacconist/dairy next door.

On the other hand, since he had to move around with a cylinder of oxygen, their grandfather had to greatly limit his independence of movement and spent his time doing crossword puzzles and watching television, but sparingly, because electricity was expensive and they didn't have money to burn.

None of the four children had keys so they had to go home after six, when their mother had come back from visiting her patients.

More often than not, Mauro turned up at the building's entrance long before six, and he would ring Mrs. Diamanti's bell to get her to open the door and let him in, and not just into the building.

Sometimes Cesaretto followed him too; he enjoyed playing tricks on the caretaker's son, who notoriously devoted himself to exploring his own body, shut inside the broom cupboard on the terrace, all by himself.

"Why are you always following me? Go and play soccer." Mauro didn't have much patience.

"Mr. Filippo burst my ball, the one who's always got a headache."

"Get the porter's son to give you a ball."

"He doesn't know how to play soccer."

"Here. Here's 100 lire. Now go away."

For Cesaretto, nothing was more persuasive than money, and Mauro set an example for him in this regard.

Usually he would convince the caretaker's son to come down to the courtyard to look for someone with a ball, seeing that his makeshift playmate didn't have one either.

JUNE 1978

Lina was in the courtyard too, playing hopscotch with other girls who lived in the building.

"D'you want to see my sister's bum?" Cesaretto once asked the caretaker's son.

"Dunno." He wasn't very enthusiastic. "What can you see?"

"Her bare bum."

"But what does your sister have to say about it?"

"She likes showing her bum. She shows it to Michelino too, but you've got to give me something in exchange."

"Two packs of stickers?"

"Haven't you got 100 lire?"

"I'll go and ask Mum. Wait for me?"

"Okay. I'll wait here. But hurry up or Lina will have gone."

In the garden in the courtyard there were lots of trees where the children would play hide and seek. Michelino, Cesaretto, and the caretaker's son joined Lina, who was already ready and waiting behind a tall, broad pine tree.

Michelino had booked first and Cesaretto collected the money: "First the cash: 100 lire just to look and 200 if you want to touch her bum."

Michelino pulled out 200 lire, while the caretaker's son was calculating if it was worth it.

Lina was wearing a lightweight yellow skirt that was lifted up with every breath of wind, or even if she just jumped. Everyone saw her knickers, always and anyhow.

She signaled to Michelino and turned around, slightly lowering her blue-flowered cotton knickers.

Michelino bent down and looked at Lina's bottom without saying a word while she laughed. He stretched out his hand and squeezed her flesh.

She laughed even more loudly and he ran away.

Lina still had her knickers pulled down, so that if anyone came she could say she had to pee.

"So, what do you want to do?" Cesaretto was fed up with keeping guard and hurried the caretaker's son.

"I've only got 100 lire."

"So, look and that's it."

The shy boy fished out a coin and went to hide behind the tree.

Lina was crouching down. "Hurry up. I really do have to pee now."

"Can I watch?"

Lina wriggled around a bit and moved her bottom in front of the boy's face; the color had drained from him and he looked as white as a sheet.

"Why do you want to watch while I pee?"

"Because I don't know how girls do it. I want to see where it comes out."

Lina squatted and urinated, but the caretaker's son didn't see anything except a little pool with a rivulet running from it. Afraid of dirtying his shoes, he jumped backward.

"Now show me how you do it," Lina cheekily dared him.

"I'm embarrassed."

"So was I, but if you don't do as I say I'll call Cesaretto."

At the thought of having to face the forceful Moretti, the caretaker's son accepted the deal: "No, no. Okay. I'll let you watch."

They went up to the terrace; he felt embarrassed and that he wouldn't be able to go, but Lina stayed close to him, pleased as Punch: "Let's go there, behind the aerial mast. Okay?"

"Yes, but I don't want to pee much."

"Well, try."

She watched him and waited; he took out his willy, which had got a bit hard, and he had difficulty getting the urine to come out: "Move over a bit, or I won't be able to do it."

"Gosh! What a lot of bother! Come on, I let you see me peeing— you're not keeping your promise. I'll help you. I'll make a noise so you'll want to pee."

He stood there with his willy, which hurt a bit, in his hand and strained to make the urine come out.

"Psss, psss, psss," hissed Lina, as if she were calling a little bird.

Suddenly the jet of urine arrived, much more than they had expected— a nice long stream that made a well-defined, uninterrupted arc.

JUNE 1978

Lina clapped her hands, delighted with her discovery. She was so pleased she almost wanted to touch it.

The boy smiled, thinking about how well he had done and how happy he had made her.

"Will you show me again tomorrow?" Lina said, scratching herself under her skirt.

"Yes. But don't tell your brother."

Then they went back down to the courtyard, he went home, and she went back to her game. Cesaretto thought that he needed another 100 lire to buy a Super soccer ball.

In those days, anyone who had a color television set was a sort of king in the neighborhood, and Michelino's father was one of them.

"My dad's bought a color TV."

"Really?" Lina never watched television; in the evening there was the news and then her brothers always wanted to choose, and anyway the TV they had at home was black and white and the button for the second channel always got stuck so when you had to switch it back to the first channel their father got annoyed because it didn't work. Then one day Mum had the idea of putting a toothpick there to hold down the first button and it worked. However, every now and then Cesaretto dropped it and it got lost and then Dad got pissed off again.

"Yes," Michelino wanted to make an impression on Lina.

"And what do you see?"

"Colors. The faces are pink and the clothes all different colors. Then when they do the technical tests for the signal they show you a multicolored striped ball."

"And what can you hear?"

"Voices, the same as black-and-white TV."

Michelino liked Lina a lot, but he wanted to be sure he didn't look foolish: "But you like the caretaker's son, don't you?"

"Well? . . ." Lina was noisily chewing strawberry-flavored gum, one of those large pieces that filled your whole mouth and they said that if you weren't careful you could even choke.

Michelino got embarrassed talking to Lina, and more than anything else he was embarrassed about the 200 lire he had given Cesaretto to look at her bum. But it didn't bother her.

She would always avoid him, perhaps she didn't like him much, and yet he had lots of toys and a new bicycle.

"Would you like me to teach you to ride a bike?"

She was bored with being stuck there listening to Michelino: "Dunno. What if I fall off?"

"No, you won't fall if I'm there. I'll hold you. I've got two new stickers, nice ones—would you like them?"

"I don't like stickers, and anyway Mum doesn't like me sticking them on things."

"I've got 500 lire."

"Give me it!"

"What will you give me?"

"I'm going. Mum'll be home in a bit."

"For 500 lire, will you let me touch you there?"

Lina pretended not to understand: "There where? You've already touched my bum lots of times."

"Not your bum." Michelino blushed and realized he had said something stupid. He looked down at the toes of his trainers.

"Give me 300, but I'll touch you," she had countered.

Michelino didn't understand: "But where's the fun in you touching me?"

"I've heard that men like it if you touch them where they pee."

Curiosity led Michelino to accept the offer and, in addition, he would still have 200 lire left: "Quickly then. Let's go inside where the boilers are."

They ran off together, pretending they were playing hide and seek. They slipped into the dark and silent room.

"The game'll be starting soon." Michelino was in a hurry to try out this new thing, but he didn't want to show it. He undid the buttons of his short trousers, and Lina started laughing.

"Shush. They'll hear us."

JUNE 1978

"Don't you have trousers with a zip?"

"What's it to you?"

"Money first." Lina was a person who liked to be meticulous. "And you have to take it out yourself because I'll be sick if I have to touch your pants."

She took the three coins and put them in the pocket of her blouse.

Michelino had taken out his willy, and Lina, turning away, touched it with a finger and ran off at once.

He thought he had wasted 300 lire.

Lina was looking through the balcony railing; it was hot and everyone had their windows open, the World Cup was on, and all the men were watching television.

Her father and Mauro were drinking beer and Cesaretto orange squash. Mum had gone to visit the caretaker to get a bit of fresh air. Mum couldn't care less about soccer, and neither could the caretaker.

It was so quiet you could have heard a pin drop if it hadn't been for the loud noise of the televisions that echoed throughout the neighborhood like a single voice.

She didn't care about the World Cup either, nor did Granddad, who stayed in his tiny room with his memories and his oxygen cylinder, staring at the closed window because, even when it was hot, he was afraid of catching a cold.

Lina thought that she didn't know how she could think—it was difficult to think anything, especially when it was so hot and the only good thing was those breaths of air in the evening.

She looked at the courtyard through the railings; cats were moving undisturbed from one garden to another without worrying about the caretaker and the blows she used to rain down on them with her broom.

Michelino lived in the building opposite; in his living room window you could see the light from the television, which was a bit green and a bit red, not sky blue like the light from black-and-white sets. But the sound was the same, the sound of the World Cup.

The sun had sunk behind the blocks of flats and the tops of the pine trees but you could still see.

Lina thought that she could think about something important, about Michelino or perhaps the caretaker's son.

The sound of the television was always constant, then suddenly the whole building shouted out, the whole neighborhood, her whole house; it was the World Cup, and when it's the World Cup men shout.

That evening they shouted so loudly that no one heard that Grandfather's cylinder had run out. He didn't manage to shout as loudly as the other men.

They noticed him when their mother came back, and called the nurse, who hurriedly replaced the cylinder with a new one and then called the doctor.

At the time, Lina thought that perhaps her granddad had died of fright because of the shouting and she realized that she had had an important thought.

Thirty Years Later

They say that the neighbourhood has changed completely. Now everyone minds their own business and there aren't children in the street anymore; they say it's dangerous.

Mothers take their children to school and go to collect them by car, even if they only have to go five hundred yards; they no longer have the time to walk, but they have time to double-park. However, some women do walk—the Filipinas, the Moroccans, the Eastern Europeans—in short, the women who don't have cars.

They closed the parish recreation center—no one went there anymore anyway—and the fields where they had cross-country running have become building land and construction has already started.

In the middle of the avenue they've made a traffic island; at least that's what they call it, but really it's a cement step where you have to stop to check the traffic before crossing the other half of the road, but because it's too small sometimes it creates a huddle of old people who look like a flock of birds on a power line.

In my building a few people are left along with my mother, who is now just a tenant but still has the old habits of a caretaker. Mrs. Moretti and her husband went to live in the country, in Poggio Mirteto, because they said you couldn't breathe in Rome anymore and at a certain age you need fresh air.

The flat was taken over by the daughter, Livia, who had got married; Cesaretto took over Mr. Filippo's workshop; Mauro seems to drift in and out of the neighborhood; and Lina . . .

I found Lina again.

It appears that she is working as a physiotherapist and has taken the place of her mother at the hospital.

There are lots of different types of massage, but you know if you look through the ads in the papers what sort of massage they mean. Usually I go to reliable people, relying on word of mouth, but once I wanted to try the classified ads. You can take your pick from names suited to beauty salons or prostitutes: Centro Luna, Jessica, Studio Solange, Tatiana.

I chose one so out of place that whoever had placed the ad must have been new to the game: *qualified physiotherapist available for massages, reasonable prices.*

It was even in my old neighborhood, so I decided to make an appointment.

It was quite a scene when I arrived: a small, scrupulously clean room with a smell of bleach and camphor, folded towels on a bed covered with a blue paper cloth. It looked real; perhaps she was one of those who do role-play—nurse and doctor, patient and nurse.

I imagined her coming in wearing a Red Cross nurse's bonnet and white garters visible below her unbuttoned uniform.

Instead, through a side door, there entered a small woman with a ponytail, a penicillin-green smock, and a rather haggard-looking face, although she was still quite young—she could be my age.

She says to me: "Please lie down. Where does it hurt?"

I had made a mistake: she really did do massages, and I didn't know what to say except "Sorry, I've made a mistake."

I felt sorry for her as well; she was someone who definitely worked because she had to. I remembered that one of my knees had been bothering me for a while, and so I decided to take advantage of my mistake to do something useful.

While she was preparing the liniment I tried to strike up a conversation: "Do you know, I used to live near here years ago."

She didn't seem very interested, but out of politeness she replied: "Really?"

"That's right. In fact I was born in this neighborhood. Every now and then I come and visit my mother, who still lives here."

She had started to knead my left calf. First she had warmed up her hands, but I still shivered. Who knows why one specific memory out of the many from my childhood came to mind.

"Do you know the Blue Angel bar?"

"Yes, but it's not called that anymore. An Egyptian took it over—I really couldn't tell you what it's called now."

"Were you there that time when Renato Zero came in?"

A wide smile brought the color back to her pale face: "Renato's great. Yes, I remember that. I was playing in the courtyard when at some point we heard this screaming from the street and then all us kids ran off to see what was going on.

"'It's Renato, it's Renato,' they were shouting. There was already a mass of people on the pavement and in front of the bar and, being small, I couldn't see a thing. I even stamped on someone's foot so hard it'll still hurt, poor thing. But do you mean you were there too that day?"

I stretched out my leg and propped myself up on my elbows: "I'm the son of the caretaker at number 15."

She cleaned her hands on a cloth: "I'm Lina, Lina Moretti."

We could have told each other so many things, about our families, work, how things were going, but she had gone bright red and I put my trousers back on, ready to get the money out of my wallet.

She waved it away: "No, it's fine. I don't want your money. It's a pleasure. In fact, if you come back, for you it's free."

Inside the Body of Roma

SOFIA NATELLA

A journey is always through time and space.
The only possible vital dimension: speed.

In Medias Res: Milestones, Altars and Drainage Channels

When he entered the body of Roma for the first time, he felt lost.

It seemed to him that he had suddenly been awakened from a whole life of sleepwalking and flung at the center of her, among alleyways, streets and green spaces. He clung to her body so as not to be swept away, to keep himself anchored in some way to reality, and the more he held her breasts or held her wrists above her head and pushed himself into the depths of her vagina, the more he seemed to slide further, however, at a speed he couldn't control, exploring all her places (the Circus Maximus, the Ara Pacis, the Imperial Fora, Piazza di Spagna, Trastevere, the Campo dei Fiori, the Villa Borghese . . .).

While he was entering her—his mouth open with amazement, his breathing against the wind that filled her, impossible to put up any resistance—he felt himself transported through a landscape in which immaculate palaces and churches, majestic and indestructible ruins, windows like mirrors and statues, triumphal arches, villas and avenues of maritime pines and palm trees rose up and towered over every corner. And yet, that same sensation of traveling made him feel trapped in a maze, going round in circles between the same four streets, staying within range of the crossroads—always within reach of her, always held by her imperial gaze and in the grip of her legs, his lips harpooned by her teeth—at the mercy of that womancity who continually changed his view of her while staying motionless, disorientating him. The taut and exposed nerves (like cables in midair between the pylons) revealed the possible electrified routes to reach orgasm, causing electrocutions through contact with water. But he couldn't help but repeat the same itinerary, the same identical movement, the same thrust of the pelvis, without being allowed any detours. *Was it his cock that was guiding him, or was she leading him?* Inside Roma, he was aware of the beauty contained within every moment, extracted from time and developed instantaneously in a fresco [eternal]. His consciousness had been ravished, while the rest of him continued to pulsate.

Suddenly he heard himself cry out: he was falling into the body of Roma, traveling through all her layers and swiftly overflowing into an ejaculation, before being sucked under by her subsequent spasm.

He had seemed to catch sight of fires and red debris in her eyes, as he was coming. But he immediately forgot it. Now it was dark and the face of Roma hadn't changed.

BEFORE

Centurions, Gladiators and Sibyls

He had come to the party without having been invited, but he was with Dean and the man at the door let him through, impassive in his granite-like stance. A small invisible woman took his coat and vanished before Dean had finished saying "Let's go and get something to drink," gliding with his shiny lace-up shoes through the penthouse. And they drank, as much as they talked, shaking hands; they undid the top buttons of their shirts so they could drink and talk more easily, light cigarettes, smile, the muscles of their faces tensing and relaxing repeatedly, revealing subtle wrinkles at the corners of their eyes. The whiteness of their teeth and their shrill laughs merged with the bass emanating from the speakers, the beat of the music that was thumping out tunes and internal punches, trying to get out. The girls shouted their names, trying to make themselves heard as the room became hotter and hotter. They shouted even when they weren't saying *nice to meet you, Sara/Agatha/Marlene/Zoe* in their evening dresses and with their hairstyles that rose up like hair-sprayed scaffolding; they shouted with their bracelets that crashed against each other as they fell to their wrists, with their dangling earrings that slapped against their necks. They shouted while they clattered their heels as they repeated the same dance steps—left, right, a sway of the hips. The loft was packed and he hadn't yet worked out what the party was for. Tacked onto the wall there were lots of photographs of a girl, being hugged by her parents, in a mausoleum of memories in color. He grabbed a bottle and leaned against the wall, near the large window, studying the unknown metropolis (New York, London, Paris, Shanghai, Moscow, Sao Paolo, Rome itself . . .) through his reflection.

SOFIA NATELLA

Morituri Te Salutant:
A Vision of Sugar to Wet the Sand of the Arena

The music stopped with a jerk; silence arrived like a whip crack. Then there was a jingle of silverware on crystal, and everyone—with a concurrent movement of their neck/head/eyeballs/feet—turned toward the apex of the party. Roma was in the middle of the room—the room, in turn, in the middle of the large house—and it seemed that geography had been created because of her, Roma as the single dominant temple. The guests were standing around perfectly upright, but keeping their distance, as if in reality the girl took up much more space than her body, enclosed in a sphere that made her, at one and the same time, sacred icon, emblem, monument, mythology, dreamlike manifestation. Her black hair fell straight to her shoulders like a cloak of night, an extension of her dress, which then faded into nylon. The only touches of color were her lips and nails, her shoes, the inner corner of her eyes: all red. The only contrast was her skin: white. From her shell of silk and varnish, the girl greeted her guests with her eyes, thanked them by altering the tilt of her chin slightly, addressing first one part and then another of her arena.

Someone at the back shouted "Happy birthday, Roma!" raising his glass, and then everyone echoed him, raising the glasses that the waiters had just refilled, repeating in unison the wishes they had just heard.

Then the guests arrived—ambassadors of oppressed lands: radical chic types, dandies, intellectuals and artists, young entrepreneurs, promising sports people—paying their respects in an orderly line. Bunches of flowers that gathered together whole gardens, cards and gift-wrapped presents that Roma accepted and unwrapped with a polite lack of haste, pulling the ribbons with the tip of her fingers, lifting lids of precious card, always smiling, raising and lowering her gaze with clockwork precision, hiding the pain on her covered gums, just above her teeth, behind her soft and indolent lips.

Preparations for a Civil War

Roma drew closer without holding out her hand to him. He looked her in the eyes, and he seemed to do it from below, although he was taller than her, and she was wearing heels. He felt he needed to explain his presence: "I'm a friend of Dean's. I've recently moved here and he brought me to the party." She asked: "What's your name?" He replied: "Happy birthday." He couldn't get over her height.

A Rite of Pan

They could hear the whirring of an aircraft that was flying over them, searching for a point over which to evacuate, and the ground swaying below them, becoming more and more fragile and soft, ready to swallow them up. Their bodies were in a state of alarm. The siren was pulsating blue and red behind the thorax; it was flashing on and off through veins and arteries, on their faces, shading them with colored darkness and nocturnal transmissions, the rest of the room a nonexistent backdrop: white, green, blue, *who knew? Who cared?* Blood was deserting the high levels of the brain to pour into the streets, gushing, collecting lower and lower down, surging, and every movement needed effort to counter the flow that would have dragged them in another direction, toward a heavier center of gravity, below the focal point [one toward another, there, now]. Synchronized with the circular movement of the siren, they carried alcohol to their mouths, they opened them to say something, they broke off to let the other person speak, they smiled earnestly, then they drank again, producing silence. A single sustained beat that whistled indistinctly, the result of millions of internal collisions that cancelled each other out. The contemporaneity of action and reaction was a game of tennis in which both players hit the ball at the same time, leaving it hanging in the void, its shadow cast between the red ground and the white line of the net. Their immobility broke every law of physics.

SOFIA NATELLA

Gladiators as Pigeons on Top of a Monument

She was in front of him as they climbed the stairs, until they reached a small door squeezed in under the wings of the roof. She turned the key: "This is my room" and gave him time to look around to gather details and impressions of her, keeping her from having to tell him about herself. Roma must have been younger than she seemed—she could be eighteen, nineteen at most, while he was already over thirty—and yet she seemed ancient, outside time. A painting to admire behind golden barriers and red cords, which came closer to him, making him enter the forbidden area. He felt in danger, too full of blood. He was sure that he would have left, once he had entered into any sort of contact with her.

Visiting the Imperial Suburbs

The contact between their lips seemed supernatural to him, as if she could look at him with her skin. The epidermis of Roma was the Coliseum, an eye in every arch, like an architectural version of the prismatic eye of a fly, breaking down a single vision into a multitude of perceptions. Each paroxysm surrounded him, all around him. The touch of hands revealed that they weren't made of the same material: the differences between his body and that of Roma opened up to him under his feet, exposing the chasm that separated them, the closer they were. He ran his hands along her sides (the borders) and, lifting her dress, he uncovered the panorama. Her stomach—a wide square with a dry fountain in the center, her navel—and her abdomen polished by millennia of footsteps, her ribs to be ascended one by one, until he arrived at an altar from where he could admire her seven hills: her cheekbones, her nipples of red earth, her buttocks, her mons veneris.

Roma sat on the edge of the bed, to offer herself up to him in a last vision of the whole, before disappearing into the details of their close contact. Her legs, slightly open, invited him to enter.

FROM THAT POINT FORWARD

How Many Escape Routes Exist in a Siege?

He left the room where Roma was sleeping, her abdomen sinking under her ribs, her feet poking out of the bed. He went down into the half-empty house with his shoes in his hands, his shirt carefully tucked in to his trousers again, his blood still incandescent. The shrieks of the few people left penetrated through the muffled volume of the music. They were reduced to mere bodies: crumpled, dragging themselves across the floor, shuffling their feet and knees, giggling and vomiting, or else propping up other bodies at the bathroom door, or against a thousand other invisible doors, one falling into another almost by accident, through other doors open between them, with their mouths wide open and their tongues that moved in an overlapping of interpenetrating levels (he seemed to see Dean's tongue twisted around that of a girl with a flower dangling in her hair, Dean's penis projecting toward the unknown girl). They were all outside, outside their cages and their empty rooms, the only full and locked room—occupied by Roma. The way out must have been in there.

When the exhausted waitress brought their jackets and they left the apartment, the feeling of being imprisoned—in a bas relief, in a state of cardiac arrest—clung to him with both sleeves.

SOFIA NATELLA

The Phallic Detail in a Sacred Building

"But where have you been all this time?"
"Around."
"Ah, I see. Did you have a good trip, eh?"
"Yes."
"That thing was great, wasn't it?"
"Who was that girl?"
"Ah, just some girl."
"No, the birthday girl."
"Why? Do you want to do her?"
"No. Does she live there on her own?"
"Do you want to marry her?"
"No."
"Well, you should. She's extremely rich, you know?"
"I thought she might be. A lucky girl, she could be an artist[*] if she wanted."
"Not that lucky, to be honest. She's a little luxury orphan." [†]
He stood there with his mouth open. It seemed full of salt.

---

[*] He had grown up in the provinces, because there houses cost a third of what they cost in the city. When he had begun studying, often he had had to use old torn sheets as canvases on which to paint. The poor quality of the support had resulted in him getting lower marks than he should have during his studies because the colors seeped through the fibers, making the brushstrokes blurred. However, this technique, completely accidental, had won him a certain amount of attention, at the end of his course.

[†] And in fact she was. As Dean told him, the girl lived alone in a penthouse of 2,500 square feet with a terrace, on the top floor of a period building, which had belonged for generations to her family, where from time to time her guardians came to visit her. As for her parents, they had both died when she was thirteen, from food poisoning when they were in Mexico to celebrate their wedding anniversary. Now she had reached twenty-one, and she was about to take control of her inheritance.

Carved with the Point of an Ice Pick

He kept on looking at the hand where he had written her number, which he had then copied onto a piece of paper, which finally he had stuck up in the windowless bathroom in the hotel, to stare at it in secret. One day he had called it, eager even if only to hear the answering machine switching on. He wanted to hear Roma's voice: it flowed and faded into silence like a river—the Tiber?—which ran through her and then left her, covering huge distances, through channels, upstream through the urethra, to finally surge inside him. He stayed there with the receiver in his hands and his hands in his groin, as if he were intent on masturbating over the phone, the rhythmic delay of the signal, his ejaculation and his smile held back by the silence. Then she responded. "Hello?"

But he wasn't ready. Roma repeated "Hello? Who is it?" He said: "It's me." Roma was smiling at the other end of the line.

Retractable Drawbridge

As the elevator was ascending, he was panting, his breath fractured on thousands of stairs. Roma opened the door in a dressing gown, with a finger marking her place in a book of comic strips. *Wasn't she going to her classes? What did she still have to learn? What did she do all day?* Roma *existed*.

"Do you want something to drink?"

The house was empty but she occupied all of it, spreading out in an exploded mass that carried her every movement—of her neck, eyes, every single finger bent and then outstretched—beyond the confines of her body. He already felt inside her, while he sat alone on the sofa.

When Roma appeared with the coffee, the silk fell, exposing her shoulder. That moment between the slipping of the fabric and the movement of her hand was enough to make her pupils dilate, revealing the true depth of the well. Then the breach closed again rapidly, trying to vanish among the colors of the rainbow. The archaeological feeling that he had had that first night drilled deep into him, and became clearer.

It was the sign of another city inside her, a subterranean city that guarded a mysticism of pagan rites and violence, and that Roma had buried under opaque surfaces, which covered the blue of her veins. Now he knew it clearly: Roma was lying, concealing, despite the extensive exposure of herself, disguising her heart with that clothing, that face and that polished immobility. The pillars on which Roma stood were made of bone. He sensed this because at times her skin felt empty under his hands, and she flinched—imperceptibly, but she flinched—when this happened. He sensed it because from her warm and clean body he heard the howling of an icy wind, escaping through the porousness of marble and the gaps between the cells. His body tossed and turned, his fingers and penis tense like diviners probing every possible access route.

The Tourist Trail of the Wind in the Baths of Caracalla

Towers and skyscrapers of ash detached themselves from the cigarette, falling on the floor. Standing in front of the large window and in front of the outspread city, Roma asked herself what it was about him that had attracted her, and made it impossible for her to free herself from a sense of excitement and menace. It was something that related to the concept of comparison. The most modest origin, the rougher skin, the appearance of a beard every forty-eight hours, the more pungent smell, forms that stood out whereas in her they turned inward (Adam's apple, penis, and, the other way round, chest), the different proportions of the same parts of their bodies, the disorderly arrangement of the clothing, the insistent gaze which pressed into her (some of his glances seemed to her to be out-and-out attempts to break through), the different deepness of the cavernous voice, the greater physical strength. She wanted to understand, and she liked understanding, how she was different from him, studying him like a unique specimen in his own natural ecosystem (the bedroom, the bathroom in the morning when he was shaving, the deserted study, the underground passages of the Metro, the art galleries, the art supply shops, which he chose with obsessive calm). The differences created a lack of balance, a dizziness that terrified her; she sensed a destructive energy in the tension that allowed vaulting and arches to remain standing. Roma pushed herself against him—against his chest, under his shirt, her head in the hollow of his armpit or in the niche between his neck and shoulder—to seek out a hiding place in which to count with closed eyes. The closer she got to him, on top of him, the more she could hide in his shadow. She closed the window (the hyperventilating sky streamed between the buildings). It was fear, and loving him was the only way to hold it at bay.

Postcards from the Capital as Tourist Information

He used to collect postcards of Roma that he stuck on the wallpaper of his room and then copied in his paintings in details and wide-angle views. Roma appearing from a fold between the sheets, the ridge of a hip bone like a roof, an elbow like a tooth, the toes like a series of bell towers, a blood vessel that runs across the eye like a rivulet in the park.

He photographed her everywhere, violating her image and her actual dimensions. In the street, on the balcony, sitting on a bench, while she was eating a sandwich or the cuticles around her nails. While she was putting on makeup, laughing, sleeping, while they were fucking, shifting locks of hair and limbs, arranging them in different poses, trying to capture on film fragments of an encrypted map.

A Pantheon of Cells

The elasticity of his eye had increased. During intercourse he was able to see Roma unbelievably close up, penetrating her surface to such an extent that he could break her down into details and incomplete components. In the same way, closing his eyes, he managed to make his gaze pull back until he could see the widest views that set Roma within the world. The entire process made visible the overflowing of Roma into reality, and of reality into her. Her skin was paved with cobbles, her limbs were level crossings and bridges, her pelvis the atrium of a castle or a turned dome, her heartbeat a bacchanal, her orifices the gods of the Pantheon. A waste bin was the final stretch of her intestine, the plan of a building traced out the structure of her cells, the advertising displays impulses in her brain. Roma was everywhere, even inside him. *Wasn't this the correct concept of 'art,' of 'wonder'?*

He got into the habit of looking at himself in the mirror with particular attention, trying to study the effect that she was having on his body, certain that he would find her crouched in a dark corner.

Outings to the Baths

He dreamed that while he was bathing in a fountain—the Trevi fountain?—and he was calling her, asking her to join him, from the wrists of Roma poured cascades of small coins, which settled on the bottom. That feeling of separation stuck to him.

When he talked to her, when he rubbed himself against her bottom to make her feel how hard and large he was, and when he then entered her, Roma seemed like a well-preserved statue in an apparent state of grace. She remained still, as if any gesture were just a different arrangement of the same figure: a repositioning rather than a movement. She allowed him to deploy her, to arrange her body, to place it on the bed, to open her legs, to fill her mouth. But it was a concession of her passive will, not the result of active desire. While he felt more and more corroded, infected and shattered by her, Roma remained intact, immune, inanimate. Her body was a pretext, but she was elsewhere.

The Exact Location of the Mouth of Truth

The upright obelisk helped him to find the direction to follow. The thighs of Roma were always accessible, so he could quickly get to where he wanted. Perhaps too quickly. If he altered his route—now a finger to soften the anus, knuckles to slide over the clitoris, lips to circle the big toe—or delighted in getting lost, lingering in the fluctuations of intercourse instead of trying to reach orgasm, he heard the banging of the shutters as they closed, the hiss of bars sliding to bolt the street doors, the crash of blinds lowered too quickly, death that raced to disguise itself as a mime, pretending nothing had happened in the center of a square.

However much he thrust into the depths, he felt that Roma was revealing only her wrapping: polished facades and ruins, triumphs and attractions for tourists, rich viewpoints and friezes, zigzagging scooters and dance halls; essentially, what everyone saw, what everyone stopped in front of, following the directions and ignoring the existence of the damp and flawed substratum where the rats ran. Yet what was forbidden to him was the one place where he wanted to go. At the risk of continuing an erosion that had lasted centuries, rubbing inside her until she was worn through.

La Dolce Vita in a Polluted City and the Fascism of Beauty

Looking at himself in the mirror, he saw both a beggar and a worn-out puppet. The sun, the trees, the churches, the art galleries, the cinemas and the theatres no longer gave him a thrill. Neither were his work nor the holiday a relief, nor holding Roma by the hand, walking along wearing Hollywood-style sunglasses or watching her coming out of a dressing room, or fucking her in the morning, half aware of having gone to live with her enough for him anymore. It only helped to crush his purple eyes and to make his shirt come untucked from his trousers, making a uniform out of that exhausted appearance. The image of

Roma towered over him with her chin held high and ambushed him at every corner, depriving him of the most intimate freedom of thought.

Spartacus Rebels, Wearing a Tie, and Organizes a Gangbang in His Mind

He didn't want to hurt her, no.

But he wanted to soil the perfect image that was sleeping by his side. Shatter her shell between his fingers to reveal the living flesh. He wanted to see her flooded, put to fire and sword, infected by epidemics, trampled, beaten, stained with the sand and blood of the arena. Reduced to an expanse of red ground with no roads.

He imagined her sweaty and in tears, dressed in clothes torn at the knees, by her breast, her sex. Rome subjugated and enslaved by hunger, yearning to be replete at night, finally an ordinary mortal.

One cigarette after another, a vision of the body of Roma, besieged and possessed by two penises, or maybe ten, surrounded by men who plundered her of all protection, vanity or dignity, she was burning up and the smoke went to his head. Which was going round and round in circles, repeating the same sequence of mental images: Roma on her knees between four men, sucking them two at a time with an impossible mouth, the detail of Roma's hand lifting a penis to her mouth and making it disappear between her lips, all the openings of Roma filled at the same time, without allowing her a way out, Roma subjected to barbarian desires, Roma who allows herself to be sodomized by an endless series of men who stand in line behind and then inside her, Roma with her tongue tense, the enlargement of her bloated pupils equal to that of her pinched nipples, Roma flattened against a wall before being shot by his cock, the distance between Roma's fingers as she grips another member, the tilt of the wrist and the stroke of the hand needed to squeeze it. At last, him pissing in her arse, or coming. He wanted to inundate her, replacing the white of her marble skin—cold—with the hot whiteness of his sperm, which would burn her.

You Too

The walk to Roma's house didn't help to get rid of his hangover. The remnants of the Long Island iced teas were still circulating around his body and made him float, along with Roma, Dean and Martha (the girl his friend had met at the party), as they walked along the pavements, and then took the elevator. They fell onto the sofa, exhausted; that small amount of exhilaration [because of the recent success of his exhibition] was enough to keep them going for another half an hour, chatting before their collapse. Dean mixed rum and Coca-Cola in glasses: "Let's play a game. Each person tries to imitate the animal they'd like to be and the others try to guess what it is." Martha started to beat her arms—a hummingbird!—and Roma got down on four legs, stretching out in long paces. He and Dean watched her from the sofa, mouths and glasses suspended in midair, uncertain. Dean said "I think it's a puma," and then Martha, "No! It's . . . I can't make up my mind if it's a dog or a wolf." Roma went to sit down between the two men, her feet hidden under her legs, her lips glued to the straw. She said: "I am . . . " He concluded: "You're both a bitch and a wolf."* His stare bore into her like a dagger, the silence formed a crack in the ceiling. Dean and Martha lowered their eyes, embarrassed; his stayed focused on Roma, wild. He was imagining taking her hand and resting it on Dean's cock; in fact, he wanted her to do it herself, and then take it in her mouth right to his balls, while he pulled aside her moist panties and moved her head. Her head that then swayed toward him, her head that then pushed between Martha's legs, following the rhythm of him and Dean, who were screwing her from behind, first in turn and then together. Roma sensed in his stare a magnetic excitement that stopped her looking away, enticing her in a clairvoyant state that allowed her to probe into his thoughts through his eyeballs. *Did she really yearn for him?* In the tension of that contact—sustained, exclusive, by now unbearable—they weren't aware of Dean and Martha bidding good-

---

* The she-wolf, in ancient Rome, represented a prostitute

bye to them and leaving. They continued to pulsate. The distance between them was a paradox.

He sprang at Roma, crushing her under his weight, forcing her to open her legs under her skirt, pressing his lips against her, then his erection against her knickers that—it was true—were moist. Her fluids were gasoline, his cock the torch that set them on fire.

I know you like it, I know you like it, now I'll fuck you how you like it

Roma struggled, but too weakly. With one hand, he held her, with the other he gripped her neck, her pupils dilated, along with the rest of her. Roma wanted more, and he would have *dared* to give her what she wanted. To burn.

You want to be fucked like a whore, I know you want to be fucked like a whore

He wanted to make her surrender her defenses, hammering inside her with that red iron, slapping her breasts and face, branding them, using force to hold her legs apart, while she shouted *no, no,* and writhed, pushing him away, but she continued to kiss him and to grow wet, as if to bear the heat better. She thrust herself backward with her chest sinking into the sofa, or she tried to hit him, but attempting to keep him at a distance made their genitals join tighter together; they were throbbing one against the other, incandescent by now. Every touch of hands, mouths and tongues produced a burn, lifting the skin, leaving the living flesh exposed.

I know you like it, I know not even this is enough, you want it in the ass, right? I know you want it in the ass

He took her and made her kneel on the floor, with her face pressed against the sofa, then he pulled her toward him, holding her by the hair. A black lock had stuck to her face, her makeup had melted and lined her cheeks.

I love you like this, you're a whore like this

Roma arched her back. When he entered her ass a cry escaped from her throat. He stopped her mouth with his other hand: he wanted nothing of what she felt to escape her. She had to hold it inside, everything, that scorching magma (the body that oozed lava, the soul scattered in ashes, the walls and the bridges that tumbled down one after another, charred). He fucked her harder and harder the more she tried to rebel, subjugating her, eager to see when and how much would be *enough*; and the more she twisted against his cock, burning, her movements becoming more frenzied, the more he enjoyed it and he fucked her hard, compelling her to come dangerously close to orgasm, to the point of fusion. He could sense it from how she was biting his fingers, from how her muffled cries weren't of physical pain but caused by a more intimate laceration, a wound from which truth overflowed. She liked being violated, broken and terrified by his strength, by his rampant desire, being fucked in that brutal and dirty way. She liked feeling full, she liked feeling that cock that worked its way into her, that enlarged her and tore her, that consumed her and forced her to yield, to renounce her eternity. It was a process of drilling, demolition and devastation. And Roma wasn't fighting against him, who was fucking her, driving it into her ass, she was fighting against herself, so that she didn't entirely enjoy that *taken* being, so that the flames weren't too red or wondrously rising too high, because the pleasure would have destroyed her. She couldn't let herself be the one who soiled the white of the marble, who knocked the heads off the statues.

His hands harpooned her hips, the impact of his thrusts bent her and unleashed her, making her surrender. When he came inside her, he felt Rome's orgasm frantically gripping his cock. But it was a pleasure that she couldn't endure.

They smoked a cigarette close to each other, without touching. A thin smoke emanated from their mouths, the slow dying of the fire under the rain. The aircraft had disappeared. Everything had passed.

AFTER

A lot of time passed before they could meet again. Centuries in which many stories were written, in which he had imagined endless stories about Roma—Roma at gala dinners, Roma studying in prestigious universities, Roma getting plastered in disguise in rooms without windows—and, in fact, in which many stories were written in tabloid magazines. Or maybe it was only a year. A year in which Roma had discovered via notification from the bank that her guardians had fallen from favor and had squandered her fortune on bankrupt investments and satisfying vices, or the other way around—things wouldn't have changed because of that: Roma's inheritance was a *tabula rasa* with six zeros. The group of friends had broken up, migrating toward more prosperous company, without even making excuses. During that year Roma—by now of age and popular—had had to suffer the humiliation of seeing bailiffs for the bank—it seemed to her there were hundreds of them, whole phalanxes in overalls, but in reality there were no more than five or six—taking out of her house her armchair, designer lamps, rugs, and Chinese vases. Furniture and objects went out of the door without even being crated up, as if they were impatient to leave Roma. With her lips taut, the cigarette she was smoking between her fingers, letting ash fall to the floor, she watched sofas, beds and wardrobes in pieces going out of the windows and out of her life, to then be piled up in the truck together with tons of other things that had been hers and that she wouldn't see again. Dispossessed and plundered of everything that she had believed would always remain in her possession, Roma had had to go out into the street and watch—hidden in her coat—the new owners who were throwing her out of her house forever. And she hated them, above all because they had kept none of her furnishings. In that house there no longer remained anything of her. She had nothing left of herself.

Franchised Stoning: The Guardian Gods Favor Fortune by Administering Misfortune

He didn't realize straight away. She was asking him *what would you like?* in a snack bar, the ridiculous cap pulled down on her head as far as possible in order to eclipse with the visor her lifeless, automatic gaze, or—counter–tray, tray–counter, smile pre-set by the company policy—to hide the parting of her too shiny hair. He wasn't quick enough to leave her a note with the tip, nor the courage to talk to her. He paid and that was all, knowing that it would never have been enough.

Are You Looking for Trouble?

Roma was keeping watch over the pavement, hidden by the switched-off lights of the restaurant, casting her gaze out onto the cement beyond the window. With her elbows resting on the counter, her back parallel to the floor, her apron hanging down at right angles like a tongue or a curtain, she was wondering *who would he catch, this evening?* chewing the visor of her cap. The owner rubbed himself against her buttocks, coming out of the kitchen. Then he rested a hand there, saying "It's late. You should go home" too close to her neck. She let him do it, and he didn't notice that she had emptied the tip box. The roar of rain and horns had covered the clinking of the coins in her pocket.

The City of a Thousand Fountains

The water was cold when he got into the shower. He was in a hurry to get washed. He had undressed quickly, tearing off his clothes as he would have liked to do to her, to free her from that filthy uniform. He scrubbed so hard that his skin turned red, imagining that he was also washing away his sense of guilt and the body of Roma, to give it back its original glory. *Would soap have proven sufficient?* His head and face were white, one hand leaning against the wall, the other running over his cock, making the glans appear and disappear, together with the still unspoiled vision of her. His orgasm burned, and he felt it was coming out of his eyes.

Souvenir

The outcome of the following days was a repetition. The projection of her movements on the white wall; the mental reproduction of the smell of the different parts of her body; the reorganization of the details of Roma through the photographs that he had held onto and the subsequent enlargement of those same photographs; the development of new erotic fantasies that involved her, trying to picture her as he had seen her that first time: pure, unalterable, untouched. The memory was the only protection he could offer to them both.

NOW COMES THE END

I Bring You My Severed Head as a Gift

It was Roma who sought him out. He saw her opposite the exit of his studio, her cleavage crossed with blue tracks, livid with cold sweat, wrists and ears adorned with costume jewelry, her clothing from a local market copying the designs of the leading fashion houses. The badly bent metal spokes of her umbrella carved her face pierced by dark red lips into an irregular area of shadow. It looked as if the red were trickling down her chin as she talked. He wasn't listening to what she was saying. He felt his fingers tingling and the sky sizzling above them.

(The clock hands dissolve into waves and aqueducts)

They were in front of the window of a hat shop when the storm broke. Neither of them suggested going into a café. In Roma's room the double bed took up all the space, the entire floor seemed to be made of springs. She scraped against the wall as she went to close the curtains, then she climbed onto the bed and from high on her pedestal she held out her hand to him. The difference in their weight on the mattress made their eyes align for the first time.

(Coincidence and overlap)

He explored the quiet and desolate suburbs of Roma from afar: the epidermis, so worn that it had become transparent, almost failed to separate her from the world. He could sense in the mystic whispers that wriggled under the skin the swarming of a dancing madness that was distorting her, pushing her breasts, her buttocks, her cheek bones toward the outside.

Where was outside actually situated? The screeching of horns and voices in the crowded streets and the squares in quick succession, the insistent press—in the veins, in the blood—of the traffic, guided him toward the one possible destination. All the streets led to the center of Roma. She was the one to lead them inside her.

As he was getting closer—holding her hands, which were getting nearer and nearer a contact—he could hear the distant call, then more and more piercing, of the ancient city in flames: from her cunt escaped scalding steam, from her eyes thick smoke, her mouth wide open to invoke the melodrama. She seemed to be begging him to save her with frantic movements of her eyelashes, but she wanted to drag him into the fire together with her. In the destruction of her life, in the decline that the bankruptcy had forced on her, Roma had discovered a taste for the devastation that was needed to trigger cycles of rebirths and small deaths like time bombs, planning or else grasping the moment of explosion. From that evening when he had sodomized her, the inevitable process of dismantling her interior city had begun. The friction between their bodies had opened up a channel in which their blood mixed and polluted, flowing in opposite directions. Roma's desires had been dismantled, becoming his reality; his desires had spread through Roma with a transfusion, instilling violence and corruption. The more he continued in his ascent, the lower she fell.

It had begun by accident, accepting small gifts and that historic buildings were demolished, that jewelry and works of art were sold off, allowing whoever could do her a favor or be useful to her to occupy her rooms, changing them however they pleased. She liked to feel used, that not even an inch of her was being wasted, left to collect dust. She wanted to make herself fecund. But making simple, unedifying concessions wasn't enough for her anymore. She wanted to be burned to the ground, to see her foundations sinking into the earth.

(*Collision*)

INSIDE THE BODY OF ROMA

The impact reawakened an epicenter in every cell. They juddered, compelled to flow one over another, dispersing on trembling hands and lips, as their clothes slid to their feet, making both of them violatable, their flesh naked, on which they beat heavily. With hands, with tongues, which landed blows at random, wandering wildly. From the face to the ass, from the ass to the cock and the cunt, from the cunt to the thighs to the feet, then hurriedly returning to the breasts, tightening the grip on hard nipples, biting, scratching the back and the ribs. Then they started to repeat the same path all over again, rubbing his cock and her cunt there where they were most sensitive, each time using even more the rigid blanket of streets and surfaces of skin, revealing the seismic contraction of the musculature, the glittering blades of the nerves, the darkness of a chasm. His cock was there in the middle, and she climbed onto it in order to swoop down into the well, taking him inside.

A soft howl escaped through her teeth, carrying an odor of fever, and she invited him to stab her and fuck her *harder harder harder* in that wound already open between her legs, inflicting the thrusts herself then and fucking herself, slapping him to make him fuck her harder, resisting in order to submit even more. He twisted her wrists behind her back, forcing her to turn around, thrusting himself into her mouth until she was almost suffocating, and then spreading her thighs again and that cunt that she kept so tight, when she wanted to feel it more, making him fuck her with a violence that he wouldn't have known to use on his own, and that she asked of him. The blade plunged all the way to the bone, making the marrow spill out of its channel.

He was almost exhausted, and Roma didn't know where she was wettest. To wear herself out, she liked to draw out the seconds, hold them inside her until she could unravel them in little momentary eternities, to consume in a glass sphere together with oxygen, condensing them and transforming them into sweat. He caressed her liquid back, her breasts, he slid into the groove between her buttocks, caressing her then with her own fluids, smearing them on her face and all over her, making her lick them from his fingers or his cock, which she strove to suck. Now he could discern the speed of Rome, the simultaneous existence of time and space in the movement of their bodies, until they overlapped in a single history. In a repetition, a ritual.

He spat between her buttocks and she slid in two fingers. Then the glans entered, forcing slightly, then the rest straight after, as far as it would go. Roma arched her back, offering him her hair to pull tight, pushing her pelvis backward to feel him more, her throat exposed to be sacrificed, on the point of death.

The rhythm of the thrusts increased with the rain. The drops were smashing against the windowpanes, slamming, expanding and dripping, like their bodies, which were delirious, foaming at the mouth.

I want you to come inside me, I want you to piss inside me, I want you to fill me, fill me, fill me, fill me

The aircraft released its cargo. The river that ran through Roma started to swell, plentiful, excessive. His white spurt was enough to make it overflow. Flooding the pavements, the cellars, the houses, submerging the museums, the alleyways, the churches, even the tallest bell towers, managing to wash with an orgasm even the feet of god.

A brief note from the author: *The idea that forms the basis of this story—a story about the city of Rome as a woman, and about a woman as the Eternal City, and about the journey through her/it in time and space—came to me on a train, returning after a short visit to the capital (to launch my novel* The Arrangement of the Internal Organs*). I had written about two pages of it, which I have reworked here, the first and last scenes. Only a few months after that I would read* Crash *and* The Atrocity Exhibition *by J. G. Ballard; in some respect this story was a precursor, and maybe it's a homage to them, entering and then blossoming in my unconscious mind without me being able to hold it back or being aware of it, until the story was almost finished.*

Mr. Baby Gigolo

MARIROSA BARBIERI

A bottle of champagne and a packet of Marlboro Reds.

That's what my signora had for breakfast: strawberries drowned in alcohol, mixed with smoke and lots of laughter. After a night of sex between scarlet sheets, never satisfied, her mouth wanted more.

We went to a hotel a couple of times, when the desire to possess each other was intense. So intense that we tore off our clothes and made love on the recently polished parquet.

We fucked on the floor and our bodies chafed against rugs that were already threadbare and worn. She would fake her orgasms and we ended up body against body, one on top of the other, like two old sacks.

I had got to know my signora, the tone of her voice, always calm, warm and mellow. I had discovered that nothing could satisfy her, not even three hours of sex.

I knew everything and nothing about my signora. She didn't like to talk about herself. She was my last signora.

I started out as a gigolo partly for fun and partly to find myself. Gay . . . straight? That had been my uncertainty ever since I lost my mother.

I lived wrapped up in my meandering and fickle sexuality. I sought out my mother's clothes and wore them like a call girl. I would make myself up in front of the mirror so I looked like a woman, and I ended up looking like a whore, but a well groomed one. I would ring my eyes with pencil and eyeliner until they were two thick circles. And I spent hours swaying my hips. Then, the fashion show at an end, I would throw myself onto her bed and cry; I smeared everything with makeup: her sheets, her pillows, her lingerie, until I looked like a Pierrot dug up from the grave.

I wasn't aware of my penis: I didn't become aroused next to a girl dancing in a club; my eyes didn't even stray to my next-door neighbor, who every day, her tits swollen with milk, fed her two baby twins.

I became a pallid and sickly figure. I got bronchitis. I cured it with an overdose of cough drops. I slept, opened my eyes, closed them, went back to sleep again. I died, and then came back to life one day when they called me through a sex channel.

I saw adverts for high-class gigolos, the sorts who have the stomach to fuck classy eighty-year-olds, lonely and willing. The women who use their money to buy jewelry, cars, and sex, and for a few hours of company will put their hand in their pocket. Those old ladies who are crazy about nothing and everything.

You needed guts to make out with an old reprobate of nearly ninety with bad breath and drooping breasts.

At least they didn't expect anything. They let you go and then come back without prattling on. Without lingering on the doorstep with that pining look of someone who already thinks they're your girlfriend after a few hours in your company.

The old reprobates know. They have perspective, they know about settling for what they can get, about filling up the lonely hours, about flesh on flesh, about those minutes ticking away like the tolling of a bell.

Yes, I liked making out with those old ladies. I had little experience with immature girls. I became intimate with bodies that were flaccid and treated badly by time, or by a faithful partner or a fleeting lover.

I liked not knowing what secrets those old, violated temples were hiding. And almost always I went home without having discovered those secrets. And then it was always different. Some women asked me to kiss them, some to masturbate them, some to have penetrative sex, some to take them roughly. I discovered the old world of old ladies. Of those fur-clad benefactresses who go to mass on Sunday or enter raffles on Thursday.

There was a place where I would pick up my old ladies. It was a café on the corner between Via dei Caduti and Via della Libertà. There I met my signora. And it was a meeting like all the others.

That day my usual table was taken. She was there, a French woman with a snub nose. Large breasts restrained with difficulty by a lace bra that peeped out from an eye-catching décolletage.

She was looking down and blowing on her cup of tea, and the clinking of her tea spoon was making me fidgety. I loosened my tie, walked briskly toward the table and then stopped in front of her. Her ebony-colored eyes met mine and then she lowered them.

"Can I help you?" she asked me.

She had class, my signora. She turned her neck like a swan; she had a long and very taut neck, with the odd crease when she relaxed. Her hair fell onto her totally straight shoulders. She was blonde and, despite the warmth of the air, was well wrapped up, aside from her décolletage.

She stood up, moved toward an empty table, picked up a chair and held it out to me politely.

"Can I get you a tea?" she said to me as if she had known me for years.

I sat down. With one hand she spun around her cup of tea, with the other she played with her hair. Her hands were pale and slender, her grip rather weak.

"No, not tea, just a coffee. A black coffee," I said to her.

"I like this city," she told me.

"Rome's wonderful," I replied.

"I live near here," she continued.

"I live in the neighborhood," I answered.

She smiled, but it was a demure laugh.

My coffee arrived. I dropped the spoon. I bent over to pick it up and saw her legs: smooth, bare, well proportioned, covered by just the delicate mesh of her stockings. My signora was wearing heels and a skirt that fell to the knee. I pictured myself entering her. Her legs were still attractive and trim.

"Do you often come to this café?" she asked me.

"Every day," I answered.

"You can see everything from here," she continued.

"Everything?"

"People, the traffic, ideas, hustle and bustle."

"Why are you here?" I asked her.

"To have company."

I too had sat in this café so many times so as not to feel alone. The soft music, the distracted faces of the people, their features confused by the emotions they experienced—worry, indifference, loneliness, joy—all this kept me company as I hunted for new old reprobates.

She looked at her wristwatch, jumped from her chair and was ready to dash off.

"I'm very sorry but I have to go."

"Where are you going?"

"I'm going home, gigolo. It's been a pleasure meeting you," and she headed toward the door after having left the money and a tip on the table. She had caught on that I was a high-class fortune hunter.

I didn't want her to go. I should have followed her, run after her, said something to her, anything, even just to thank her for the coffee. I started to run to catch up, but when I turned the corner she had disappeared. Her walk, her lithe hips, her determined wiggle were imprinted in my mind. I would have liked to take her hand, lead her into a bathroom and fuck her, until I felt her come.

It wouldn't have been enough for me to wait for her.

When I was little I would wait for my mother. I didn't sleep at night and I would open the window in my room. The neighborhood slept, my uncle snored and I listened to the breathing of the darkness that was deeper than ever. The night breathed heavily, it inhaled and exhaled all the waiting. A son coming home, a husband going out, a prostitute walking the streets. Waiting has a shameful taste. You sense that it's there but isn't there.

The day after, someone knocked on the door. I opened it. I was in my underwear and looking dishevelled. I looked at the silhouette in front of me

MR. BABY GIGOLO

from the bottom up and recognized those tapering legs. Then the waist, the bulk of a thousand items of clothing covering her body. Then I recognized her eyes. It was her ...

My gaze rested on her breasts; they were almost invisible there were so many layers covering them. Her voice interrupted me.

"Can I come in?" she asked me.

I moved out of her way. White trousers were visible under her raincoat. She wasn't wearing lipstick. I saw the natural color of her lips; they were even more pink than I remembered. Her peach-like neck was bare. I would have liked to plunge into it like a vampire.

"Hi, gigolo," she said to me. Then I led her into the lounge and she made herself comfortable. She handed me her raincoat.

She smiled. But she had no energy left. I watched her. Her arms were folded and she was looking straight ahead, staring at the photograph of my mother on the table by the wall.

"Aren't you going to undress me?" she asked me suddenly, "that's what I'm here for." And she took off a woollen jumper, then another and yet another, but left on her vest. She lay down on the sofa. I started to get aroused. I felt my dick expanding and throbbing.

I moved closer and asked her if this was what she really wanted. She nodded and covered her face with her hair.

I sat down next to her and took her hands from her face. Her hair slid away and I looked at her closely.

"How did you find me?" I asked her.

"I asked about you at the café."

"Do you know my name?"

She smiled.

A kiss on the lips. Fresh breath, skin slightly lined, her mouth a shriveled peach. The most beautiful old woman I had ever seen.

I slipped off her vest. It smelled of fabric conditioner. Still covering her breasts was the black bra, a deep black, almost funereal. I lowered the straps and put her hands behind my back. She lay still and focused on me. Her hands had already reached down to the zipper of my trousers.

"How old are you?" she asked me.

"Two," I told her.

She feigned a distracted smile then unzipped my fly.

I unhooked her bra: her breasts sank down on each side of her chest. The shape of two champagne glasses, drunk from many times, almost a lifetime. The signs of a faded past; a long scar on her right breast.

"I've had cancer."

"A beautiful old lady with cancer," I thought and I didn't give a damn.

I took off her trousers. Thick black knickers covered the stain of her vagina. She stopped me with her hand.

"I'm ashamed."

"Why?"

"Because you're a baby."

She put a hand on my cheek and turned me toward the light from the window. A trickle of sunshine flowed across me. Against the light my beard seemed more fresh-faced than usual. It was evidence of my youth.

"You're a child," and she laughed.

I felt at ease in this role and I became aroused. My pleasure increased; my member felt stifled under the rhythm of those words, but I held back my ejaculation . . . I wanted to come between each of us exposing our bodies.

I pulled off her knickers angrily. Like a wild animal throwing itself onto a carcass that smells of fresh blood. A forest of tousled hairs on her pubic mound. I would have had to create an opening there in the middle.

I pushed my way through, I dropped my trousers, I opened her legs and entered her. She wasn't damp. It was easy to go in, impossible to pull out.

I came inside her. I lingered in that warm home, in that cradle of childhood, in the mature flesh of a mother.

"I have a son," she told me after I came.

"I didn't ask you that."

"But I told you."

I would have liked to know, in fact.

I would have liked to know if there was another man in her heart, someone else who made life pulse through her. Not just any man but a son. No one is able to make you live the way a son does.

I licked her nipples. They were soft to the touch, wilted, bent over by the circular motion of my tongue as it directed waves of saliva.

"How old are you?" I asked her.

"Signora, call me signora," she told me.

The idea excited me. Her pubic mound was smeared with my sperm.

"Get rid of it," she asked me.

I licked her greedily and cleaned her. I didn't understand her request but I did it, completely enslaved by her commands.

"Get dressed again," she ordered me and she regained her poise.

"How old are you?" I asked her again.

"Three," and she found it entertaining to pull a tuft of my hair.

This time, at the door, I saw in her eyes the light that women have when they feel they're already yours after an hour of deconsecrated sex.

She wasn't my usual type of old lady, but a woman who was absolutely a mother, virginal.

The next time we met at her place. Her home. We spent two hours together. We talked and fucked and then talked again, then fucked again. She was married.

"A difficult marriage," she told me.

He was a businessman. And she had been swallowed up by that desperate, stultifying routine.

"We lived in both the USA and Europe. We're two strangers. Two lives that meet up, share an appearance of domesticity."

"Does he love you?" I asked her.

"He doesn't love me. He's alone."

Love and loneliness, the perfect marriage, an unfathomable relationship: I love you because I'm alone and I'm alone therefore I love you.

Her house was beautiful. Tasteful decor. A few too many ornaments to fill the gaps. Her bed a cold and crumpled alcove.

You could smell a male scent between those sheets. Perhaps someone before me had dipped into her charms. I was beset with jealousy, a morbid and uncontrolled jealousy.

"Do you have another man?" I asked her forcefully.

"Perhaps, perhaps not," she said to me with the look of someone who enjoys leaving you in a state of uncertainty.

I pulled down her trousers angrily. I wanted her again. She was mine. I wanted to mark my territory, like a dog pissing outside its kennel.

"I don't want to," she said.

I didn't listen to her.

I lowered her knickers, I put my arms round her waist and I slammed her down onto her stomach on the sofa. I took her from behind. I entered her violently.

With my hand I brushed her face and felt a tear. I stopped. My penis withdrew. She went back to being a piece of dried-up flesh.

I did up my trousers and asked her to forgive me.

"I'm sorry, I was an animal."

She regained her composure and went into the kitchen.

She went to the sink. I could hear her breathing quickening, faster and faster. My heart was beating so frantically it wouldn't stop.

She took a cigarette from the packet that was lying on the table. She lit it and turned around. She breathed in smoke. She exhaled anger.

She picked up her handbag and took out a check. The ash rained down onto the piece of printed paper. She wrote down a figure—500 euros—and waved it under my nose.

"You're a professional gigolo," she said to me, inhaling angrily.

It was time for me to go. I left.

Three days without seeing her. The fourth day, I waited for her on the doorstep. She didn't go up, she didn't come down, she didn't go out.

I knocked on her door; she wasn't there. I needed to touch her and to apologize to her in a way that perhaps I had never done before. The fifth day I waited for her again outside the entrance to the building. It was evening: eight o'clock in the evening.

I huddled in front of her door, like a drunk who has found shelter. I fell asleep.

I heard soft footsteps coming up the stairs, getting closer and closer, more and more tentative. I recognized them.

I opened my eyes slightly and saw a silhouette.

She was tired. A woman with a purple scarf covering her head and breathless from hurrying. She leaned against the banister and looked down at the ground, tracing her steps, one by one.

She saw me; I saw her. Our eyes met and we knew each other for the first time and rediscovered each other. It was her.

She turned and tried to flee. I caught up with her and grabbed her arm.

"Where are you going?" I asked her.

The scarf slid off, leaving her head bare. A light down covered her skull. It was like new-grown grass, fresh, young, clean.

She was embarrassed and lowered her naked head. She put up some resistance.

"Where do you want to go?" I asked her.

"Why are you here, little boy?" she asked me, furious.

"To see you."

"Go away."

I pulled her toward me and hugged her. I kissed her bare baby's head. I smelled the scent of rose and vanilla and she let herself go.

It was the first time I had fucked a woman with cancer, a mutilated breast, fresh from chemotherapy.

You need guts to fuck an old reprobate with bad breath and drooping breasts. You need a heart to do it with a woman who is ill.

That evening I licked her all over, I sucked her skin, her breasts and her pussy. I moved my tongue inside her and swallowed her viscous liquid.

She surrendered herself completely, exhausted, withered. That night she was feverish. I stayed with her. I slept beside her.

I watched her all the time, kissing her neck. She got up to put on the wig that she had put away in the wardrobe. I stopped her and told her that she was more beautiful as she was. She looked like a new-born baby.

"You're a crazy baby gigolo," she told me with wild eyes, and her teeth started to chatter from the cold.

I covered her with my body, I dried her cold sweats and I stroked her forehead as she vomited away the cancer in the bathroom.

I had never done this. What the fuck was I doing there, in her home?

"I'll write you a bigger check," she said to me between one retch and another as she kept hold of the cantilevered toilet.

"Consider it a bonus. Tomorrow I'll feel better."

The following day we went to the seaside.

I took her to Ostia. We ate fish, a frugal lunch. Then we booked into a hotel room, a five-star hotel, as high-class as she was, and we washed each other. She got into the shower fully clothed.

"I haven't done this for years," she said, laughing. I joined in her laughter, which became hysterical, childish, lighthearted.

I got in, dressed, too. I noticed her blouse sticking to her breasts, her skirt becoming tighter, more black, more waterlogged.

We laughed even harder and she brushed the hair from my forehead. I listened to the noise of the water battering against our alien bodies. Suddenly our laughter became a distant echo. I took off her sodden wig and threw it down onto the floor.

"Hug me," she asked me. "Don't make love to me, not now, not yet. I'm afraid."

I held her tight with all my force, until I was hurting her. I could hear her bones creaking under mine.

"Wash me," she asked me.

I unbuttoned her blouse, I slid off her skirt, her slip, her knickers, her bra. I took off my shirt and rolled it up. I wrung it out and ran it over her body. I started from her head and stopped with her feet.

I kissed her big toe, then her legs and her knees.

"Don't move," she ordered me and I stayed there, dazed, in the rain of the shower, at knee level, while she ran her hands through my hair and caressed me.

A tear fell from my eye, I lifted my head, the water blurred my vision, and then she said: "Why are you here?" And she leaned her back against the glass wall of the shower. "To fuck me or to fuck yourself?"

"Tonight you ... tomorrow, who knows," I replied.

She asked for strawberries for breakfast, in our room. She liked to pour over them the champagne that she found in the minibar of the suite.

Then she would light a cigarette and I would inhale the smoke with her. "It's bad for you."

"It does me good," and she would light another, holding it in her other hand.

She told me that smoking made her aware of the intensity of life.

"A cigarette is like life," she would say. "You inhale it, you exhale, and then there's nothing left but ashes."

She didn't want me to call her by her name; I had discovered her identity by peeking at the hotel bill. She was my signora and I was her baby gigolo.

That was enough.

She stood in front of the mirror, her gaze fixed and sharp: one of those cutting looks that you never forget. And her soft hands, covered in rings, swept over the supple outline of her lips.

A sexual charge, concentrated blood, air, thought, passion. That is what I was when I was by her side. I proudly penetrated that small, moth-eaten body and I came and I cried.

I didn't hear from her for a long time.

She said to me: "I'm leaving. I going to find my son," and she disappeared.

I drowned my drunken pleasure in other pussies. Haggard and drooling women, a few even attractive, but I missed her drugged taste so much I started to feel ill. I searched for her in my bed and I tossed and turned. I masturbated, thinking about her.

My penis became hard and swollen as I pictured her embracing her son. Then it deflated when I thought about her smiling with him and swelled up again at the thought of having her near.

I flailed about, I was restless, I turned over between the creased sheets, I sought her with my hand.

The heart of a son had met the dick of a male and the two became confused, mixed up, both ending up in that one woman: mother, sister, friend, ill old woman.

The tenth day I went to her house and I waited for her, as I always did. The waiting was more agonizing than usual. I lit a cigarette in front of the entrance and I surrendered myself to the music coming from an out-of-tune piano above me.

It was pleasant listening to that disenchanted rhythm. I imagined I saw her climbing the stairs, without her wig, naked. Naked as I'd never seen her before, like snow that has just fallen and is still pristine.

And then I imagined undressing her, taking hold of her diseased breast, squeezing it, squashing it and hurting her.

I imagined lifting up her skirt, ripping her tights and making an opening under her slip and masturbating her. I imagined making her come there, on the landing, while her neighbor looked on from the door next to hers.

I imagined all this before shattering my head against a voice of marble.

"Who do you want?" asked a very distinguished man in a jacket and tie, as he came up the stairs and headed toward my signora's door.

"Who are you?" I asked him and my heart jumped out of my chest.

He was a middle-aged man, perhaps her husband: the lonely and disappointed businessman who was brandishing funeral notices on which I could see the name of my signora.

She was dead.

She had chosen to die in the way the most compassionate animals die; she had withdrawn, enduring the cancer far away from me, from her baby gigolo.

What do I still have of her?

The fading perfume on my pillow, her bare head that rejoices in my arms, her lacerated breast and that night under the shower when she asked me if I was fucking her or fucking myself.

Today my answer has changed: I want to fuck myself and leave this world of old, life-sucking reprobates.

The Steel-Scaled Mermaid

MARIA TRONCA

She lived in a hole on the seabed—it had been dug by crabs—and she stayed there all the time, with her tail hidden, her elbows resting on the sand and her chin on her hands. She revealed only her head, neck, and perfect breasts, with their light pink aureoles and long, large nipples adorned with golden starfishes with a hole in the center of each. A shark had grabbed her and had almost ripped off her tail; he had torn out her fins and all the indigo and silver scales. He had left her naked, with transparent skin that showed her bluish veins, rosy blemishes, blood red patches, and long dark and swollen scars. He had grabbed her while she was dancing and singing outside the great blue grotto, where her sister and her gorgeous lover, a triton with a beard and silver hair, were exchanging red hot kisses. She was dancing and protecting their privacy, stopping anyone else from entering the cavern of pleasure. He had been spying on her for a while; he wanted her, he desired her with a passionate ruthlessness, but he knew that he would never be able to have her. He was a fish and she a mermaid, and her human part could never have desired him or loved him. His lust grew from day to day, together with his anger and frustration, so he had decided to kill her. If he couldn't have her, no one would. And that evening in late summer he had lain in wait for the two lovers to enter the grotto, for her to be alone, distracted by the dance. He had moved closer, silent and lethal, and had taken her from behind. He had opened wide his horrible, monstrous mouth and had closed it on the center of her tail, very close to the scales that hid her soft, secret lips; a tangle of flesh, blood, bones, and hate. She hadn't cried out straight away, because she hadn't realized what was happening. The surprise had stopped her from feeling anything at all. Then the pain of that brutal bite had enveloped her in a transparent shroud and the sensation of sharp teeth embedded in her body had clouded her mind. The red of her blood had merged with the deep blue of the depths of the sea and she had let out a hiss, as if she couldn't breathe and was desperately sucking in the air to fill her lungs. Her screams had burst forth immediately afterward, while he was trying to carry her away, to finish her off in a quiet spot. But tritons had arrived; they appeared from nowhere, like ghosts, armed with their golden tridents. They had surrounded the assassin and one at a time had run him through, without saying a word, aiming at his sides, his abdomen, his heart. He hadn't even tried to defend himself, he stayed motionless, staring at them with a strange smile in his dark eyes, waiting for the bites of their tridents. And when he had collapsed onto the sand of the seabed, he was still smiling, his mouth half open, deformed in a ghastly grin. She had fainted, almost dead, but they had saved her. For her wonderful indigo-colored tail, however, nothing could be done; the scales hadn't grown back and the scars couldn't be hidden. She was ashamed of that single leg, lame and disfigured, reduced to a poor piece of sad and scarred flesh. From that day on she hadn't danced again with her friends and sisters, she hadn't sung and she hadn't made love anymore. She didn't touch and she didn't let herself be touched by any mermaid or triton, and she had almost forgotten what it meant for her sex, hidden under the indigo and silver scales, to pulsate under the delicate touch of another tail, to tremble under the skilful hands and eager mouths. Now her flower of flesh was exposed like a wound one could see the lips, once swollen and now withered. Closed. And when she heard the moans and groans of pleasure enclosed between the rock walls of the grottos near her hole, she remembered when she was the queen of pleasure. The most exquisite, the most passionate. The most imaginative. She used to organize wonderful parties that were attended even by half-human and half-sea creatures from far away, from other seas, remote oceans, attracted by the renown of those incredibly beautiful events.

The mermaids decorated their colored hair with transparent anemones and seaweed, they hung corals around their necks and wrists, and seahorses on their nipples. They combed the scales on their tails and waited with fire in their bodies for the dancing to start, excited by the thought of new encounters. The tritons polished their muscular and hairless bodies with the oil of the puffer fish and tied their long hair with garlands of starfish. She would always arrive last, and her entrance into the great blue grotto always created a stir. She roused their souls, overwhelmed their senses, excited their bodies. She would have a look, a greeting or a hug for each of the invited guests, a seductive smile for her favorites, a kiss for her lovers. And she was always the one who started the amorous dances; she would take a mermaid or triton by the hand and, in the center of the cavern with its walls of blue rock, she would move sinuously, irresistibly. Her lips were sweet, her tongue left scorching trails on the skin, her hands touched the most sensitive points. Even the water in the deep sea simmered with desire, and everyone's eyes were fixed on her and her companions. She always offered herself with a smile; she would recline on a rock, almost clinging to it; she would bend over and let her sex—rosy, hairless, juicy as a fleshy fruit—appear from under her indigo scales. Eager for someone to eat her sex, suck it, enter it with strength and passion, without restraint. Then she would close her eyes and wait. And after a moment she would start to feel hands and mouths, who knows how many or whose, that touched her all together, making her lose her mind. She would open her lips, sure of finding a soft and fleshy nipple and a hard and salty member. She felt her flower of flesh melt and drip with the juices of pleasure, and she felt other fingers, other tongues, other fins bring her to the edge, taking her beyond it. And finally she would cry out with pleasure, her mouth open on another mouth, her exhausted nipples ablaze, her buttocks lifted up and her sex spread and filled with hard and hot flesh.

He was a craftsman and goldsmith and had a strange power over precious metals; between his hands they melted like the sex of a woman in the grip of pleasure. He was able to create leaves of gold, of silver, of platinum that seemed to be as thin as veils; he spun metals, making them look like the hair of angels, and he created marvelous, unique jewelry. He displayed his creations in the window of a little shop that looked out onto the sea, where he worked and lived, and there wasn't a single person, male or female, young or old, who didn't stop open-mouthed when they were passing by, staring at the rings in the shape of flowers, the necklaces studded with silver teardrops, the brooches that looked like live butterflies, ready to beat their wings and fly away.

Once, a few years before, he had found a steel rod on the beach, come ashore from who knows where, that shone more than any other metal in the soft light of the early morning. He had taken it home and had discovered that the strong and bright alloy responded to him much more than the noble metals; working it gave him a deep feeling of satisfaction, moulding it filled him with a subtle pleasure that thrilled him and made him feel as powerful as a god. He had started to make jewelry using steel and sand, steel and glass, steel and fishing nets, steel and shells, abandoning gold, silver and precious stones.

He was a nondescript young man, neither handsome nor ugly, and when he walked down the street nobody noticed him, but it just took a woman to see what he was capable of making for her to be captivated, seduced by the beauty of those magical jewels. He, however, pretended not to understand this and avoided any type of approach; he didn't have a girlfriend, he was bashful and very shy. He didn't think about sex; when he wanted it he pleasured himself alone, with his eyes fixed on the sea shimmering in the distance, dreaming of creatures with gold or silver hair.

That evening at the beginning of the summer he was walking on the pier, thinking about the next piece of jewelry—he wanted to make a small brooch in the shape of a shell—and suddenly he heard it again, after twenty years. A fisherman was telling it to a group of tourists: the legend of the scarred mermaid. He knew the story, his grandmother had told it to him when he was small, but over the years he had forgotten it, bottling it up in a corner of his mind, and he hadn't thought about it again. And now, listening to the words of the old man with his sunburned face, it returned powerfully to his memory, worrying him and fascinating him as it had done when he was a child.

The slow voice of his mother's mother had caressed his ears again and he could still see her in his mind, sitting on the wicker seat in front of the sky-blue door of the little house with its pergola, on top of a hill that looks out onto the sea. He went to live there during the summer, as soon as school finished, and every evening she would tell him a magical story. And it routinely ended with the phrase: "Is it true? Is it made up? It all depends on you."

She used to smile at him with her gap-toothed mouth and give him a kiss on his forehead. She had told him the story of the mermaid with the scarred tail one night when he was suffering from sunstroke; he couldn't sleep, he had a headache and she had put damp cloths on his head and had held his burning hand. She had started to talk suddenly, looking out of the window, into the distance, beyond the sea that was sparkling under the light of a moon that looked like an enormous orange. But that time his grandmother had chosen the wrong story, because her words, instead of cooling and soothing her little grandson, had inflamed him even more, making his temperature soar and his temples, his eyes, all of his body burn. In the end he had collapsed, exhausted, and had dreamed about that tortured tail. All night. And he had continued to dream about it for as long as he stayed in the little white-and-blue house: the unhappy mermaid had bewitched him and he looked forward to going to bed, so he could see her again. He had fallen in love with a fairy tale. But then the summer had come to an end, he had returned home and he started school again. She disappeared from his dreams and from his memory, replaced by real life.

And now she had come back, now that he was a man with desires that he didn't have as a child. The thought of the scarred tail has sent a powerful shiver down his spine, an electric shock, like when a moray eel had brushed against him. And his member had reacted instantly, it had raised its head, turning to stone in his trousers. No woman had ever managed to have such an unsettling effect on him.

That night, laying on his bed with its white sheets, freshly laundered, his body naked and tanned, he had called her, hoping she would come and find him in his dreams. And she had fulfilled his hopes, that night and all of the following nights. He saw her as she caressed her injured and naked tail, he felt her suffering while she watched her fellow creatures delighting in frenetic dances of love. He spied on her every night and regularly woke up with his member hard and moist, short of breath and with clenched hands. With the passing of the days he became convinced that it wasn't a fable, that she really existed, that she was calling him, that her tears were a plea for help.

So one morning, early, when the sun was still sleeping and the sea breathing peacefully and fragrant, he went to the port and bought a fishing net with a fine mesh, a very fine mesh. For days, at dawn, he went down to the beach, to the exact spot where he had found the first steel rod. He knew that for the work he had to do it was important for the sea to give him the materials he needed. And finally one day the enormous watery wilderness fulfilled his wishes and let him find a thick and shiny steel pole that sparkled like a diamond. He ran home with his precious haul and started to work the hard and cold material that responded to his desires, eager to please him. It was like an onion losing its skin, layer after layer. From the thin sheets he created fish scales, some as small as fingernails, others as big as rose petals. By day he worked on the steel tail, at night he dreamed about his mermaid, and in the morning he would wake up shaken by pleasure and ashamed. Because that horribly disfigured, bare and exposed tail drove him crazy. He liked it as it was, covered in dark and swollen scars, grazed and flayed, with white and reddish patches. This was also the reason why he was making a new tail for her, not only to make her happy but also to enjoy a single moment of joy. He knew that when he gave it to her, to put it on, she would have to reveal her scarred fish-like leg and he would finally be able to admire it up close. And perhaps touch it, run his fingers over every single scar, brush against those healed gashes that made her brutally thrilling. Follow their path with his tongue, knowing that they were much more sensitive than the rest of her skin, living flesh that asked only to be inflamed with pleasure, to tremble and pulsate again. Just the thought of it made him hard, he felt his mouth watering and his chest burning with emotion and arousal. And so he would lower the zipper of his trousers, take it in his hand, and give himself pleasure, thinking of her and all the wonderful sensations that he would have been able to make her experience if only he could have her. Even for just an hour. And one day he finished his masterpiece, he fastened the last thin plate of steel shaped like a scale, he checked that the long hidden fastening worked, and he rested it gently on the floor. The smooth steel tail shone with an unnatural light, too bright, dazzling. It was exquisitely beautiful and he smiled, thinking of his grandmother's words: "Is it true? Is it made up? It all depends on you."

He was certain that it was all true, and he sensed that she was waiting for him.

The following morning he got up early, took a turn around the whole house, as if he wanted to imprint it in his eyes, and he put on his swimming trunks. He closed the door, hid the key inside a terracotta pot that was packed with geraniums and dived into the sea, with the gleaming tail folded up inside a bag that he slung over his shoulder. He didn't have oxygen cylinders, just a mask, but he was sure that he wouldn't die: his love, his desire, and his obsession were his oxygen. He would breathe the magic of the legend of the scarred mermaid. He swam out into the open sea, gave a last look at his house, at the village, and the shore, now far away, and then dived down. He went deeper and deeper, following an invisible path that he didn't know he knew. He met the first fish among the underwater gardens, he saw the hills covered with seaweed, the forests of coral and sea anemones and the mountains of dark rock. And he didn't lack air; he wasn't breathing although he seemed to be doing so. When he had reached so far into the depths, where no man had ever gone, he saw the first triton, who looked at him as if he were a ghost. He continued swimming, sure of the right direction, as other tritons and a few mermaids peeped out of the caverns and clefts hidden between the gigantic sponges. "A human," they were whispering, more astonished and fascinated than frightened, "a human who swims and breathes like a fish." And they followed him, curious and incredulous. He smiled and his heart started to beat faster because he knew that he had almost arrived. She was watching the somersaults of some grains of sand disturbed by a very slight current. She had her usual sad and resigned expression, her eyes lowered. But suddenly she raised her head, alerted by something, not a sound but a sensation, and she saw him. She widened her eyes, alarmed and unbelieving, and tried to hide herself inside her hole, but it was too shallow to hold all of her and her entire head remained outside, with her long indigo hair that danced tenderly and sinuously around her face. He smiled at her and moved slowly toward her; he was tired and excited. He forced himself not to think about her hidden tail because he would have become hard straight away and would have made the wrong impression. He stood in front of her, he opened the bag and he pulled out the marvellous sheath of steel scales that sparkled so much that she had to close her eyes a little. She didn't understand immediately what it was, but when she realized she parted her red and fleshy lips and murmured "Oooh!" "Come," he said to her, signalling to her with his hand, his eyes fixed on the round opening that was hiding the tail of his desires. She shook her head; she didn't want to let him see it. "Please," the young man's eyes implored her. "Turn around," she told him through a movement of her finger. He shook his head and offered her the tail, but he held it at a distance. She ran her tongue over her mouth, her eyes were gleaming. Then she came outside, darting from the hole in a flash, revealing her naked and tortured fish leg in all its splendor. He stayed motionless, staring at her, recognizing every inch of flesh, every shred of frayed skin, every scar and broken and mended vein. She tore the steel tail from his hands and tried to get into it but didn't succeed because it was too narrow. He let her try for a while, smiling and enjoying the sight of the elegant long leg that was dancing, contorting, showing itself to be wonderfully indecent. She looked at him pleadingly and he took her new garment from her hands, opened up the fastening and put it on her. It was perfect: it looked like her own real skin, and it suited her extremely well. She hugged and kissed him, first pressing her lips hard against his. Then opening her mouth, offering him her tongue and seeking out his. When they tore themselves apart, she was ablaze; he was thinking about her naked tail. She took him into the great blue grotto and stared at him with shining eyes, she leaned over at ninety degrees and offered him her hairless sex, forgotten for too long. He moved closer to her, hugged her and murmured in her ear: "Get undressed." She stayed still, astonished; she didn't understand. But when she realized what he wanted, she moved away and said to him "No!," violently shaking her head, her face like thunder.

"Please . . . I want it so much . . . I want it the way it is, with your deep scars . . . imperfect, terrible and beautiful. I want to caress it, kiss it, hold it . . . naked." She was shaking, with her eyes as blue as the depths of the sea in his, brown like the earth, imploring her. And it was just at that moment when he saw it, within his eyes, her naked tail, imprinted in that gentle and loving gaze like a brand. Slowly she undid the fastening and the tail of steel scales opened, her mangled leg wriggled out and she placed it in front of him. Proud and regal. He seized her by the hips, he lifted up her tail and he laid his mouth on her bare and exposed sex, brushing against her with his lips. Then he started to place little wet kisses on every inch of every scar, of every graze, scratch, and swelling of the skin. He made her glide up and down, he turned her around and around, searching out all the pinkest, most maltreated patches of skin, and he tasted them, licking them, he sniffed them, he rested his cheek against them, rubbing gently. She let him do it, abandoning herself in his hands; she felt like a precious doll, loved and desired. The rock walls of the great blue grotto made her sighs and her moans rebound and they merged with the slow lapping of the water. And little by little she felt the passion she had thought dead coming back to life, the energy and the strength of her desire. Her body was responding again, more than before. The kisses and caresses to her scarred tail flowed through her to her nipples, which became swollen and taut, to her breasts, which regained their vigor, to her lips, which opened up greedily, and to her flower of flesh, which started to throb with pleasure. She had come back and he was aware of it. He had felt her stiffen and had feared that he had gone too far, that he had hurt her. That he had offended her. He made her glide toward the bottom and he made her rest the point of her finless tail on the sand, looking into her eyes. And his heart skipped a beat because her eyes were full of promises and they shone with a untamed fire. But also with something greater and more profound. Now it was her who was leading the game, who was caressing him, sniffing him, licking him, passing her tongue over his tanned and smooth skin. She was curious about this creature who excited her and moved her, so similar and yet so different from the tritons. With a now uncontrollable eagerness, she took off his swimming trunks and found his hard penis. It was almost the same as those of her fellow creatures. She took it in her mouth and he thought he would die. She sucked it, licked it, and kissed it, but suddenly she let it go and he thought he would die for a second time. Again, their eyes met, she started to play with his mouth, nibbling at his lips, gratifying herself with his tongue, taking away his breath and feeling his heart, which was beating loudly and powerfully. And when the urgency to feel him inside her became unbearable, she folded her scarred tail and knelt down on the soft sand of the grotto, offering to him her naked and swollen sex. He did the same, placing himself behind her, and he gave her what she wanted. What he could never have imagined could happen. They moved slowly, with the rhythm of the waves that washed in and out of the grotto, of the invisible currents, perfectly synchronized. He rested his chest against her back and held her breasts, his face buried in her hair, his lips against her ear. And as he was about to explode he said to her: "I love you both. You and your tail." She remained motionless and suddenly felt something blossoming inside her, right in the center of her chest, a deep and overwhelming urge. And finally she laughed, with joy. Again.

Have You Come Yet?

FRANCESCA CANI

If there were something magical about waking up in the morning with the person with whom you went to bed the night before, Christian wouldn't have been able to explain it. Certainly, that day, when the rays of the midday sun glided over his eyelids, the sensation of having someone important next to him spread through him, so much so that it forced him to ask himself some questions. From the depths of his insides to the tip of every strand of his tousled hair, across his tattooed skin, riddled with holes from his piercings, a long shiver of pleasure ran through him. Buried in the covers was Linda, petite, young, ruffled like a chick just out of the egg. Chris didn't know how to distinguish between the feeling of affection, the passion of last night, and his own profound need to be at the center of someone's life. In less than a second he convinced himself, rationally, that he was in love.

Strange for him, who, with his Viking charm, had no rivals in town. His fiery red hair had always attracted women, fitting perfectly as it did with his statuesque physique and acting as a bright brushstroke of color that caught the eye. There were women who were mad about him, and there was himself, eternally indecisive, never fully satisfied. And then there was that small problem that had led to his brother Fil, the psychologist, calling him a "serial lover." But that didn't mean much if you looked at it more closely. In his relationships he ended up alternating young, obliging girls with women who were older than himself and more domineering; the only thing they had in common was that he had never left a woman first. He had always been dumped.

As he rolled out of bed and trudged around the room looking for clothes, he felt so light-hearted that not even the thought of the next seven hours as a waiter at the Napoli Bella pizzeria would have irritated him, for once. He headed toward the bathroom and brushed his teeth, at the same time running a squirt of gel through his ginger hair with one hand. Linda was still sleeping and let out a whole series of irresistible, throaty whimpers in her deep sleep. She was so beautiful and tired out after a night spent going around the clubs together with DJ Chris that he was genuinely moved and let her sleep, leaving her with the keys to his flat.

Before going out he breathed deeply and tried to fix in his memory every detail of that heavenly vision. The unmade bed, Linda's pale body, her slender ankles that poked out from under the duvet, revealing her small and delicate feet. He had managed, the evening before, to disguise the usual chaos by quickly shoving everything he had found on the floor into the wardrobe. Chris decided to take a photograph on his BlackBerry just in case his memory played any nasty tricks.

And yet there were details about the previous night he definitely would not have forgotten: the power and beauty of the turntables, his languid movements on the equalizers, several hundred sweaty bodies shaken by the vibrations, and Linda in a pearly white dress that left her whole back bare. He had platform dancers dancing for him no more than three feet away, but Linda was the most desirable in the room by far. With her blonde hair loose and slightly damp from the sweat, it just so happened that she craftily rubbed against his jeans as she was passing with a drink in her hand. Chris had played all night as horny as a boy contemplating his first girlfriend.

"Are you pleased to see me?" she asked, moving her lips, moist with gloss, closer to his ear. Chris's only answer was to take hold of her hand under the turntables. Linda's hand had paused on his aroused member.

"Is there anyone who could take over for you?" she asked him, gently tightening her grip.

Chris stared at her and then beckoned to a boy he always took along with him as a trainee musician. The young man was grateful to be put in charge, even if only to cover his absence. Chris followed Linda to a VIP area, a secluded alcove draped in dark-colored velvet. Chris signaled to the bouncer, a madman with a striking tattoo on his head, and then closed the two flaps of material behind him. Linda, sipping the last drop of vodka from her frosty glass, moved toward him to unbutton his shirt. She ran the glass over Chris's hot skin and then, as if by doing so she had been able to extract the taste of the alcohol, she avidly licked the damp trail that the ice had left on the DJ's chest. Chris reacted with such impatience that Linda let out a little cry. He threw her down onto the semicircular banquette, untied the bow at the nape of her neck, and the sheer, opalescent voile that covered her breasts glided downward. Chris pulled down his trousers and bowed down between Linda's open legs. He drew aside her pink thong and entered her, clutching in his hands her silk skirt.

Impaled like that, Linda finally felt in the right place. Physically joined to the man she had courted and led on until she had obtained his sole attention. She was shaking and aroused in a way that had never happened to her before. She let Chris take more and more generous parts of herself; she allowed him to suck and bite, while she did nothing but tease him with the ice. When he asked for her mouth, she moved away, eluding him, leaving him trembling and dissatisfied, free just to brush his lips against her neck.

"Stay still," Chris begged her, dazed by the sensual motion of the girl's pelvis. "Stay still or . . ."

Linda covered his mouth with hers, tightened her arms around Chris's neck, her legs encircled his firm buttocks, and she let herself be lifted up by him. She sunk her fingers into his silky red hair, she stroked the back of his neck, she explored his mouth that tasted of alcohol and salt. Chris totally lost control; gripping Linda's small buttocks he exploded in a long and devastating orgasm, followed immediately afterward by the satisfied feeling of fullness that had swept through Linda's petite body.

That was what had made him so elated and head over heels in love the next morning, when he woke up with the warm body of Linda still clinging to his.

Later, whizzing along in his old Fiat Punto into the center of Mantua, he stopped at the pasticceria to order the most high-calorie, heart-shaped cake, with the most icing, that his cousin could make for him. As he went into the pasticceria he shook his head as he read the shop sign GENTLE BREEZE OF THE SOUTH; he had insisted for a long time that the shop should be given a more glamorous name, but in the end Mirko had won, as had Mirko's total devotion to Alfredo, his partner who was originally from Palermo.

"Hey, lads! How's it going?" he began, too loudly, as he crossed the threshold. The silence in the shop was soothing and matched in intensity only by the smell of the cakes.

"Hi, Chris!" Alfredo greeted him, sticking his head out from the kitchen. "Mirko, your cousin's here!" he shouted in the direction of the door that led to the upper floor. Upstairs in their flat, Mirko spent hours opening envelopes and worrying as he worked out their accounts for the previous months.

"This place is really great . . . " Chris commented, feeling rather awkward. "It just needs a bit of music." And a few more customers wouldn't hurt, he thought as he drummed his fingers on the counter.

"Everyone's having lunch now," Alfredo said, making excuses, as if he had read Chris's mind, and opening wide his small, dark, and sunken eyes.

Chris nodded and stuck out his lower lip to corroborate that great truth.

"Chris, hi! It was nice of you to come . . . We haven't seen you since the opening," Mirko said. Thirty-two years old and with a slight physique, he retained the high cheekbones and long legs of the Borghi family. He had dark, curly hair and an open smile. Alfredo, his partner, was the complete opposite: short, chubby, and with his deep-set eyes ringed with bluish shadows.

"Good food for free, cousin, I couldn't miss that," Chris winked with his habitual easy-going manner. "And then I've got a new girlfriend . . . Well, she's special and we're spending a lot of time together . . ."

"Mmm, I get it," said Mirko, unexpectedly interested. "That's quite another story . . . What's the new one called?"

"Linda" said Chris, smiling angelically.

"A nice name . . ." Mirko and Alfredo echoed each other. "We want to see a photo!" added Mirko.

Chris took his BlackBerry out of his pocket and scrolled through the pictures looking for the one he had taken just a few minutes before. He found it and showed it to the two men, whose only response was to equip themselves with pen and paper and start to take notes.

"Linda . . . Pretty, *very* young, dainty." Mirko weighed up every syllable. "I can definitely see the color: white chocolate icing with lilac sugar flowers. I'd suggest violets and . . ." He stopped to study Chris's reaction, his beatific and dreamy expression encouraged him. "Buttercups, perhaps."

Alfredo, on his piece of paper, was sketching a heart with one cut slice pulled out slightly. "I'd say a heart, but not the usual banal heart for lovey-dovey lovebirds," Alfredo said, using his index fingers to put his words in quote marks. "This is an open heart, unattached, free. It says: try me and you won't regret it."

"Lads, I leave it in your hands," sighed Chris, delighted. He ran a hand through his bronze-colored hair and gulped. With such a present, what sort of passionate thank you would he receive in return?

"Perfect. And now the most important part. A base of sponge soaked in sherry and layers of cream, milk chocolate, and . . ." Mirko stopped, thoughtful.

"Zabaglione," Alfredo pronounced.

"Mmm, the eggs will do you good, believe me . . . " said Mirko, putting his arm around Alfredo's plump shoulders.

"Yesss." Chris had completely lost track of the time. He worriedly looked at his watch and realized that it was only a quarter of an hour before his shift started. "Guys, you're amazing! I'll come and pick it up this evening when I get off work. It'd better be something with 'special effects'." And with that he rushed out, leaving the two pastry chefs engaged in drawing the design for their new creation.

That same morning, two blocks away, Filippo Borghi's consulting room was brightly lit by the sun. From the third-floor window you could see numerous passers-by wrapped up in heavy overcoats and bulky scarves. It wasn't as if it was freezing cold, but the air was damp and the sun was just starting to peek through the morning mist. In Mantua, Thursday was market day and had been for time immemorial, and the inhabitants would never let themselves be put off by the humidity from attending such an event.

"Doctor, do you have children?" A baritone voice rang out and was immediately deadened by the walls of the consulting room.

For about ten minutes, Fil's mind had been working on two different frequencies. On one, there was the session with his patient, which maintained a solid, steady connection; on the other, he was disturbed by a thought that was running through his brain incessantly. The response to his message from Marisol, his Facebook girlfriend.

"No, not yet . . . but I'd like to have some," he replied honestly, without censoring his answer. God knew how much he would have liked to have children. He had been married for five years, and he had never given up on the idea of a large family. He would have liked at least three children, three tender heads to caress and to see running around the park.

"Would you like to have them even if they weren't yours? Biologically, I mean."

Fil was stunned for a moment. He didn't know the patient in front of him very well, a man of about fifty, handsome, if a bit past his best, but full of charm and experience. The man, a certain Massimiliano Avanzi, had contacted him the week before, and this was his second session of analysis. He was in Doctor Filippo Borghi's study in order to relieve the tension that had built up over the last few months, stuck as he was in a complicated marriage and a stressful job.

"Do you mean, would I adopt a baby? Yes, I'd adopt a child. But you're not here to talk about me. Are you possibly thinking about adoption?" Fil responded.

"In a way . . . "

A long silence followed. In the study only the peaceful ticking of the clock and the rapid clicking of Fil's fingers on the keyboard could be heard. He recorded: "Unfulfilled desire to be a father? Question further."

While he waited for the time allotted to the patient to come to an end, Fil followed the thread of his own thoughts. He felt more like that man than he would have liked to admit. And that affinity that he could sense existed between their lives prevented him from working impartially. He would have liked to suggest that the man listened to his own biological clock and that he told his partner what he wanted, and if she too felt ready . . . At that point babies would undoubtedly have come.

Instead, after having restored the silence inside himself, he arranged a new appointment for Massimiliano Avanzi in his electronic diary.

In that very moment in Alba and Enrico's house a perfect silence reigned. A whole day dedicated to her new job: looking for a job. Alba hadn't imagined that it was such a tiring activity. She pushed her chair away from the desk and for a good ten minutes she sat motionless staring at the ceiling. She yawned and took her eyes from the ceiling to rest them absent-mindedly on the screen of her computer.

A yellow banner with the words "you've won" flickered on and off above the results of her search. She was looking for pictures to illustrate the text she had written. A new meaty post for her blog was on the home stretch. Her hundred regular readers would have been delighted, but unfortunately that wouldn't have satisfied her. She even had to admit that the blog didn't involve her as it had done at the beginning. When, six months before, consumed by the boredom of a spring day, she had put together a blog, she hadn't thought that it would have found a following. Especially because she hadn't thought that a few bits of nonsense and some gossip about her family could be of interest to anyone. She had had to change her mind; day after day the number of followers grew and her gossip began to get a very respectable number of hits.

For some time now she had no longer asked herself whether telling the world via the Web about her own life was ethically correct. Alba, the very person who embodied the height of human unproductiveness, had managed to find a handful of people who followed her and paid attention to her. There were pseudonyms and a whole heap of security measures: she never gave the names of the places where they met and she didn't provide details that would make her protagonists identifiable, but just the fact that they were real stimulated the imagination of many readers.

The curiosity of the public had kept her in a good mood between one job interview and the next. The comments had galvanized her, but what could she do now that their lives seemed to have become so normal? The DJ was in love (again) and had cut down his number of gigs in the clubs; Fil was now developing into a tragic character, hostage as he was of his mad wife; and what could you say about cousin Mirko? Well, he was the most normal of them all in his particular traits. And her? Was she still interesting? Certainly, her readers were starting to wonder whether the great potential she was endowed with would ever result in something good.

On the monitor a fuchsia banner with hard-porn images of naked girls was promising immediate and totally live delights. Alba checked the number of visits to her blog and immediately afterward clicked on the hard-porn Web site. "Fuck! A hundred users online just at the minute!" she murmured, even though she was completely alone in the house. On her extremely honest blog there was only one . . . A crazily spontaneous idea began to force its way into her brain. And what if it wasn't enough just to describe things? Instinctively, she activated the Webcam on her laptop and for a good twenty minutes left it on, filming all the neatness and silence that ruled in her home.

When she heard Enrico coming in from work perhaps she didn't calculate mathematically the lifespan of the batteries or the accuracy of the framing, but she moved away from the computer and left the camera running.

The day after, Alba approached the computer with a mixture of emotions that blurred her vision. The anxious wait for Enrico to leave and go to work had ended. She had managed to gulp down just half a yogurt and a cup of coffee while her fiancé watched her, worried about her lack of appetite. Now that she could go and check on the results of her filming, Alba was nervous and more impatient than a poker player with a lucky card in her hands. She prolonged the pleasant feeling of uncertainty as long as she possibly could and then checked the countdown of visitor numbers.

For a few seconds she couldn't breathe, she almost would have preferred it if the computer hadn't filmed all night, then a thrill ran through her and slowly she broke the connection. Five hundred links just to see Enrico and her talking about the bills, getting ready to go to bed, and then sleeping all night. Alba was seized by the most intense feeling of dizziness she had ever experienced in her life. She grabbed her mobile and immediately invited the whole family for a lively supper at her house.

She had a shower, singing, and experimented with at least eight different makeup looks before finding the one that could work for the evening. In the meantime, all the people she had invited had confirmed, and as soon as she was certain that she had a full cast she sent a post to her blog's notice board. The moment had come to put a face to her characters.

The first to arrive were Chris and Linda, clearly in love and clinging to each other like two koalas. As they moved they radiated an unsettling sense of déjà vu. Alba had witnessed the exact same scene so many times before that she was sure that before the end of the evening someone would have put their foot in it by getting the name of the newcomer—Linda—wrong. The youngsters had brought cans of beer that Enrico, grateful for the distraction, had taken charge of straight away.

Naturally, Mirko and Alfredo had brought dessert, or rather they had literally emptied the pasticceria, judging from their cake tins. With their arrival, the dining room came alive with voices and noise.

Alba's exhilaration increased with every greeting, with every kiss, and even before having supper she was aware that her stomach was stricken by terrible heartburn. While she was sucking an antacid, she tormented herself about not being able to serve the antipasti and because of the frustration of having to sit still on the sofa and wait for the drugs to work.

When the doorbell rang, Alba decided she wouldn't wait any longer, she rushed down the stairs to welcome Teresa, Filippo, and the inevitable little King.

"Ciao dear, you look well," lied Teri, kissing her three times on the cheeks.

"No, but you are . . . fabulous . . . are you using a new conditioner?" Alba asked her, weighing up ringlet by ringlet the elaborate hairdo of her brother's wife.

"You noticed? I've changed my hair stylist!" As they went up the stairs Alba worried about the successful outcome of the video and at the same time tried to keep the group of guests together in front of the camera, with the same diligence of a sheepdog tending its flock. Teri expanded upon who or what was "in" and what merited a dismissive "out," articulating the words with contempt and with a slight curl of her upper lip.

They talked on a variety of levels: from the intelligible in the group made up of Alba, Enrico, and Fil; through flippant and flirtatious with Mirko, Linda, and Chris; to going beyond the limits of the absurd with Teri, who had trapped a nonplussed Alfredo in a heated monologue on the pedigrees of King and Princess. This was all accompanied by excellent food and plenty of wine and beer. Dessert took the shape of an elegant chocolate-colored box. It was the incredible heart-shaped cake that Chris had dedicated to Linda. The surprise made the young woman go red in the face.

It was right at the moment of dessert that all eyes focused upon Fil, who, raising his glass for a toast, made the announcement that would change his life forever.

"Guys, it's great to be here, around this table, all together like in the old days. This evening I've returned to my childhood with you all; I'm reliving the nicest, most carefree part of my whole life and that for me is . . . relaxing, calming, soothing . . . "

"Go on, Fil!" Chris spurred him on, miming the act of drying his tears with his napkin. Everyone laughed.

"That's just what I mean, Chris; at any moment I expect to hear you having a tantrum because you don't want to eat anything green . . . like in the old days."

"That's not nice of you. Green things disgust me," Christian pointed out, furrowing his red eyebrows. Linda hugged him in a maternal gesture.

"And what if I told you that soon we could need another place at the table?"

Everyone held their breath while the idea of having a baby, a new generation, filled them with a blind euphoria, similar to being drunk.

"Yes, we're trying to have a baby!"

There followed shrill cries and a confused chain of hugs. Teri stiffened, put King on the floor so no one could crush him in the confusion and put up with the shows of affection of all the family, one after another.

On the other side of the camera, anyone watching, initially curious, was getting totally bored. Alba's attempts to make the scene entertaining had made it resemble a type of South American sitcom aimed at an early-afternoon audience. People smiling too much, over-large gestures, background chatter and a perfectly second-rate storyline. And then they'd also thrown in the announcement of a virtual pregnancy . . . banalities for those people watching on the Internet.

The interest of those who were on the other side of the screen unexpectedly increased when most of the group made an exit to tidy up the kitchen; Alfredo took refuge in the bathroom, and, as usual, Enrico went outside to smoke. Linda was clinging to Chris on an armchair as far away as possible from Teri. Teri's clutch bag vibrated persistently; she took out a small white mobile phone and put it to her ear, covering it with her hair. She instinctively moved away from everyone, but, unknown to her, she went and stood within range of the camera.

"What are you thinking of?" she yelled furiously. She was having difficulty controlling her emotions after the wine she had had to drink to get through the evening. "You can't call me whenever you like!"

A long silence followed in which her eyes widened and for a few moments she stared at the black eye placed at the top of the computer monitor. "There's no excuse, you shouldn't have been listening," she squeaked at the height of the horror. "No, it doesn't concern you! Anyway, we'll talk about it tomorrow."

Having said that, she hung up, gave a snort, and lowered the laptop screen, thereby breaking off any lines of communication with the outside world.

The next day, one person at least had taken Fil's words extremely seriously and reacted by questioning their own brief existence. Linda was lost in her own thoughts for a long time while from the bed she watched Chris who, with growing enthusiasm, was preparing his bags for a DJ gig that evening. She gazed at him as she ran her fingers through her long blonde hair and carefully examined the locks for split ends, an automatic action that hid her rapid internal plotting.

Chris's MacBook was switched on at the desk and for twenty minutes had been copying the same minimalist techno rhythm. The young man's head rocked backward and forward in time to the music, while, bent over his bags, he was packing cables and electronic equipment in a large sack with a camouflage pattern. Every three minutes on the dot he had to pull up his trousers, which, because the waist was exceptionally low, continually slipped down, leaving his boxers prominently on display.

It was a scene Linda had witnessed so many times before, but—and perhaps her PMT was a factor—that morning it made her suddenly insecure and nervous. After all, she hadn't fallen in love with a waiter with a passion for videogames or something harmless; she had met him the first time at one of his gigs and, she had to admit, she wouldn't have gone to bed with him straight away if he hadn't been so striking and fierce on the turntables. And then there was his flaming red hair, his high cheekbones, his square jaw, and his fair, stubbly beard.

She had been struck immediately by his urban, trendy appearance; the tuft of auburn hair, always windswept. And his green eyes had captivated her, and then there was his piratical manner, his look of the beautiful and the damned. A combination of special effects that even in the current moment prevented her from seeing him for what he actually was: the same fascinating lad who would have spent all night on the turntables with or without a woman controlling him, with or without her. Just the thought of all the girls who would have thrown themselves at him produced in her mind a kaleidoscopic vision of bare shoulders, tattoos on the neck, long legs, high heels, and skirts so short they revealed the girls' buttocks with every movement.

"Don't sulk, love . . . " he cajoled her, jumping onto the bed and unexpectedly rolling around with her.

"No! Leave me alone . . . " she said, irritated.

"Someone's woken up in a bad mood this morning. Someone needs a pastry or something sweet . . . " Chris, ignoring her pleas, stroked her small, firm breasts. "Or else someone needs . . . " He slid her hand inside his trousers and licked her ear, while Linda lay there frowning, imprisoned under his body.

"That's not the point. I don't want you to go on your own this evening," she murmured without conviction, while with every caress from her lover the doubts receded to make way for the shivers of pleasure that resulted from the scorching contact with his skin.

Chris's fingers moved brazenly under her clothing. Linda's breathing quickened until it was rapid and shallow. The bodies of the two young people stayed stuck together like magnets; every one of his movements was mirrored by an imperceptible change in the position of her body. Linda was so small that Chris's muscular and tattooed back hid her completely, buried as she was in the covers. His perfect lips found no peace on the young and pale skin of the blonde Linda. She was smooth and inviting with her melting blonde pubic hair, and she smelled of orange blossom-scented shower gel. He removed her vest and shorts with such skill that Linda found herself naked without realizing it. But that was normal, and when he made her giddy with his kisses, she was lost.

Linda, nude under the gigantic body of her man, was happily exposed to his attacks. Chris's rough jeans pressed down on and rubbed against her pelvis, drawing little cries of surprise from her. It was thrilling feeling him ready through his clothes. He made her wait and tremble under his hands; he enjoyed the feeling almost until he could no longer wait for the sensation of possessing her naked body. Then he pulled off his T-shirt with a single hand while with the other he felt her slender neck in search of the most sensitive points.

Although her eyes were half closed, Linda followed with growing desire her man's every movement until, impatient, she began to unbutton his jeans.

Chris smiled smugly, aware of his own charms. She sat up to kiss him and bite his lip.

Supple and lithe as a cat, he took off the last few items of clothing and knelt down in front of the white and enticing body of the young woman. He raised her up, grasping hold of her buttocks, and entered her with a single motion, smooth and strong at the same time. She moaned quietly, losing all her willpower and every thought between the urgent thrusts of his huge member.

Linda didn't last more than five minutes, because, when Chris took her like that, because he wanted to make her forget her worries or to get around her, he was able to sweep her into a delirious state in which her sole objective was pleasure.

As he followed the rhythm of Linda's sighs, Chris broke out into a sardonic smile. "That's impossible, you've come already . . . " he murmured, touching her to find proof: the moist trail of pleasure that wet her between the legs. She burst into a high-pitched scream and wriggled when he brushed against her clitoris.

"You have, you've already come!" crowed Chris, ecstatically admiring the cheeks red with pleasure of his beloved. Linda was about to protest but Chris pulled out of her. He rested his penis on her stomach and then dragged it damply over her navel and her small, delectable breasts. He lightly touched her neck and moved it toward the girl's plump lips. She took it into her mouth and Chris let out a moan as, kneeling next to her outstretched body, he turned her onto her side and placed her so that he could enter deep into her mouth. He sunk his hands into her hair and started to rhythmically move her head closer.

"Oh, my God!" he groaned as she sucked his member.

He put a hand on her breast and pinched her nipple. It was too much; he had to bring that sublime agony to an end. With his hands, enormous compared with Linda's tiny body, he rolled her over again so that he could spill his semen inside her.

Linda, smeared with sperm, was still regaining her strength when she heard him going off to the bathroom and filling the bath. Chris came back into the bedroom, took her in his arms and offered her a hot bath. He would have left her there, beautiful, wet, and "branded." Linda smiled thoughtfully when she heard the sound of the door to the apartment. She lingered in the bath, playing with the bubbles, and relaxed. After all that frantic sex, he wouldn't even have looked at another woman.

If for some people the problem is how to trap love and contain it, for others it is how to make their love bear fruit. For some time Filippo and his wife had given up on erotic games; indeed, quite some time had passed since the last time they had had intercourse, but finally they had a common goal.

Fil and Teri came out of the medical laboratory arm in arm. Their legs felt like jelly after the zealous nurses in white jackets had taken a huge amount of blood for the routine tests and genetic checks that were necessary to have the strongest guarantees of conceiving a healthy child. They had also asked Fil for a sample of seminal fluid to analyze, and of the two he was definitely the most distracted.

"Would you like a nice breakfast at the bar? We've earned it, haven't we?" Fil broke the silence and squeezed his wife's hand to attract her attention.

"Mmm," she said laconically.

"You seem thoughtful," noted Fil, aware that perhaps "thoughtful" wasn't the right adjective; "pissed off" was rather better.

"I was thinking that taking care of the puppies and at the same time conceiving a baby will be difficult . . . "

"So we'll sell a couple of puppies and just keep the one you like best." Sometimes Fil was worried about his wife's vacuous comments. He knew her well; they had shared five years of marriage and two before that when they were engaged. He kept on telling himself that every time, as a psychotherapist, he came up with a fitting diagnosis for her. "And you'll see it'll be natural . . . having a child, I mean."

They went into the bar and Teri sat down impatiently, continually checking her watch. Fil noticed her restlessness despite being busy enjoying a filled croissant and an extravagant cappuccino.

"Do you have an appointment?" he asked her, because he really couldn't imagine what she could possibly have to do. She had been to the hairdresser two days before and the re-doing of her nails was marked down for the following week on the calendar.

"To be honest, yes. I have to see a possible owner for one of our puppies." Teri seemed to weigh up syllable by syllable everything that came out of her beautiful mouth. She barely touched the steaming cup of tea with her lips before setting it down again on the saucer without having taken even a sip. "It's a guy who lives in town, not far from here. He can certainly wait a few minutes." Teri smiled and looked her husband unflinchingly in the eye while with a foot she pushed under the table the bag that was hopping about to the rhythm of the ringing of her cell phone.

An hour later, in a flat in the center of town, not far from Fil's office, his wife was taking off her coat, frowning. After having arranged it on the back of a chair she sat down, very annoyed, on the soft white leather sofa. Hurrying her and then not being there waiting for her, calling her on her cell phone while she was out with her husband, this wasn't behavior that she would have put up with for long. Teri grumbled, rummaged around in her bag, pulled out a mirror and lipstick and set to work giving her lips a hint of strawberry color. Then she took off her knickers from under her suit skirt. She straightened her jacket. She studied herself in the mirror that covered the wall opposite. The room looked more like a photographer's set than a doctor's consulting room. Teri was beside herself with rage, more and more excited by her feelings of resentment. She shook her head, took off her suit and bra. She admired her body, sculpted by the gym, and nodded, pleased with the slimming effect her suspenders had on her buttocks. She picked up her coat and put it on, loosely tying the belt at the front.

When the man she was waiting for came in through the door to the apartment, she jumped up from the couch. She reached him in front of the door and gave vent to all her frustration by throwing a powerful backhander that hit him full in the face. The man, about fifty with greying hair and a rather neglected beard, didn't move back an inch. She let her coat fall to the floor; he didn't show even the intention of wiping away the trickle of scarlet blood that was flowing from his lower lip. The only perceptible sign of a reaction was the rhythm of his breathing, which quickened until it became feverish as he started to move closer to Teri.

"No!" she said imperiously, pushing him away from her. "It doesn't work like that!"

"First, you need to tell me what was so urgent that you couldn't wait for an hour." Teri slapped him a second time, this time with her left hand because her right still hurt from the previous impact. She hit the man on the cheek, scratching one of his eyelids with a nail. The man didn't react this time either.

Teri wasn't more than two inches shorter than him; when she thought about it rationally she found it odd that she had certain feelings for a man who was much less attractive than Fil, but when that man was standing in front of her she wasn't responsible for her own actions. He held up his wrists to her, in a way that was anything but submissive. She gripped them so firmly that she left a purple mark on his pale and sensitive skin. Then she pulled off his tie and used it to tie him up, knotting the material tightly.

"I've seen your husband again . . . " the man whispered in Teri's ear. The pronouncement had all the weight of a confession of a sin, murmured with downcast eyes and through gritted teeth. Teri stopped herself giving a start, but a shiver ran through her as she shook her head to show her disapproval.

"That's no good . . . Someone has been very naughty," she reprimanded him crossly while she slowly moved up his instep with the heel of her shoe, driving the stiletto in deeply.

Chris was just finishing his shift at the pizzeria. It was late at night and the streets of Mantua were deserted and silent. He had tidied up the chairs in the restaurant, helped the manager to close up, and checked that the dishwashers were switched on. He wasn't planning on going to bed straight away, despite feeling incredibly tired.

At home he had a demo tape to finish and send as quickly as possible to the producer for whom he wrote pieces of minimalist techno music, pieces that the most famous and well-paid DJs would play at their gigs. A poor consolation, but always better than waiting around in a half-empty restaurant staring at the ceiling. There was room for music and nothing else in Chris's mind at that moment, so he ignored Linda's text messages that were bombarding his cell phone with the regularity of a stopwatch, one every two minutes and twenty seconds. Mainly terse and threatening messages.

Chris gave an annoyed snort. He checked the strength of his magnetic stare in a silent conversation with the large mirror in the restaurant. He felt handsome, desired, the focus of a new love, and already quarrelsome. A thrill of excitement ran down his spine.

DJ Chris in love was a magnificent arctic fox, perfectly camouflaged, super-fast, and always ready to escape. Behaving like a hunting dog didn't work as a way of getting close to him; quite the opposite: it provoked in him his instinctive need to be desired by others.

It was past midnight and Chris rushed out of the pizzeria as if there really was a pack of ferocious dogs on his tail. With long strides he headed toward his car, parked down the street. By the time he noticed Linda curled up on the backseat, it was too late to slip away. Chris cursed the day he had entrusted her with the keys to his apartment and his car; he blamed himself for having given in to his feelings of affection.

He opened the door and sat down, leaning over the girl. Small and childlike, she was all wrapped up in a fleece that was too big for her. She had pulled the sleeves down so that they covered her fingers, which were clenched into fists; her blonde hair was tied back and the hood partly covered her face. Even so, Chris realized that she must have been crying: trails of mascara lined her cheeks.

"What are you doing here?" he asked her, his hand brushing her bony knee under the tight jeans.

She sniffled and then grabbed his hand, grateful for the contact. "My mom drove me here. She says she's fed up seeing me unhappy in my room, waiting, and so, basically, she dumped me, like she always does . . ."

Chris sighed, the arctic fox in him wasn't completely made of ice. "Okay, come to mine. You can stay with me tonight."

Chris put off sending his CD to the producer and spent all night clinging to Linda's warm and trembling body. Spending a whole night on the sofa with a girl without having sex required all his willpower. He weakened a bit and had a couple of intense erections, but he resisted. He cradled the small blonde head resting on his chest and stroked Linda's back, until the breathing of the young girl became steady.

The Gallant Adventures of Colette and Renate

MAYA DESNUDA

Inside the Laclos Palace in Paris | June 1755

Colette Laclos and her close friend Dorette, the viscountess of Plessy—much talked about at one time—lie languidly on a couch. Their pale white bodies are supported by tight bodices that reveal the generous powdered curves of their breasts and nipples like swollen mulberries ready to be sucked forever without ever drying.

Dorette plays with the red silk ribbon that holds up Colette's white stockings, caressing her shapely legs, as if it were a precious mantle. Her friend reciprocates, sliding between the immaculate cage of whalebone slats of the viscountess's pannier, searching for more intimate and wet apertures.

Dorette can feel those hands making their way, brushing against her hairless mons veneris; she already feels a drop of honeyed desire moistening the lips of her shy vulva. She lets her head fall backward as she feels those fingers penetrate her with greater velvety resolve, and her gaze wanders out of the window, to a distant dot. But the dot seems suddenly to get much larger.

In the sky, something seems to be moving closer. The viscountess, expert handmaid of Diana, all at once rejects the damp attentions of her lover, springs to her feet like a cat, and reaches over to the nearby closet. She takes the musket, always kept loaded, points it toward the window, cocks the hammer, and the index finger of the barely dressed huntress tenses to pull the trigger.

But then Colette, with a decisive gesture, deflects the weapon upward, shouting "No, stop!" and pushes her friend away from the window frame.

Dorette, in a surprised tone of voice, says: "But . . . what are you doing? Can't you see? It's a hawk right outside your window!"

"Yes, I can see." Colette watches the noble shape of the bird circling in front of the window. Then the hawk sets off like lightning and banks sharply, coming to rest on the windowsill.

Not frightened at all, Colette moves closer to the predator, admiring its magnificent appearance. The hawk stays still, standing proudly on its talons. Colette notices a crimson ribbon around one of its legs, at the base of its plumage. Without hesitation, but holding her breath, she reaches out to the bird to turn the ribbon and to untie the knot, to which is attached a small envelope.

The envelope is closed with a wax seal with the symbol of the serpent Ouroboros. Colette breaks into a smile full of light and complicity. She can't wait any longer.

In the meantime the hawk resumes its flight toward the woods that at one time surrounded Paris. Dorette, half undressed with her sex still hot and moist, has been left to watch the scene, astounded and incredulous.

Colette breaks the seal, opens the envelope, and takes out a recently written letter.

"If you are now reading these words, you are the woman who sublimates the 'rubedo' into elixir.

"I have need of you, as you do of me, to reach the 'path to the essence.'

"I will wait for you under the pomegranate tree in the Bois de Vincennes, tomorrow night.

"Come alone and remember, under your cloak you will be ready to glorify all your lust, you will have nothing to regret. I will give you what will lead you to the supreme pleasure.

"The taste of your kisses mixed with your blood intoxicates me still.

"Your humble servant . . ."

She had wondered what sort of man he was. And she had hesitated in formulating one of her hasty judgements. There was something unusual. A halo of mystery that hovered around him. It might have been those gestures of his, lacking in the affectation typical of the dandies who were regular guests in her drawing room. In him, everything was clear-cut and yet in semidarkness. Even Dorette, usually so wry toward her gallants, had been rendered speechless this time. And she had guessed that jealousy had gripped the generous and wicked heart of her sweet friend. But there was nothing she could do about that. That damnable man had roused something in the depths of her soul. Something that she hadn't even believed she still possessed. And now he was actually challenging her. With a hawk and on her own hunting ground. He was daring. But that was good. She detested weak people. The baron, however, was manly, and this stirred the female blood that roared through her veins.

Naturally, she would have raised the stakes if the young man, perversely provocative, thought that it was sufficient just to arrange a meeting with her in order to win. He overestimated himself. And underestimated her. She would make that clear to him very soon. She must seek out the address of Madame de Valmont. The celebrated courtesan would help her. Since she had retired she had devoted herself to the schooling of future courtesans and had created a court of love that Colette wasn't averse to frequenting occasionally. And not always under her main identity. And she would make use of her alternative identity to meet the mysterious baron.

Colette hastily called her maid to help her dress and asked for her carriage to be prepared. She simply had to go to see Madame de Valmont.

"My dear, you are astonishing, and at my age, believe me, it isn't easy to be surprised by anything anymore." Louise Richelieu, better known as Madame de Valmont, observed the woman she considered her goddaughter with a satisfied smile. She was extremely beautiful, but she had the beauty of a young soldier: elegant, refined and absolutely ambiguous. Her long black hair had given way to a shorter, rakish style, her hair tied at the back of her neck with a simple velvet ribbon. The uniform of a royal guard was perfect. The red-and-gold braid at the shoulders emphasized the harmony of Colette's body. The white trousers tucked into the high black boots hugged her bottom and her legs in a shameless and provocative fashion. She had bound her chest, of course, but she couldn't do anything with those round, pert, firm buttocks except conceal them with the tails of the uniform. The sword hung at her side and the gold hilt shone at the waist of the young, proud military type who smiled back at her in the mirror of the boudoir of her dear friend Louise. She would have worn a mask and a cloak over the uniform. She knew how to ride like a man. Better than a man. Her entrance would not have gone unnoticed into the park of the country residence near Versailles.

Louise had already seen about writing an invitation in her elegant script to her court of love, and Colette had run the card between her thighs so that it bore the true signature of the invitation. If the baron was the man she sensed he was, he would not have hesitated. Now the die was cast and she trembled, anticipating the effect that the following evening would have had on him.

Her face lit up with playful mischief at the thought of that man, so virile, who would have looked for her among the half-naked ladies present at the court, while she, on the other hand, would have been drinking with the men, with Dorette in her arms, pressing her masked face between her breasts, licking them avidly . . .

She wondered if he would become aware, and if, when he realized, he would have been able to play along. She believed he would, and for this reason she had played that so dangerously intoxicating card.

Come along, mon petit bijou, there are still lots of details to be sorted out so that the court tomorrow evening is perfect. Stop gazing at yourself and let's get on . . . Believe me, that baron of yours will be eagerly awaiting you. He is more of a man than you can know . . . He won't disappoint you, Madame de Valmont gives you her word!

Court of Love at the Valmont Palace | Evening

Colette, in her gallant clothing of a man of arms, had definitely not aroused any suspicions among those present when she entered the elegant drawing room, in which her lustful patroness had organized an authentic court of love. Just like the renowned Eleanor of Aquitaine, long-term heiress of the most famous of Venetian courtesans, Veronica Franco, in Madame de Valmont's establishment one met dissolute scions of the court of Versailles and bold cavalrymen as valiant in maneuvering their sabres as they were vain about handling their other equipment; unscrupulous prelates who, under their cassocks, certainly didn't hide their more perverted passions; and men of art and intellect—free thinkers, they called themselves, at a time when science, which was catching a glimpse of the early flares of the Enlightenment period, philosophy, all the arts, were being put at the humble and joyful service of the arts of love.

And, above all, in that court, the place of honor was held by women. Sophisticated and confident, they revealed and unveiled the secrets that governed the art of love. How one gives, how one trades, and how one takes.

Colette—the soldier—lay with the courtesan Dorette in her arms, stretched out on a couch, just at the entrance to the sumptuous drawing room, completely lined with mirrors, including the ceiling, so that every member of the court could enjoy every gesture and every act of endless lust committed in that communal boudoir.

If her mysterious baron had replied to Madame de Valmont's invitation (countersigned with her intimate essence), she would certainly have seen him appear in that mirrored door. As the capable man of arms that she was at that moment—although hers weren't arms of war, but rather extremely sharp blades of polished seduction—she found herself in a strategically perfect position to dominate the whole court; every step Renate took would be noted and followed. Mmm . . . She was already looking forward to the scene!

Dorette was trying to divert the attention of her lover—her knight—offering her the fruits of her swollen breasts, made even more ample by their overflowing lace corset. She was sure that this mysterious baron wouldn't have been able to gain rights over her precious Colette; the imprint of their moist caresses, like bitches in heat, was stamped on every drawing room in Paris. So who was this man, the man who had so thoroughly possessed the thoughts of a woman famous in the whole of France, and surely beyond as well, for not letting herself be possessed as much as for controlling the coupling of aristocrats, officers, high-ranking cardinals and stable boys! Yes, what did he have that was special, this almost unknown baron? she asked herself. The only definite information about him was that he wasn't part of the local nobility but that he was related to the tsarist crown. There was a lot of talk about him, but there wasn't a single witness who could swear to the truth of even one of the many rumors that had appeared within their circle of friends. Rumors about oriental sexual ambiguities worthy of a Moorish pirate, and of mystical, almost supernatural, powers; in short, gossip and indiscretions full of mystery. Dorette, the lips of her lover plump from sucking her swollen nipple, was discovering to her amazement and anger that she too was captivated by the thought of Baron De Lituan. Oh, come along . . . I wish this prank were over with soon! thought Dorette to herself. So let her fuck him this very evening, like the skillful, high-class prostitute she was. And then let her return passively under her sheets, run her through with leisurely kisses and lash her already dripping pussy with her tireless tongue.

Dorette noticed the attention of her alert friend. She looked toward the entrance. A man, with an agile physique and a cat-like walk, wearing a mask and a tricorne hat, wrapped in a black cloak closed with a brooch depicting the serpent Ouroboros, was now entering the room.

Colette abandoned the breast she was gently encircling; from under her mask her watchful eyes didn't lose their hold on the gentleman. So here he was. It's him. One of Colette's animated smiles sparkled below her mask.

The gentleman, under a close-fitting black damask frock coat, moved as quickly as a spectre against the hazy walls. He approached attentively to pay the expected compliments to his host, Madame de Valmont; a subtle glance of understanding between Colette and her patroness acted like a spring that, once disturbed, snaps shut the trap on the unsuspecting mouse who has come to savor his piece of cheese. Colette felt amused and enraged at the same time. How could he? . . . she asked herself.

Upon her word, she didn't think he was so weak, so unsure of the outcome of the challenge he had issued to her with the hawk, that he was surrendering himself to the easier court of Madame Louise. Besides, he was abandoning the invitation, or rather the promise, to wait for her under the pomegranate tree. Oh, what a contemptible being. But now he was in the trap he would pay dearly for such impudence.

While she was lost in these thoughts, Colette realized that the cowardly young man had disappeared from view. How was it possible? . . . She rapidly searched the mirrors, on the walls, on the ceiling. Nothing.

It was impossible to hide in that drawing room! He couldn't have evaporated! She searched out Louise with her eyes; she too seemed to be wearing a worried expression.

Ah, what an insolent little man! The desire rose in her to suck him, for her own enjoyment, like an oyster, then to throw him away among the remains of other men who lacked a backbone. While she was pondering the most agonizing and lustful revenge, she saw the slight shadow of Renate reappear. His face was covered by an elegant Venetian Bauta mask with gilded decorations. For an instant she caught a dark glint in his eyes. But the baron was too quick for her to be able to intercept his gaze.

Here he was again, on the opposite side of the room; Colette was wondering how he was able to escape her sight and then materialize with such deftness in another part of the totally mirrored room. By God, this man seemed more like an eel than a mouse. So much the better. Colette adored hunting and definitely hunted better than a man. The poor baron will lend more savor to the game, she thought.

She got up to go over to him; she didn't want to lose him now. From the supple way he moved he seemed rather effeminate; she hadn't noticed this detail the first time she had met him at the reception for Monsieur Diderot.

Finally the baron turned. Colette gave him an ambiguously interested look . . . she definitely wanted to enjoy herself! Their eyes met for just a second. The baron backed away as if nothing had happened, to then vanish, swallowed up by one of the openings that led to the terraces of the property. Colette, emphasizing her proud military bearing, went out to meet him.

Now they were both outside the room. The "soldier" set her sights on the young man with the Venetian mask. Determined not to allow him a way out, she wanted to see him in a corner, forced to submit to the indecorous desires of a rough tomboy in arms. Strangely, the baron didn't seem to put up too much resistance. He didn't make as if to escape from that sordid siege—which, to all appearances, was what it was. On the contrary, he let himself be approached, turning his back on the soldier who was coming straight toward him, keeping his mask always turned into the darkness. Colette smiled under her simple mask, pleased. So the baron was what he appeared to be and, moreover, he truly seemed to welcome the attentions of a male lover; how delightful it would have been to play the game right until the end!

Colette was so close to the young man that she could feel the heat radiating through the damask jacket; those shoulders communicated something alluring. The young man, still with his back to her at this point, couldn't be unaware of her presence. The soldier planted her arms on the balustrade to prevent a possible attempt at escape.

The cat is entitled to its measure of sadistic play with the mouse, by now without any hope of salvation. She was amused and thrilled by thinking that Renate believed she was a full-blooded "him."

Ah, how she regretted not having endowed her otherwise perfect disguise as a man with one of her ceramic delights, one of those that, as a rule, she shares intimately with Dorette's vulva. Surely it would have made the moment more enjoyable for both of them, or so it seemed. The young baron now appeared to be yielding to the will of the soldier. Colette took advantage of this to press her breast against the baron's back.

She felt him pulsate with pleasure. There was something strangely familiar to Colette in the way in which the boy was surrendering his back to the attack from the soldier.

The baron's mask finally turned, and now they looked into each other's eyes, but it was a challenging look thrown down with the gauntlet of the most perfidious lust.

Colette—the cat—resolved to press down her paw on the now defenseless Renate—the mouse.

She drew her mask closer to the face of the baron. She could hear his breath tense under that Venetian screen, almost as if it were amplified by a closed room. She gently lifted the lower edge, just enough to uncover Renate's mouth and to open it slightly in a moist caress of lips and fingers, until she heard his breathing almost fading away into sobs. She wasn't expecting such entrancing delicacy in kissing a man, and to think that she had kissed, tasted, sucked, and bitten so many in her life. The baron knew how to surprise, even at this juncture, thought Colette behind one of her musical smiles.

Now the cat wanted to see it through to the end; the game was now drawing to a close for the mouse.

Colette confidently untied the baron's mask. The light shining from the torches revealed a marvelous pale complexion, with lips delicately sculpted from coral and two stag's eyes . . .

No. Doe's eyes!

Colette couldn't move . . . What sort of a joke was this!? It was a girl, but . . . her cloak had a clasp with the symbol of the De Lituan family, and, more than that, her invitation to Louise's court of love was the one that had been delivered to Renate.

Her astonishment was turned to ice by the crystalline voice of the woman.

"Madame, I have to remind you of your rendezvous . . . someone is waiting for you under a pomegranate tree tonight, don't you remember?!"

Inside the Laclos Palace in Paris

Colette was smiling as she finished sealing the letter with the wax, stamping her imprint into it, an image of her full lips.

She had decided to deliver the letter personally. She would go to the place arranged for their meeting and would leave Renate a sign . . .

Night. The branches of the tree indicated by Renate are moved by the light breeze. Colette is ready. The place is still deserted. Renate is expecting her to obey this time. And the presumption of that man is limitless. But soon it will backfire on him. Colette takes off her stockings and the silk reflects the moonbeams in a flash of light. In one stocking she inserts the scarlet envelope that contains the letter for Renate, and she ties it to the lowest branch of the tree. Mission accomplished. With a leap, the young woman gets back on her horse and gallops away as the echo of her laughter lights up the darkness . . .

Hours pass. In the depths of the night, a figure wrapped in a black cloak dismounts from his horse right under the tree. The figure is clearly outlined against the pale light of the stars.

He looks around. She isn't there, but it's strange; it's as if he feels her perfume enveloping him just the same. How is it possible? That damned woman really is a witch, thinks Renate. An impossible and fascinating witch. Then he sees it. It is swaying gently in the breeze. The scarlet flash of the paper illuminated by the moon. He grabs the stocking impatiently, ripping the thin fabric, and opens the envelope as if the paper burns between his fingers. It is too dark to read. In the carriage he will be able to light a lantern. He walks quickly over to the carriage and gets the coachman to give him a lantern. He can't wait. He has to know. What further trickery is this? What scheme has that witch concocted this time . . . The words penetrate his soul like knives . . . Fuck!!!

"*The day in which you will meet me, you will have no escape. Simply.*

"*You will not be able to focus clearly on the situation. You will not understand,* or perhaps it won't even be important to understand, who is the prey and who is the hunter. The roles have so little meaning . . . in the right circumstances. Between us they will have no meaning at all.

"Ours will be an elegant chess match. A game of poker in which the stake can be just one thing: everything. Neither of us would be interested in anything less. And the art, the perfection of pleasure that mixes with the sublime existence, like a pure feeling, requires its tribute.

"Soul and blood. Sweat and sperm.

"Ecstasy doesn't satisfy itself. It doesn't restrain itself. Nor does it govern itself. One abandons oneself to ecstasy.

"It will be like this between us, I have no doubt. I know. I feel it inside me. It will be a fight to the last breath. No holds barred. An instinctive fight. Atavistic. Between the feminine and the masculine. A seductive and seducing fight. No. Not a courtship. A fight. Or, if you prefer, a tribal dance. The instinctive celebration of existence at its truest core: Eros.

"It is thanks to Eros that I understand you clearly. I read in you my sweet, cruel evening game, with crystalline clarity. You are already the mirror image. You write about yourself, on pages that you cover with interwoven words, about the total harmony of living. Free. Actually and ironically free.

"It is seductive, the freedom of smiling at one's own world, while one re-creates it on a sheet of parchment. This about you seduces me and mirrors me. Completely.

"The smiling truth of the variations of pleasure that you relate emerges clearly from the pulsing tangle of words. It is magic that becomes liquid desire between my thighs.

"If I were a man. Well, I would have wanted to be like that.
"Anarchically free.

"The day in which you will meet me. You will have to surprise me. It is in your nature. Like in mine is seduction. The day in which you will meet me you will have to raise the stakes. You won't be able to help it. The throbbing carnality of desire between us will force you to do it.

"*My carnality and your desire.*

"*An unfamiliar game.*

"Details, suggestive fragments that shatter the desire that now makes my eyes cloudy, as I hastily scroll through your words written in an elegant and strong hand on these precious sheets, my gentleman of mystery.

"*Mmmmm KHAMEL . . .*

"A court of love in essence. A delight dear to the medieval troubadours. Courtly love, contrary to what one has always believed, was far from platonic in many of its concrete expressions.

"A dissolute and poetic court. With a master of ceremonies who holds in his hands the red thread of the variations of pleasure to which the participants abandon themselves with nightly desire.

"My body throbs at the thought of being the queen of that court, the subject of Khamel. Desire becomes liquid between my thighs. A burning flame in my stomach. I have a longing now. A longing for cock. And not only that. A longing for hands, tongues, mouths that pursue me eagerly, intertwined, indistinguishable. A longing for pussy. As well. A powerful longing, intense as the perfume that emanates from my pulsating vagina. Now. You can feel it, can't you?

"And it goes to your head, it sends icy shivers down your spine. It makes your buttocks shake and your cock rise. You read me and you want me. There is no dividing line between the two things. Your hands grasp the delicate crimson paper that holds my words. You want to be that man tamed with violent possession. Dominated, weakened, used and filled. By me.

"But it isn't the moment. I don't have a fancy for it yet. Seduction is a wide, encircling spiral, the coils of which tighten progressively and inexorably.

"You are fighting now against your own desire to belong to me. Totally. Fight. That is what I want. Anyway, the outcome is inexorably only one: MINE.

"The day after. When your skin will tell the world of the marks of my possession. And mine will tell of the sublime violence of the fight. The day after I will make a story of it. I will tell a story like Scheherazade because an audience plays an integral part in certain pleasures. And it is right that it's like that. I will tell a story for us. For me and for you. For the mischievous smile that will cross our faces at the moment in which the court will meet again to delight in our flaunted pleasure.

"Now I will leave you, seductive lover of the sublime. My coils are tightening around you soft and inexorable; you can feel them and you fight, but they will wind around you, inexorable yet insubstantial, gentle like my nails that scratch the delicate skin of your buttocks, like my teeth that trace whirls of violet circles on the skin of your back.
"Dream of me because this is all you can do, dream of me . . . again and again until you blur the horizon between reality and your constant reveries. Dream of me, my handsome gentleman, and who knows . . . perhaps the dream will become reality for at least a moment.

"Can you see me? I am certain that you can. You are capable of it. Your soul sees me beyond time and space.
"I smile. About you. With you. In you.

"Au revoir, mon cher serviteur.

"Colette"

Renate doesn't even know how he managed to get to the end of that letter. Desire has been tearing him apart since the very second line. All the patina of indifferent sophistication that he has so skillfully constructed for himself has shattered into pieces. Now he is naked. A man naked and full of desire, for a rebellious and dangerous female who for him will be the first step to hell.
But he wants her and he will have her. He too knows how to play that game . . . and soon Colette will get the opportunity to become aware of that. Ah, if only she gets the chance to realize that! He would have made sure

that she was branded by his desire. In an indelible fashion. He would have forced her to surrender, to then fall to his knees at her feet. There wouldn't have been winners, nor losers. Not if things turned out the way he wanted them to. In the end, it was what she wanted too. He was sure of it.

The carriage drives away in the mist of dawn, with its cargo of violent and excited thoughts . . . Soon, very soon, his torment would come to an end. And she . . .

Les jeux sont faits!

The Night I Went Away

CRISTIANA DANILA FORMETTA

This is not a story.
It is a letter.

Your face. That's my problem. I can picture your eyes, your mouth, the crease in your chin when you smile, your hairline, the shape of your ears; but it's useless, the details get lost, they disappear, and I can't see them anymore. If I managed to hold onto them I could finally say good-bye to you, without necessarily having to relinquish your memory, or the memory of the face that every day I imagine I can see on the pillow.

But this isn't possible; you don't allow me to do it.

If I try to note down your name in the list of things I have already seen, already experienced, you change. In every way. Your features, your expression, and even the way you grind your teeth in the mirror as you scrub at them with your toothbrush. And suddenly, in front of me, there is someone new, someone to discover. A face to caress with the same passion as the first time. The passion of true love.

Because of this I can't let you go. Not completely, at least.

Leaving you means losing all my memories. No trace would be left of your face, and soon I would no longer even be able to explain to other people why you, out of so many men, made such an impression on me. Why it was you and not a more handsome man, perhaps. Fuckably handsome. And likeable, intelligent, but not *too* sharp. In short, a man who is easier to manipulate, who cannot read what is inside my heart, like you do. I feel an insistent and childlike need to hold onto something for myself, something I can bury, like a treasure to be hidden deep within my flesh. Instead, for you I am an open book. There is no secret number, no code book, no magic word, no vocabulary or language that you don't know yet. And perhaps it would be an idea to invent one if only to forget it again, so that everything becomes incomprehensible and loses its meaning, and its spell.

My left hand has gone numb. If I try to move it I feel a slight tingling at the tips of my fingers. I persevere. I bend my thumb a little, my index finger, my middle finger, my little finger. Last, I move my ring finger. I move it up and down twice, rubbing my ring against the pillow as if I were trying to hollow out a furrow, to mark out a border between night and day, between darkness and light, between the right thing and the wrong thing. Just like that night.

My hand had gone to sleep, grasped tightly in yours. You were holding it steady and still as you slept next to me. My hand had become heavy, sluggish from the sex and the caresses that follow these violent and uncontrolled hours, hours of abandon that, paradoxically, one would never want to abandon.

If I close my eyes I can stop time, I thought. If I close my eyes I can see only your face. Still. I see you inside me, as you whisper to me to be quiet, to not move.

If you move I'll come straight away, you said. Yes, perhaps you too wanted time to stop at that moment, like that, with your hands in my hands and your legs between my legs. Together we are a strange beast that goes against the laws of nature, a wolf with two heads; a wolf voracious and starved of kisses, of your mouth so close to mine.

Don't move, you gasped when you opened my legs wider, and you gripped my wrists so tightly that it hurt.

What a waste of effort for a body that had become light from the magic. I felt weightless, insubstantial. I was made of air, a sky full of clouds that sex would sweep away. No more obstacles, no more barriers. No limits to what you could do or say.

Sex is a language too, and your body was saying that, after that night, I would have meant much more to you. More than the woman who was laying herself naked before you at that moment, more than the animal that was demanding your caresses. Your warm and strong body was telling me everything. It was convincing me again that you needed me, that you desired me more than this. It was shouting to me that you wanted to come, that every one of my moans was making it more difficult for you to hold back the moment, and every sigh was inviting you to live in my skin, now, and never ever to leave.

Stay, you said, tightening my fingers in yours, before giving way to sleep. And you said it so softly and at the same time so decisively, as if that one syllable contained the meaning of a world, our world, that has no time or space.

It is the world that sleeps between the sheets. It is a universe made of words and promises, of expressions of love that are shouted out at the top of one's voice, without fear of offending or hurting, without fear that one's feelings are so deep and boundless and so exaggerated that they could explode, in the end, like an enormous soap bubble.

Stay, you said. Because it was the simplest thing to say. And you said it simply, you said it with the self-assurance of someone who is sincere in their delusions.

You asked me to stay because there are things that cannot change after a certain point. Or perhaps you asked me because there are things that suddenly change everything.

Change. Of course. It seems easy when you say it. But now the word doesn't help me. It is because I am set in my ways, the classic plodder averse to change. Even when I write I need a system, a structure, a rigid outline to adhere to. I work on it for days, or even for weeks, and then, when everything is ready, everything is clear, finally I get down to work. Except that I realize, at the last moment, that you are not part of any system, structure, or outline. Because you know everything about me, but I know nothing about you. I don't really know you and I can't write about you as I would about anyone else. First I have to subvert the outline, take the structure apart. I even said this to my publisher, and he very nearly agreed with me. But when I sent him the first draft, his response was a blunt *no*.

(*No, this does not work. No, it requires a happy ending.*)

Imagine the effort I had to make not to tell him to go to hell. And imagine how hard it is for me to not call you now and tell you all about it.

No, you can't imagine. You have never thought about how much this choice costs me, because you think you know me and you have always believed that I was a coward, someone who backs down at the last moment.

Okay, this time you have won.

If I had found the courage to tell you earlier what I had inside me, with no doubts or fear, perhaps things would have gone differently between us. Or perhaps not, who knows. Perhaps nothing would have changed or maybe things would have been even worse. Make your memories suffice, then. Content yourself with my face, glued to the window of the train, fixed and motionless in an idiotic expression, not saying anything, not even *I love you*. Not even if you ask.

Go to hell. The truth is that my publisher is right: one never starts a story from the ending.

Readers don't like it; readers don't really want to know how it ended. Readers want to be taken on a ride, they want a dream, an illusion, they want the certainty that after the storm will always arrive the calm. They want simple and clear characters, who know how to tell black from white, not like you and me, who crawl around in a shadowy area like a badly printed copy. Readers expect two superheroes, not normal people who smugly make a mess of their lives. And you and I are no good as protagonists, not even in a penny dreadful. But do you picture a life together for us?

I did, damn it.

I wrote about us two, without saying anything to you. I imagined days, months, years, and I started to write about walking hand in hand, about children, wrinkles and greying hair, illness, death, tears, laughter. Without saying anything to you. Our future, our life, without ever opening my mouth. Without telling you how it really ends.

This is the trouble when I write; I have lots of good beginnings but never a decent ending. Perhaps I should put all these notes together and come up with a sort of Dada novel, but who would buy it apart from you?

You who read my heart as if it were a book and only now realize that I have torn out the last few pages. But I had no choice; there were too many phrases stolen from love stories. And I don't believe in love stories; it is a luxury I can't allow myself. It would be like admitting that I made a mistake by getting on that train that took me away from you for the final time. The dear old Turin–Naples night train. Nine hours to get home, nine hours without falling asleep, nine hours of the same repeated questions. Those questions that no woman—and I do mean none—should ask themselves after their marriage.

(If I did the right thing in getting married. If I did the right thing in marrying Luca. If I did what I did only because I hadn't yet met you.)

But nine hours on a train wasn't long enough to come up with a single decent answer, a remedy for this cold.

Only your hands have the warmth I want. The touch of your fingers on my breast. The breath of your mouth between my thighs. Your tongue that forces its way into the depths and reaps its liquid pleasure. *You are a drenched rose*, you would say, while with your lips you would caress every petal of this flower, and then you would enjoy making me moan, pushing hard against the warm and moist flesh.

There was no longer silence, but neither were there words. Pleasure was the only sound you wanted from me, when you took me like that, on all fours, and you would lift my skirt without any time to protest. Without any wish to protest.

Love and lust burn in the same way. A fire runs through the body and reduces it to ashes. The flames envelop the foundations, penetrate every cavity, until an explosion of fire forces you to arch your back, to push your chest upward with a start, to beg *now, please*, and other profane entreaties.

A fire that heats and that consumes.
That consumes itself, as is only right.

I feel cold in my heart, now. In my hands, in my arms. Cold in my face, that no longer laughs. There is a blade of ice that pierces my face and that holds back those beautiful forced smiles that I could produce so well before. Now, however, smiling takes more of an effort; sometimes it hurts, it hurts a lot.

Since that night I have suffered from a sharp and persistent pain in the middle of my chest. But I choose to blame the cold and not your absence.

The cold of Turin is still in my bones. Today it merges with the memory of your resigned face and with the composure of that kiss, which one can't even call a kiss, but merely a last, cursory resting of your lips on mine.

Your mouth. There, this is a detail that I remember well. And even your teeth.

How odd it is remembering your teeth now, the incisors that protruded just a little, the way you used to smile at me, so childlike, so irresistible. You used to lower your eyes slowly and you used to pass your hand over the nape of your neck, to downplay with that gesture the laugh I had forced from you. A laugh that you knew how to turn into a sneer every time you felt the need, like timid people do when they suddenly become aggressive. And they attack. Without thinking about it for even a second. And they don't know how to stop anymore. They don't know when to stop.

Your mouth. Teeth. Lips. Tongue.

Perhaps the mouth is the gateway to a deeper intimacy. And kisses, bites, were the desecration of my closed consciousness. They invaded my private life, which was made up of the walls of my home, of dreams put to one side and stored away, like Sunday's biscuits that are already stale the following day.

They entered my days and my nights, those bewitching kisses. But now they are no longer here. There is just the cold.

The first twinge arrived on Friday when I was on the train. I was almost falling asleep when I felt that the ice of our good-bye had reached all the way to my heart. On Saturday there was a brief respite, but by Sunday the pain had returned, stronger. I spent the following week lying in bed, convalescing, trying to fight an illness whose name I could not reveal to anyone, not even to my doctor.

I can picture the bitter smirk you have on your face. Probably you are thinking about Luca, and about the fact that he is a doctor. But Luca was the last person who could cure me, and there is some irony in this, I have to admit. However, I have never thought of myself as one of his patients; indeed, if you really want to know, Luca does not have patients, he has only clients. Clients who pay regularly to hear him say that they will live for a few more years, despite their excessive cholesterol levels. Clients who give him their trust and economic stability, not to mention that subtle sense of well-being that he loves so desperately.

And I love it more than him, you know?

I love the security that Luca is able to give me, despite people thinking that writers eat only bread and poetry all day.

There, I have said it.

I love the money more than I love Luca. But you knew that, too, right from the start.

What you do not know is that too many times I have run the risk of calling him by your name and I have dreamed that you were in his place. Your body, your smell. Your mouth that kisses me, that delves between my legs. Because it is your mouth that I want. And your breath, which slips between my teeth when I reread these words aloud.

Damned words, books and writers. Damned cinema and all the arts.

When my publisher suggested writing that essay on Godard with someone else, I turned up my nose. I work better alone, and anyway the idea of acting as your nursemaid didn't appeal to me at all. I didn't know you then, but your reputation had preceded you. You talked too much, you drank too much, you fucked too much. You were erratic, rude, unsociable. Okay, you write well and you throw yourself into things, so much so that if you are in the mood you can work day and night, and do in a few weeks what others take six months to do. But first you need someone to keep you away from the bottle and from tarts.

The trouble is that you are half French, half *maudit*. If I had given you a free hand, the essay on the films of Jean-Luc Godard would have become an essay on your emotions, and it would have had the smell of lit cigarettes and rumpled sheets. I had to stop you somehow, and curb your imagination before it took flight. I had to take you beyond the frame of a stereotype, beyond the black and white, beyond the fleeting vision of Jean Seberg's neck, which had made you fall in love during that early, enchanting passage of *Breathless*. Instead, things turned out differently, and it was my fault.

What surprises you now? After all, you never really believed that, between the two of us, I was the *sane* person, the more intelligent person. What makes me different from you is just this heart of stone, and even that is insignificant, a pebble if you compare it with a mountain. Like after an earthquake, in the evening everything collapses. Every evening everything collapses. Something inside me breaks into a thousand pieces, and the day after I have to put it back together one piece at a time. It is an endless job that requires patience and pride, and even makes me doubt that balance that was apparent in my actions, my work. But perhaps in this world there doesn't exist a single sane woman. It is the truth, or have you already forgotten the first time we made love? I was wearing a pleated skirt and an innocent expression that went well with all the rest of me. Do you remember it, that face of mine? Have you ever seen it since? It has been lost, just like my faults, or your apologies. So don't defend me now. It was me who put myself forward, you just gave me space. It was me who pushed myself further, to make you believe that everything was permitted. In and out of bed. Because it wasn't about you screwing me; it was about me wanting to screw you. It was always and only me.

I became the puppet and the puppeteer, for you who wanted everything, even love.

And you were good at talking about love.

You used to say that I was your good morning, that my smile gave a different rhythm to the passing of the hours, that distance was the only thing that saved you from doing something reckless or making unforgivable mistakes, that waiting for the next encounter was a sublime pleasure, to fill with gratuitous obscenities and rationed sweetness with a skill worthy of an alchemist. Your words used to prepare me for sex; the telephone would ring and I was ready and hot, like you wanted. Protected by the distance between us you let yourself go and you talked so much, too much. You said that the next time you would have licked my pussy for longer, that you would have made me come so many times, fucking me with your tongue, and only afterward, *a long time afterward*, you would have screwed me properly, in every position, in every opening. You used to describe it in the minutest details, and you were vulgar and filthy, but also exciting.

You were made for this. You were made of this. Of flesh and flames.

Of words spilling over me like sperm.

The more I listened to what you would have done to me, how you would have done it, the more I was mesmerized by that vice you were injecting into my blood like a poison.

You used to say that it was the fault of my feet, too beautiful for you not to be driven mad by them.

You used to like to lie on the bed and watch me walking with bare feet around the room, wearing just a bathrobe, until I would go and lie down next to you. Then you would kiss my ankles and out of habit I would rest my feet on your shoulders so that you could continue.

My skin is as soft as a baby's, and you used to bite it gently, first one foot and then the other, exactly like one does with babies. Once I even took a photograph of you while I was tickling your nose with my big toe, playfully, and you insisted on having a picture.

Who knows what became of that old Polaroid. Perhaps you threw it away in a fit of anger, or perhaps you kept it in your wallet, next to the one of your wife, and every time you look at it you say to yourself that this is the real madness.

Don't trust coincidence: we chose each other, you and I.

In the books we had read and that passed from hand to hand, in the films watched on television in some hotel room, in the music snatched from shopping centers and held close to our ears so it couldn't escape. In beds shared in various places, in distances and crossroads. We chose each other from the very first day, in that café, when you insisted on paying the bill.

You opened your wallet to pull out the money, but I stubbornly grabbed your wrist to tell you to leave it. You then clasped my hand and lifted it to your nose; you said something about my perfume that I can't remember and, straight afterwards, almost absentmindedly, you showed me the photograph of your wife and your daughter that was peeping out of one of your pockets. You were walking on a knife-edge but I didn't say anything. For weeks after that meeting there was nothing more, except for Godard.

Lovers always have something special that connects them, a place that has a secret meaning, a song. We, however, had Godard: snatches of black-and-white film without any music. Our soundtrack was the street, the railway stations where you watched me arriving, the monotonous whistle of passing trains, the screeching of the rails, the noise of metal overwhelming the banal tunes of advertisements that both of us pretended to hate.

We were bodies in transit, distracted travellers who lost their way from station to station. No one paid any attention to us, no one seemed to notice how long our embraces lasted. But you would press your body against mine so I could clearly feel the erection that was rising inside you, and you stayed like that, motionless, unable to regain your composure. You would hold me tight and move slowly against my skirt, taking my breath away. Only then would you let me go, having done this so I would be persuaded to rush to the nearest hotel.

I remember one hotel, particularly awful, near the Rome Termini station. The rooms were decorated in an Arte Povera style and reproductions of eighteenth-century paintings hung on the walls. In ours there was even a plastic cherub's head standing on the bedside table, an object that was so ugly we didn't know whether to laugh or cry or ask for a refund.

You touched my side, under my blouse. Your hands were cold and made me grimace. You immediately stopped.

Did I hurt you? you asked me. But it was only that you had icy fingers.

Sometimes you could be so considerate: if I had backache you would turn pale; if I felt dizzy you would dash to a pharmacy to buy me aspirin. Pain was a fascinating emotion for you; you saw it as a sort of ransom and it didn't matter to you if it were me, you, or the whole of mankind that was suffering. Indeed, third-party pain was your favorite; you took it on your shoulders extremely willingly, because, even if you didn't want to admit it, it made you feel a better person. The pain eased your sense of guilt and balanced the harm you were doing to your wife and daughter. Therefore you persisted with those questions, because you lacked the simple courage to apologize.

So it was better to suffer, better to be punished rather than face the reality and admit that there has always been something wrong in you, in me, in this vice we carry with us. A cowardly carnality that left us naked and stunned.

Leave your shirt; it takes too long with these buttons. Help me with my skirt instead.

Slow down; there's no hurry. She thinks I'm busy correcting proofs.

Well done! Carry on with that story about proofs and you'll see that one of these days you'll find your suitcases on the doorstep.

Impossible: the house is mine.

The money, however, is hers. You hardly write best sellers.

Be quiet; don't use your mouth for talking. You pulled down your trousers and lit another cigarette. I knew that trick; you had done it before. You thought that smoking while I gave you a blow job would teach me a lesson, but instead it ended up with you almost choking on the smoke, so much so that you put the cigarette out halfway through, right on the cherub's forehead. I smelled the stench of melting plastic and resin, and I laughed.

What are you laughing at?

Nothing, it's just that . . . I was thinking about the cherub's head. When they notice they'll make you pay twice what it's worth.

Oh, fuck you! Both you and that monstrosity.

You moved away and looked at me. I looked at you, with new eyes.

From the waist down you were naked; from the waist up you were in a good copy of Versace. As a whole I found you a man who was strong enough to love but weak enough to be loved. Love, that word again.

You like to see me look like an asshole, don't you?

You didn't expect an answer. Perhaps you didn't want an answer. You wanted to take me to bed, that was all. It was much simpler like that. Damned simple.

Come here.

Why?

Because I say so.

The beds in hotel rooms aren't made for pain, they aren't made for remorse. They are made for screwing, and only for that. And when you screwed me you knew that finally I was at peace. Your prick filled me completely, and every thrust carried me closer to ecstasy. I almost felt as if I were flying.

But what use is flying, when it's easier to fall, to trip over your illusions and crack open your head? Believing that, in the end, love prevails over everything is a bit like chasing rainbows, looking for a crock of gold. But in books it always works out. Only in books, though. Real life is more complicated.

Why don't you say it was a mistake? you asked me.

It that what you were thinking? That it was all a mistake? But you closed your eyes, you hesitated. You endlessly put off answering. The sex had exhausted you and you didn't feel like talking any more.

Under those conditions I could easily have got the better of you. I could have run away, told you to go to hell, or I could have cried and had a crisis of conscience. Naturally, I didn't do any of those things. Nothing right, nothing respectable. All I did was determine the rules, precise rules. I lay down limits and conditions.

I made things clear, and I decided where, how, and when. Only because I wanted there to still be a where, a how, and a when.

I have a soft spot for difficult types, for those men who never have to ask, but in the end always ask too much of you. They ask you to give them everything you have, starting with respect for yourself. Because these men take away your strength, your dignity, your dreams, and your ambitions for a calm and happy life. And if you let them, they also take away your heart, piece by piece.

Luca is not like that. Luca will never be like that. This is why I married him and not someone else. Because Luca doesn't know how to hurt women. He doesn't know women and can't make them cry. And perhaps he isn't interested in knowing how they think or what they really want.

For Luca, asking questions is an odd thing, almost an eccentricity. But I don't have these taboos. I don't believe in superstitions, and I doubt that curiosity is seriously capable of killing the cat. Rather, curiosity is how trouble starts, with one question too many.

So why did I ask you about her?

You are forty-five. You have a wife, a rebellious daughter, and a dog that gives even burglars a warm welcome. You have a nice house with a small garden, and you sleep in a comfortable and large bed that almost entirely fills the bedroom. You also have a refuge, an old bachelor apartment that you weren't able to give up, not even after your marriage.

I need it so I can write in peace, this was your justification. In fact, the place looked like it was meant to accommodate no one except its owner. The first time you took me there I noted the practical and basic furnishings, made up of solid and sturdy furniture, starting from the unusual built-in wardrobe hollowed out from one of the walls. That wardrobe, inherited from the previous occupant who worked as a dressmaker, was possibly the only trace of an extraneous presence. The one and only, because there was no mark, smell, or scratch that made one think that another person might have passed through that flat. Maybe a woman. A mother, a friend, a whore. There was nothing.

So far, I seemed to be the only woman who had ever entered that house; even your wife was barred.

Do you really love her?
Of course I love her.

Of course you love her. What a stupid question.

You love her like you loved, for years, that plaque for sporting achievements that they gave you when you were a boy, the one you proudly displayed on your mantelpiece so that your friends could see it, but then you forgot to dust it, or at least you only did it once.

You love her; it's obvious. But it isn't like before. All of a sudden, you realized you loved her a bit less. So you stopped looking at her, without asking yourself why. You stopped touching her. Without there being a real cause, a reason.

Naked, next to me, I brushed your lips with the tips of my fingers. I stroked your chest, I slid down to your stomach, scratching your skin with my nails. Then you pushed a lock of hair from my face, and I wondered how many times you had repeated that same gesture with your wife. Was it different with her? Was it something else?

I wanted to know, to ask you about yourself, about her, and about us, too. But after every question you became a bit larger, more important. And it is still my fault. I let you grow so that you would hold onto me. I took you under my wing in a stupid and dangerous game, without thinking about the risks, the traps that you hide just below the groin.

Screwing me came naturally to you. Like looking me in the eye.

The missionary position, you used to say, *is undervalued.* Perhaps because today people are scared of intimacy. People who want love also learn to fear it, to fight it, to turn their face away from a stare that is too intense, that wants to know everything, that expects to know everything.

When you screw me all I can do is surrender. I wanted this love, even if at the beginning I thought I could keep the situation under control. Your kisses had no effect on me, your words did not excite me, but my body ... Christ, my body yielded to your every thrust, as if I were a rag doll to be twisted and turned in a hundred different ways.

When you screw me all my body can do is welcome you. It is fertile soil under the rain; it is moist pussy in your hands. Your fingers caress me inside, and my face takes on a serene and contented expression as if by magic. I don't need to tell you how much I enjoy it; I don't need to tell you *I love you*. You know that very well; it is written across my face.

You know that when you screw me I become helpless. Cries break off my words and make them brutal; they transform them into savage echoes, into songs and praise to your prick. Naked and dressed in you. In a bed or on the ground, with the freezing tiles as a pillow. On the ground like dogs, and I know that put like this it sounds unromantic, but at least it is more real.

Reality doesn't care about gentleness and foreplay. Sometimes reality makes you desire a man so intensely that you ask him to leave it, to not waste time undressing, but to come inside you straight away, with his tie still wrapped round his neck and his trousers pulled down to his knees. Reality takes away your inhibitions, urges you to touch, to bite, makes you say senseless things, obscene phrases, words that you would never say to your husband, although he begs you to say them. And you aren't my husband. You are an inconvenient love, the indecent and vulgar voice that calls me by name.

I miss your voice now. I miss those narrow hips I harbored between my legs, your coarse beard that scratched my face, the imprint of your mouth on my breast. This is the first of many marks you have left in my memory: lines, cuts, wounds of a youth you passed through at a run, falling, going around in circles. I think about you, about those moments, and I ask myself what I can do to keep you, to hold you here inside me, breathless, locked in the yearning for an emotion that becomes more unbearable every day.

In my memory I let myself be overwhelmed by your flesh, by your nerves. Your desire fills me, fills the voids, and creates new ones, more aching and deep, that today I carry with me together with your name, four syllables stifled on my lips, in an intimate and secret struggle that accompanies the stillness of your absent body.

Some days the memory is stronger, so I go out and search for a safe haven, a place where I can rest my head for ten minutes. In short, a hiding place where no one can find you if you want to be on your own.

My city is full of places like this, you know? Places that Luca does not know. Bars, clubs with soft lighting, dance halls he would never enter.

Today I was in a club called Caffè Blue. It was the first time I had gone in but the barman greeted me as if I were an old friend. Inside there was a very beautiful girl wearing a pair of torn jeans and a colored T-shirt who struck me because of the very sweet way she was hugging her boyfriend. I asked for the same beer she was drinking, and I started to investigate those little tics that could help me to get to know her better.

There is a difference between holding a glass with all five fingers of the hand or with only four, keeping the little finger raised. And it is these actions that, wordlessly and conclusively, distinguish us as people.

That girl, just like me, was a five-finger woman, and I imagine that if I had had a daughter she would have been like her when she grew up. On the other hand, if I had had a son, he would have ended up resembling you.

Your son. Our son.

When you found out that I was pregnant you asked me to stay with you. To leave Luca. To leave everything. You were ready, you said. You loved me, you said. And I almost started crying from happiness.

I have always wanted to have a child, maybe a boy, who would grow up strong and free like I would have liked to be. I would have brought him up in an open and independent way, I would have taught him to be his own master, to think for himself, and to take important decisions without feeling constrained by duty or impositions.

I would have named him after you, because you have a nice name, a name that wasn't your father's or your grandfather's first, a name that would have been yours and his.

Yes, I would have called him by your name, and I would have loved him with all my heart. Like I love you. Still.

Go to hell if you don't believe me. Go to hell if you say yet again that I ruined everything.

In your memories of childhood the sky is blue and full of stars, loves last forever, and dreams come true easily. You wanted to dream again, my love. That is all. You desperately wanted it and you were ready to do anything, even to lie to yourself and to believe that you wanted me right until the end. But it doesn't work like that. As adults, it never works.

Stay, you said. But you didn't really think that.

You asked me to stay because you were convinced that it was the best thing to say. Perhaps because your marriage had reached the end of the line, perhaps because you hoped you were getting a second chance to be a father, I don't know. However, I know that love had nothing at all to do with it. That night you needed only an emotion, an illusion.

The night I went away. The night I did not return again.

It was the last time you touched me, the last time you tenderly ran your fingers through my hair, the last time we watched *Breathless* together. And when you said that you wanted to stay with me because you loved me, and not because you felt alone, it was also the last time you lied to me.

It was not me who left you. You left me.

This is the truth that you don't recognize.

You said that I was cruel and selfish. A whore, a bitch. You even said that I had got rid of you and your son with a single blow, and that I went back to Luca as if nothing had happened, without any regrets or remorse. And yet I still have the cheap ashtray that I stole from that café in Turin, at our first meeting. Isn't that funny? Me, who never believed in the power of objects, in the end I have transformed even that piece of trash into an unforgettable memory.

But that's how it is. This is the truth.

I think about you every day and I keep going.

Dorothy Is Going Home

ELISELLE

1. The Dream

I dreamt that I was leading an army.

I dreamt that I was a general.

I dreamt that I was fighting against a dark and savage enemy.

I dreamt that I was about to lose the battle.

I dreamt that I risked losing everything.

I dreamt that, so as not to lose, I had to make a choice: enter a mirror, thick and black as pitch, and pass into another dimension, or be defeated. Forced to choose: either that or chains. I chose the mirror.

I wasn't afraid of seeing what was on the other side. I only wanted to know what I should do so as not to be beaten and so as not to fade over time, dying in vain.

I dreamt that I entered the mirror, and only by doing this did I begin to understand the minds of my enemies, managing to assume control of them.

I dreamt that by doing this I even felt their desires. And their desires, suddenly, became mine. And I, to my great surprise, became their desires.

I dreamt that, in this way, I was winning.

I dreamt that, in this way, I was becoming queen.

2. The Scarecrow

"We're not there yet."

The eyes that analyze the walls, explore every corner of the room.

I see him shaking his head, frowning. He tries hard, as if he were solving who knows what nonsensical equation, as if he were considering the future of the world. As if the destiny of mankind depended on his decision. With that expression on his face, that he would like to look interesting. Those calculated gestures that strive to convey certainty. To at least keep up appearances.

For me, on the other hand, they are starting to get on my nerves.

"I really don't like it, you know? We need to think it over. We need a system here."

No, we don't need a system.

All I need is a sharp knife.

To sink it into your throat.

"Without a rational plan I'll end up ruining my holidays. We need to be well organized."

A chill silence follows. Then, once more, his voice, which starts to fill my ears with senseless remarks again.

Senseless, *for me*.

"It's not just about choosing a color, it's about choosing one so that it goes well with all the rest. And it's about finding a considered solution. We don't even know what style to adopt: I'm still undecided between Long Island and Zen. We could even use both, dividing the flat precisely into two halves, in a logical way. That way, each person, if we like, will be able to have an individual zone. In my opinion, maintaining the separate areas is a good idea."

Logic. Reason. Order.

It isn't. A good idea. At all.

Creating the illusion of keeping within separate areas isn't exactly what I want, spending my life deceiving myself about something that doesn't exist.

I would like to say this, but I stay silent. Impatience besets me, it is a vulture hovering over my carcass. It is slowly picking me clean, it is feeding on my flesh. It is soaking up my energy. Bit by bit, leisurely. With a steady rhythm. Indifferent to everything else.

"I don't feel like spending the holidays doing test after test, repainting everything over and over again, and I don't think you do either, so we have to think about this very carefully, Dorothy. Dorothy? Dorothy, are you listening to me?"

No, I'm not listening to you.

I'm not listening to you anymore.

I'm thinking about something completely different now. I am picturing something completely different.

I am thinking about him, that he is fucking me. That he is grabbing me by the hair. That he is running his tongue over my throat.

I am thinking about this so intensely that I have to slide a finger over my skin, just under my ear, to check that it isn't wet from his saliva. I revisit the feelings of my memories and I feel hot between my legs, in the center of my stomach. A warmth that rises and reaches straight up to my brain and clouds my mind.

I am breathing too quickly. I am losing control.

I have to get out of here.

"I know you're under stress, Dorothy, I understand. I am too. But if you make the effort and listen to me for just a second, we'll sort this out straight away and won't have to think about it anymore. So, are you ready?"

No, I'm not.

I'm not anymore.

I am far away. In another place. A place that you can't reach. And if you don't stop annoying me with your nonsense about the room and the flooring and the color to paint the walls that matches the furniture and doesn't ruin your crap holidays, if you don't stop it, I will kill you.

I will drive a blade into your neck. I will sever your artery.

Then I will cut off your head, like they do with traitors. Or martyrs. You choose.

You decide how you want to go down in history. However badly it goes, you will get to heaven.

The heaven of those who talk, talk, talk.

Who talk, though they don't have a brain.

3. The Secret

The tongue that thrusts between my legs.

A finger, inside, exploring mysterious depths.

Lips that search for me, lick me, taste me.

Persistent hands that caress my feet, massage my legs, travel over my body. That grasp my breasts and inflame them. That grasp my hair and ruffle it. That grasp my hips and pull them forcefully. Toward you.

You, who enter, making space for yourself between my flesh. Your space.

You settle in, inhale, start to move, to push according to an instinctive, primeval rhythm.

You hold onto me with the strength of desperation.

I, who am fire, and I catch fire under your fingers.

The eyes that drown in mine, the gaze fastened on yours. Liquid.

The kiss, an intense wait. Senseless.

I receive you, I moan, I let myself go, I surrender.

You don't frighten me. What you are doesn't scare me.

The skin that trembles, waiting for the wave.

When I come, I become sand, I drift away.

Sucked down by the undertow, dissolved in the water.

Together with you.

4. The Tin Woodman

"Whatever happens, you and I will stay friends."

That is what he had said, without caring about anything, breaking in two my naive purity. For someone without a heart, he wasted a fair amount of time on sentimentalities. Now that I see him again, I realize that he hasn't changed. He is just the same as before, although ten years have passed.

He shrugs off those words as if he had forgotten them, as if he had never said them, and smiles at me, arrogant. He bares his white teeth and I look at him, bored. Distracted by his motionless, complex being.

I retrace those moments, those moments of parting. They don't hurt so much anymore. Perhaps it is true that time heals all wounds. Perhaps it isn't just a fairy tale.

"Because I love you, you know that."

He had added this immediately afterward, to sugar the pill. Or perhaps because he had felt bound to do so. Or again, seeing that they are phrases that one usually says when one ends a relationship, he had learned them to perfection and wanted to show them off, to prove to me how diligent he was. How clever he was to have learned them by heart.

I never asked him which of these was the real reason.

Maybe there wasn't a reason.

Maybe it was just that he didn't know what else to say.

After ten years, here he is again, in front of me, talking to me, bestowing his judgements and unasked-for advice, as if nothing had happened. Here he is again, without a shred of self-respect, telling me all about what has happened in his life, *complicated* he says, as he stirs his coffee. With a drop of milk and lots of sugar, of course: some habits don't change.

Some meetings that we describe as fortuitous are certainly determined by a will greater than yours.

Or by your unconscious desire to harm yourself.

"Who would have ever said that a wild one like you would have let herself be caught?"

Me, wild.

In this adjective, so wrong, there is his alibi.

He never really understood me. I see that only now.

I was in love with him, hopelessly. And when one falls in love one can be stupid, one can be crazy, one can be fragile, but not wild. One accepts everything, passively, sacrificing oneself to one's own executioner and even thinking that that is right. A flair for sacrifice, when you're in love, comes naturally.

He has never seen me be wild. He doesn't even know what it means.

I remember that his repertoire from back then included other phrases: things such as "if I leave you, I'm doing it for you" or "you know you'll always be the best" or even "rather than lose you as a friend, I'd prefer to end our affair before the relationship between us sours, before we end up hating each other."

A succession of banalities, of unoriginal rubbish, thrown in my face without any dignity.

Here he is, now, my first love: a loser destroyed by life, who sees only himself, reflected in the metal of a licked teaspoon.

I don't know whether to be sad or relieved.

"Living together, marriage . . . I'm not ready yet for that sort of thing."

I would like to say to him: you will *never* be ready. And even when you think you are, you will end up making a poor deluded girl unhappy. You will soon get tired of her, maybe at the very moment when she becomes pregnant. Poor thing.

I would like to say this, but I stay silent.

"It's nice seeing you again: in the end you lose touch with people—work, commitments, different company, you know how it is . . . "

No, I don't know how it is.

If someone wants to see you, they pick up the phone and call. They arrange something. They get off their ass.

If someone doesn't want to see you, they disappear. Like you did. Full stop.

"So, let's make up for lost time: what's new, Dorothy?"

I shrug my shoulders. I hold the cup, I take a sip of coffee. Black, no sugar: even in this we are different.

He isn't exactly a person to whom I would confide my secrets and my uncertainties, without hesitating.

With someone like him, I really wouldn't know whether, or how, to start.

5. Half-asleep

A series of snapshots without any logical connection.
    The thought that continues until dawn.
    A white dog that whimpers at my feet.
    My mother who is dying in a hospital bed.
    Wet towels, hung out in a green sunset.
    A violent whirlwind that shakes the house.
    The sign that reads *fourth mile*.
    The wicked witch with the poppy head.
    The amber necklace lost in the wood.
    A quarrel between drunks at a bar.
    The prostitute in the middle of the street.
    Frayed jeans, hanging on long purple braces.
    Red shoes, with black ribbons and five-inch heels.
    The wisp of smoke from a cigarette that has never been extinguished.
    A starry night in a cornfield.
    And, at the end, before sleep, you arrive. You find your way into every thought.
    You creep under my skin and you don't ever go away.
    An orgasm shakes me, makes me quiver.
    Until, exhausted, I slide, then fall, into sleep.
    Worn out from so many visions.

6. The Cowardly Lion

"I would have liked to have been just a bit braver, but now it's too late."

I look scathingly at him and he lowers his eyes. He looks terrified. I almost feel sorry for him.

Now it's too late. Now you've had it.

When it was a game, it was alright. Now that the game has become serious, now that the rules have changed, fear arrives and takes charge. But you can't escape anymore, *not now*.

Trapped in a perverse mechanism, like a laboratory animal.

"Courage isn't something they give you. You have to practice it day after day, you have to pay personally, stand up for yourself. To be honest: this has never been your speciality. At least not with other women."

He holds his head in his hands: he doesn't have the strength to answer back.

He looks so bewildered that he doesn't even seem himself. He who, until a few days ago, every Wednesday entertained me on the backseat of his car, in a car park on the outskirts of the city, and used to boast about making me come three times in a row. Our regular appointment.

He laughed about it.

"Only with me do you come like that," he always said, at the end.

Gymnastic orgasms. Never intense enough.

Orgasms to forget. To drown my uneasiness.

Desperate orgasms. To avoid heartache, sweet temptation, an implacable cage.

The fate of my existence.

Compelled to fuck to leave a memory behind me.

Compelled to come to break free from a shadow.

Compelled to delude myself that sex for the sake of it could help me move forward.

Compelled to make my life easier, in the face of a real commitment on the horizon.

"So this is the urgent subject you had to talk to me about," I say to him.

Instead of hitting me he floods me with tears, and I am here to respond to the confessions of a repentant playboy.

I wasn't the only one, I was one of many. I knew that from the start; that was why I accepted.

No emotional involvement, no promises. What begins ends the same night, it runs its course in a few hours, and the following day everything is as before. The wonder of having sex with no expectations amplifies the sensations, because you know it could be the last time. You let yourself be touched, licked, penetrated everywhere, without barriers, without limits. Without either demarcation lines or inhibitions. Everything is permissible, nothing is forbidden. And when you go home and you find it empty because he, your partner, is still out with his friends, you have a shower to wash away the odor, to prevent him from realizing you're such a whore: it is almost liberating.

You feel alive.

You feel free.

You feel *yours*.

"Do I know her?" I ask.

He shakes his head.

I knew that every evening he saw a different woman. I had Wednesday, but I know that his diary was always full. He reserved for me his confidences about the *others*. I was the *trusted friend*.

Confidences are what can make a purely sexual relationship dangerous. It is complicity that makes two lovers unpredictable. It isn't sex. Sex is merely a stopgap. The intimacy that develops afterward, that is a time bomb.

However, the problem doesn't arise, because from tomorrow I won't see him again: I can only despair at having lost my erotic toy. A real shame. We were on the same wavelength, in that regard.

"You're ravenous this evening, you're eating that ice cream with a relish that's almost embarrassing," he says. "You're not pregnant, are you?"

He tries to joke about it, to lighten the mood.

I put in my mouth a spoon heaped with chocolate chip ice cream and whipped cream and, without looking at him, I gather my poison on my tongue and use my sting.

"I'm careful. I don't have to trap anyone."

He takes it. He doesn't respond.

Sometimes, *saying* something, and not checking one's words, is really liberating.

7. The Reflection

How much can a woman endure?

How much can she torment herself before she says enough?

How far can she push herself before she realizes that she is finished?

How far can she postpone the moment when she comes to her senses and finds the strength to move forward?

I ask myself this continually, but I don't know. I don't know.

Small, unexpected traumas that make the rot rise to the surface.

You suddenly see your first love.

You are suddenly left without your lover.

And you find yourself, alone, taking stock.

You began your romantic education with a relationship that was lost from the start and you have continued with pointless affairs, framed by foolish acts and wasted words. You have grown up with the idea of putting your life back on its feet, canceling out past mistakes, avoiding repetitive and unhealthy patterns, and you have reached thirty convinced that you would have done it. You have matured while repeating to yourself that you wouldn't waste any more of your time with the wrong men. You chose one on a theoretical level, because he didn't particularly thrill you but at least he represented security, the guarantees you were looking for to achieve your goal: the curing of your paranoia. He gave you the illusion of having found your own level and all this carried on for a while, until the house of cards collapsed.

Until the Wizard of Oz, who you had asked for advice, turned out to be a farce, a fool, an everyday fake.

You spent months betraying him. Betraying the man you were soon supposed to marry. You switched off your brain and wasted your time in a clandestine relationship, sticky and inconclusive, just so you didn't have to think about what was really important, just so you could postpone your appointment with the truth.

Sex? It isn't an issue of secondary importance: when you look for it elsewhere, it is a sign that something isn't working. Sex is the great revelation: it shows that you are running away from your responsibilities, essentially, because you don't want to have them, those responsibilities. Because you aren't ready, because it isn't the right place, the right time, the right person.

But then does he exist, the right person?

Perhaps he does, for a limited period of time.

The only man who has ever possessed your mind, your cunt, and your heart, managing to make all three come at the same time, disappeared among the affairs of the past. But he is still there, still present. He is an obsession. You keep on seeing him, in your dreams, in visions, in erotic fantasies, with the constancy of a torment, with the force of the forgiveness that you do not want to allow yourself.

Pure self-destruction, with no allowances.

Him. The man of your secrets. The man who left too deep a mark, who entered every cell of your body, and who has never gone away. The man you can't forget.

The moral is soon reached.

It isn't enough to find a man with whom you can share every day: you will get tired.

It isn't enough to find a man with whom you can have sex every now and then: it will end.

Too simple, after all.

It could be less complicated, your life.

You could decide to not get married, and upset everything.

You could run away. Leave everything behind you and not think about it anymore.

You could search for the man of your *secrets*, make up for the moments you have not lived through together, create new ones.
You could start again. Just start all over again.
Without getting tired. Forever. Endlessly.

8. The Meeting

"Bitch."
Your tongue slithers and moves inside his mouth.
Your hand strokes the rough fabric of his jeans and follows the shape of his erection.
Your feet free from the red shoes. Your legs twisted around his waist, his intense fragrance that clings to the skin and to the hair and creeps into the veins, like a needle that delves inside and moves pitilessly, mingling with blood.
He who repeats to you "you're a bitch" in a hoarse voice, whispering, and the tone in which he says it is a bullet at close range that goes straight into the brain.
The almost painful wait for his fingers on your face, at the back of your neck, clenched in your hair. Fingers that rummage, eagerly, fingers that grab, obsessively. Fingers that tear. Fingers that you would like inside you, but you feel that it isn't yet the right moment.
You only need to imagine that he is yours, for an instant.
To make him want you again, make him want your fantasies, your lips around his cock.
You were searching for him for too long, you wanted answers for too long.
To cure yourself of your obsession: your objective.
You kiss him and close your eyes but then open them again to search for his and you find them there, a breath away, following you in turn. Your eyes meet and inside you it is like a tremor, an eruption of white-hot lava, while your bodies touch, unaware of your clothes, and provide no respite.

You wanted this moment.

You devoured sex, burning and evaporating a drop of the thirst you had. But it isn't enough. You want more. You have visions and dreams and fantasies to fill. An hour is not enough.

You want to torment his lips, absorb the emotion, contain the adrenalin, and mix them up together with his taste, to come again.

You arouse him, you kiss him again, deeply, you find it hard to breathe.

The thrill is an unexploded bomb, you can feel it between your legs, throbbing, pressing.

You say, quietly: "You want it too, do you feel it?"

You surprise him with a subdued laugh, amused, while you caress him more intensely to drive him mad and break down his resistance, all his resistance, to the last drop. You succeed. He towers above you now and he lowers his jeans, then his briefs, he lets you take his cock in one hand while you seek out and grip his balls with the other and you make him cry out when you start to suck him, following his desire, instinctively knowing how to move, moistening him with saliva and reaching orgasm together with him.

He brushes aside your hair. He wants to watch while you do it.

He whispers "I'm coming" and you like the way he repeats it once, twice, three times, quickly, urgently, as if he were letting himself be dragged along by the current and everything was now past, irretrievable, forgotten.

He murmurs "I'm here" and it is as if your mind were exploding together with his member. As one.

Then he sinks down at your side, and without realizing you think about the moment when he will no longer have this urgency, this desire, this lust for you. It has already happened, you know what it feels like. And for a second, in the silence of the night, your heart surprises you. Your heart, unexpectedly, in the middle of the night, amazes you. For a second, in the night, your heart skips a beat. And everything seems to stop, while the world keeps turning.

9. The Vision

The Emerald City has disappeared.
    It was here a moment ago, and now it's not.
    The Wizard has fled in a hot-air balloon.
    He has gone forever, he has decided that he will not come back.
    For the Tin Woodman he has left a cloth heart.
    The heart is crimson, covered in pins, it is still, it doesn't beat.
    A mere imitation that will be no use to him.
    He made the Cowardly Lion drink a potion.
    The potion is poisonous, in a few hours everything will come to an end.
    He will be able to forget his mistakes and in death forgive himself.
    To the Scarecrow he gave a brain of mud.
    Mud is just mud, it drips and doesn't stop.
    He will drown in it, unwittingly, persisting in his error.
    He hasn't left anything for me. I am the only one whose hands are still empty.
    I am the only one who, whatever happens, will have to muddle through on my own.
    Simply alone, using my own strength.

10. Neglect

I ask myself if I am doing the right thing. If I shouldn't reconsider. If I should continue along this road, if it is already too late for me to stop. His frozen stare as I packed my bags and went out of the door, out of our ex-future home and out of his life without saying a word, without explaining, that stare I will carry inside me as long as I live. But I can't carry on like this. It is stronger than me.

DOROTHY IS GOING HOME

Searching for and meeting again the man from my past was a mistake, but it was also the only way to be free. Making love to him again, I know now, was the best mistake of my life.

It reconstructed the broken wires. It reopened the connections. It rekindled the light.

It revealed the truth that I longed for and that I couldn't see, because I was wandering in the dark.

It illuminated a part of my life that no longer belongs to me.

It allowed me to jettison the dead wood of my empty trophies.

It short-circuited my false certainties.

It cancelled out years of obsessions.

It showed me the answer: *let go of everything, take your time, go back to square one.*

The answer was always right in front of my eyes, but I was blind, too frightened to understand.

The answer, so simple: Dorothy, go away.

Put on your red shoes and go away.

So, this time Dorothy has decided.

Dorothy has made her choice.

In the end, Dorothy put her red shoes on her feet.

In the end, with no more uncertainties, Dorothy is going home.

Random Constructions

ALINA RIZZI

This will be the hell that everyone talks about:
still wanting the things
of life and feeling that one is standing in the wrong room.
                    —Daria Menicanti, "Autumn"

The man is old but he pretends not to know. She, in his memories, is simply young, beautiful, vital. Nothing more than what the man feels about her. She could be a construction in his mind, a folly. Perhaps he invents. Perhaps he tells himself about a desire never realized. But it isn't possible to discover this: there are no clues. The man is telling his story and it doesn't matter to him if anyone listens. He starts at the end, because he needs to untie the knots.

"And then my wife found out everything," he is saying.

The usual anonymous telephone call gave her dates, places, and times, with meticulous accuracy. I didn't think I had many friends, but I always suspected invisible and bitter enemies, ready to strike like snakes at the first favorable opportunity. Which naturally arrived, and at the worst moment, when she, not asking for anything anymore, had hooked me so well, so thoroughly.

Never again, said my wife categorically, looking me straight in the eye. Imagine! Of course, I agreed. She was exercising her sacred right. Never again, definitely, I told her. Don't worry. Anyway, it was just a game, an act of bravado, an adventure. An exciting and entertaining chase after a shapely pair of legs, a cheekily short skirt, a provocative mouth. A boyish rush of blood to the head.

Immature, ungrateful pig, she hissed through gritted teeth, without moving a muscle in her face. How could I deny it? Rhetorical accusations, but fair accusations that could be thrown at any fifty-year-old man. Yes, because in the meantime eight years, more or less, had passed. A boyish prank that lasted almost a decade, unbelievable, a sort of regression, kept firmly under control, however. Anyway, one meets so many girls in miniskirts and high heels. So many with dyed hair that looks natural, honey blonde, like real. All with that lethal appearance, when the admirer is fifty, between fifty and sixty to be exact. Would-be Lolitas in search of Pygmalions. But really I never had what it takes: I don't know how to protect, reassure, comfort. I don't even have much time to spare, and so there were clear understandings right from the start. We see each other and that's it, nothing more. And the fear of getting old and then dying doesn't go away even then, even if she's thirty years younger. It will be because of this that when my wife said it had to end I didn't lose any sleep. I knew that it could happen, and in the end it happened. It didn't seem to me that I needed to make a song and dance about it, so to simplify things I told her over the phone. Anyway, I hate the weeping, threats, or whatever else could have happened. To me it seemed all clear and clean. There wasn't much to discuss and so I broke up with her. A nice neat break, like chopping off a hand or an arm. A strong gesture, effective and satisfying. A pragmatic man doesn't vacillate: he is the manager of his soul.

The pain, the real pain, I mean, wasn't expected. It followed a couple of months later, perhaps three, in a sudden and subtle way. I was crossing the road when from behind the corner of a building popped out a girl in a miniskirt, with shoes like stilts. I didn't stop, I didn't hesitate for a second more, and yet inside my stomach, or thereabouts, I was aware of a sharp spasm, a clear and deep twinge. It is desire, I told myself confidently, calmly. Arousal, nothing else. I'll be faithful even, but I certainly haven't taken a vow of chastity. Who would turn their nose up at a soft and inviting body, uniformly firm, energetic, vital? Two hours in a nondescript motel and I would go back to my pursuits more convinced than before. Then the girl turned and I was disappointed. Not that she, the other she I mean, was the ideal of beauty, not that she was perfection. She was she and that was enough. The eyes, the mouth, the breasts, the bottom, the legs, they were hers.

Anyway, I had a coffee in the bar opposite and drowned the cramp in my stomach. With everything I had to do, I didn't need to waste time on useless thoughts.

The second time the pain reappeared, still wearing its pleasant mask, I was driving outside the city. The business appointment had borne fruit, I was relaxed and happy, as much as one can be on certain September mornings when the sun carries with it already squandered remnants of summer. I was driving in not too much of a hurry, traveling along the same old road, the one that crosses the flat and silent countryside like a river, when I noticed the car. It was at a distance from the roadside but perfectly visible, on the bank of a river. Against the body of the car, in full sun, she irreparably blonde and he just a bit taller, entwined, embracing, breathless, feverish. It was a fist in the stomach, an unendurable surprise. I just had time to recognize the gestures and then they had already disappeared, they had fled together with the river, the plane trees, the bushes still in flower, the warm and fragrant air, the limpid sun, the outstretched and welcoming sky.

I realized that I was gripping the steering wheel tightly, that I had accelerated without meaning to. Go away, I was thinking, let it be, nothing has changed, it doesn't interest you, it doesn't concern you. That was true; in fact, it didn't concern me. I was fine. The pain inside, beneath my ribs, wasn't my concern. I could easily ignore it, it wasn't really a tragedy. Even if that was the place, more or less. I remember that there was a similar river, probably the same one. And it was summer, it was hot. June or September, it doesn't make much difference. She was clinging to my jacket, her lips moist and insatiable, her eyelids fluttering. I was breathing in her hair, my hands all over her, my blood like a roar in my wrists. Love, she was whispering against my mouth. Quiet, quiet, quiet! What need was there for words? Don't say them, not now not ever, don't do it. But she was laughing. Her tongue, her small teeth, her neck upturned. Liquid and hot.

By December it was already too late. She, nestled under my skin, sucked dry my strength and determination. She was invading my certainties like an illness, eating away my defenses. She pawed inside my chest and suddenly surrendered sweetly, languid and yielding. To forget and resist, that was my goal. I know I can be very determined, I always know what to do.

If I phoned it was to not have any doubts, to be reassured. In the end, what did it cost me? I wasn't jeopardizing anything with a phone call. And then, after a year so, many things change and you get to miss the memories more than the reality. And the nostalgia distorts things and people, changes the colors and tones. It isn't reliable. So it's better to narrow the gaps, better the brutal but realistic impact, which sweeps away every hope, which cleans out the past and dims your regrets. It was a solution: I have always been very rational. Because of this I phoned. And I learned that she had moved to another city, perhaps to another country. No, they couldn't be more precise, they didn't have information about her, they were simply the new tenants.

Good. I sighed with relief. Everything had worked out just as I had expected. It had been easy and efficient. Even if I had wanted to make further enquiries, I wouldn't have known where to begin. And anyway, it wasn't my intention to inquire further. Things had sorted themselves out in the best way possible, for both of us, surely.

I could go back to dealing a bit more seriously with my work and my family. In conclusion, with my life, with my normal life, which could still be okay. Anyway, one can't live in the skin of someone else, within the reality of just anybody.

To tell the truth, I did make a few inquiries, as far as it proved possible. They said that she had moved to England but that she would be back sooner or later. It wasn't a final solution, hers, she certainly intended to return after a certain length of time.

Excellent, I thought. Better for her. Even if I didn't understand what she had gone abroad for. Wasn't she happy at home? Anyway, I often say to myself, sooner or later she'll come back. Maybe to the same city, it's very likely. Or somewhere else. In reality it makes no difference to me. I certainly can't spend my life on the phone in the hope of tracking her down in some village or other. What would my chances be? In any case, it can't be ruled out that she'll return to where she lived for so many years, it would be the most logical choice. She could even look for me one day, just to find out what's become of me. Out of curiosity. There wouldn't be anything odd about that. Obviously, I won't be here waiting for her to call, I'm not fifteen and if I want feminine company I know where to find it. I have no problems in meeting pretty and enterprising young women. In any case, I'm not interested in what she'll do with her life. It doesn't concern me, just as it didn't concern me then. And then really a lot of time has passed and things change. If she calls I'll be pleased to say hello to her, but that's all. After all, why shouldn't she call? We were together for seven years and we could have stayed together another seven, or ten, or twenty, if what we know happened hadn't happened. We were good together, I don't mean to deny that. She would agree, I believe. So she'll call, I'm sure of it. I don't make myself ill over any woman, you must be joking, at my age. But I'm here. If she calls, I'm here.

I hardly ever go out. And I've certainly not forgotten her.

And anyway, why should I forget her? What should I have done?

The desk is cluttered with sheets of paper, pencils, books, Post-Its in various colors, blue and red felt-tip pens. The phone rings. The woman answers without raising her head, but simply stretching out her hand to where the receiver should be.

Yes?

Good morning.

She lays down the pen calmly, after having put the top back on. She frees the wire of the phone, which has curled up on itself. She leans back in the chair.

RANDOM CONSTRUCTIONS

Outside the window a green field, a vigorous hedge, pines, patches of light blue sky.

Well, thank you.

Yes, two years I believe. Really a long time.

In her diary, open in the middle of the table, a shopping list, orderly notes, the date of a birthday, old cancelled appointments.

A wonderful spring, I agree. Let's hope it lasts.

Beyond the half-open windowpanes, down in the street, the chatting of two women who are going for a walk, the shouts of a child who runs ahead.

I work, see friends.

Yes, I've traveled, I needed to.

On the wall a strip of wallpaper is peeling off; it ought to be fixed.

Changed? I would definitely say so, luckily.

Good, and you, good-bye.

The woman hangs up calmly. She chooses a blue pen from the earthenware vase and goes back to correcting the sheets of paper.

The days are getting longer, soon summer will be here.

It will be hot again. Like then.

⁂

The water is dark, cloudy, barely rippled by a light breeze that curls the waves far from the shore. One side of the tree leans in the lake like a ship, long and narrow. On the balcony, white and polished, one can imagine being on the deck of a cruise ship. The rooms, all in a row, are the cabins. Mostly empty.

They are sitting on plastic chairs, side by side, which are covered with towels so that they feel more comfortable. Their feet resting on the balustrade, their hands linked, their gaze following the ducks that are moving away from the pebbly shore. They breathe slowly, in the sun.

For a few minutes she has pretended she can ignore their naked bodies in the glaring light of early afternoon. She was focusing her gaze on his eyes, so as not to let it drift elsewhere, almost holding her breath with the effort. Then she had to surrender. Give in to the facts, however painful. So her gaze traveled over his shoulders and his thin chest, much thinner than years before. And his arms, where the skin seems lacking in substance and sometimes forms creases. It is frail, thin skin, which easily becomes covered with hematomas, abrasions, which turns red if she rubs herself back and forth against him. There is a lump in her throat but she has to resist. She strokes his grey hair, telling herself that it doesn't matter, that it makes no difference.

He seems to read her thoughts.

"Grey," he says, resigned.

It doesn't matter to her, he wants it not to matter to her. She grazes his neck with a kiss. What does the flesh matter, after all? But equally he can't deny the evidence, he can't stop himself remembering when his thighs were more solid, more muscular thanks to hours spent windsurfing, or perhaps just thanks to being a few years younger. He recognizes his dark veins, blue, that line his right leg because he had those before as well. Will she get them too, in ten or twenty years? Along with the empty flesh, the delicate nails, the thinner bones?

She gets to her feet with a jump and looks at herself reflected in the window behind the man. The shiver of horror fades away as soon as she encounters her own mirror image, the soft and rounded curves, the smooth and compact skin, bronzed by the sun, with no shadows, spots or streaks on display. She smiles, cheered up, but with a vague sense of guilt. Because of this she hurries to embrace the man: she seeks forgiveness for her shameless and dazzling youth.

"You're beautiful," he murmurs to her.

Of course she is.

She pulls his face against her breasts and brushes his short and thinning hair, almost white, with her slightly open lips. She cradles him to console him for what he has lost, as if she could sense his regret. Then she sits down on his thighs, slowly. Desire is something different, something more vital:

what she offers him, with his chest swollen with nostalgia, is a silent consolation.

But it doesn't matter: after two years it's still him.

***

If she counts up to fifty without ever getting distracted, he'll call. She senses it. Or else she should try something more difficult, for example, repeat three times in a row an old tongue-twister: she sells seashells on the seashore, the shells she sells are seashells I'm sure. Will that work?

She ought to dry her hair, she's cold. But if she switches on the hair dryer she's bound not to notice the possible ringing of the phone. So she slips it into her pocket, so she can feel it vibrating at the right moment.

But she still can't make up her mind to do anything. And in the meantime it has got late. Upset, she takes off her make-up in front of the mirror. Her gestures are restless, mechanical, a necessary contrast with her interior apathy. She shouldn't be so weak and vulnerable, she doesn't have a reason to be. The fact that her senses are in a daze isn't helpful and it irritates her. She rebels, running down the stairs, with her bag under her arm, the car keys in one hand and her jacket in the other. She flees as if from danger and dashes out into the street.

The ringing erupts together with the warmth of the sun that hits her full in the face. She gasps in the bright light with her hand clutching the phone: she feels exposed, surprised.

Instinctively she takes refuge in the dark lobby of a building, she turns to face the wall and lowers her head and shoulders, bending over the telephone in a protective recess. She answers almost breathlessly.

"Yes?"

Now she is smiling.

"I was expecting you."

Barbara is a brunette. She has a mass of smooth, thick hair that falls heavily onto her shoulders. And pale-colored elongated eyes, a thin mouth with undefined edges. She is prettier when she doesn't wear sunglasses, because she has a kind look.

Like her body: smooth, plump, small breasts, wide hips, sturdy thighs. She is already tanned, like all the brunettes at the beginning of July. Her black bikini makes her look daring, provocative. Perhaps despite herself.

Next to Laura she creates a strong contrast. Because Laura is blonde, golden, tiny. With her narrow, masculine hips, her thin legs, her round breasts liberated in the sun. They chat freely to each other, unconstrained, sitting close, gleaming and smelling of suntan oil. They smile often. They are beautiful in the sun.

Laura knows it. She can see them both from outside, as if she were a spectator, slightly aloof but attentive. She observes through the eyes of the old man in the distance. She observes their young, full bodies, almost naked, and feels an unspoken but intense pleasure.

She imagines the old man there next to them, watching them, drinking in their every smallest gesture. She wouldn't invite him to join them, not that. She doesn't miss him because Barbara is exquisite and satisfies all her senses. But she would let him watch, fanning a secret fire. The pleasure that he would experience, from a distance, she experiences under her own skin when, out in the waves, she stretches out her arms and pulls the other woman toward her, to brush against her face and hair. To breathe in her scent of sweat and salt, to weaken next to her, silently, under the eyes of the bathers, so alert, so oblivious.

He watches her enter the parking lot quickly. Get out of her car, smile, move toward him, dancing beneath a very long pink skirt. Her short T-shirt leaves her stomach exposed. She has high heels and feet crisscrossed with black straps tied around her ankles. He can't even move for the thrill.

He stands with his arms open, like in a sign of surrender. Not even a hello. She merely hugs him and plants a gentle kiss on his lips, removing his every defense.

"I can't believe it," he mutters, taking her hands, holding her a few inches away from him to look at her again, from her feet to her hair, ruffled but straight.

"You're beautiful, a vision."

Inside his chest vibrates a sound that is like singing, music: Laura, Laura, Laura.

All talk is superfluous: it's enough for him to have her there, in his arms, laughing, exposed and damp with sweat, to feel his soul turned upside down as if by a sudden beating of wings.

They get into his car, which he immediately drives off the highway, entering unknown villages, sun-drenched and half-empty squares, in search of a bar with tables outside. Here it is, by the side of a pond: girls in bikinis, ice-cold drinks.

She is telling him about Barbara, about how she was sweet and sensual. He can picture her through her eyes, he can enjoy her as if he had seen her and touched her. He listens but at the same time he watches Laura, who talks and talks and laughs every now and then, and drinks her Coca-Cola through a straw, then she leans forward to kiss him on the lips and to stroke his neck.

"You should have been there, we were gorgeous. You could have watched us in the shade and you would have loved us."

He nods, persuaded, and stretches out his hand to stroke her hair.

"What do I have to do to have this life together with you? Get divorced?"

She doesn't reply, as if she hasn't heard him, and continues her detailed account of the day spent on the beach with her friend.

After a while they get up from the table. They walk arm in arm on the grass. He slides his hand under the edge of her T-shirt and caresses her furtively. Laura responds with a passionate kiss, clutching at his jacket, whispering that she wishes they had a bed.

"Of course, honey. Me too," he replies breathlessly, "but not today, you know it's impossible."

She protests, irritated, but in the meantime strokes his wrists and rubs her pelvis against his groin.

She is lovely, delicious, delightful, and red hot.

She says: "I love you. Let's do it now."

He tilts her head back and licks her neck. He would like to immerse himself in her hot and pulsating body, melt in her, lose himself in her blood.

"I have to go, honey," he manages to murmur instead.

And tearing her away from him is like amputating a limb, pulling off shreds of living flesh with his own hands. He smiles at her simply to persuade her, to hide from her his burning pain, the scream that can't explode outside the confines of his own body.

"How can you go right now?" she asks him.

He doesn't have any explanation, apart from the usual.

"We'll see each other next week," he suggests, despite knowing that the hours will be interminable and the days an eternity. And that next week will doubtless be thrilling but that won't make up for the emptiness that eats into him beneath his ribs, now that he blows her a kiss through the open car window and drives out of the parking lot. An emptiness that seems to get a bit larger every time he lets her go, and it really is too often, while she is still smiling at him, resigned or perhaps quietly knowing, as if she had found some meaning in that repeated departure.

Matteo is tall, muscular and strong: a strapping man. He always wears designer jeans and checked shirts of quality fabric, sometimes Lacoste polo shirts. In both summer and winter he wears deck shoes. He drives a convertible sports car. He has the latest model cell phone and dreams about living in California, because he went there once, and he says that there no one does anything. He married a fat, rich woman, just so he could build his own little California on the outskirts of Milan. In fact, he spends his days breaking in wild horses and buying houses over the phone. Sometimes he phones Laura, he warns her that he's on his way and five minutes later he's at her door. He goes up, they hug on the stairs, he puts his tongue in her mouth straight after having said Hi, how are you? When he leaves, on the other hand, he says bye, be good. In between the greetings, for about twenty minutes, sometimes half an hour, they have sex on the marble worktop in the kitchen, him with his trousers pulled down to his knees, her with her short skirt pulled up. Maybe in the meantime he asks her if there's any news, but Laura never has any, not for him. She doesn't feel any need to tell him anything at all, and anyway she knows that he would respond with an "Oh, good" even if she were describing a walk on the moon. They don't have conversations: they just moan and sigh locked tightly together, him with his forehead damp with sweat, while she tries to concentrate a bit. For Matteo, Laura is a stolen and reinvigorating interlude. For Laura, Matteo is a lottery: sometimes she wins a quick and comforting pleasure, sometimes she doesn't. However, she accepts the risk, because sometimes she needs a man who she doesn't have to think about afterward. Matteo is good for this: he has a good physique, he's young and willing.

Joking, he says he would happily be a gigolo. In reality he already is a gigolo, officially from the moment he started wearing a wedding ring.

"Will you call me?" he asks Laura when he kisses her at the door and rushes off, eternally late for some appointment. But he never listens to her reply.

She closes the door and goes to wash up the glasses they used, then goes back to her desk and carries on with her work.

Spaghetti with seafood, lobster, a fruit tart, ice-cold white wine. Laura really eats only when she is with him and forgets her fear of getting fat, of not being attractive to him. But then, he is devouring her with his eyes and every now and then he feels her thighs under the tablecloth, or he bites her shoulder, puts her fingers in his mouth.

Around them the pergola of vines and wisteria creates a corner of comfortable and calming cool. He often calls her "darling." He says to her "I love you" without lowering his eyes or his tone of voice. Laura pretends not to attach much importance to it, so as not to frighten him, so as not to push him away, believing he has gone too far. The reality is that all those "darlings" and "I love yous" descend to her stomach along with the food, they fill her up and satisfy her with a secret pleasure. Nothing like this ever happened, two years before.

They leave the restaurant under a blazing, unbearable sun. He complains about it.

The air-conditioning in the car isn't enough for him. He says he feels incredibly tired, that he woke up at dawn, he has traveled for hours.

"It'd be better if you went back to work now," he tells her resignedly.

Laura protests, however. The heat raises her spirits, the sun breathes vitality and strength into her. She wants to stay with him, to make love.

Completely useless. He is willing to hold her, to devour her with kisses, to slide his fingers under her dress, to pick her up in his arms like a lightweight doll. But no motel, no bed, no sex.

"I'm sorry too, darling, but I can't complain: I've already had my share of happiness for today," he explains to her.

Laura looks down in silence. Her eyes are shining and she doesn't even know if it's because of anger, frustration, or who knows what.

The man lifts her face with two fingers, he looks at her.

"I'm old, tired, worn-out. Haven't you noticed?"

She shakes her head vigorously, she doesn't want to hear it, because she already knows everything. And then she leans her head against his chest, clings to him, lets herself be cradled.

And, cradling her, the old man cradles himself a bit as well. For a few moments. Then he moves away decisively, he turns back to the car. He prefers to go straight away and know that she is willing, taut, yearning, rather than disappointed and annoyed. Because it's like that that he would fuck her, after two hours in a nondescript room in the middle of the afternoon, with that heat and hours of motorway driving and a too large lunch behind him. He would never be able to contain her vitality, her youth, her eager emotions. To give her what she needs.

He turns on the engine. Then he turns it off and goes back to kiss her. In an instant, he pictures everything. Losing his head, for example, catching hold of her, carrying her away, far away, on the lake. He sees himself booking an elegant room, one that doesn't stink of smoke like all the motel rooms. He watches himself fling open the windows looking out onto an inlet of cool dark water, order ice-cold white wine, strawberries and cream. The bed is huge and welcoming. They have a shower together. Her hair is wet, smoothed back, and there are smudges of mascara under her eyes. They go to dry themselves on the terrace, under the sun that shatters into purplish reflections. Afterward, naturally, dinner in the restaurant, with an abundance of candles, music, fresh flowers. No schedules and no hurry. He pictures her tight-fitting dress. And later an entire night for them, for whispering in the dusk, for making love, for falling asleep pressed against each other. At dawn his thinning hair on the pillow, his body warm with sleep, his arms that open invitingly.

"I'll phone you tomorrow," is all he says to her.

She doesn't respond.

"You're still the one who's making the choice. You know that, don't you?" she merely asks him, before he leaves.

No, it's not about a choice anymore, but she'll tell him that another time, perhaps tomorrow, if she ever has the courage and the strength.

A café like any other, a day like any other.

Barbara is smoking in silence and listens.

"Yes, he's getting older. He expects more for himself, for his life, and because of this he demands much less of me: he just needs a kiss, a hug. He says that that's happiness already. That without me, without seeing me, without touching me, he has experienced emptiness, death."

Laura can believe it.

And Barbara? It doesn't matter much: she isn't interested in the old man, she's not there because of him.

"But I've grown too. I expect more for myself as well. And because of this I can't be content, I don't know how to give things up anymore. Away from him I've discovered freedom and life. I want a lot now."

Laura thinks about Matteo then shakes her head: no, that isn't desire. Not that magnificent but vacant body. And yet, unfortunately, nor is that intense but now fragile body of the old man. Is wanting a bridge between the strength of youth and the passion of maturity, between the past and the future, perhaps wanting too much?

Barbara has no answer to offer her, but she doesn't impose any limits on desire.

She exhales a ring of smoke and takes Laura's hands in hers on top of the table.

"If you can't find a bridge," she tells her, "build one."

"Are you still angry?" he asks her, hesitating.

"Definitely," she answers him.

He guesses the real answer from the tone of her voice. The word is unambiguous but the silence that follows it suggests something more articulate and deep, which isn't about need as much as desire. A desire that can't be suppressed. In fact, Laura is in no hurry to be there with him, she doesn't ask it of him. Laura just wants him to be there and to continue to be there. That's what the silence hints at. The silence of both of them that, in some way, heartens them. Now he is driving fast, northward, relaxed. She is accompanying him. They tell each other about what has happened over the last few days, who they've met, their disappointments. Even what they have eaten for lunch, plans for tomorrow, the plot of a film watched on television, of the last book they bought. Words that stream past along with the miles, along with the minutes and the hours. Sometimes the line cuts out because of interference or a tunnel, which distorts the shortwave signal. He calls her back straight away, she doesn't even make as if to go back to her interrupted work. Together they plan their next meeting: they choose the restaurant and the time. Laura pictures the dress she is going to wear for him. It doesn't matter much if they will see each other or not, shirking other commitments and appointments: the plan they have in common is already a bond.

"I'd like to take a trip with you," he is saying to her.

"To have you with me all day, to talk to you, look at you. And in the evening to fall asleep together and then wake up by your side."

"Don't think about it," is Laura's reply.

"Wouldn't you like that?" the man insists.

She closes her eyes.

"We don't need it," she answers, trying to sound confident.

Their wounds, absolutely unavoidable, they will lick later.

He knows that and lets the subject drop.

Then he stops at the service station to fill up with gasoline. Laura hears him joking with the person at the pump, then he asks for directions and pays in cash. He hasn't even thought to hang up, as if he wanted to keep her there by his side, despite the physical distance. He seems not to be aware of the hours passing, but Laura doesn't mind: they are traveling together, in spite of everything.

Now he gets into the car again, starts the engine, fastens his safety belt and returns to the highway.

"What are you working on today?" he asks her.

She continues the interrupted conversation, with lips that barely touch the receiver, conscious of his attention. Until it gets dark. Then she lights the lamp and, with the first shadows that envelop the desk, pictures a man, who drives holding a phone in his left hand and the steering wheel in his right; it's uncomfortable and dangerous but nevertheless he is incapable of breaking off their communication and that thin but real wire that binds them, mile after mile, weaving the plot of an indestructible secret.

The Feelings Don't Come Back

GRAZIA SCANAVINI

There was a moment when I thought that everything could start again.

I was wrong.

The feelings don't come back. They remain inside you.

It's August, the hottest that I can remember. Stopped at a traffic light, I lower the window despite the heat; I want to smoke. I search for the lighter at the bottom of my bag, which is sitting on the passenger seat. How is it possible that I can never find one? There must be at least six in the bag, I'm certain. While I rummage through the bag I feel drops of sweat beading on my face, despite the air-conditioning. There it is. As I light the cigarette, I look up at the car standing next to mine; I sense that I'm being watched.

No!

A palpitation.

Oh god! I don't believe it. Is it him? He smiles at me with that smile I know well. A second that lasts an eternity. What do I do? I smile but I must look like an idiot and my heart is choking me: it's beating so fast that it's not letting the air get through and I feel a lack of oxygen throughout my body. The hot sweat on my face suddenly becomes cold. Shivers. My hand is shaking and I drop the cigarette. I struggle to find it.

Right inside my bag. Fuck! I don't have the courage to raise my eyes. I feel like I'm dying, but I want to die looking in my bag, not at him. I find the cigarette—it's burning the plastic of a packet of paper tissues. I take it out of my bag.

It's pointless, him continuing to look at me: I'm not falling for it!

A horn honks behind me.

Yes, yes, you're right, sorry! I put the car into first gear and set off, looking straight ahead at the road that has to take me far away. A long way away.

My heart is going to burst out of me, I'm certain of it. It doesn't have the necessary room to stay in my chest; I can feel it in my throat; I'm sweating again.

God, please, make it so he's turned off! I can't bear to look: if I see him there again, what will I do? And what the fuck is he doing in Ferrara? Another red light . . . No, please!! I stop but I'd love to accelerate. I shut my eyes; I don't want to look at him. I pretend to be distracted, I raise the window, and I increase the volume of the radio.

Go, go!! Go green, please!! Nothing. It's the pedestrians' turn to cross. What do I do? Light a cigarette? If I smoke now I'll die, for certain; I'm already short of air as it is! I shut my eyes, again, and again the car behind me honks.

Yes, yes, I'm going! I turn left; if he was on the right, he'll be going straight on or turning right, no?! I get onto Via delle Poste and only when I stop at the zebra crossing at Via Garibaldi do I find the courage to look in the rearview mirror. A dark car, like his. Fuck!!

I set off again and I drive to the end of the street without looking in the mirror again. I think about where I could slide the car in so there's no chance of him coming alongside me. Via Ripagrande, yes! I drive into it, hoping that my heart will calm down because if I carry on like this I won't be able to do anything anymore. At the roundabout I can't resist: I look up into the rearview mirror, careful not to move my head—I don't want him to notice. I just raise my eyes and the dark car is there, stopped less than a couple of feet from mine. I look inside: extremely long blonde hair! It's a woman, but the tension doesn't relax yet. I turn right, I enter the street where I live, and the blue car carries on.

It isn't him; it's a woman. You can calm down now. I park and sit there, looking in the mirrors. No one in sight. I close my eyes, lean my head against the steering wheel, and my heart seems to slow down, trying to find peace. My thoughts don't, though. A thousand images run through my brain. That door of dark wood, the brass key, the dress that glides over my body, leaving it completely naked.

I open my eyes again and lift my head from the wheel. My body seems numb; my muscles feel stiff as if I have run for hours and hours. I am soaked in sweat. I take my bag and keys; I just want to go into my flat. A last look in the mirrors. Still no one. I get out of the car and walk toward the main entrance to the building's lobby. My head's spinning. I feel dazed like that afternoon in Venice, crossing the Rialto bridge. As I'm putting the key in the lock, the door bangs suddenly from inside. I jump.

"Hi, Livia!"

"Ah, it's you, Angela! You gave me a scare. I was miles away . . . How are you? Everything okay? I haven't seen you for a while."

"That's true. I go out early in the morning. I changed jobs recently and I'm running around like mad . . . but it's better to be working, considering how things are at the moment . . . Tell me what you've been up to?"

"Everything as normal, the usual things . . . work, study, commitments, you know. I got back from vacation a week ago and I can't even remember it!"

"Ah yes, I didn't even notice you'd been away . . . we've now become robots!"

"Listen, Livia, let's meet up one of these evenings for dinner. What do you say? This evening even, if you like."

"Yes, I'd love to . . . Let's do this: I'll make something and wait for you. What time do you get back?"

"I'm home at eight o'clock, but don't prepare anything."

"Don't worry: I'll be expecting you."

"See you later then."

Angela smiles at me as she walks off and waves.

I smile. For an instant I had almost forgotten about him, almost. I go in, close the door, and lean back against it. I think that he was there, a few feet away from me, and my strength fails me. I look at the stairs and the elevator . . . elevator, definitely. As soon as the elevator door closes, I sense smells all around me, the feeling of hands, the sensation of lips. Pleasure, pain. I feel faint.

I go into my flat. I leave my bags and slide to the ground, my back to the door. My heart seems to go crazy again. I stay still, my head tipped backward against the door. Thank goodness I left the air-conditioning turned on: the cool air on my hot skin seems to be a relief. Seems to be.

I stand up and switch on my computer. I type his name in the search engine, with my heart in my mouth. That's why he's in Ferrara . . . an exhibition of his paintings, for two weeks. I feel like I'm going mad. I knew that sooner or later he would have returned inside me; he never left.

I had met him one evening in October, the year before; a dinner at the house of a musician friend in Venice. Ten people or so, I don't remember exactly, also because I didn't know anyone except Marco, the musician. I had arrived late, as usual, and when Marco had opened the door and shown me into the dining room where everyone was already seated, he had introduced me to everyone as "the journalist friend I'm always telling you about." I had smiled; I didn't know he talked about me to anyone. Ours was a rather superficial friendship, we had known each other for three or four years but we didn't often see each other. I sat down in the empty place next to Marco and, after a bit of small talk, a pleasant convivial and rather familiar atmosphere was established. Among Marco's friends there were a couple of photographers, two bass players, a car salesman, a doctor and two painters—a girl from Berlin and him: Fulvio. A man of about fifty, not particularly tall, solid, wearing jeans and a blue polo shirt. From the moment I sat down, he hadn't taken his eyes off me. He watched me steadily, intensely, it was almost embarrassing. Nevertheless, the dinner passed by pleasantly, even if his stare somehow unsettled me. Once we had finished eating, we moved into Marco's studio. He wanted us to listen to a new piece he had written for a concert that would be taking place in a few weeks. While Marco's music was playing, Fulvio came up to me and said:

"When are you next in Venice?"

"I don't know. Every now and then I come here for work, but I'll certainly be coming for Marco's next concert."

He smiled, looking me in the eyes, and I had the feeling that he was drilling inside me. He didn't say anything else, and he moved away. The evening continued with music, discussions connected to the various jobs of the people there, a bit of chat about current affairs, and it was really nice. I often tried to catch Fulvio's eye, but after his initial question he had ignored me, making a slight and nonsensical anger rise in me. He had looked at me throughout dinner and now it seemed like I didn't exist. Perhaps he had expected me to do or say something different when he had approached me. One of the girls, a photographer, decided it was time to leave, and I did the same. It wasn't late for me, but I did it almost to punish Fulvio for not having continued what he had started.

Once I had left, as I was driving home, I felt strange. That stare had got to me, despite the fact that Fulvio was definitely not the type of man who usually had an effect on me. Physically, I really didn't like him, and during the dinner there hadn't been any particular exchange between us, just a few pleasantries.

That night I couldn't get to sleep, so I sat down at my computer, searching for information about him. A well known and highly regarded contemporary artist, his works were portraits of nude or semi-nude women, very sensual. At four in the morning, as I was deciding whether to try lying down in the hope of sleeping, an email arrived. It was him. Just one word: "Come!" Attached, there was an aerial photo of part of Venice, along a canal I didn't recognize, with an arrow indicating a building.

I replied immediately: " . . . is this a game? Do I have to guess, like in a treasure hunt?"

Inside I felt a strange excitement emerging. I didn't like him and yet I felt inside me a desire to play his game, to give in to this entanglement straight away without even knowing who he was or what he wanted from me. I had the sensation that he was getting into my head to excite me, although nothing he had said had led me to believe that except his "Come!"

A few seconds later, his reply: "Come now. You'll find the address below. Ring the bell, no one lives here but me. Come up the stairs, second floor. When you reach the door, you'll find a red blindfold. Put it on, get completely undressed, and wait."

Panic. "But you're mad! I haven't slept yet since I got home, and I don't even know who you are." Yet, what had been a mild tension at first had now become real excitement. I didn't know what had caused it but I knew it was there, and it had taken hold of me.

He replied again with the same word: "Come!"

A thousand thoughts began to meander around my mind, from a definite refusal to the impulse to take the car and leave. I looked at my clothes lying untidily on the armchair. I got up, put them on, picked up my keys and went out. There was no one on the roads and, as I drove and smoked one cigarette after another, moments of excitement alternated with moments of rationality. But the more I thought that it was madness and I ought to go home, the more I put my foot down on the accelerator.

I arrived in Venice at dawn. After parking my car, I walked in the direction of Fulvio's house, while opposing thoughts were flooding over me. I stopped in a bar that had just opened, the still sleepy barista made me a coffee and I would have liked to tell him what I was doing. As I was paying I thought: "I must be mad."

I left. I walked quickly, with the sensation of being late, with the fear that he wouldn't wait for me, that he thought I wouldn't come. I soon arrived outside number 18. A sigh, and I rang the bell. The door opened in an instant: he was waiting for me. I went up the stairs with my heart in my mouth.

I was there, in front of the door. No spy hole, so he wasn't watching me. I shut my eyes a second after having taken in my hands the red blindfold that was tied to the door handle.

THE FEELINGS DON'T COME BACK

I put it on. I got undressed. I just kept on my stockings; without them I felt ill at ease.

I heard the door opening. I was trembling.

He took my hand to guide me; he didn't say anything. I felt that I was inside a warm environment, and I had the sense that it was a large space.

"I must be crazy . . . " I whispered.

"Ssshh . . . " He didn't say anything else.

He closed the door and let go of my hand. I was naked and I sensed him behind me; I felt him looking at me. He stroked my back, with a finger I think, making me shiver. He took my hand again and led me a few steps. He made me sit down on a small, low table, cushioned with leather.

He moved away. I was in a whirlwind of anxiety, fear, excitement.

I felt him brush the hair off my neck, then a mouth gliding against my neck, then kissing it. Warm lips and a gentle tongue running over my skin. I let my head fall back and he started to kiss me and lick me more boldly, descending to my swollen and aroused nipples. I couldn't hide my arousal and I didn't want to. It was his mouth that I wanted.

He sucked and licked my breasts as no one had ever done, alternating caresses from his tongue with little bites from eager teeth. Stretching myself out, I bent and spread my legs, resting my feet on the table. He entered me straight away with his hand, two fingers, maybe three. I gave a start, feeling his fingers sinking inside me, entering without any resistance, sliding in as far as they could, wet with my arousal. His fingers massaged me inside, pushing hard while his mouth became more and more insistent on my nipples. He was caressing one breast and devouring the other. I was so aroused that I couldn't hold back my first orgasm. I felt myself become even wetter.

He didn't stop. He kept on touching me inside and his mouth didn't move away from the nipple of my right breast. He seemed to have a thousand hands: with one he was still penetrating me vigorously, as if he hadn't noticed my orgasm, without altering his rhythm. With the other he touched me all over. I was lost, completely abandoned to the sensations so that I didn't know anymore what he was doing to me.

"Enter me, please." I wanted to be fucked.

"Ssshh . . . " Without taking his mouth from my nipple.

He took my hand and guided it to my clitoris. It was what I was waiting for: I began to masturbate myself while I felt every inch of my body being stimulated. Again he seemed to have a thousand hands. I came again. I was exhausted, abandoned on the table. And he took his hand from me and moved away completely.

I felt something coming near my mouth while a hand gently raised my head. A glass. Red wine. I drank.

As I was swallowing I felt him take my wrists, both at the same time, and tie them, fastening them to the table. I had a moment of bewilderment but he started to kiss my mouth, hungry for me. His hot mouth, wet and aggressive, aroused me incredibly and I began again as I felt my ankles being grasped. They too were tied to the table, my legs bent and open. I was his. Completely. I couldn't move.

He licked my lips; he penetrated my mouth with his forceful and arrogant tongue. He entered me with a single thrust. He must have been very well endowed because I felt him make a space for himself inside me as if he were enormous. An exquisite sensation. I felt filled, and tied like that I was even more aroused. He was fucking me as if I were his property, as if he wanted to break me. I wanted to masturbate myself but the bonds at my wrists prevented me. He kept on penetrating my mouth with his tongue and I was about to come again, when I felt a mouth resting on my nipple and starting to suck. At the same time a hand began to caress my clitoris intensely. I was dizzy with arousal. Two mouths were on my body, and two hands, perhaps three, were caressing me while I absorbed the thrusts, wanted to open myself up even more. An orgasm, and then another immediately afterward, while I didn't know anymore how many mouths and how many hands were roaming my body. He carried on fucking me, with force, hard. I heard several people panting, without ever talking. He took his mouth from mine and straight away I felt it filled by a penis. It was hot, as hard as the one that was fucking me. A smell of sex emanated from it, of a woman I would say, even though it wasn't the one that was penetrating me; that one had never come out of me. I started to suck it and lick it, following its movements, bathing it with saliva to feel it sliding over my tongue. I wanted it in my throat and he seemed to understand that because he started to push, thrusting it against my throat and taking my breath away. I didn't wonder about anything anymore; I didn't know how many people there were, I simply experienced the sensations I felt. I came several times, between hands that caressed me, penises that entered me, mouths that sucked at me.

Suddenly everything ended. Everyone moved away at the same time, leaving me on the edge of a very intense orgasm that was about to wash over me. I had a moment of panic. I knew they were watching me. I felt someone approaching my mouth: a leg, smooth. I licked it, raising my head to reach the groin, although I didn't know if I was licking the inside or the outside. It rested against my mouth and, moving my face toward what I thought was the inside of a thigh, my tongue felt a moistness as it brushed against what I immediately realised were labia. A woman. I carried on licking and she offered herself to my mouth, while another mouth rested on me, licking me in turn. I thought it was a man. With my tongue I stroked her clitoris as if it were my own. I licked it with a generous and welcoming tongue, gathering the fluids that continued to seep between the labia. She had an orgasm, and her coming aroused me even more. She took my head in her hands, pulling me toward her; my face was completely wet with her. She moved away after having come against me and I felt a tongue licking my face, cleaning the fluids that remained at the corners of my mouth.

I felt the fastenings at my wrists and ankles being untied and someone made me get up, gently. He made me kneel on the table, and in just an instant I felt myself being penetrated forcefully from behind. With a decisive thrust he entered me. It wasn't the same man as before, I was sure of that. He started to fuck me violently but I felt no pain. I wanted him to do it still harder. The woman started to kiss me, delicately, licking my lips and tongue with intensity and warmth. Rising up slowly, she let my mouth run down over her neck until she could put her nipple in my mouth, which I began to lick and suck greedily. I felt hot liquid trickling between my legs and I didn't know if the man who was penetrating me had come or if it was the result of my intense arousal. A hand began to stroke my buttocks and stimulate my anus, wetting their fingers between my thighs. Suddenly a firm blow, a slap on the buttocks, which excited me even more. I felt someone crouching behind me, against my back, and pushing at my opening. The man who was fucking me slowed down for a moment as the second man pushed and entered me, causing a sharp stab of pain. I cried out, pulling my mouth away from the woman's breast, but she held me by the hair and pressed my head against her nipple. Someone slapped my buttocks again as the two men penetrated me roughly together. The pain changed in an instant; it immediately became an incredible excitement. I felt myself bursting; I no longer knew where the pleasure was coming from, as a hand now started to masturbate me. I reached an unbelievably powerful orgasm—I thought I would die—and copious liquids gushed from my vagina. A hand began to massage the liquid on my legs while the two men continued to bore into my body, which by now was completely defenseless and ready to accept any further stimulus. The woman moved away and another penis filled my mouth. Three men then.

I was on that table, on my knees, filled in every possible orifice, and I was being driven mad by the excitement of being used that way. Someone kept on slapping my buttocks from time to time, and this sudden distraction from the sensation of being penetrated was enjoyable and thrilling.

Repeated orgasms. I felt them withdrawing and re-entering me, while the gentle hands of the woman stroked my back. We came, they came too, all inside me, coming out straight after. They began to lick me all over, wiping away the juices of their pleasure, and mine. They turned me round and I found myself lying on the table again. She put her pussy on my face—it was dripping wet. I wanted to see her being penetrated but I didn't ask to take off the blindfold; I wanted to stay in my own world, and I was scared that I would be constrained if I looked into their eyes. I slid two fingers inside her while with my eager tongue I caressed her clitoris. No one was touching me anymore and I sensed that they were watching me. I thrust inside her energetically and began to massage her inside. I wanted her pleasure, and I licked her and sucked her until I could feel her tremble and hear her gasp. I pushed more intensely inside her, and she cried out, tensing her legs and contracting, while from her vagina squirted a hot liquid on my face.

She caressed my wet face and kissed me, gently at first, then she lightly bit my lips. She whispered: "Good girl . . . " The first words I had heard in that room since I came in.

She got me up and led me for a few steps. She lowered me as if to sit me down and I felt myself touching the legs of one of the men. I tried to settle myself, sitting between his arms, my back to him. He was sitting on a sofa and guided me. I sat on him, letting him slide inside me, between my buttocks, in the still open orifice. I leaned against him with my back against his chest and immediately someone in front of me started to lick my clitoris, while I moved on the man who was penetrating me. I thought about the others who were watching me and I squeezed my nipples, harder and harder; I would have liked to tear them off. The mouth left my clitoris and someone entered me. Again there were two men fucking me. I came after a few minutes; by now, time no longer existed.

They sat me on the sofa and left me there. I stretched out. Nothing mattered to me anymore; I was content and satisfied, and I wanted to exist in these sensations.

After a few minutes, she came near to me and started to tenderly stroke my face, to kiss me, to lick my ears, my neck and my nipples again. She put a hand between my legs, I was sure it was hers. The gentleness was unmistakeable. I let myself be fondled, touched, entered. By this point I felt totally relaxed, my fissures were open and put up no resistance. She kissed me and touched me. And I became wet again.

She pushed two fingers inside, then three, then I felt her whole hand go beyond my pubic bone and I had the sensation of engulfing her. My orgasm was slow and strong, while I kissed her mouth as I had never done to a man.

She moved away from me, and I heard voices coming from a room nearby, without being able to distinguish how many people could be there or even what they were saying. They must have closed the door. I stayed motionless, without asking myself anything. For an instant I thought I would have got up and left; I was worn out. But I didn't. I fell asleep.

What woke me was the touch of hands that were opening my legs. Without a word, as before. They were using my body for their own pleasure, while providing pleasure to me as well. It was a strange situation, different, maybe dangerous, but I didn't sense that it was, even if every different stimulus that aroused without me expecting it was a provocation, an invasion, a transformation that was always unrestrained and unforeseen. I felt completely captive to their wishes, and, contrary to what logic would have expected, I felt safe. A hand was caressing my clitoris, which responded immediately to the stimulation. It was aroused, swollen; I felt it pulsating and I wanted them to suck it. The hand that was masturbating me was dexterous, pleasant, warm, slow.

A few moments later a feeling of cold together with the caress of the fingers: ice. The person who was touching me was alternating caresses and the pressure of their fingers with caresses and the pressure of an ice cube. My skin shuddered in response to the changes but it wasn't the ice that was causing the shudders but arousal, again. I didn't know if it was a man or a woman, but the caresses were gentle and intense. He, or she, slid the ice from my clitoris to my vagina and with a tongue pushed it inside to then find it again. I felt the ice melting inside me and the mouth that went to recover it provided me with unknown sensations. This game lasted a long time, with me endlessly verging on orgasm without ever attaining it. Inside I was begging it not to stop; I would have liked it to continue forever. He kept on kissing my clitoris, holding an ice cube in his mouth. Between his kisses he ran his tongue over the ice, skillfully, then he guided the cube to my vagina with his mouth and pushed it inside with his tongue. He was filling me with ice, which I felt melting and mixing with the liquids of my body.

Suddenly, lost in these sensations, I felt a nipple being squeezed by something cold: a clamp, I thought. It hurt. It aroused me. The other was also soon grasped in that metal grip. The mouth had stopped, moved away. I was full of ice and my nipples held tight. I extended my hands to touch myself but someone took hold of them and turned me, making my pelvis protrude from the sofa, lifting up my legs. I felt the water dripping, coming out of my vagina, and a mouth bent over to lick me and dry it. I could still feel ice inside me and someone started to fuck me, violently. The hard cock pushed the ice all the way in. I felt it pressing against me and every time it slid out I impatiently wanted it to go back in, pushing harder. He turned me, he made me kneel with my chest on the sofa, and while cold liquid still dripped from my vagina, he leaned against me and plunged between my buttocks. The pain was intense and I cried out, but he put a hand over my mouth, continuing to thrust and pulling my head toward him, gripping me by the hair. I felt his panting breath on my neck, my nipples swelling despite the grip of the clamps, my vagina throbbing, hot, even more swollen perhaps because of the ice, wanting to be filled. I came again while he, after a few violent thrusts, withdrew to ejaculate on my back.

I sank back, exhausted, in the same position on my knees, while a mouth licked the sperm from my back. That same mouth came to lick my lips, wetting them with saliva and sperm, almost as if it were a reward.

I stayed like that, inert, then two of them took me and made me lie on the floor on my stomach. The biting at my nipples hurt now. Pressed against the floor they seemed to burn. Suddenly a feeling of intense heat on my back; small pinpricks of fire were burning my skin while someone started to lick my buttocks. They lifted my pelvis, raising me onto my knees. I was completely open in front of their eyes and at intervals they continued to do something to me that gave me a feeling of scalding, wax perhaps, that was dripping on my shoulders. They entered me, again. A man fucked me while a vibrator pressed against my anus, trying to widen it. It must have been enormous, so much so that the penis of the man who was fucking me felt tiny. My nipples, which were swelling, tight in the vices, seemed to explode. I screamed with pleasure, while the skillful hand managed to get the vibrator inside me, pushing it as far as it would go.

They left me there. Lifeless. I had come to the point where I thought I would die there, in their hands, being used for their pleasure. But I didn't care at all. I fell asleep again.

It was hours before I opened my eyes again. I wasn't blindfolded anymore. I was lying on a bed, the room was in semi-darkness, and the door closed. I was alone. I struggled to get up. I was still naked and my body was covered in little swellings, especially on my breasts and stomach. Just brushing against my nipples made them hurt.

I breathed deeply and opened the door that led to a very large and light room. It was a loft apartment, elegant and sophisticated. There was no one there. No sound. On the sofa were laid out my clothes and my stockings, which someone must have taken off me. I went towards the only door there was, next to the entrance door. I opened it and went into a bathroom, almost relieved not to find anyone in there. I had a shower. There was just one robe folded on the bathroom cupboard, freshly laundered, and a towel. I went back into the main room, I got dressed, and after a few minutes I noticed that there was a note by the stockings.

"You were good. Come back tomorrow. You have to be here at ten o'clock."

I threw myself onto the sofa, almost devastated by those words. I stayed there, I don't know for how long, maybe I was hoping that someone would arrive. I looked around a bit to work out whether it was really Fulvio's house. But there was nothing that made me think of him: not a photo, not an item of clothing, nothing. A sterile apartment.

I got up, took my bag, which they had put on the low table in front of the sofa—it must have been the one on which I had lain a few hours before—I looked at my watch: seven in the evening. I must have slept for ages.

I went out, closing the door behind me, with one certainty: I wouldn't return. I ran down the stairs and hurried during the walk to pick up my car. I just wanted to go home.

During the journey I thought again about the hours that had passed, the pleasure I felt, the intensity of the sensations. And gradually as the miles flowed past, the reality of what I had experienced seemed to drift further away.

I got home. Fulvio didn't look for me either that day or ever again. That same evening I went out to dinner with a few friends and, looking at my watch at ten o'clock, I smiled. It had been an intensely pleasurable experience. But I wouldn't repeat it.

Today, seeing him again by chance, brings me back to the thousand questions that I asked myself in the subsequent days. It hadn't been easy to rationalize what had happened, more than anything because I had been subjugated by him to the point where I let myself be used however they wanted, but without ever knowing, in fact, if he too was one of those people, if he had touched me, if he had entered me or if he had just watched me.

But now that's enough thinking about Fulvio. I have to get dinner ready for Angela.

I get under the shower, and, while I'm soaping myself, brushing my nipples reminds me of those clamps that evening. The memory of that flurry of sensations, the mouth and hand of that woman . . . I abandon myself to my hands with the desire to feel hers on my body, while Fulvio watches, attentive. I caress myself slowly, while the water runs over my skin, until I come, thinking about the hand of that woman that sank into me, plunging in beyond my pubic bones.

I get out of the shower and put on a T-shirt and a pair of panties. I switch on a CD while I start to prepare something for dinner. There are still another couple of hours, so I don't have to rush. I prepare meat and vegetables, I put them in the oven to cook, and I settle down to read a book that I bought the week before.

I fall asleep, without realizing, and the ring of the doorbell wakes me up. "Who is it?" I ask via the entry phone. "It's me, Livia. Angela."

Heavens, it's eight o'clock . . . I must have slept like a log!

"Come in, Angela. Come on up. Sorry I'm like this, but I had a shower and then fell asleep reading a book."

"Don't worry, Livia. I don't mind. You're fine as you are."

There's a strong smell in the air, but it doesn't smell burned. It must have turned out alright. Angela follows me into the kitchen, putting her bag down on a bench and a bottle of red wine on the kitchen counter. I set the table while Angela tells me about her holidays, and as I take the dish out of the oven distractedly I burn the palm of my hand. I'm always the same.

The evening passes pleasantly and we talk about thousands of things. After dinner we sit down in my study and I show Angela a few photos I've recently taken in Oslo.

"Would you like a drop of whisky, Angela?"

"Yes, go on . . . perhaps with a bit of ice . . . "

The thought of ice takes me back to Fulvio. I feel dizzy again at the thought of him being here and the thought that I could bump into him again at any time. I go into the kitchen and then return to the study with the ice bucket and the glasses. I hand one to Angela and sit down next to her on the sofa. I put ice in Angela's glass and in mine, but I'm just putting a cube in my mouth when it slides out of my hands and inside my T-shirt.

"Don't take it out!" Angela tells me.

I look at her questioningly. Angela springs at me and puts a hand between my breasts to search for the ice as she rests her lips on mine and slides her tongue in to kiss me, as if she has been waiting for this moment forever. I let her do it, and I respond to her kiss with all the passion I have in me after having seen Fulvio again. She takes the ice cube and, holding it between her fingers, she brushes it gently against my nipple, making it swollen, and then she puts it in her mouth. We continue kissing, passing the ice cube from my mouth to hers until it melts completely, while Angela caresses my breasts, over the T-shirt. Her mouth moves lower, kissing my neck and licking me, until it comes to rest on a nipple. She licks it and sucks it while I feel my arousal growing. I slide a hand under her skirt, caressing her thigh and moving it up towards her groin. Her skin is warm, smooth and delicate. I desire her, I want her. I get up and kneel down in front of her. I hold her by the buttocks to make her slide forward, pulling her toward my face.

Angela is aroused. She looks me straight in the eye, waiting for me to touch her. I lift her skirt to her hips, I pull her toward me and, as I look at her face, I rest my mouth on her thigh. I start to lick her and kiss her slowly, moving toward her groin. I gently pull aside her knickers; she is very wet. I put my mouth on her clitoris, encircling it with my lips and sucking, giving her a pleasure that is so immediate that I feel her tremble and come straight away.

"You were aroused, eh?! . . . you wanted my mouth . . . "

Angela agrees with her eyes, smiling mischievously. I slide my head between her legs again, relishing her pleasure, and I push two fingers inside her . . .

I want to make her come, with all the passion that came back instinctively after having seen Fulvio.

The feelings don't come back. They stay inside you.

The Spa

HEATHCLIFF

All he was wearing were the thin disposable paper panties, of a faint, almost transparent, white that he had just put on in place of his robe.

Francesca swallowed with difficulty. After two years working as a masseuse in the spa, at the rate of twenty or thirty massages a day, the last thing that could embarrass her was a semi-naked person, whether it be a man or a woman. In fact, her particular skill lay in appearing so at ease that the client also found it the most natural thing in the world to lie in front of her covered by only that small triangle of paper, ready to let her put her hands on their body. And ninety-nine percent of the time, she didn't have to make an effort.

But it didn't often happen that she found herself massaging a hunk like the man in front of her at the moment. To be exact, it had never happened to her. Various well-built young men had ended up under her hands, muscular and athletic, and maybe with a nice face as well, and something interesting between their legs, but there had been nothing comparable. She had felt a certain amount of enjoyment in massaging them, naturally, but that had borne no relation to the heat she could now feel spreading like liquid between her thighs.

Francesca felt hot even though under her smock she was wearing just pants and a bra, and she wondered, embarrassed, whether there was a chance she was blushing. She was almost certain she was, and the fear of her blushes revealing to him how much the sight of his naked body was affecting her made her feel uncomfortable in a way she never had before with other clients. But at the same time the prospect of filling her hands with those muscles made her tremble with expectation.

"Please lie down on the bed," she said to him, smiling sweetly, and she appreciated the slightly self-conscious smile that he gave her in reply.

He was about the same age as her, brown hair no more than half an inch long, and even shorter on the back of his neck, and an attractive, regular and masculine face, with deep-set eyes of an indistinct color somewhere between grey and dark green. But however beguiling his face, the thing that had fascinated Francesca as soon as she set eyes on him was his body. He had the good fortune of being athletic and well proportioned, and it was clear that he had improved upon nature with intense and frequent workouts at the gym; the result was a physique that left you open-mouthed, it was so well developed and sculpted. Every muscle was bulging and defined, shamelessly shown off, as if it corresponded to an individual erection for each part of his anatomy. His muscles had the same effect on her as an erection would have had: namely, that of a masculinity overflowing with strength and vigor, which promised every type of pleasure for anyone lucky enough to enjoy it.

And now that he was lying almost totally naked under her hands, the feel of that incredibly still and firm flesh was unsettling her more than she would have liked to admit. She had made him lie face down and had started by massaging his head and neck, broader and more muscular than any neck Francesca had ever touched, and then lost herself among the ridges and depressions of the wide expanse of his shoulders and his back. Despite trying hard not to think impure thoughts about that fabulous body, Francesca was more and more aroused. Also because, however pleasant the touch of her hands, none of her clients had ever let out the satisfied whimpers that he was uttering now, as if he had the deliberate intention of provoking her. They were so sensual that anyone who had heard them without being able to see the scene would have thought that, instead of a simple massage, the man was enjoying the services of someone's mouth, and services performed pretty well at that. Self-conscious, Francesca hoped that there was no one in the waiting room who could hear those grunts and get the wrong idea about the services she provided to her clients; however, she remembered very well that he had arrived together with a friend who was a dozen years older than him, and, if she had to be honest, she remembered him so well because she couldn't help looking at him too. He was definitely less handsome, but he had the same build and height, and he was even more masculine and virile.

Meanwhile, her client was having more or less the same thoughts as she was, as he felt her hands expertly kneading the muscles of his back. Her woman's touch was reawakening in his groin a desire for pussy that he hadn't felt for quite some time. Despite the relaxing music that was filling the air, already saturated with the sweet perfume of citrus and vanilla, and the disgusting stress-relieving herbal tea that they had made him drink, he felt as coiled as a spring. Or at least as tight as the front of the girl's smock, full to bursting with breasts so ample that the buttons strained. He had seen her naked skin peeping between the edges of the smock as they were pulled apart by the bulk of those generous tits, and that had been enough to trigger his desire to feel them under his tongue, and to harden the large nipples that he imagined hidden inside her bra. His friend Marco kept him on a strict diet of muscles and cock, and, after plentiful rations of hard masculine flesh, the thought of that soft and voluminous bosom into which he could sink his face was stimulating appetites he thought had dulled. He had a hard-on, and he was wondering, full of embarrassment, what he would do when the girl asked him to lie on his back. His cock would have stood upright in plain view in that ridiculous disposable paper loincloth that she had made him put on, and he had no chance of being able to hide the effect she was having on him. However, thinking it over, perhaps it was better not to hide anything, he reflected, sneering to himself. Maybe the young lady would have been flattered by the side effect of her massage . . . Federico already saw himself with her straddling his cock, her large breasts bouncing to the rhythm of the strokes with which she was pushing down on him, and her open mouth moaning and begging him to fuck her. He let out a sensuous groan, pressing his totally erect cock against the bed as discreetly as he could. He abandoned himself to the fantasies that were whirling around in his mind, enjoying the sensation of her hands on his skin. He started to emphasize with more and more shameless little grunts the feeling of well-being that the massage was provoking, perfectly aware of the sexual implications of that deliberate display of delight.

But he wasn't expecting to get a result straight away. His breathing caught in his throat when he felt them, smooth, firm and hot, sinking onto his back. Tits, large tits. Soft, but with the tips of the nipples already erect at the first touch. Francesca's brown curls tickled his skin as she pressed her breasts against him. Federico felt his cock, which was already hard, tightening and swelling even more, and his heart pumping quickly in veins dilated by the excitement. He swallowed his saliva, hesitant. He wanted to fuck, he had no doubt about that. More than just a want, he suddenly realized he had an overwhelming need for it, as if his craving for a female body, ignored for months, had exploded inside him all in one go, leaving him at the mercy of an animal and primordial instinct. But exactly because he could feel that urge simmering powerfully in his blood, the fear of making a false move and wasting his opportunity prompted him to let Francesca take the next step and to see how far she would go. Anyway, it was clear that she didn't lack initiative, judging from how her naked body was now rubbing against him, smooth and soft as velvet, so much more smooth and soft than what he was used to that it seemed to him as alluring as a new world.

Not that Francesca was usually so enterprising. She would have never dared behave in that way with a perfect stranger, however attractive he might be. If Federico had been standing in front of her, watching her doing what she was doing, Francesca would never have had the courage to take off her smock first, and then her bra and her knickers, and to lean over him to brush his sides with her erect nipples. But seeing him lying there on the massage bed, almost completely naked, waiting for her magic touch, she hadn't been able to resist. There was something so inviting in his unaware and abandoned pose, almost defenseless, that Francesca had felt the most blatant temptation stimulating her between her legs, and urging her to do with him what she wanted. It wasn't even necessary for him to participate much, although she would definitely have preferred to feel inside her the stiffness of his member. But for now all he had to do was lie still where he was, without escaping her caresses. She wanted to touch every inch of his statuesque body, rub him down with the palms of her hands and brush against him with her fingertips, but that would have been what her job entailed, and it wasn't enough for her. She wanted to caress him with her breasts, let him feel their weight all over his body, and enjoy the thrill she would give him by sliding her nipples over his skin. Then, when that game had excited her until she felt wet and hot between her legs, she would caress him with her pussy, straddling him with her legs apart, rubbing her clitoris against his firm flesh.

Federico felt her tickle his back with her hard nipples, then press her body against his as if she wanted to make him aware of the swelling of those large breasts, and the desire to fondle them grew in his hands. He moaned, and stretched his arms behind him to touch them. He let out a satisfied "oh" when he grasped one in his hand, and he gently investigated its texture, both soft and full. Then he found her nipple, and started to play with it between his thumb and index finger. Francesca's excitement spiraled when Federico's hands began to massage her breasts, and her pussy filled her with new juices. The stimulation of her nipples was causing an unbearable tension to develop between her thighs, which she instinctively sought to release in a feeling of pleasure, pressing her pelvis onto Federico's buttocks. In turn, Federico rhythmically pushed his erection against the bed, adding more spice to her rubbing. Finally, she sat astride Federico, her pussy open and crushed against his buttocks, and started to ride him while Federico continued playing with her large breasts. Her breathing became labored, and little cries started to escape from her lips while the pleasure rose between her legs, more irresistible with every second that passed. Federico would have liked to turn over, lie her down on the bed and sink his cock into her pussy, which he could feel, wet with desire, on his buttocks, but he sensed that Francesca was already enjoying things as they were, and he didn't want to stop her. His ass had never given pleasure to a woman, and the idea aroused him and made him feel the way he loved to feel: a body at the mercy of others' lust, whether those others be men or women. He would let her come the way she wanted to, and then he would throw her onto the bed and fuck her with all the fire that had built up during two months abstaining from women. "You like riding me like that, eh, little whore? Oh, but this is nothing . . . You should turn me over and ride my dick if you really want to come," he said, while he kept on touching her breasts and her nipples, and Francesca couldn't help picturing how huge his erection must be and how it would have been delicious to feel it inside her, and she came with a cry, her eyes closed and her hands clenched over Federico's, which were still playing with her nipples. Then she gradually lessened the strength of her thrusts, until she was left languidly rocking her pelvis against Federico's buttocks, her eyes still closed and with a pleasant, intoxicated, light-headed feeling.

"Hey, sweetheart, usually I'm the one who plays that game," said a masculine voice behind her. Francesca turned with a shamefaced start. The friend who had accompanied Federico was looking at her, smiling, from the doorway that linked through to the waiting room. He was wearing a robe and slippers. Completely taken up with her orgasm, Francesca hadn't heard him come in, but judging by the protuberance poking out from under the robe, he must have been there long enough to have enjoyed a good part of the show. The man came into the room and closed the door behind him, making sure that the lock clicked shut. "I mean, Federico's arse is mine, even if he'd give it to anyone, and this is the umpteenth time he's proved it. So I think I'm entitled to compensation."

"Okay, Marco . . . we'll do all the sums you want later. But for now let me enjoy myself, okay?" Federico replied, sounding fairly pissed off, as if he didn't appreciate the intrusion at all. In fact, the mere presence of Marco was increasing his arousal, but he didn't want to let Francesca know that just now when she wanted to be fucked by a man. Marco seemed to be ignoring his plea. He went up to Federico, in front of the bed, and when he was a few inches from his face he untied the belt of the robe and pulled the edges apart. An enormous cock popped out, and straight away set about goading Federico's lips, leaving copious traces of pre-cum under his nose. "Come on, be a good boy, Federico," he urged him, like he would have done with a naughty child. Federico grunted, and Francesca didn't know if it was a protest or an encouragement. But then she saw him open his mouth and take into it the glans, immense and inflamed with desire, and do everything he could with his hands to stimulate the whole shaft as well, as it was too large and long to be swallowed even halfway. She was completely disconcerted by it, but the surprise of seeing her partner giving pleasure to a man as well as to her didn't deaden her own arousal, quite the opposite. She watched Federico for a few minutes while he was engrossed with that gigantic erection, feeling the desire to taste that cock herself, for it to excite her pussy again after the orgasm she had just enjoyed. She had never had a man with a member as impressive as his, and it was as if she were bewitched. She stretched out on Federico's body, trying to touch it with her tongue and take it between her lips, but Federico was more convenient and more eager, and once Marco's huge glans disappeared into his mouth he relished it, sucking like a madman unless Marco stopped him to change rhythm or to press it on his nose and on his cheeks. But then Marco became aware of Francesca's efforts to have her share of his cock, and he intervened on her behalf. "Federico, change over now. Get up and let her lie down."

Federico got up from the bed, slightly reluctant to let go of Marco's cock. Between the unusual massage that Francesca had administered with her tits and her pussy, and the enjoyment he felt giving Marco a blow job, his cock had become as hard as marble, and it sprang obscenely from the disposable paper pants that Francesca had made him put on a while ago, and that he hastily tore off and threw away. Marco took off his robe, and the two men stood naked in front of Francesca, ready to transform a boring day at work into game of endless pleasure. Federico's cock would have seemed enormous if there hadn't been the unflattering comparison with Marco's exaggerated size, and Francesca couldn't believe her eyes. She could feel a more and more irresistible desire rising inside her to play with those two large cocks, to smother them with attention and pleasure, and to get them to fill her in turn. The two men stood one opposite the other, one at each side of the bed on which Francesca lay, and started to drag their cocks over her face and to compete for her tongue and her mouth. She greedily licked and sucked, moving from one to the other, trying to do to one the same thing she had just done to the other, delighted by the whimpering and indecent encouragement of the two. Meanwhile, the need to feel them thrusting inside her pussy as well had made her unconsciously open her legs, and the more she sucked them with her mouth the more her juices gushed slick and shining between the fully opened lips of her vagina. When Federico and Marco began to knead her tits as well, one each, massaging them and lightly touching her nipples, Francesca felt she was being driven mad by the stimulation. She clutched at the cock she was sucking as if it could fuck her in the mouth until she reached orgasm; she moaned and raised her pelvis, opening her legs wider in a desperate pursuit of pleasure. Federico inserted a finger in her drenched pussy, Marco pressed down on her clitoris, rubbing it in a circular motion, and soon Francesca started to feel such delight that only Marco's cock filling her mouth stopped her from crying out. She came with a searing orgasm, so intense that it was almost painful, which left her exhausted. But she couldn't let herself lazily savor the languid sweetness that enveloped her afterward, because the two men hadn't come yet, and they too wanted their satisfaction.

"I want to come between your tits," announced Federico, who had been entertaining that desire ever since she had started massaging him. He made Francesca get off the bed, too awkward and narrow to accommodate both of them, and moved the thin mattress that covered it onto the floor. Then he invited Francesca to lie down on the mattress and he straddled her level with her tits. He inserted his throbbing erection in the groove between her breasts, and he pushed them together above it, starting to slide his cock in the warm and soft hollow that he had created. In the meantime, every now and then he went back to stimulating her nipples, very soon arousing between her legs the desire to come again. His cock began to move more vigorously, so vigorously that at full stroke Francesca's tongue was able to tease his glans and catch the copious drops of fluid that seeped from it. Sometimes he moved from her breasts to her mouth and thrust between her lips until the pleasure became almost irresistible, and then he would pull out and sink back between the breasts squeezed one against the other.

Marco followed the scene with a mixture of envy and jealousy. It wasn't the first time he had found himself watching Federico with a woman, but his reaction was always the same: Federico looked to him more virile than ever while he was enjoying her, and that display of masculinity aroused him tremendously, but at the same time the secret fear that Federico could prefer the graceful body of a woman to the strength of his always drove him to seek to reaffirm in one way or another his mastery over him. He went to stand in front of him, his legs wide apart on either side of Francesca's head; he put a hand on the back of Federico's neck and he lowered his face onto his cock.

Federico grunted, opened his mouth and welcomed it inside with gusto, as he slid his own between the equally eager lips of Francesca. The sensation was sublime: his cock thrust into her mouth while Marco vigorously moved his own back and forth, and faced with that double pleasure Federico couldn't hold back any longer. He felt the orgasm rising inexorably from the depths of his being, rising from the center of his groin into every push he gave and received, bursting from his swollen and taut testicles until it flooded his cock with ecstasy . . . He pulled out of her mouth and sank the final violent stabs of pleasure between her tits, spraying spurts of cum on her breasts, her chin, and her throat.

Marco took his cock from Federico's mouth in time to enjoy his moans of pleasure, and the sight of Federico's member, wet with sperm and still being rubbed between her breasts, reawakened all his feelings of lust: he leaned over and started licking all that cum like a starving man.

"You like tits flavoured with cum, eh cocksucker?" Federico said to him, pushing his face onto Francesca's body. And it was true. Her large breasts inspired in him a feeling of wonder at least as great as his cock did in her; in his limited experience with women, until that moment he had never known how to overcome his reverential awe for those two rounded orbs, which, on the other hand, catalyzed Federico's attention. But now, with his nose and mouth plunging between the softness of those breasts and the stiffness of Federico's cock, and the smell and the taste of the cum intoxicating him, Marco was lost in a new paradise.

An astonished Francesca was watching him licking and sucking her tits as enthusiastically as he licked and sucked Federico's cock, and the unfamiliar sight increased the thrill she felt inside. Her nipples, tantalized by both Federico's fingers and Marco's tongue, were sending stabs of uncontrollable pleasure right down to her burning hot pussy, and a longing to be penetrated was flowing through her thighs.

As if he could read her mind, Federico turned over and got on all fours above her, his face buried in her pelvis, his cock, not yet soft, dangling and brushing against her lips, and his ass offered up to Marco's tongue. They began a bizarre sixty-nine in which Federico replayed on Francesca's pussy the things he could feel Marco's mouth doing to give him pleasure between his buttocks, while Francesca just stretched out her tongue between one cry and the next to stroke the tip of his cock. When he thought that Francesca was ready to come he broke off and began to tease her with words.

"Do you want to feel it inside now?"

"Yes . . . yes, fuck me."

"My friend hasn't come yet. He'll fuck you," said Federico, and immediately after he gave a little lick to Francesca's clitoris that made her judder with pleasure.

"Yes . . ." groaned Francesca, thinking that it didn't matter at all which of the two fucked her just as long as someone fucked her. But Federico hadn't yet finished preparing her for Marco.

"My friend is very big, little one . . . are you sure you want it?"

"Yes . . . yes . . ." she whimpered. "I want it inside me, please, please . . ."

"You want a cock so big it'll split you in two, baby?"

Francesca felt faint with desire. She tried to raise her pelvis and rub her clitoris against Federico's mouth, sure that the touch of his tongue would have been enough to make her reach the orgasm she yearned for, but Federico didn't let her. "Tell us what you want, baby."

"I want the huge cock of your friend . . . I want him to fuck me like a whore," gasped Francesca, beside herself with readiness.

Federico let Marco take his place between Francesca's legs, and Marco entered her. The way in which Federico had been arousing Francesca had given Marco the same need to fuck that used to burn in his cock when it was him talking to Federico like that, and he pushed his way into her impatiently, plunging decisively in a single thrust. He found her pussy wet with slippery liquids and open compared with the resistance of the sphincter he was used to, and he surrendered to the instinctive urge to thrust roughly. Francesca let out a cry of pain, and found Federico's cock blocking her mouth. The taste of her pussy under his tongue and the perverse relish of the words he was saying to her between one lick and the next had made him become completely hard again, and now, already, Federico wanted to come a second time. He regretted having given up his place between her legs to his friend, but he pressed his cock against Francesca's lips in search of another soft, warm opening into which he could slide. Francesca took him in her mouth, trying not to grit her teeth with the pain. Although she was fully aroused, Marco's cock really seemed to be tearing her flesh, and a grimace of agony made her tense her face at every thrust. Federico imagined he knew what she was feeling. Something not that different from what he felt when Marco bored into his ass with his twelve inches of cock, and he felt as if he were dying. But he liked it. From that lacerating pain, pleasure blossomed inside him like a flower in the mud, even more intense because of the contrast from which it grew, and it filled him thrust after thrust until he would explode without even needing to touch himself.

"Good girl . . . " he started to say to Francesca in an encouraging tone, while he gave her his glans to suck. "Good . . . like that . . . Take it all like a good little whore. Can you feel it filling you completely? . . . Can you feel it's bigger than all the pricks you've ever had? It hurts a bit now, I know what it's like, you feel open and stretched as if it was splitting you in two, but then you'll feel the pleasure behind the pain, and you'll feel that if he pulled it out now you'd want it again . . . "

It was then that Francesca started to really feel pleasure. Federico's words seemed to anticipate by a fraction of a second the sensations in her body, and soon the burning of the first thrusts became a mounting and invincible warmth that was sweeping her again toward orgasm. Federico saw the light change in her eyes in an unmistakable expression of lust, and he saw her body greedily welcome Marco's thrusts, without drawing back, but rather searching for the rhythm to enjoy them more, and even to communicate to him the same feeling. Marco kept on pushing, with slow, deep thrusts, hollowing out pleasure inside her. The unaccustomed sensation of her pussy filled him with an enjoyment that was subtly different from the one the body of a man gave him, more fluid and smooth, and he felt himself sinking into her like the sea, in a warm and dark sea where pleasure was submerging him in waves, and his cock was longing to drown.

"Federico . . . ," he said, when the waves that were seizing him came so close together that he felt disorientated, and Federico took his cock from Francesca's mouth and offered it to Marco, who clung to it like a shipwrecked man holding onto a rope. Every time he pushed forward between Francesca's legs, Federico's cock rubbed against the roof of his mouth, and every time he withdrew he tried to hold it inside with a noisy sucking, and once it came out he fondled the tip with his tongue.

Jealous, Francesca joined in the competition to catch Federico's cock in her mouth, as Federico slipped between the two of them. Marco and Francesca began to take turns to suck him, both of them hoping to get him to come and to take in their mouth a thick cascade of cum. The situation was so irresistible for each of them that soon none of the three were capable of controling their feelings any longer. Francesca and Marco were fighting over Federico's cock like two eager tarts, and while Marco's thrusts became more and more powerful and close together, Francesca's pussy throbbed and in the depths of her womb pulsated an earth-shattering pleasure that she had never experienced before. Federico read in her staring eyes her imminent orgasm and slipped his cock into her half-open mouth. "Take both of us . . . " he gasped, he too feeling that he could no longer hold back the tremor of pleasure that was trembling inside him. "Take them like a whore, fuck ... his deep in your pussy, mine deep in your throat ... make us come together, make us fill you with cum at the same time ..."

Francesca exploded in an orgasm more intense than any she had ever had. The pleasure that overwhelmed her took her into another world, so much so that she almost wasn't aware of Federico and Marco both coming at the same time as her, splashing her with sperm inside and out. She ended up with their rivulets of cum at the corners of her mouth, on her cheeks and on her throat, and lower down between her legs, and the satisfaction of feeling like a slut made her pussy throb in the final spasms of delight. Then she felt their tongues eagerly brushing against her wet skin, as each of them licked with gusto the sperm of the other without wasting a single drop. "Oh God," she sighed weakly, stretching out and opening her legs to let both of them clean her completely. "It's hard to say which of us is the biggest whore here ... "

The Hill of the Goats

GIORGIA REBECCA GIRONI

The first day of summer arrived swiftly this year, after a dry autumn and a too rainy spring that rotted the undergrowth. The leaves of the trees quiver against the purple sky, leaning up against the edge of the night like cats, and in the yard surrounding the villa there is a marked smell of moss. Antonia breathes it in deeply, then, her hands trembling, picks up her skirt at the front and moves quickly, from the washhouse to the first tree, skipping over the black earth of the estate.

It's a strange night. An eerie tension flows through everything: it slides over the hills dotted with bushes, moves along the course of the tree line, dives headfirst into the pond, making the frogs take flight, and between Antonia's girlish legs, moderating her steps. She feels her knickers full of it and clenches her thighs, trying to see into the dense black hiding between the oaks. She can't see anyone yet on the road; the track snakes silently, vanishing at times behind the hills. The moon is round and high in the sky.

Although the brightness of the moon has lit up the landscape, the darkness, between the tree trunks, seems able to swallow up everything. Digging with her big toe, hunting for pebbles, the young girl stares into the darkness for a while, uncertain about what to do, until the wind carries to her ears the echo of distant cries. The noises are faint, hardly discernible, but they don't resemble any countryside sound. She holds her breath and stands listening. The voices chant confused words that slowly take shape. "Idiot," "Devil," "Pussy"; definitely "Pussy."

It must be them; Antonia recognizes the sound of their voices. The person who said "Devil" was certainly Ferdinando, the shepherd's son: brown hair above a wide and expressionless face. That gap-toothed mouth of his is good only for uttering swearwords, like his father's: when bad blood speaks, it does so clearly and loudly. Sure enough, here he is appearing first, Ferdinando. He leaps out from behind a bend, with his hands in his pockets and a toad-like jump, and kicks something as he moves forward, perhaps a rotten fruit, perhaps a hard clod of earth, rolled into the path from a field.

The others, behind him, are more graceful. There's Giovanni, the oldest, who moves confidently even in the semidarkness, and his brother Francesco, who looks like the son of a prince, blond and charming, like the hero of a fairy tale.

With her eyes focused on him, Antonia hastily descends the steep slope that separates her from the road, tackling it in a zigzag, as agile as a goat. The young boy looks at her in turn, a flash of unhappiness in his clear eyes, before lowering his gaze again to her bare calves streaked with dirt, and then, further on still, bringing it to a stop among the thin branches of a bush.

Once she plants her feet on the dirt road, she lets her skirt go and it falls back into place.

"Why is he here too? We didn't agree on that," she mutters, her gaze black and deep, a faint blush warming her cheeks.

Francesco shrugs his shoulders; he makes as if to say something, but Giovanni quickly pushes himself forward, elbowing him.

"Because there needs to be an odd number of us," he replies bluntly.

The girl widens her dark eyes, her eyebrows form two arches on a forehead striped with her loose hair. She opens one hand in front of her and counts with her fingers, laboriously, a grimace making her look ugly: one, two, three. Still holding the middle finger of her left hand between her thumb and her index finger, she finally looks up, suspicious.

"We were an odd number before, now there are four of us."

"So what? You don't count," the boy responds, plunging his hands into his pockets, and he thrusts his groin forward then pretends to head home. "But if you're not interested anymore in getting rid of your sister . . ."

"Of course I'm interested!"

"Then there has to be at least three of us, otherwise the devil won't come. A friend from Perugia told me that."

Antonia thinks about it. The reason seems valid, so she drops her arms to her sides and drops her objections. Her arms are strong, a farm worker's arms. Her legs are strong too, as she takes a step forward, joining the group as it starts back on the path in the opposite direction. In no time at all she reaches Francesco, who is at the back of the group. His blond hair looks greenish in the moonlight, and his skin paler than ever.

Sensing her presence at his side, the boy's shoulders tense. He carries on staring straight in front of him, at the spot where his brother's head is outlined against the starry sky toward which they are moving in silence.

For a while they walk along side by side, him pretending not to know she's there next to him, and her skipping barefoot, her hands buried in her light-colored skirt. Then boredom gets the upper hand. Antonia feels it, it makes her lips prickle.

"I didn't know you knew about these things," she murmurs.

Francesco furrows his eyebrows. In the darkness they look like two thin ribbons, much thinner than hers. Quickly glancing at them, the girl runs her index finger over her own, thick and dark, before smiling slightly.

"Is this the first time?" she asks.

Finally the boy deigns to pay attention to her; turning only his eyes, he focuses on her in the shadow cast by his head. They are the same age, but Antonia seems more worldly wise: she has the allure that animals have when they're in heat. Recognizing this, he reddens. He avoids looking at her, as if the sight of her could burn, and, without even having noticed his unease, his brother gets involved in his attempt to escape.

"Leave him alone," he orders her. "He has to concentrate, otherwise the ceremony won't work."

Antonia blushes. She opens her lips, then slowly closes them. The words die in her mouth, leaving a trace of bitterness that dries her saliva. She thinks she can feel her mouth trembling. For a few feet she tries to picture it, black and dry, until her courage returns.

"How much longer now?" she asks.

"We have to get to the foot of the mountains. There's a place there that'll do," answers Giovanni, a step behind Ferdinando.

The girl looks straight in front of her. The Sibillini Mountains silently keep watch over the valley. They seem close, so close that she feels she could touch them just by stretching out her arm. The moon, too, seems close. It's a magical night, this night. A mysterious tension flows through everything; even Francesco, she smiles.

After a good hour of walking, shortly after the umpteenth pair of ash trees, Giovanni and Ferdinando come off the road, climbing the banks to find themselves in the center of a field bounded by a dense row of fir trees. Antonia, behind Francesco, leaves the path and looks at the lazy sweep of the fallow field, in which the turned earth still preserves some traces of human activity, and at Francesco, who is moving across the field, stumbling between the hollows. Further on, the trunks of the trees create a prison crowned with foliage; through its bars one can glimpse only darkness.

"Are you sure this is the right way?" asks the boy, wiping his forehead with his forearm.

Ferdinando signals to him to come closer. He is stocky and dark; on closer view he looks like a sinister spirit.

"It was my father, who's a shepherd, who told me about this place. A place that looks exactly like Hell's Gorge."

"There's water?" Antonia cheers up.

"No, stupid. It's a place where witches used to meet."

At this claim, the young girl holds her breath. Her eyes light up, fastening on the dark-haired boy's face like a trap, but her body flees hastily to Francesco's shadow.

Ferdinando twists his mouth into a crooked sneer.

"To get there, we have to cut through the woods. We'll be there in about ten minutes," he says, and already he is looking forward to her taste, his fists hidden in his pockets. After a last long look he turns his back on the two to move toward Giovanni, who is waiting in the shade of the tree trunks, black and grey like a ghost.

A few moments more, a last glance at the moon and at Antonia's face, and it's time to leave the familiar road behind them.

"Keep right behind me. If the group stays tight, we'll avoid the wolves."

As confident as the devil's son, Ferdinando moves rapidly in the shadows, climbing with the agility of a spider. After awhile the others too, getting used to the dark, are able to make out the faint unraveling of the path, which between turns and sudden drops creeps through the folds of the undergrowth. The shepherd's son is quick, he plants his feet firmly on the ground and grips on the slopes with the soles of his shoes; when the incline is too steep he uses his hands and arms, clinging to the rock, hanging onto the low branches of the trees, which loom up out of the void as if they wanted to hold them back.

Between the leaves, round cats' eyes appear and disappear. Every sound seems solid in the middle of the night; Giovanni breaks out in a cold sweat, Francesco jumps at even the faintest rustling. And when Antonia huddles up against his side as well, he gives a start but doesn't say anything.

The darkness is thick and damp. Safe from being seen, the girl's hand finds the wrist of the blond boy and fastens onto it, more and more firmly, until she can feel the rapid palpitation of his blood running through his veins. It's a strange sensation, which makes her close her eyes slightly, as is denying herself that contact once they get beyond the scrub, after all that walking, which suddenly seems too brief.

When the first moonbeam reveals the end of the path, breaking through a gap between the bushes and leaving traces of light among the white leaves, Antonia is already far away: her figure is outlined against the thick tangle of the undergrowth, pale and uncertain, and she moves as in a dream in the eyes of Francesco, who, motionless, follows every sign of her disquiet. Her skirt gathered up on her hip and her left arm tensed, her hand searching for a support, the girl bends forward and disappears behind a low branch, then reappears higher up, pulling herself up the umpteenth climb. Her impetuousness leaves her with tousled hair. A final push, a groan snatched from her half-open lips, and there is the pasture promised by Ferdinando: a still expanse of grass that curves gently toward its distant edges. In front of them, the Sibillini Mountains raise their peaks toward the sky. Francesco looks at them, coming back into the light. Then he looks for Antonia.

She is sitting on the ground. Lifting one leg at a time, she bends over the soles of her bare feet: sometimes she brushes them with her open palm; at others she moves closer until she is almost touching them with the tip of her wrinkled nose, her attentive stare boring into the center of her black-tinged flesh. The blond boy sees the back of her neck covered with dark waves lifting and falling rhythmically; when the tattered clouds free the moon, he also catches sight of her profile, which suddenly becomes pale only to then sink back into the blue-grey of the night. She is near her toes, now. Francesco imagines their smell: the thought lodges in the center of his stomach and lies there smouldering.

A few feet from her, Giovanni seems to be consumed by the same fire: he lingers over the remains of a bonfire, his hands plunged into the ashes, and furtively casts glances full of silence in the direction of the girl. Although he ought to light the fire, he can't stop staring at her. From the loose neckline of her dress, her small breasts heave; her skin tightens over her wide breast bone and trembles with her every movement. Giovanni could watch her all night, soaking his pants with desire; he almost can't breathe, the strain is so great, and when Ferdinando leaps out behind him, waving a makeshift torch, he loses his balance and ends up kneeling on the grass.

It's just a moment, and Antonia lights up like the fire. Francesco sees her emerge suddenly from the darkness, her face buried in the sole of her foot, her upper lip brushing against her heel, and the thought planted in his stomach grows suddenly, spreading like wildfire. Antonia senses him near her, a breath of wind carries his smell, and she looks up with a start. She stares at the blond boy, the son of princes, charming and golden like in a fairy tale, and slowly takes her lips from her dirty skin, revealing a hint of a smile. She lowers her foot, straightens up, and turns her back on him.

The skin on her arms burns with the reflections of the fire and her hair is streaked with red and bronze, and this image is what stays with Francesco. Beyond, Ferdinando skips like a satyr. He throws branches into the flames and claps his hands above his head; he unbuttons his shirt hurriedly, revealing curls of thick hair on his chest, of which there was no trace that morning; his face, transformed by the light of the bonfire, doesn't look like him anymore.

From below, Ferdinando looks enormous: he is outlined against the starry background, strange and wild, showing his hairy chest bordered by the fluttering of the fabric, and his hair ruffled around his face. His eyes, compared with the stares of the other three, are shot through with quick flashes of red; on his lips his smile is intense, it reinforces the thread of tension that increases with every moment. It's no more than a shudder. As are his words, deep like the shaking of the earth and yet light, weak, as flesh is weak. In Giovanni, who had stopped hoping. In Antonia, squatting on the ground. In Francesco, who keeps his distance, his wish to run away almost stronger than his wish to stay, to plunge his head into that dark pleasure, almost until he gorges himself on it.

"It's time to start," announces Ferdinando, then he bends down, grabs a stick from the fire and points it toward the girl, signaling her to get up. Great sparks rain to the ground, extinguishing in the grass, as she obeys, unsteady on her legs.

"Have you put them on?" asks the boy abruptly, as soon as she is facing him.

Antonia tilts her head. Her hair brushes her bare forearm.

"Yes," she replies.

"Show me."

This time she stays silent, her thighs stiffen under the heavy skirt. She swallows, she bites her lip, she raises her eyes for just a second.

"What are you waiting for? Show me, I said," he insists. He is talking about Antonia's sister's underwear, which she stole that evening from the chest of drawers, and, obediently, put on instead of her own. She thought she would have shown it proudly, straight away, but now that the moment has arrived she feels the lace burning against her skin, it seems almost red-hot, and the tension she senses makes her tremble slightly. Out of the corner of her eye she looks for Francesco, who is standing behind her, then she looks at Ferdinando's ankles because she doesn't want to look him in the face. No one does anything to stop what is happening, so she takes hold of her skirt and for the umpteenth time lifts it up to reveal her bony ankles, her strong calves, her bruised knees, and, higher up, her long, firm thighs, on which her hair is paler. She pauses for just a moment more, then the boys see it in front of them, the exposed underwear, her little sex that thrusts forward to counter the weight of the material, bulky between her folded arms.

Antonia keeps her back curved backward and her head high now, in a show of pride. Sparks flash across her severe stare, animating her otherwise unreadable expression, but only Francesco notices them, and only for a second, before looking back at her rounded, ample bottom, which under the lace embroidery reveals a dark crack. There, in that safe place, there's the custodian of the secrets of sinful pleasure, the pleasure one has before marriage, among the bales of hay, and that one can enjoy fully. Just knowing this makes the boy's member sway like a pendulum, forcing him to hold his breath. He would like to go closer and stretch out his hand, cup it under that wide bottom, let her welcome it there and stay like that, forever; and while he is imagining this she opens her legs—slightly, just a hint—and seems to invite it.

Now the position of the little opening is identifiable, even in the shadow of her clothes. Antonia pulls the material higher, and it becomes obvious. From behind, he can make out a cotton flower, which with her every breath lowers its petals and reveals her brown frizzy pubic hair. Francesco feels a thrill; he grabs the crotch of his trousers with his right hand and squeezes hard, to suppress the feeling, but his pleasure, instead of being stifled, leaps out all of a sudden. With every spurt the boy buckles more, once, twice, three times, until he awakens, drained and panting, in a new and vivid world, run through with dozens of words.

"It was your idea," he hears.

Antonia is still standing there, her skirt raised. Ferdinando is holding the makeshift torch up straight. Giovanni, red in the face, is panting, standing between them. He holds out his hand. He takes a step forward. Once he is in front of her, he grabs her genitals firmly. He doesn't even look her in the face, he just stares at the swelling that rises under the pink knickers, feeling it between his thumb and his index finger. Her hair tickles his palm. He can't wait any longer.

"To call the devil, I have to burn them," he whispers. His voice sounds choked, he keeps on staring down, to where his fingers don't stop moving.

Antonia tenses her buttocks instinctively.

"What do you have to burn?" she stutters in a loud voice.

"Your sister's knickers."

"Her knickers?" She scowls. Then she looks up at the sky, puzzled. "Are you sure the devil will appear then?"

"He'll definitely come."

"Okay. I'll take them off," she says, but when she is about to let go of her skirt, Giovanni stops her.

"What is it?" Antonia grumbles, looking him in the face. He doesn't stop staring at the swelling of her pubis, pressing against the lace fabric; he is breathless and his face is all red.

"I'll take them off," he stammers.

"What did you say?"

"I'll take them off you," he repeats loudly, and his face gets even redder. "The ritual says I have to."

Under her fixed gaze, he bends forward; he changes position three times, self-conscious, before he decides to kneel down in front of her. On his right the fire burns in tall flames of red, in front of him the pink knickers are so close that they fill his field of vision. The curls of her hidden pubic hair push to escape. Giovanni can smell them. He releases his grip reluctantly, in order to hold the edges of the fabric, and when he lowers the underwear half an inch, Antonia's smell gets stronger, striking him full in the face.

She has a pervasive aroma, Antonia, that makes his head spin. It is an eager smell, pungent, that invites sex, piercing the center of desire like a long pin. Giovanni feels completely addicted. Even if he wanted to stop he couldn't, but, after all, who would ever want to deny themselves such a discovery? With a tug he lowers the knickers halfway down her thighs and her smell hits him harder, leaving him open-mouthed. Confronted by his blank stare, finally free of the constraint of the fabric, the girl's pubic hair begins to rise. It exposes the red wound underneath, which protrudes like a tiny tongue. Higher up, a narrow, dark opening.

Giovanni looks at it from below: it seems to be smiling, that opening, and in the slow acquiescence of Antonia, who is swaying on her legs as she tries to regain her balance, it opens up a bit more, revealing everything. He puts his right hand back in position. He raises his stiff index finger, the nail fringed with black, and he prods at the edges. Then, timidly, he makes it disappear into the opening as far as the first joint.

Antonia, silent, widens her legs a bit more, and when his second finger finds its way into her, she glances over at Ferdinando, who is smiling at her with that crooked sneer of his, and at Francesco, behind her, curious to discover what emotion is passing over his handsome features, astonishment or desire, need or compliance. Once she finds his familiar face, however, all she can see there is herself, and she is merely obscene, standing with her legs apart, in front of a young boy contorted like a hunchback.

Francesco, crouched down, is aware of the cold of the ground permeating the canvas of his trousers, there on his knees sunk into the grass and on an ankle, bent awkwardly. His white face reflects the pallor of the moon, in his wide-open eyes the figures of his three companions are clearly outlined. Once the veil of passion has slipped from his eyes, everything is more brutal, almost sickening: Antonia's nudity, who stands there with her knickers pulled halfway down her legs, and the expression of Ferdinando, who is as still as a guard, keeping watch over the moment armed with a long stick. But for Francesco the worst thing, the most horrible of all, is the mask that has fallen over his brother's face: completely in thrall to his own needs, the face of the boy has become more bloated; his eyes have become sunken, small and shining; and his lips are now motionless, flung open like those of a demented person, red and all wet with saliva.

While he is exploring the inside of the girl with clumsy movements of his wrist, his small member protruding from his trousers like the tip of a knife, Giovanni lets out a hoarse panting. His nostrils dilated, he stays tuned to the tension that runs through his belly and then starts again wildly, moving his fingers in Antonia's body like pistons. His desire is so strong that it threatens to shatter him into a thousand pieces and that's how he feels, like a fuse that has been triggered, that he is rapidly being worn down by an ever greater need. The only thing he wants—that he has ever wanted—is a step away. Swallowing, he slides out his fingers and he buries his face there, so deeply that he can't breathe, and he anchors himself there.

He is in the redness, now. His hands, held tight on the creamy buttocks, search out new paths. His mouth is greedy; in his eyes glow flashes from the wood fire, which create shadow puppets as they blend with the fire of his flesh. The scenarios that form in the boy's mind only feed his passion, so he sinks deeper, indifferent to her hands that, in his brown hair, tighten and pull, scratching his skin, trying to keep him at a distance. He doesn't want to stop; he squeezes to the last drop. He doesn't even hear her voice.

In Francesco's eyes, Antonia tosses and turns: she clenches her thighs, with tensed hands she grips the back of Giovanni's neck in an attempt to tear him away from her; but however much she tries, Giovanni is too strong. He buries himself between her legs like a man possessed, and when, finally, with a slap of her palm on his forehead, she manages to push him away for a second, he rises up like a wave of sea spray, overwhelming her. He grabs her wrist. With his other hand he fumbles with his trousers, trying to undo the button, which suddenly comes off.

Pressed against him, the girl cries out; she tries to free herself with violent tugs. Short of breath, she stiffens her shoulders. Her skirt falls back over her thighs. Giovanni, sensing his goal getting away from him, opens his eyes wide, lets go of his trousers, and plunges his arm inside her skirt, searching through the fabric for the lost nudity; then he takes hold of his trousers again, twisting Antonia's wrist harder to stop her from trying to escape, and again throws himself into the thick folds of the skirt.

The girl, however much she tries, isn't able to get free.

"Let me go!" she squeals, but Giovanni isn't listening to her; all he cares about is rediscovering her sunken wound, and when for the umpteenth time it disappears beneath the folds of her dress, he bares his teeth, snorting like a bull and letting go of Antonia's wrist in order to hold her by the hips, pushing her onto the ground, he lifts up her skirt, reversing it onto her chest. He grabs her pubis with force.

From below, Antonia widens her eyes.

"What are you doing?" she screams, grabbing Giovanni's wrist with both her hands. "Stop it! You're hurting me!"

"It was your idea."

"You're hurting me, I told you!" she keeps on shouting, but he doesn't answer her cries anymore, he just settles himself above her, his knees on the ground. His penis, as dry as a twig, is now seesawing between them as if it were trying to take aim. This is the time to call the devil, it seems to be saying. Giovanni thinks he can hear its voice, while Antonia squirms and he, to hold her still, puts his hands around her neck and tightens them, tightens them as much as he can, ravenous.

It is time. The foliage of the fir trees rustles in a gust of wind. Ferdinando beats his thigh with his free hand, marking out an ancient rhythm. Giovanni lowers his behind. Francesco, on the ground, flinches. He is shaking like a young goat, and his palms are damp with sweat. Antonia is choking. He can hear her low gasps rumbling between the mutterings of his brother.

"You'll kill her like that!" he would like to shout out, but his tongue is motionless, heavy in the center of his mouth, so he gets up and runs toward him, toward the white buttocks that show above his lowered trousers, toward his curved back, and pushes him as hard as he can, charging at him with his shoulder.

Giovanni rolls to one side; he ends up against the legs of Ferdinando, who, as he recoils, drops the torch. The end of the stick explodes in sparks on the grass, reflected in the dampness that flows quickly. Higher, it illuminates the glances of the two friends. Their eyes gleam, absurdly, showing from their depths the flames of damnation.

Francesco and Antonia run across the field and throw themselves down the slope hand in hand; her skirt balloons up like a bride's veil, following in the wake of her leaps, and he advances first, a blond condottiere. Behind them, disadvantaged by their later departure, Ferdinando and Giovanni set off at a run: Francesco can hear their grunts and panting, the sounds carried quickly on the wind that now freezes the back of his neck. Not even the thought of wolves is as terrible as the idea of being caught, so, once they reach the edge of the firs, the blond boy slips between the trunks, entering the darkness purposefully, and feels his way until his sight returns.

When he stops, behind the trunk of a tree, his chest rises and falls rapidly. Antonia spots the movement of his lightweight shirt and a shadow of warmth fills her breast. She huddles up to him, trembling. The pulsing of the boy's blood prickles her cheek; beyond that sound, from somewhere, she hears their pursuers moving. The wood confuses the echoes of their steps, which bounce from one trunk to another, becoming distorted.

Thoughts become distorted too. Francesco counts them on his fingertips, untangling the sequence of events that have brought them to this point. His breathing is shallow; the smell of Antonia's hair pricks in his nostrils.

"We should get to the road," he whispers after having thought about it for a while. The undergrowth continues to send out the low noises of its interior—they run on spider's legs, show the teeth of the wolf, open the wings of the owl—and getting to the road seems the only solution. Besides, Antonia's smell is too recognizable; Francesco can almost see Ferdinando and Giovanni setting out on their tracks, following their trail with their noses on the ground, like diabolical dogs. Just thinking about it sends shivers climbing up his spine.

"Do you have any idea where we are?" he asks, trying to overcome his trembling.

The girl raises her head. She looks at him with her large dark eyes and shakes her head.

"And do you have any idea what happened?"

She shakes her head again, the waves of her hair brushing her face. Francesco tenses his shoulders.

"I thought you'd already done it, before," he murmurs, staring at the tangle of branches that blocks the view.

"No. It was the first time for me, too."

"Really?"

"Mmm."

"And did he? . . ."

She frowns. She clenches her thighs and buries her hands between her legs, as if to check. No, he didn't have time to violate her; she sighs, and shakes her head. Francesco, feeling the rubbing of her head against his shoulder, sighs in turn, then stays silent for a while, trying to gather his thoughts, which have scattered inside him like a large pack of cards. When he remembers what they need to do, he holds tightly onto that thought: the only solution is to reach the road, he repeats to himself, so they can go home. If he remembers correctly, the track ought to be to the east. If moss on trees always grows on the north side, then he ought to go right and then straight on for quite a way.

"Do you feel up to walking?"

Antonia nods, uncertainly, then she leans on the arm he offers her.

"Hold onto me. Somewhere to the east there should be the end of the wood, and the road. Once we've got out of here, the moonlight will guide us: I'll have you back in less than no time."

The girl nods again, all of a sudden she seems to have lost her resourcefulness somewhere. Probably it's Giovanni's fault—Francesco exhales, cautiously moving away from the tree trunk he had leaned on—and how could he blame her? Not even he, who is his brother, recognizes him anymore, with his bloodshot eyes and that strange hair that has sprouted on his chest, poking out at the neck of his shirt like an embroidered border.

Sinister things are happening tonight. A strange tension runs through everything, even the ground beneath their feet and the air in their lungs, which suddenly seems to have become too thin and goes to their heads. It's all wrong. The world is whispering and its voice is full of dangers, he realizes, leaning against a precarious branch, and almost ending up on the ground if it wasn't for Antonia, who helps him keep his balance.

Francesco snorts, widening his nostrils. He takes a step forward, then reconsiders. He grabs the insecure branch with his right hand and slides it out of the tangled foliage from which it has detached itself, breaking cleanly under the weight of some animal, then he lifts it up in front of his face. It is a short and sturdy branch an excellent club. Stabbing its end on the ground, he explores the terrain where his eyes can't see, then he raises it again and brandishes it in the air before him.

"I don't know if the devil really has anything to do with this, or perhaps it's some poisonous plant, but I guarantee that I'll take you home," he promises.

Antonia, listening to him, tightens both of her hands around his wrist, and the two start walking again in silence.

The undergrowth is damp with odors. Over the stench of a carcass, the boy and girl smell the creeping scent of the water that flows lower down in the gorge. Somewhere there must be a stream, says Francesco to himself, and as if it wants to prove him right, after a bend the noise of the current reaches his ears. It is a tremulous and crystalline sound; it comes up from below like a murmur.

"Wait for me," he says to Antonia, and he advances alone in the direction of the gurgling, leaning through a dense patch of shrubs. When his face emerges from between the leaves a current of cold air hits him. After a few seconds the shadows take shape. A deep gorge appears, wedged between two steep walls, on which nothing grows.

"We can't get through this way," he mutters, retracing his steps. "Do you remember if we crossed a stream on the way here?"

Antonia is leaning against a low branch, her hands held together, one above the other. When she hears his question she revives, but just as her words are about to rise to her lips, a sudden sound from above bursts onto the scene, shaking her like a dry leaf.

Francesco is paralyzed, his knees bent and his abdomen tense. At last they have reached them. He lifts his head and sees their eyes, yellowish in the dark, shining like cat's eyes.

"Brother!" Giovanni calls him, leaning forward to dominate the scene. "Brother, wait for us!"

The blond boy screws up his eyes, trying to focus: his brother is stooping, crouched on the ground like an animal, and he is anchored firmly on the slope, his bare chest bristling with hair and his hands twisted into white claws. Behind him, he can just glimpse the sneer of the shepherd's son. Seeing him, Francesco tightens his grip on the stick.

"Go away!" he yells.

"Brother, wait for us!" Giovanni repeats, sniggering. "We'll share her!"

Antonia cries out when she hears his plan. The sound is enough to reawaken the predatory instinct of their pursuers who, sticking out their red tongues, start to eat into the distance between them again, descending the drop with agility. The girl watches them getting closer, her hand on her heart. Her white face no longer displays any emotion.

"Come here!"

Francesco pulls her by the arm. At his touch, she gives a start. In his eyes now, her whole world is reflected.

"There's no way out!" she cries. "They'll get us!"

"No, I tell you! Come with me, we'll follow the gorge!"

The blond boy drags her into the undergrowth, beating down a wall of leaves and thorny branches, and pulls her further until they get to the overhang. The chasm is bordered by a thin strip of earth, which runs along free from obstacles. Francesco takes the path decisively, moving low so as not to slip. The wind blows on his face and arms; it slaps against Antonia's skirt, which sticks to her legs, and turns her hair into a lash.

Even if the other two are faster, he doesn't give up: pulling her like a madman, he guides Antonia along the slippery path, keeping her leaning in to the slope as much as he can. They are smeared with mud now and they merge into the darkness, but the eyes of the two possessed boys are able to see in the dark, so they spot them just the same. A leap, and they are on the path. A jump, and they grab hold of Antonia's skirt with both their hands.

"Ah!" she screams.

"We'll share her!" Giovanni drools, transformed by evil, but his brother doesn't give way to his fear. Instead of going on alone, he pushes Antonia behind him. He is between them now, and instinctively brandishes his stick to keep them at a distance. He doesn't think he can hit them, but in the heat of the moment he strikes the chest of his brother, who slips backward. The terrain is viscous, the shrubs growing on the walls of mud are few and low, so the boy, when he loses his balance, can do nothing but stretch out his arms and open his mouth in a silent plea for help, which goes unanswered.

Events moves rapidly. While Antonia clings to Francesco's waist, his brother overbalances and bumps into his friend behind him. The two boys roll together down into the gorge and plunge into the blackness with a sob. The girl sees Giovanni's head open up like a seed, there against a rock, and his brains spill out. Ferdinando, on the other hand, lifts himself up. She sees him raise his hand. Her eyes focus on him, then go back to showing just fear, her sense of responsibility for what has just happened so intense it makes the earth shake.

Antonia hugs Francesco. His body, under her open palms, shakes violently, like the heart of a sparrow. His face is ashen and he is damp with sweat; his eyes are spheres of blue, in the darker blue of the half-light.

"Have I killed him? Have I killed my brother?" he stutters, breathless.

She hugs him tighter. She sinks her face against his side.

"No, you haven't killed him!" she lies. "I saw them get up again! They're both fine."

"But how? . . ."

"They went further along the gorge. They'll climb back up the path to the road, like we meant to do," says Antonia, looking at him with her large dark eyes. Her eyebrows are furrowed with fear and her cheeks are pale and full like the moon between the leaves.

"If they were to cross our path again . . ." she worries, and Francesco, seeing her like this, tightens his hold on his stick.

"No, it won't happen. We'll take another route. We'll find shelter somewhere and wait for morning. We can't let them get us. I don't want them to hurt you."

Antonia, hearing his words, embraces him even tighter; her warmth quickly creeps over Francesco's chest, and he holds her close to him.

"Let's follow the path wherever it leads. We're almost there," he assures her. She nods and kisses his knuckles, then she starts walking, sweeping him along in her shadow.

The two of them move through the twists and turns of the undergrowth, going up slopes and plunging down again, one next to the other. The forest is dense, there are no safe places, and the atmosphere is so oppressive it makes their heads spin. Francesco has almost lost hope when, scrambling along a narrow strip of land between the trees, the path opens out onto a plain. Then he opens and closes his eyes, astonished.

"What *is* this?"

"A spring," whispers Antonia, pulling him a step forward to draw him out of the shade of the trees. "They say that fairies live in places like this."

The spring tumbles out in the middle of a small green clearing; all around the trees create a thick tangle of trunks, beyond which nothing can be seen. Between their roots grow fungi, which speckle the ground with white; their bark is green with moss.

Above, the sky is visible, and the moon is reflected in the center of the spring. The noise of the water is a soft murmuring.

Francesco looks around, he sees the colored patches of violets and lily of the valley, and the reeds that curve at the edges of the pond, bent by the touch of the warm breeze. He hears the buzzing of an insect, then the song of a cicada. A toad dives in. A reptile slithers through the grass.

Antonia is already close to the water, her skirt lifted up to bare her ankles. Dreamily, she dips a toe in.

"It's such a beautiful spot, to rest," she murmurs, but something seems wrong to Francesco, as if something rotten were hiding beyond the beauty of the place.

He stiffens and takes a step backward.

"Don't you think there's something strange here?" he asks.

"Something strange?" she whispers. "Do you think there are spirits here?"

Noticing her fear, he joins her, and with every step he feels his blood pumping faster. The warm rush soon fills every part of his body. He has brandished a stick against his brother, saved a girl from an assault, crossed the wood without a guide ... Now that he is opposite Antonia, he is a man as he never has been before. He brushes the hair off her cheek. He leans over and kisses her forehead.

"We can wait here till daylight; it's safe," he says, then helps her to sit down on a rock, takes one of her feet in his hands and washes it with the water from the spring, cleaning the mud away. Then he takes the other, gently. First the sole, then to top of her foot, then her ankle.

His movements are leisurely. Her skin responds, tingling, while with his right hand Francesco follows the shape of her ankle, up along her calf, a bit higher, until he remembers that under her skirt she isn't wearing anything and he stops, respectful.

She doesn't draw back; she settles herself on top of the rock.

"They say that water keeps evil spirits away," she says.

"Water?" he responds, bewitched.

"Wash the evil from me."

Antonia's words gently dart inside Francesco then plunge deeper, to the center of his pale stomach. He furrows his brows, feeling them tighten, and looks up at her. He can't have understood, he thinks, and yet suddenly she is there, still and perfect, with her shoulders freed from the straps that sketch two graceful curves over the fullness of her small breasts.

Her lovely face, encircled by her long hair, seems that of a Madonna. Even now, as she repeats "Wash the evil from me," gradually opening her thighs to welcome him, bowed on the ground before her, almost as if he were a worshipper at the entrance to the temple.

Francesco has never seen anything more perfect. Hesitant, he slowly stretches out his hand and pauses close to her curly pubic hair, his fingers warming on the fine skin of that secret place. He would like to slide into her and give her children, see her abdomen fill up with sunlight, but in his astonishment, every intention dies and all he can do is look at her, his throat dry, his eyes moist.

"I don't know if I can," he whispers.

Antonia then brushes his hair with her hands. Gently, she guides him to her.

"I'm a virgin," she confides. "Take me from behind."

It is almost dawn. The present is tinged with blue, sunk between the first rays of light that filter through the foliage. In the cold shadows the animals are waking; some crawl, others creep into the earth. Some of the white fungi have rotted, others have sprouted up; their round caps rise from the black of the soil. Antonia, moving toward them, takes one between her fingers. She snaps it from the stalk and crunches it between her teeth. It tastes of earth. And of algae. And of grass. Like Francesco.

As she thinks of him again, she turns her gaze. The boy is there, asleep, his limbs abandoned on the grass. Looking at him, she smiles. He is curled up, like before he came into the world, and he is so handsome, with his hair tousled around his face, and younger than she has ever been; so much so that just looking at him fills her heart.

Antonia moistens her lips with the tip of her tongue. It doesn't seem real to her that he has become hers, and through such a chance. The youthfulness for which she desired him in the end betrayed him, she sighs; it's like that for many people. Satisfied, she turns her back on him and starts walking again, slipping into the blue of a bend in the wood, beyond the low branches. She goes past a bush. There, she meets the creature.

It is sitting on a stone, as black as the night just past. Its broad chest covered with bristly hair, its narrow waist crisscrossed by the lines of pulsing muscles, its navel bulging, as big as a fist: it has always been here, its arms resting on its thighs, its hands still, its hoofs sunk in the ground.

THE HILL OF THE GOATS

Looking at its mask, Antonia smiles. Today it is wearing a horse's head; from its empty stare one can glimpse the absence of thought. Now it is lifeless. From its taut sex drips a thick slime; it reaches the ground, attracting dozens of slugs and snails. Squatting down, the girl takes one between her fingers: she turns it round, studying its shell, then she gets up again and throws it into the undergrowth. She is drawn to the horse's head now. She grabs it by its sides, taking it off the creature. Finally she puts it on again. A thrill shakes her. She turns, opens her arms, and gallops over the mountains.

A Dyptich: Absinthe & Piercing

FRANCESCA MAZZUCATO

1. Absinthe

A glass of absinthe is as poetical as anything in the world. What difference is there between a glass of absinthe and a sunset?

—Oscar Wilde

He pulls me towards him and I press against him to fill myself with him as much as possible. I sink my face into the pillow to suffocate the cries of pleasure that accompany our movements and our words. I know that the more licentious the sex, the more intense the pleasure, but I still try to stifle my gasps.

—Salwa Al-Neimi

[I look at you]
It is nice to look at you, to watch your hands, hands that have glided over

me and have lingered for such a long time, with such a need to "feel" my skin in every fold, along every tiny edge. Your hands are large and beautiful, with the little fingers slightly crooked, that type of imperfection that makes them still more desirable. Every imperfection increases desire, feeds it.

[Languorous] I am like this. Naked, under the sheet. I feel a bit dizzy.

The room is completely closed, the key swings and I note a number similar to so many others.

A number that has memories that flow through its digits. The furnishings are similar to others too.

The rooms I end up in with casual lovers, pursuing my desire, making space for it every time I want, reading in the eyes of a handsome man, after a meeting, after a few words, the need for another body, the certainty of the pleasure that will follow, the urgency of possession, the rooms in which we inevitably find ourselves for that necessary intimacy, savage, deep, devouring, are the same, even in different cities, they are carbon-copy rooms designed for lovers who have to overcome time, the countdown and the usual ending, the familiar ending, almost always a silent parting.

[Similarities] I notice only imperceptible, minute variations in the furnishings, in the position of the beds or the balcony, in the traces that sometimes remain and that I find of the people who loved each other here before us.

—Are we floundering around? Or is there a real desire?

I ask questions that leave all the unsaid things hanging in the air, all the possible interpretations. They are treacherous questions, ambushing questions, I know that. I love ambushes, I feel a strange pleasure in making the possible reactions trouble.

After, I have to admit, these meetings don't last and I feel free to ask, free to let myself go, free to fuck up every hypothesis or to pull out of my hat new and inconceivable ones.

[In the meantime]

They are moments of liquid and ephemeral pleasure, when one is naïve one exchanges words destined to die in the morning, words with mistaken nuances, words of love, or of need or of urgency. I have learned not to do this anymore. "Words of urgency" do not exist. One cannot say it, it is intangible, it cheats you, it exists but it doesn't have an outline that can be described, you can't capture it. Only living it and feeling it is possible.

Before, before the carnal splendour begins, I make myself more mysterious by keeping silent. They have told me often that my presence is enough, I intoxicate them, I drug them, I magnetize them.

Silent, I imply mysteries that aren't there. I let secrets hang in the air that I couldn't reveal. I have none. My indecency, eager to be filled, appears by itself, the rest is an artful frame, perfected over time.

I am needy, like them, like everyone. I am looking for an illusion but I have learned not to count on it. I am looking for a reason but I have learned not to have a definite one.

I listen, during, to the sound that is never absent, it comes with pleasure, it is like a lute, it is the moan, the climax. If one talks, everything is void. After, still wet with you, dazed, sated, I say what I think. Deferred observations.

You are grateful to me and you have the look that denotes satisfaction without shadows. I wasn't expecting it. You threw me onto the bed after a few caresses and you stripped everything from me. You kept your clothes on, you made as if to spread my thighs but there was no need, I understood and I opened my legs before you, I let you look, at length. You, standing, in front of the wide, comfortable, and warm double bed. You looked at my waxed sex, my smooth sex, my velvet sex, you asked me to open my labia slightly so you could see better. I did.

You kept going. That stare ran through my body, made me feel like a virgin and a whore, indecent and desirable. Perhaps you knew that. You took a long time to take your eyes from my clitoris, from that secret area that I allowed you to absorb, then, still dressed, you sat down next to me and, with your fingertips, you began to caress me. And to touch, to touch touch touch. It was difficult to maintain that mysterious silence. That delicate touch of yours was a wonderful torment. With wide-open legs, I let you.

In that room, the same as so many others. Knowing that I could seem pathetic, looking for something I wouldn't get, didn't diminish anything.

A DYPTICH: ABSINTHE & PIERCING

You were there. I was there. You got undressed and finally it happened. I was able to destroy that empty space that I wanted not to fill, I was able to let myself go, to cry out and to come.

We found ourselves on the same wavelength, modulating that language of pleasure that resembles a childish language made up of guttural sounds, little cries and starts.

One is like that, during orgasm. One becomes a newborn baby again.

[Ancient hungers]

You answer my question.

—You came. I tasted the flavor and I heard the music. Not yours, mine. When you come inside me something rings out. It is already the second time and I believe that there will be others. Then you laugh. You look at me. You laugh in a not unpleasant way, you don't create dissonances. But I only smile. I am fluid, lascivious and abandoned.

—You're right. But I don't know if that means something. It could be just my body reacting. An automatic mechanism.

Too many questions, I know. It's not what one does. One doesn't do it before and one doesn't overdo it after. You measured the tempo, it was an adagio, and then there was the fortissimo, but without surprise. As if everything was natural, normal. Flesh and life, our bodies united.

I talk in order to demythologize. I don't want something of me to be tied to this moment. Will it last? Perhaps there will be another meeting? I don't know if you belong to that group of men to whom one can permit this. A meeting requires effort, thorough and lengthy pedicures, the feet rubbed several times with perfumed oils, complete depilation, massages, manicures and hair. I do this. Every time, with almost obsessive devotion. Like a Zen ritual. But I would like to see you again. I know that we aren't about to leave each other, but now, picturing our good-bye speeds up my heartbeat. This springtime Paris is alluring. You're not bad, quite the opposite. There is something feverish and crazy in the way you seduce. You get to the point slowly. I thought you didn't want it, that those words were enough, that brief touching of hands in the suburban brasserie where I was reading and you were typing on your laptop. You didn't hurry me, you were smiling, nodding, a coffee, a look, a bland compliment. And yet. I'm not mistaken about looks. Your first look burned with sensuality, there was already an embrace and an orgasm in your eye. We adhered to the rituals. It was right, there are tempos and rhythms, one needs to be the conductor of one's own orchestra of pleasure.

It wasn't difficult to find the hotel. Paris seems to offer glass doors and spiral staircases with dark pink carpets, seductive possible alcoves, one on every corner, the choice was mine, no, you choose. In the end, we left it to chance.

—Do you want something to drink? In my opinion, you ask yourself too many questions, and, by drinking everything that I give you, drinking it slowly, the outlines of reality will become blurred. That's good, isn't it? You'll see.

You move toward me with a green bottle. There are two glasses, sugar, a pierced spoon.

—I'm bringing you the green fairy. It's nice to be able to count on a magic fairy every now and then, don't you think? It helps. It takes you to those areas you need.

—Wait.

You say to me first.

—What?

—Pull off the covers, open your legs.

I do. Fluids, saliva and sperm have left a stain on the sheets, my labia and my sex are those of an indecent woman. In fact, I have enjoyed a lot of pleasure and I have had multiple and symphonic orgasms. [You are amazed]

You go back to looking and nothing more, as at the start, as you did before everything came to an end.

—What are you doing?

—I'm looking at it, after. After it has held me, after it has contained me, after it has throbbed together with me. I don't know if I like to look at it more before or after. It's always magnificent, and looking at it is admiring the only real work of art.

I was thinking about this before, as I was preparing the fairy.

You'll see. You need to be precise to prepare absinthe properly. And then it comes. That suspension of all solidity, which we need. That I need.

[Naked]

A naked man is vulnerable. Without the things that defend him and represent him in the daily battle of social success.

I have this privilege. I look at you. Naked and unafraid.

You have looked at much more intimate things. We help ourselves to this privilege as if it were a delicious dish.

Naked, but not with an erection. There is something harmonious about it all the same. I would like to taste it again, and again with a finger so I would suffocate in that torpor where you have brought me, with your member pressed inside and your hand on my neck or inside as well, if I want it again ... now my heart is pounding and my breathing is too fast. I slow down. I need to change direction.

You have a bottle of absinthe and you manage to surprise me, truly this time, I'm speechless. I wrap myself up in the sheet again and I watch you pour the liquid with its color that is already beginning to hypnotize me. A shiver.

Pleasure that runs through the spine and stops there, where you have just been looking, at length. Twice. I smile. But perhaps it is a grimace. I don't know anything anymore. I don't know this Paris anymore, which played its part in our first meeting. I don't know anything about men anymore. Where did my unshakeable certainties go? Where?

You are handsome. You surprise. You stare at my sex as if it were a diamond.

You suffocate me with the charm of someone who knows how much suffocation can increase enjoyment.

What else?

—Absinthe? Was it in that briefcase that you never let go?

—It could have been.

—But we don't need it. We don't need ...

—No, I want to love you and avoid madness. It's needed for this.

You say that word that usually isn't said, not at the first meeting, not when we found ourselves here by chance, or perhaps not by chance, but it's the same thing, and you looked at me, I exposed myself "indecently," you showed yourself to be fragile but satisfied, and this, after our cries that took us back to our birth, to hunger, to everything that is primordial and primitive in our lives, after me giving my hands to you to bind them, on the sheet like a shroud (profane, marked with necessary blood, revealed and revealing), no, I didn't think you could be the person to use that word. To love you. Love.

—Do you think it can help? Why?

—There's your pleasure, mine on yours, inside yours, next to yours, there's this room, airless, damp, dirty and perfect, there are terrible moments that our bodies make magnificent, there are paths of flesh that join us together, it would be easy to go mad. It would be easy to not be able to do without it.

—You say that.

—You say it too, but not in words. Words mean fuck all. Your body counts. You say it with that, with your body, with your labia, the way you part them, the way you welcome me, the way you stifle a cry, the way you don't hold back a moan, the way you bite your lip, the way you open them slightly, you say it with your sex that you tighten, you say it with your legs that you let me spread apart, with the smile that appears on your lips, at the end, when you come.

It's true. What happened reveals a carnal evidence that I can't counter in any way. In the minibar there is already some red wine. I don't understand the reason for the absinthe. Perhaps it's a question of scenography. It has an effect. I had a lover a long time ago (who knows how long ago, I don't remember, but it was a period of a ripe, stupid, need to love and to believe in irresistible meetings, like that one, I still believed I could have more than two meetings, even three, and when I started to desire him, that lover, to feel I was nothing without him, incomplete when he was absent, everything ended, crumbled, all that was left was a nothingness that stuck to my skin for painful months, until I said enough, I don't want this "hurt," I don't want these burn marks left by what was a great love affair, no more crumbs, I will know how to avoid them), this lover brought with him, to every meeting, a special arrangement for listening to music, I don't know what it was but the sound that came out, the tune that radiated, seemed to me to be softened and flawless. He used to put on various things, but mainly Wagner. Yes, Wagner. Who I have never ever listened to since. To him it seemed ideal, and to me too, with him. But Wagner didn't fill the "without," the emptiness, the missing limb, the wound of absence, the announced and deferred ending, the non-presence. So. So I have always been suspicious of stage sets, of extra things, of things used as ornamentation, in a meeting of bodies, in afternoons that become night, expanding the time endlessly, skillfully avoiding the wearing effect of words, the predictability of asking yet again what hurts, consenting, letting them look in silence, in a suspension that doesn't create misunderstandings or suffering, duty, illnesses.

It shouldn't create loves either.

—To love me?

—Yes, to love you. This, what is happening between us, is love.

He answers me and puts down the small tray with the precious-looking vial full of green liquid.

Is this love?

[Perhaps] It could be. Who can say, before or during? It is in the traces that it leaves and in time and only in what you take from it. When you lose it, when it tears you apart from a distance, when it remains the only loss that you would like to erase from your memory, and perhaps even from reality, if an instant replay existed, because love turns couples into assassins, killers, each one of the other. In this, it's necessity.

If it were so, I ought to flee, flee immediately without letting you understand anything, without giving you any coordinates (you would drown your perplexity in absinthe, your initial astonishment, my absence, and you would forget quite quickly, I know).

And yet that word, so hackneyed, so worn, so dusty from the occasions when it was suffocated by what wasn't said, or said at the wrong moment, or whispered too quietly to cross the barriers of blood, tears and delicate pain, yet that word still wields, despite everything, a sort of malign power.

In me too. By then I thought of myself as a queen. A whore-queen who doesn't fill the silence, who doesn't shy away from embarrassment, who looks for pleasure and then goes, with Paris her accomplice, with the untamed Seine watching what happens, with its motion that, every time, from those exaggerated parapets, makes me think of jumping, of delirium, of a journey with no return. I thought by now I was far from this frailty. To believe that somewhere there is a meaning, a man, a possible connection, a oneness charged with that magic that beginnings have and that doesn't fade, doesn't wear out over time.

Yet I carry with me the memory of the bodies of lovers I had afterward. It took months but I learned, once again, to let myself go. To not avoid opportunities. France was my accomplice, Paris nurtured me. And I stayed.

And if a lover after having looked at and "seen" my body like he did, says this to me, says he loves me, I feel myself sliding, no, it can't happen to me again, I feel that letting myself go can be a temptation, a new possibility, a glimmer of an offer that doesn't leave me unscathed.

—Absinthe then?

—Yes.

It could be honey or condensed milk, or another liquid to be licked. It has this color that slowly hypnotizes you if you look at it.

—Will you lick it from my lips?

—We'll drink it. If you dribble, I'll lick it.

—Dribble?

—It could happen. And then you know that absinthe, like a poem, encourages love? Oscar Wilde wrote that. He drank a lot of it. He appreciated it and he extolled its powers, and he talked about the aniseed there is in it as the strongest aphrodisiac in the world, but . . .

I make to stand up.

—We don't need anything that "encourages" anything and I don't need love either. Now I'm going and you can finish your private little party with the green fairy without me, who . . .

You hold me by the arm, move everything out of the way, throw me down onto the bed, you are above me and kiss me, your mouth devours my mouth, more than anything else your mouth sucks, bites, feeds on my lips, my face, my saliva, me. Something unprecedented and never experienced, my head's spinning, torment and love, the unbearable chimera of the possibility of being "one," together seizes my heart, again, after that time, but I mustn't think about Wagner and about . . . no.

Absinthe is an extremely pure distillate and the one you brought is produced by strictly following the ancient nineteenth-century recipe with the perfect method for guaranteeing the taste, the bouquet, and the correct color. It needs sugar and a silver spoon that looks like a pierced spatula, and you take one from a bag like you're extracting a jewel.

We drink, then put everything on the floor, I feel the liquid burning me inside, while your eyes never move from mine, and, in this entire, surprising whole, I feel myself boiling inside and out, and it is true, outside, reality dissolves, and the outlines disappear, you come closer.

—Let yourself go.

You kiss me and you taste of blood and alcohol, I taste like that too, of blood, alcohol and desire, you slide inside me with your unstoppable cock, I hadn't noticed but you had reached a climax during the preparation of the two glasses, looking into my eyes, looking at our indecent "stains," my nipples that you had maltreated splendidly.

—Don't stop, let yourself be taken.

I let myself go completely and you take me and you are inside me but you also are me, and all the heat burns inside me but it is a magnificent burning, the heat of life, the heat of sensuality that breaks down every boundary between our flesh, every barrier of words that then crumbles and collapses, that then solidifies and shatters, I let myself be taken and I am yours, you are inside, you spin me around, you transport me above you and I move, I let myself be moved, by you and by invisible wires, your penis inside me is the source of endless pleasure that becomes a torment and then unequalled well-being again, but perhaps I should go, I still remember the immense betrayal of the Wagner man, of that void that remained, of his leaving, of that nothingness he left me, and that, after, he made me go from the murmurs of an inconceivable ecstasy to desperation.

But you, us, here, in Paris, in an interior that resembles so many others and no other, we are here, yes, I feel myself coming, I let myself go, I cry out, perhaps I dribble, you, on top of me, take me, devour me with kisses, lick me, I am alcohol that you swallow, we mix the moods of absinthe with the words of absinthe with caresses drunk with absinthe.

I don't remember, after. I fell asleep. I was asleep for a long time, a muted light entered through the windows, while what I remembered was a shadow, first, and then it became night, deepest night.
You're not here.
I don't remember your name, and perhaps I didn't even ask you what it was.
There are small green drops on the sheet on the bed, which looks like a battlefield, it looks like a clot of liquids and signs, it looks like what happened.
There is a page from a ruled notebook, an ancient page.
You have written "I love you, I will always love you."
I read it. I have a headache but the remains of the alcohol are vanishing. My clothes are on the floor, scattered.
Of you, there is not a trace.
I could at least have asked you your name.
I could have asked you where you lived, more or less, in which area.
I hadn't asked questions, in my commitment to silence.
Now you have disappeared, you're good. You're capable of triumphant exits.
I had realized that you weren't a two meetings type of man.
I fooled myself only for a moment.
After, I realized my mistake, and then it would have been a pointless, impossible fight with the past.
The Wagner man, the one in the city on the lake, the man who constructed a musical stage set that he varied [Bruckner, Bach sometimes], that very handsome man with his grey hair and amber-colored eyes, like the stone in a ring that he gave me and I kept, during the "sleeping–waking of

sex, alcohol and surrender," he was there, he superimposed himself on you several times, he was next to me, he was whispering to me, he was putting a hand on my face (the traditional, damned, necessary caress), it was you, it was him, the man who doesn't leave me, the man who, despite everything, is still an omnipresent ghost and doesn't let me be, the man I loved, I love, and I will love forever.

Your green fairy has performed a tiny bit of magic.

It's insignificant, it hasn't made this ghost I carry with me disappear. This pain, which sometimes I relive and which still bleeds inside, enchains me, releases me. The need to rediscover something that can never be found again still lacerates. Something that remains like a scar, like a wound that bleeds, empties and becomes infected. It becomes infected in an instant, it takes nothing, it becomes disgusting pus, it becomes a memory that still upsets me, those tears wept into the river return, and the temptation, now, by every river to let myself go, as I endeavored to that time, when perhaps it was only a duck swimming past that held me back. If not, it would have taken nothing to stop that pain. That immense, incredible pain. I know.

This is what remains of the greatest love, an infected wound. A chain forever, the memory of sighs shattered with a hostile reality. With a different life.

I already knew it, fairy with your tiny spells, fairy of stupefaction and nothing else. (He was teetotal, the Wagner man.)

Excellent scenography, I will note you down in my notebook, nameless man. You abuse the word "love," you know how to look good and give orgasms and disappear without a word, between meetings that comprised a collection of moments and perhaps a few tears, because, touching the note with my thumb and my index finger, I feel them descending, against my will, sweet like that liqueur, they stream down my face and fall on that abandoned sheet of paper, that misbegotten and glorious declaration.

2. Piercing

All this to tell you that I miss you and that I can't find the antidote. All this to tell you that the fact that I miss you doesn't hurt me nor does it cure me. All this to tell you that your memory is the greatest harm that I do to myself. But this harm is the only way in which I can still love myself and breathe you in.

—Efraim Medina Reyes

The snow takes me back to the winter from this intangible and indefinable weather that has surrounded me for some days. I am coming back. In February, not long after the beginning of the month. Two days only. It isn't long until I come back. Perhaps a fortnight, perhaps less. It isn't long until this return, but to return to you I don't have to wait to get on a train. I had foreseen it [I knew]. You are in all my lines. You are in all the trails of words that I leave. You are in the spaces, curled up in the parentheses. You are there. I sense you. I have dreams that blend into various shapes and colors [pastel and grey, foam, lips, skin, organic liquids, tongue, yours]. I have reasons for returning but my desire for you still gnaws at me although my writing satisfies, partly, what eludes me like honey that drips, what I can't keep. [obsession? love? a question of gradations] I remember the last year, the period in which an "us" existed, an "us" that I felt etched in my flesh. That you loved and about which you wrote to me. An "us" of words of love left as old lifeless messages.

[nothing in my wound has ever really healed] I can't avoid them resurfacing, those memories of flesh, those caresses with your eyes, that "us" that seemed to me to slowly strengthen [we never understand anything about life, nothing], that continual excavation in the most intimate part of me. You knew how to do it, you know how to do it. I write you an e-mail.

February 2011, do you remember? It was magic and marvelous. Now I know that I can't reach your other place. Or if I reach it, you resist, you erase, you remove. You're able to. I'm not. I can't and I don't want to, I don't give time this advantage. There was something tender and warm that we shared, essentially they were fragments of eternity, something infinitesimal and extremely powerful. I took care of those fragments. I preserve them. They are precious, I don't grind them into oblivion. I know. The rest became a piercing. And the piercing was left.

[there are no other words, the wound was something to crave, in the troubled monologue of whoever seeks pain/love]

I desired our pleasure and I sank into the abyss on outstretched wings as if I were that swan I talked to you about and about which you were stiffly and rigorously ironic. [The swan, the Limmat, that edge] Serious things for me, vital. But you were joking. I liked your joking then. That austere irony like certain streets of the city to which I am about to return, to which I will always return, and to which I came for long months more for you than for the city. Whereas before I belonged only to the city, I had become yours, and the city was just a setting. It doesn't matter. The city doesn't make me atone for it, it knew that it wouldn't have lasted, there is a wisdom in the façades, in the landscapes, in the points of light, and in the views. The city was confident that I would return to it and only because of it, it knew my return was imminent.

It was a question of waiting. Cities can do that. Cities are suited to being loved with passion and obsession. They don't inquire, they don't ask if we have thought about them, they don't conspire, they don't tire, they don't smother. You can love cities however you like. You will find them again. Each one with the answers you seek, those most secret answers. Each one with the chaos and abysses that you want. The most intense. We, however, aren't suited to receiving passion. We are brittle, wounded, badly stitched together, with edges of scars that stain us with blood and with who knows what else and we want that. The savage laceration. We long for it. [I long for it]

So. Probably I won't get to your other place [wherever you are or protect yourself], at present. I know. Or, anyway, I imagine. You don't forgive. You take offense and you cherish that offense among the things to avenge or assert, even only in silence. I know that inflexibility of yours that becomes cruel. [dematerialized sadism]

A pity.

February would be wonderful for sharing multicolored sweets and to let them dissolve softly in our mouths.

[the ones that for a long time I thought were Swiss but that are French, the ones we ate naked, covered in sweat, wet with each other, after having coordinated our shudders in unison, among all that electric vitality]

February would have been wonderful for making peace with the past, exercising the necessary forgiveness, crumbling the rigid schematic, with a bit of irony and even flippancy. It really would be a magisterial gift if you could find again what it was that led you to cast aside the inflexibility typical of your behavior and of your country, the charming inflexibility that doesn't suit you, that you use as a weapon when you would like only to come closer without defenses. I know about you and about your wounds. You have soothed my old scars, becoming the only piercing in my life that I want to wear as a decoration. You are, you are the only piercing, and as an everlasting decoration I carry you together with the memory of the blood you have sucked. From that wound, from my past. This united us. The piercing unites. In a territory that is deep and mystical, at times. Of an "obscene" and majestic mysticism. In that mysticism we know how to find each other again. In that mysticism we recognize each other. Then, it was the rift, the lack of understanding, the demand, the fear. The insults and the ferocity that bites weren't long in coming, they lie in wait, even if it seems that their own love has immense wings to unfold and nothing can ever bite, nothing can ever make that pure pain flow, that only a scream, even a muffled one, that only a scream, even a silent one, can soothe.

The absence [the white void], the one that eats you inside, arrived with the silent space and with the nothingness. That void full of questions, yearnings for sharing left maimed and imploded. That void filled with fingertips that have become rough, writing and writing about you, like in that song that you loved and I loved.

[picture of us, we are smiling, far from masks and melodramas but with only gentle tenderness, and we are listening to the song and we . . .]

I know, my impatience splintered the mystical perfection of your brutality [in that semidarkness], perfect brutality, of ropes, masks and whips, burning brutality, dribbled and bitten. You put it on a stage of unmade beds and hackneyed bathrooms but with style and a soundtrack. I stopped listening to what I considered our music for a while.

[far from Bruckner so as not to feel my heart breaking, it is already a cutout, a collage of recycled pieces, my ventricle, you know] Now that music is a rift, it enters inside me and penetrates me like you used to, but its intangible evanescence produces an inexpressible anguish.

I would need, but I don't beg, of course.

[the bandage, a start]

You, who covered my eyes *before* so that your fever remained a private madness, an unsuppressible need, sorrowful lament, almost a litany with open lips, to be aware of and not to see, unless through the mesh of the fabric.

It was soft, of lace, black and delicate, it spoke its persuasive language, convincing, guiding through the shadows as if it were nothing.

You, who left me floating, I was waiting for you but perhaps in reality I was no longer there, there was nothing carnal, specific, true, it was that abandonment, it was that need for you that you never satisfied, you wouldn't have been able to.

And yet. I always came back, and, left alone. I screwed up my eyes in the wind and I licked my lips by the river, and it was as if the rope, as if the rope that you gracefully tied in the semidarkness, in the light of the sun or in the blue warmth of the evening one could no longer untie. You did this. This happened to me.

You imprisoned the storm that I had inside, you controlled it, you held it tight. You did it for a long time, with the slowness and the folly of a score that launches into the attack and involves the musicians and the conductor until it makes a whole concert hall erupt with enthusiasm [like you used to erupt, with pleasure, sometimes during, sometimes immediately afterward, and between music and orgasm there was no difference].

The dissonances came in unexpected clusters like disenchanted ghosts capable of rape, they came later and they weren't easy to sustain: because there is an afterward, there is an outside that overwhelms and devastates [after the moments in semidarkness, the necessary penetration, the urgency].

And yet with you I surrendered, swallowed by a similar intensity I was searching for an epic of unmade beds, a wet epic, gushing and thirsty poetics, I was searching for something that made a difference, and your hands on my body were a different touch from all those I had known before, never experienced again afterward. They were, your hands, an unfamiliar radiating energy and electric truth. [carnal, of course, the rest was hypocrisy and pretence or else escape, so often, so much and unnecessarily]

That isn't what I'm writing to you, the e-mail was finished before, and it won't have a reply, it won't have forgiveness, it won't have a smile, it won't have a pardon, it won't have caresses of indulgent words, it won't have glittering crystals [your eyes, so often], but it will have that nothingness that invites oblivion. That has already invited oblivion, forcing it to dilute, to kill.

And yet. [I know that we are stuck, tied. In some ways it is fate, or rather a predestination]

My words are pregnant with hopes and needs aborted in the blood in which we delighted, rejoiced, wounded again, to add blood to blood, life to the life of that pleasure of ours, which was nourished, wounded, licked, soothed, fed, stretched, discouraged, discovered.

You. You drew so much nearer without imposing any brakes before that deep and precious intimacy. [I made a gift of it to you, the gift remains, my body belongs to you]

Plundered, that intimate pierced secret part became literature through desperation and desertion. [the death of love doesn't follow, but you gave it urgency, they will be personal accounts, it will be your "without"]

I'm coming back. In February, not long now. Very soon, come to think of it. My fingertips type, sometimes I have to stop and cover them with hand cream, or pass them over my lower lip to calm down, my whole body is involved, the writing demands it, one can't get around the obstacle, think it unimportant, to leave unharmed. I can't and I mustn't, I insist on the incision, on that single cover and on those, so many, invisible and present

A DYPTICH: ABSINTHE & PIERCING

[being aware of the piercing is a way of breathing you in again, of sensing in the absence a clot of truth that hasn't been erased] I am coming. The confirmation of my ticket has already arrived. I have to do it, I want to do it. I can't bear for too long the absence of the city I love where the boundaries of pains—loves—fates become fluid. So I don't think about what the cost is [emotional, actual, physical, psychic]. I will write more, I will write about convergences, about arrivals, about hopes, and about you, but I won't send you anything, writing is a fundamental action in that still lascivious loneliness, I know that I will fill notebooks, and I will note down details and bits about real life picked up in the bar almost next to the hotel. [writing, in every way and in every sense, is a perversion, it is the self-same obsession, and only by writing is one authorized, if one knows what it means to be consumed, to make oneself body-word, body-novel, drafting words of saliva and sperm that taste and can be recognized as literature]

That bar, I spent my real Christmas there, you know? [it was a December of conflicts] It was lit up and festive. I spent long and tender mornings letting myself be pampered by the owner, full of consideration, taking notes on the large and convenient marble tables. I stayed, I watched.

I let the hours flow by. Reading. Correcting drafts. One in particular. Immersion in erotic words that seem far away [I want to and I have to write about you still, about your kisses that devoured me to excess, stunned, I allowed you, about your orgasm that caused me torment and tears, about the smell of skin and hair that I can't forget, about your being inside me, about my being for you, [an offering], about this I would like to write again and again [one always recounts one's own piercing, every writer does it].

I must do more as well, my duties take me far away but I don't stop, I can only write if I am damaged, only then do my words become powerful and you are and remain my piercing. Echoes of the East, hives of honey, organza, lives put into the most banal newspapers, daring constructions [a writing of intimacy and courage, they said], always beds left in the semidarkness, that remains a constant. I try, I know, I succeed. That bar, what a marvel, you see? I'm satisfied with very little. Almost nothing. I guarantee I won't forget and I don't. I went there in the evenings as well, that early evening and the long evening that the neighborhood divided by the Langstrasse doesn't deny you, through the windows I watched bits of the fast-flowing city, iridescent lights and tired passers-by. Every day I imagined that I saw you arriving unexpectedly, needing me [perhaps you do, you'll never say so], full of enthusiasm, a man no longer frightened by the abyss, a man who wants me. That's how I thought of you. I imagined, every day, noticing you at the corner or meeting you with a start in the hall on my return. But it didn't happen, it shouldn't happen. It couldn't, you couldn't.

[I listened to Bruckner in my earphones and also a bit of Haydn, it used to make you think of me, you said from Munich, it used to make you want me and it enchanted you, it makes me think of impermanence, which is something I know]

I used to sleep well in the bed on my own, and I was fine in the morning, when the view confirmed where I was. And now, there is the restlessness that allows no respite. Regret kneads my soul and I rediscover that warmth, that incredible enjoyment we shared. Together, naturally. We wanted it for so long and with such force that it seems impossible, but it's true. There is no antidote for your absence, there is no remedy for the piercing, once it has happened it remains, one learns to live with it as one does with a chronic illness.

And what else is it, an absence?

[I dream of them, the ropes, certainly, the clamps everywhere, your strength in taking me, the run, the fever, the skin that renews itself and beckons, the tongue that doesn't stop and dares, that breathless "everything," I dream of it, I find it again and I also watch it disappear in the morning]

In the meantime, I "learn" a neighborhood that seems like a heart. The muscle and the core, metaphor and truth, it beats and lives. Langstrasse. I buy necklaces and rings with a pearl in the center, excessive and beautiful, from Amos, the stallholder who also tries to woo me. [pearls, now I know what appeal, what meaning and what message they convey, you have taught me this and I see the truth of your sentiment from the looks I receive and that focus only on my embellished décolletage, on my hands with that single pearl that gleams. Pearls and their power in the imagination] Wearing them I think about showing them to you, sometimes. I search for you in the spaces, I search for you in the crucial moments. It happens. I felt I was gradually freeing myself, more than healing a habit to be ignored, a presence not to be nurtured, once you disappeared, once oblivion lightened [I can't do it, the city can't, nor can the swan].

Certainly, this neighborhood seduces. Its throbbing draws me in between the smiles and an unexpected friendliness. Here isn't a place for cajoling and offers to the defenseless [I am dissembling, perhaps]. And yet there are moving exceptions. The lightened implacability of Zurich. There is so much around. The things I have overlooked and that I am coming to retrieve. What I glance at through the windows, flowing quickly through the streets or close to the walls on the pavements. Everyone with a different wound, with an incision, a story, exhaustion, rage. Like us. So similar in the same insanity.

[And that me, feverish, arched, needy, offered, tremulous, cut, savage, shameless, melodramatic, open, pleading, cultured, different, breathless, that woman that you knew, that you wanted and revered, that you let go, that you stopped following, that woman made up of literature, with the soul of flesh and the body that becomes writing, with the fingertips for sale so as not to forget, with the bitter longing for your gaze on the doorstep, that woman, she deserves a smile, a forgiving hug, a renewed caress]

That giving of oneself. It remains. Only for you and for my womb that trembled for you and with you [shock, earthquake] between the incomprehensible and the mystical, in that narrow, precious space.